$\mathcal{V}$OICES OF THE $\mathcal{S}$OUTH

The Hills Beyond

Also by Thomas Wolfe

NOVELS
Look Homeward, Angel
Of Time and the River
The Web and the Rock
You Can't Go Home Again

STORY COLLECTIONS
From Death to Morning

NONFICTION
The Story of a Novel

PLAYS
Mannerhouse
Web of Earth (monologue)

Thomas Wolfe

THE HILLS BEYOND

Louisiana State University Press
Baton Rouge
MM

Copyright ©1935, 1936, 1937, 1939, 1941 by Maxwell Perkins as Executor
Copyright © renewed 1969 by Paul Gitlin, Administrator, C.T.A. of the estate of
    Thomas Wolfe
Originally published in 1941 by Harper & Brothers
LSU Press edition published 2000 by arrangement with the Estate of Thomas Wolfe
All rights reserved
Manufactured in the United States of America

09 08 07 06 05 04 03 02 01 00
5 4 3 2 1

Library of Congress Cataloging-in-Publication Data

Wolfe, Thomas, 1900–1938.
    The hills beyond / Thomas Wolfe.
        p. cm. — (Voices of the South)
    Contents: The lost boy — No cure for it — Gentlemen of the press — A kinsman of
his blood — Chickamauga — The return of the prodigal — On leprechauns — Portrait
of a literary critic — The lion at morning — God's lonely man — The hills beyond.
    ISBN 0-8071-2567-9 (pbk. : alk. paper)
        1. Southern States—Social life and customs—Fiction. I. Title. II. Series

    PS3545.O337 H54 2000
    813'.52–dc21
                                                                    00-038441

The paper in this book meets the guidelines for permanence and durability of the
Committee on Production Guidelines for Book Longevity of the Council on Library
Resources. ∞

Contents

* * *

CONTENTS

The Hills Beyond

The Lost Boy

I

LIGHT CAME AND WENT AND CAME AGAIN, THE BOOMING STROKES of three o'clock beat out across the town in thronging bronze from the courthouse bell, light winds of April blew the fountain out in rainbow sheets, until the plume returned and pulsed, as Grover turned into the Square. He was a child, dark-eyed and grave, birthmarked upon his neck—a berry of warm brown—and with a gentle face, too quiet and too listening for his years. The scuffed boy's shoes, the thick-ribbed stockings gartered at the knees, the short knee pants cut straight with three small useless buttons at the side, the sailor blouse, the old cap battered out of shape, perched sideways up on top of the raven head, the old soiled canvas bag slung from the shoulder, empty now, but waiting for the crisp sheets of the afternoon— these friendly, shabby garments, shaped by Grover, uttered him. He turned and passed along the north side of the Square and in that moment saw the union of Forever and of Now.

Light came and went and came again, the great plume of the fountain pulsed and winds of April sheeted it across the Square in a rainbow gossamer of spray. The fire department horses drummed on the floors with wooden stomp, most casually, and with dry whiskings of their clean, coarse tails. The street cars ground into the Square from every portion of the compass and halted briefly like wound toys in their familiar quarter-hourly formula. A dray, hauled by a boneyard nag, rattled across the cobbles on the other side before his father's shop. The courthouse bell boomed out its solemn warning of immediate three, and everything was just the same as it had always been.

He saw that haggis of vexed shapes with quiet eyes—that hodgepodge of ill-sorted architectures that made up the Square, and he did not feel lost. For "Here," thought Grover, "here is the Square as it has always been—and papa's shop, the fire department and the City Hall, the fountain pulsing with its plume, the street cars coming in and halting at the quarter hour, the hardware store on the corner there, the row of old brick buildings on this side of the street, the people passing and the light that comes and changes and that always will come back again, and everything that comes and goes and changes in the Square, and yet will be the same again. And here," the boy thought, "is Grover with his paper bag. Here is old Grover, almost twelve years old. Here is the month of April, 1904. Here is the courthouse bell and three o'clock. Here is Grover on the Square that never changes. Here is Grover, caught upon this point of time."

It seemed to him that the Square, itself the accidental masonry of many years, the chance agglomeration of time and of disrupted strivings, was the center of the universe. It was for him, in his soul's picture, the earth's pivot, the granite core of changelessness, the eternal place where all things came and passed, and yet abode forever and would never change.

He passed the old shack on the corner—the wooden fire-trap where S. Goldberg ran his wiener stand. Then he passed the Singer place next door, with its gleaming display of new machines. He saw them and admired them, but he felt no joy. They brought back to him the busy hum of housework and of women sewing, the intricacy of stitch and weave, the mystery of style and pattern, the memory of women bending over flashing needles, the pedaled tread, the busy whir. It was women's work: it filled him with unknown associations of dullness and of vague depression. And always, also, with a moment's twinge of horror, for his dark eye would always travel toward that needle stitching up and down so fast the eye could never follow it. And then he would remember how his mother once had told him she had driven the needle through her finger, and always, when he passed this place, he would remember it and for a moment crane his neck and turn his head away.

He passed on then, but had to stop again next door before the music store. He always had to stop by places that had shining perfect things in them. He loved hardware stores and windows full of accurate geometric tools. He loved windows full of hammers, saws, and planing boards. He liked windows full of strong new rakes and hoes, with unworn handles, of white perfect wood, stamped hard and vivid with the maker's seal. He loved to see such things as these in the windows of hardware stores. And he would fairly gloat upon them and think that some day he would own a set himself.

Also, he always stopped before the music and piano store. It was a splendid store. And in the window was a small white dog upon his haunches, with head cocked gravely to one side, a small white dog that never moved, that never barked, that listened attentively at the flaring funnel of a horn to hear "His Master's Voice"—a horn forever silent, and a voice that never spoke. And within were many rich and shining shapes of great pianos, an air of splendor and of wealth.

And now, indeed, he *was* caught, held suspended. A waft of air, warm, chocolate-laden, filled his nostrils. He tried to pass the white front of the little eight-foot shop; he paused, struggling with conscience; he could not go on. It was the little candy shop run by old Crocker and his wife. And Grover could not pass.

"Old stingy Crockers!" he thought scornfully. "I'll not go there any more. But—" as the maddening fragrance of rich cooking chocolate touched him once again—"I'll just look in the window and see what they've got." He paused a moment, looking with his dark and quiet eyes into the window of the little candy shop. The window, spotlessly clean, was filled with trays of fresh-made candy. His eyes rested on a tray of chocolate drops. Unconsciously he licked his lips. Put one of them upon your tongue and it just melted there, like honeydew. And then the trays full of rich home-made fudge. He gazed longingly at the deep body of the chocolate fudge, reflectively at maple walnut, more critically, yet with longing, at the mints, the nougatines, and all the other dainties.

"Old stingy Crockers!" Grover muttered once again, and turned to go. "I wouldn't go in *there* again."

And yet he did not go away. "Old stingy Crockers" they might be; still, they did make the best candy in town, the best, in fact, that he had ever tasted.

He looked through the window back into the little shop and saw Mrs. Crocker there. A customer had gone in and had made a purchase, and as Grover looked he saw Mrs. Crocker, with her little wrenny face, her pinched features, lean over and peer primly at the scales. She had a piece of fudge in her clean, bony, little fingers, and as Grover looked, she broke it, primly, in her little bony hands. She dropped a morsel down into the scales. They weighted down alarmingly, and her thin lips tightened. She snatched the piece of fudge out of the scales and broke it carefully once again. This time the scales wavered, went down very slowly, and came back again. Mrs. Crocker carefully put the reclaimed piece of fudge back in the tray, dumped the remainder in a paper bag, folded it and gave it to the customer, counted the money carefully and doled it out into the till, the pennies in one place, the nickels in another.

Grover stood there, looking scornfully. "Old stingy Crocker—afraid that she might give a crumb away!"

He grunted scornfully and again he turned to go. But now Mr. Crocker came out from the little partitioned place where they made all their candy, bearing a tray of fresh-made fudge in his skinny hands. Old Man Crocker rocked along the counter to the front and put it down. He really rocked along. He was a cripple. And like his wife, he was a wrenny, wizened little creature, with bony hands, thin lips, a pinched and meager face. One leg was inches shorter than the other, and on this leg there was an enormous thick-soled boot, with a kind of wooden, rocker-like arrangement, six inches high at least, to make up for the deficiency. On this wooden cradle Mr. Crocker rocked along, with a prim and apprehensive little smile, as if he were afraid he was going to lose something.

"Old stingy Crocker!" muttered Grover. "Humph! He wouldn't give you anything!"

And yet—he did not go away. He hung there curiously, peering through the window, with his dark and gentle face now focused and intent, alert and curious, flattening his nose against the glass. Unconsciously he scratched the thick-ribbed fabric of one stockinged leg with the scuffed and worn toe of his old shoe. The fresh, warm odor of the new-made fudge was delicious. It was a little maddening. Half consciously he began to fumble in one trouser pocket, and pulled out his purse, a shabby worn old black one with a twisted clasp. He opened it and prowled about inside.

What he found was not inspiring—a nickel and two pennies and—he had forgotten them—the stamps. He took the stamps out and unfolded them. There were five twos, eight ones, all that remained of the dollar-sixty-cents' worth which Reed, the pharmacist, had given him for running errands a week or two before.

"Old Crocker," Grover thought, and looked somberly at the grotesque little form as it rocked back into the shop again, around the counter, and up the other side. "Well—" again he looked indefinitely at the stamps in his hand—"he's had all the rest of them. He might as well take these."

So, soothing conscience with this sop of scorn, he went into the shop and stood looking at the trays in the glass case and finally decided. Pointing with a slightly grimy finger at the fresh-made tray of chocolate fudge, he said, "I'll take fifteen cents' worth of this, Mr. Crocker." He paused a moment, fighting with embarrassment, then he lifted his dark face and said quietly, "And please, I'll have to give you stamps again."

Mr. Crocker made no answer. He did not look at Grover. He pressed his lips together primly. He went rocking away and got the candy scoop, came back, slid open the door of the glass case, put fudge into the scoop, and, rocking to the scales, began to weigh the candy out. Grover watched him as he peered and squinted, he watched him purse and press his lips together, he saw him take a piece of fudge and break it in two parts. And then old Crocker broke two parts in two again. He weighed, he squinted, and he hovered, until it seemed to Grover that by calling *Mrs.* Crocker stingy he had been guilty of a rank injustice. But finally, to his vast relief, the job was over, the scales hung there, quivering apprehensively, upon the very hair-line of nervous balance, as if even the scales were afraid that one more move from Old Man Crocker and they would be undone.

Mr. Crocker took the candy then and dumped it in a paper bag and, rocking back along the counter toward the boy, he dryly said: "Where are the stamps?" Grover gave them to him. Mr. Crocker relinquished his clawlike hold upon the bag and set it down upon the counter. Grover took the bag and dropped it in his canvas sack, and then remembered. "Mr. Crocker—" again he felt the old embarrassment that was almost like strong pain— "I gave you too much," Grover said. "There were eighteen cents in stamps. You—you can just give me three ones back."

Mr. Crocker did not answer. He was busy with his bony little hands, unfolding the stamps and flattening them out on top of the glass counter. When he had done so, he peered at them sharply for a moment, thrusting his scrawny neck forward and running his eye up and down, like a bookkeeper who totes up rows of figures.

When he had finished, he said tartly: "I don't like this kind of business. If you want candy, you should have the money for it. I'm not a post office. The next time you come in here and want anything, you'll have to pay me money for it."

Hot anger rose in Grover's throat. His olive face suffused with angry color. His tarry eyes got black and bright. He was on the verge of saying: "Then why did you take my other stamps? Why do you tell me now, when you have taken all the stamps I had, that you don't want them?"

But he was a boy, a boy of eleven years, a quiet, gentle, gravely thoughtful boy, and he had been taught how to respect his elders. So he just stood there looking with his tar-black eyes. Old Man Crocker, pursing at the mouth a little, without meeting Grover's gaze, took the stamps up in his thin, parched fingers and, turning, rocked away with them down to the till.

He took the twos and folded them and laid them in one rounded scallop, then took the ones and folded them and put them in the one next to it. Then he closed the till and started to rock off, down toward the other end. Grover, his face now quiet and grave, kept looking at him, but Mr. Crocker did not look at Grover. Instead he began to take some stamped card-board shapes and fold them into boxes.

In a moment Grover said, "Mr. Crocker, will you give me the three ones, please?"

Mr. Crocker did not answer. He kept folding boxes, and he compressed his thin lips quickly as he did so. But Mrs. Crocker, back turned to her spouse, also folding boxes with her birdlike hands, muttered tartly: "Hm! *I'd* give him nothing!"

Mr. Crocker looked up, looked at Grover, said, "What are you waiting for?"

"Will you give me the three ones, please?" Grover said.

"I'll give you nothing," Mr. Crocker said.

He left his work and came rocking forward along the counter. "Now you get out of here! Don't you come in here with any more of those stamps," said Mr. Crocker.

"I should like to know where he gets them—that's what *I* should like to know," said Mrs. Crocker.

She did not look up as she said these words. She inclined her head a little to the side, in Mr. Crocker's direction, and continued to fold the boxes with her bony fingers.

"You get out of here!" said Mr. Crocker. "And don't you come back here with any stamps. . . . Where did you get those stamps?" he said.

"That's just what *I've* been thinking," Mrs. Crocker said. *"I've* been thinking all along."

"You've been coming in here for the last two weeks with those stamps," said Mr. Crocker. "I don't like the look of it. Where did you get those stamps?" he said.

"That's what *I've* been thinking," said Mrs. Crocker, for a second time.

Grover had got white underneath his olive skin. His eyes had lost their luster. They looked like dull, stunned balls of tar.

"From Mr. Reed," he said. "I got the stamps from Mr. Reed." Then he burst out desperately: "Mr. Crocker—Mr. Reed will tell you how I got the stamps. I did some work for Mr. Reed, he gave me those stamps two weeks ago."

"Mr. Reed," said Mrs. Crocker acidly. She did not turn her head. "I call it mighty funny."

"Mr. Crocker," Grover said, "if you'll just let me have three ones——"

"You get out of here!" cried Mr. Crocker, and he began rocking forward toward Grover. "Now don't you come in here again, boy! There's something funny about this whole business! I don't like the look of it," said Mr. Crocker. "If you can't pay as other people do, then I don't want your trade."

"Mr. Crocker," Grover said again, and underneath the olive skin his face was gray, "if you'll just let me have those three——"

"You get out of here!" Mr. Crocker cried, rocking down toward the counter's end. "If you don't get out, boy——"

"*I'd* call a policeman, that's what I'd do," Mrs. Crocker said.

Mr. Crocker rocked around the lower end of the counter. He came rocking up to Grover. "You get out," he said.

He took the boy and pushed him with his bony little hands, and Grover was sick and gray down to the hollow pit of his stomach.

"You've got to give me those three ones," he said.

"You get out of here!" shrilled Mr. Crocker. He seized the screen door, pulled it open, and pushed Grover out. "Don't you come back in here," he said, pausing for a moment, and working thinly at the lips. He turned and rocked back in the shop again. The screen door slammed behind him. Grover stood there on the pavement. And light came and went and came again into the Square.

The boy stood there, and a wagon rattled past. There were

some people passing by, but Grover did not notice them. He stood there blindly, in the watches of the sun, feeling this was Time, this was the center of the universe, the granite core of changelessness, and feeling, this is Grover, this the Square, this is Now.

But something had gone out of day. He felt the overwhelming, soul-sickening guilt that all the children, all the good men of the earth, have felt since Time began. And even anger had died down, had been drowned out, in this swelling tide of guilt, and "This is the Square"—thought Grover as before—"This is Now. There is my father's shop. And all of it is as it has always been— save I."

And the Square reeled drunkenly around him, light went in blind gray motes before his eyes, the fountain sheeted out to rainbow iridescence and returned to its proud, pulsing plume again. But all the brightness had gone out of day, and "Here is the Square, and here is permanence, and here is Time—and all of it the same as it has always been, save I."

The scuffed boots of the lost boy moved and stumbled blindly. The numb feet crossed the pavement—reached the cobbled street, reached the plotted central square—the grass plots, and the flower beds, so soon to be packed with red geraniums.

"I want to be alone," thought Grover, "where I cannot go near him. . . . Oh God, I hope he never hears, that no one ever tells him ——"

The plume blew out, the iridescent sheet of spray blew over him. He passed through, found the other side and crossed the street, and— "Oh God, if papa ever hears!" thought Grover, as his numb feet started up the steps into his father's shop.

He found and felt the steps—the width and thickness of old lumber twenty feet in length. He saw it all—the iron columns on his father's porch, painted with the dull anomalous black-green that all such columns in this land and weather come to; two angels, fly-specked, and the waiting stones. Beyond and all around, in the stonecutter's shop, cold shapes of white and marble, rounded stone, the languid angel with strong marble hands of love.

He went on down the aisle, the white shapes stood around him. He went on to the back of the workroom. This he knew—the little cast-iron stove in left-hand corner, caked, brown, heat-blistered, and the elbow of the long stack running out across the shop; the high and dirty window looking down across the Market Square toward Niggertown; the rude old shelves, plank-boarded, thick, the wood not smooth but pulpy, like the strong hair of an animal; upon the shelves the chisels of all sizes and a layer of stone dust; an emery wheel with pump tread; and a door that let out on the alleyway, yet the alleyway twelve feet below. Here in the room, two trestles of this coarse spiked wood upon which rested gravestones, and at one, his father at work.

The boy looked, saw the name was Creasman: saw the carved analysis of John, the symmetry of the s, the fine sentiment that was being polished off beneath the name and date: "John Creasman, November 7, 1903."

Gant looked up. He was a man of fifty-three, gaunt-visaged, mustache cropped, immensely long and tall and gaunt. He wore good dark clothes—heavy, massive—save he had no coat. He worked in shirt-sleeves with his vest on, a strong watch chain stretching across his vest, wing collar and black tie, Adam's apple, bony forehead, bony nose, light eyes, gray-green, undeep and cold, and, somehow, lonely-looking, a striped apron going up around his shoulders, and starched cuffs. And in one hand a tremendous rounded wooden mallet like a butcher's bole; and in his other hand, a strong cold chisel.

"How are you, son?"

He did not look up as he spoke. He spoke quietly, absently. He worked upon the chisel and the wooden mallet, as a jeweler might work on a watch, except that in the man and in the wooden mallet there was power too.

"What is it, son?" he said.

He moved around the table from the head, started up on "J" once again.

"Papa, I never stole the stamps," said Grover.

Gant put down the mallet, laid the chisel down. He came around the trestle.

"What?" he said.

As Grover winked his tar-black eyes, they brightened, the hot tears shot out. "I never stole the stamps," he said.

"Hey? What is this?" his father said. "What stamps?"

"That Mr. Reed gave me, when the other boy was sick and I worked there for three days. . . . And Old Man Crocker," Grover said, "he took all the stamps. And I told him Mr. Reed had given them to me. And now he owes me three ones—and Old Man Crocker says he don't believe that they were mine. He says—he says—that I must have taken them somewhere," Grover blurted out.

"The stamps that Reed gave you—hey?" the stonecutter said. "The stamps you had—" He wet his thumb upon his lips, threw back his head and slowly swung his gaze around the ceiling, then turned and strode quickly from his workshop out into the storeroom.

Almost at once he came back again, and as he passed the old gray painted-board partition of his office he cleared his throat and wet his thumb and said, "Now, I tell you ——"

Then he turned and strode up toward the front again and cleared his throat and said, "I tell you now—" He wheeled about and started back, and as he came along the aisle between the

marshaled rows of gravestones he said beneath his breath, "By
God, now——"

He took Grover by the hand and they went out flying. Down
the aisle they went by all the gravestones, past the fly-specked
angels waiting there, and down the wooden steps and across the
Square. The fountain pulsed, the plume blew out in sheeted
iridescence, and it swept across them; an old gray horse, with
a peaceful look about his torn lips, swucked up the cool mountain water from the trough as Grover and his father went across
the Square, but they did not notice it.

They crossed swiftly to the other side in a direct line to the
candy shop. Gant was still dressed in his long striped apron, and
he was still holding Grover by the hand. He opened the screen
door and stepped inside.

"Give him the stamps," Gant said.

Mr. Crocker came rocking forward behind the counter, with
the prim and careful look that now was somewhat like a smile.
"It was just—" he said.

"Give him the stamps," Gant said, and threw some coins down
on the counter.

Mr. Crocker rocked away and got the stamps. He came rocking back. "I just didn't know—" he said.

The stonecutter took the stamps and gave them to the boy.
And Mr. Crocker took the coins.

"It was just that—" Mr. Crocker began again, and smiled.

Gant cleared his throat: "You never were a father," he said.
"You never knew the feelings of a father, or understood the feelings of a child; and that is why you acted as you did. But a judgment is upon you. God has cursed you. He has afflicted you.
He has made you lame and childless as you are—and lame and
childless, miserable as you are, you will go to your grave and be
forgotten!"

And Crocker's wife kept kneading her bony little hands and said, imploringly, "Oh, no—oh don't say that, please don't say that."

The stonecutter, the breath still hoarse in him, left the store, still holding the boy tightly by the hand. Light came again into the day.

"Well, son," he said, and laid his hand on the boy's back. "Well, son," he said, "now don't you mind."

They walked across the Square, the sheeted spray of iridescent light swept out on them, the horse swizzled at the water-trough, and "Well, son," the stonecutter said.

And the old horse sloped down, ringing with his hoofs upon the cobblestones.

"Well, son," said the stonecutter once again, "be a good boy."

And he trod his own steps then with his great stride and went back again into his shop.

The lost boy stood upon the Square, hard by the porch of his father's shop.

"This is Time," thought Grover. "Here is the Square, here is my father's shop, and here am I."

And light came and went and came again—but now not quite the same as it had done before. The boy saw the pattern of familiar shapes and knew that they were just the same as they had always been. But something had gone out of day, and something had come in again. Out of the vision of those quiet eyes some brightness had gone, and into their vision had come some deeper color. He could not say, he did not know through what transforming shadows life had passed within that quarter hour. He only knew that something had been lost—something forever gained.

Just then a buggy curved out through the Square, and fastened to the rear end was a poster, and it said "St. Louis" and "Excursion" and "The Fair."

II—THE MOTHER

As we went down through Indiana—you were too young, child, to remember it—but I always think of all of you the way you looked that morning, when we went down through Indiana, going to the Fair. All of the apple trees were coming out, and it was April; it was the beginning of spring in southern Indiana and everything was getting green. Of course we don't have farms at home like those in Indiana. The childern had never seen such farms as those, and I reckon, kidlike, they had to take it in.

So all of them kept running up and down the aisle—well, no, except for you and Grover. *You* were too young, Eugene. You were just three, I kept you with me. As for Grover—well, I'm going to tell you about that.

But the rest of them kept running up and down the aisle and from one window to another. They kept calling out and hollering to each other every time they saw something new. They kept trying to look out on all sides, in every way at once, as if they wished they had eyes at the back of their heads. It was the first time any of them had ever been in Indiana, and I reckon that it all seemed strange and new.

And so it seemed they couldn't get enough. It seemed they never could be still. They kept running up and down and back and forth, hollering and shouting to each other, until— "I'll vow! You childern! I never saw the beat of you!" I said. "The way that you keep running up and down and back and forth and never can be quiet for a minute beats all I ever saw," I said.

You see, they were excited about going to St. Louis, and so curious over everything they saw. They couldn't help it, and they wanted to see everything. But—"I'll vow!" I said. "If you

childern don't sit down and rest you'll be worn to a frazzle before we ever get to see St. Louis and the Fair!"

Except for Grover! He—no, sir! not him. Now, boy, I want
to tell you—I've raised the lot of you—and if I do say so, there
wasn't a numbskull in the lot. But *Grover!* Well, you've all
grown up now, all of you have gone away, and none of you are
childern any more. . . . And of course, I hope that, as the fellow
says, you have reached the dignity of man's estate. I suppose you
have the judgment of grown men. . . . But *Grover! Grover* had
it even then!

Oh, even as a child, you know—at a time when I was almost
afraid to trust the rest of you out of my sight—I could depend
on Grover. He could go anywhere, I could send him anywhere,
and I'd always know he'd get back safe, and do exactly what I
told him to!

Why, I didn't even have to tell him. You could send that child
to market and tell him what you wanted, and he'd come home
with *twice* as much as you could get yourself for the same
money!

Now you know, I've always been considered a good trader.
But *Grover!*—why, it got so finally that I wouldn't even tell him.
Your papa said to me: "You'd be better off if you'd just tell him
what you want and leave the rest to him. For," your papa says,
"damned if I don't believe he's a better trader than you are. He
gets more for the money than anyone I ever saw."

Well, I had to admit it, you know. I had to own up then.
Grover, even as a child, was a far better trader than I was. . . .
Why, yes, they told it on him all over town, you know. They
said all of the market men, all of the farmers, knew him. They'd
begin to laugh when they saw him coming—they'd say: "Look
out! Here's Grover! Here's one trader you're not going to fool!"

And they were right! *That* child! I'd say, "Grover, suppose you

run uptown and see if they've got anything good to *eat* today"—
and I'd just wink at him, you know, but he'd know what I
meant. I wouldn't let on that I *wanted* anything exactly, but I'd
say, "Now it just occurs to me that some good fresh stuff may be
coming in from the country, so suppose you take this dollar and
just see what you can do with it."

Well, sir, that was all that was needed. The minute you told
that child that you depended on his judgment, he'd have gone
to the ends of the earth for you—and, let me tell you something,
he wouldn't *miss*, either!

His eyes would get as black as coals—oh! the way that child
would look at you, the intelligence and sense in his expression.
He'd say: "Yes, *ma'am!* Now don't you worry, mama. You leave
it all to me—and I'll do *good!*" said Grover.

And he'd be off like a streak of lightning and—oh Lord! As
your father said to me, "I've been living in this town for almost
thirty years," he said—"I've seen it grow up from a crossroads
village, and I thought I knew everything there was to know
about it—but that child—" your papa says—"he knows places
that I never heard of!" . . . Oh, he'd go right down there to
that place below your papa's shop where the draymen and the
country people used to park their wagons—or he'd go down there
to those old lots on Concord Street where the farmers used to
keep their wagons. And, child that he was, he'd go right in
among them, sir—*Grover* would!—go right in and barter with
them like a grown man!

And he'd come home with things he'd bought that would
make your eyes stick out. . . . Here he comes one time with
another boy, dragging a great bushel basket full of ripe termaters
between them. "Why, Grover!" I says. "How on earth are we
ever going to use them? Why they'll go bad on us before we're
half way through with them." "Well, mama," he says, "I know—"

oh, just as solemn as a judge—"but they were the last the man had," he says, "and he wanted to go home, and so I got them for ten cents," he says. "They were so cheap," said Grover, "I thought it was a shame to let 'em go, and I figgered that what we couldn't eat—why," says Grover, "you could *put up!*" Well, the way he said it—so earnest and so serious—I had to laugh. "But I'll vow!" I said. "If you don't beat all!" . . . But that was *Grover!*—the way he was in *those* days! As everyone said, boy that he was, he had the sense and judgment of a grown man. . . . Child, child, I've seen you all grow up, and all of you were bright enough. There were no half-wits in *my* family. But for all-round intelligence, judgment, and general ability, Grover surpassed the whole crowd. I've never seen his equal, and everyone who knew him as a child will say the same.

So that's what I tell them now when they ask me about all of you. I have to tell the truth. I always said that *you* were smart enough, Eugene—but when they come around and brag to me about you, and about how you have got on and have a kind of name—I don't let on, you know. I just sit there and let them talk. I don't brag on you—if *they* want to brag on you, that's *their* business. I never bragged on one of my own childern in my life. When father raised us up, we were all brought up to believe that it was not good breeding to brag about your kin. "If the others want to do it," father said, "well, let *them* do it. Don't ever let on by a word or sign that you know what they are talking about. Just let *them* do the talking, and say nothing."

So when they come around and tell me all about the things *you've* done—I don't let on to them, I never say a word. Why yes!—why, here, you know—oh, along about a month or so ago, this feller comes—a well-dressed man, you know—he looked intelligent, a good substantial sort of person. He said he came from New Jersey, or somewhere up in that part of the country, and he began to ask me all sorts of questions—what you were like when you were a boy, and all such stuff as that.

I just pretended to study it all over and then I said, "Well, yes"—real serious-like, you know—"well, yes—I reckon I ought to know a little something about him. Eugene was my child, just the same as all the others were. I brought him up just the way I brought up all the others. And," I says—oh, just as solemn as you please—"he wasn't a *bad* sort of a boy. Why," I says, "up to the time that he was twelve years old he was just about the same as any other boy—a good, average, normal sort of fellow."

"Oh," he says. "But didn't you notice something? Wasn't there something kind of strange?" he says—"something different from what you noticed in the other childern?"

I didn't let on, you know—I just took it all in and looked as solemn as an owl—I just pretended to study it all over, just as serious as you please.

"Why no," I says, real slow-like, after I'd studied it all over. "As I remember it, he was a good, ordinary, normal sort of boy, just like all the others."

"Yes," he says—oh, all excited-like, you know— "But didn't you notice how brilliant he was? Eugene must have been more brilliant than the rest!"

"Well, now," I says, and pretended to study that all over too. "Now let me see. . . . Yes," I says—I just looked him in the eye, as solemn as you please—"he did pretty well. . . . Well, yes," I says, "I guess he was a fairly bright sort of a boy. I never had no complaints to make of him on that score. He was bright enough," I says. "The only trouble with him was that he was lazy."

"Lazy!" he says—oh, you should have seen the look upon his face, you know—he jumped like someone had stuck a pin in him. "Lazy!" he says. "Why, you don't mean to tell me——"

"Yes," I says—oh, I never cracked a smile—"I was telling him the same thing myself the last time that I saw him. I told him it was a mighty lucky thing for him that he had the gift of gab. Of course, he went off to college and read a lot of books, and I reckon that's where he got this flow of language they say he has. But as I said to him the last time that I saw him: 'Now look a-here,' I said. 'If you can earn your living doing a light, easy class of work like this you do,' I says, 'you're mighty lucky, because none of the rest of your people,' I says, 'had any such luck as that. They had to work hard for a living.' "

Oh, I told him, you know. I came right out with it. I made no bones about it. And I tell you what—I wish you could have seen his face. It was a study.

"Well," he says, at last, "you've got to admit this, haven't you—he was the brightest boy you had, now wasn't he?"

I just looked at him a moment. I had to tell the truth. I couldn't fool him any longer. "No," I says. "He was a good, bright boy—I got no complaint to make about him on that score—but the brightest boy I had, the one that surpassed all the rest of them in sense, and understanding, and in judgment—the best boy I had—the smartest boy I ever saw—was—well, it wasn't Eugene," I said. "It was another one."

He looked at me a moment, then he said, "Which boy was that?"

Well, I just looked at him, and smiled. I shook my head, you know. I wouldn't tell him. "I never brag about my own," I said. "You'll have to find out for yourself."

But—I'll have to tell *you*—and you know yourself, I brought the whole crowd up, I knew you all. And you can take my word for it—the best one of the lot was—*Grover*!

And when I think of Grover as he was along about that time, I always see him sitting there, so grave and earnest-like, with his nose pressed to the window, as we went down through Indiana in the morning, to the Fair.

All through that morning we were going down along beside the Wabash River—the Wabash River flows through Indiana, it is the river that they wrote the song about—so all that morning we were going down along the river. And I sat with all you childern gathered about me as we went down through Indiana, going to St. Louis, to the Fair.

And Grover sat there, so still and earnest-like, looking out the window, and he didn't move. He sat there like a man. He was just eleven and a half years old, but he had more sense, more judgment, and more understanding than any child I ever saw.

So here he sat beside this gentleman and looked out the window. I never knew the man—I never asked his name—but I tell you what! He was certainly a fine-looking, well-dressed, good, substantial sort of man, and I could see that he had taken a great liking to Grover. And Grover sat there looking out, and then turned to this gentleman, as grave and earnest as a grown-up man, and says, "What kind of crops grow here, sir?" Well, this gentleman threw his head back and just hah-hahed. "Well, I'll see if I can tell you," says this gentleman, and then, you know, he talked to him, they talked together, and Grover took it all in, as solemn as you please, and asked this gentleman every sort of question—what the trees were, what was growing there, how big the farms were—all sorts of questions, which this gentleman would answer, until I said: "Why, I'll vow, Grover! You shouldn't ask so many questions. You'll bother the very life out of this gentleman."

The gentleman threw his head back and laughed right out. "Now you leave that boy alone. He's all right," he said. "He doesn't bother me a bit, and if I know the answers to his questions I will answer him. And if I don't know, why, then, I'll tell him so. But he's *all right,*" he said, and put his arm round Grover's shoulders. "You leave him alone. He doesn't bother me a bit."

And I can still remember how he looked that morning, with his black eyes, his black hair, and with the birthmark on his neck—so grave, so serious, so earnest-like—as he sat by the train window and watched the apple trees, the farms, the barns, the houses, and the orchards, taking it all in, I reckon, because it was strange and new to him.

It was so long ago, but when I think of it, it all comes back, as if it happened yesterday. Now all of you have either died or grown up and gone away, and nothing is the same as it was then. But all of you were there with me that morning and I guess I should remember how the others looked, but somehow I don't. Yet I can still see Grover just the way he was, the way he looked that morning when we went down through Indiana, by the river, to the Fair.

III—The Sister

Can you remember, Eugene, how Grover used to look? I mean the birthmark, the black eyes, the olive skin. The birthmark always showed because of those open sailor blouses kids used to wear. But I guess you must have been too young when Grover died. . . . I was looking at that old photograph the other day. You know the one I mean—that picture showing mama and papa and all of us children before the house on Woodson Street. *You* weren't there, Eugene. *You* didn't get in. *You* hadn't arrived when that was taken. . . . You remember how mad you used to get when we'd tell you that you were only a dishrag hanging out in Heaven when something happened?

You were the baby. That's what you get for being the baby. You don't get in the picture, do you? . . . I was looking at that old picture just the other day. There we were. And, my God, what is it all about? I mean, when you see the way we were— Daisy and Ben and Grover, Steve and all of us—and then how everyone either dies or grows up and goes away—and then—look at us now! Do you ever get to feeling funny? You know what I mean—do you ever get to feeling *queer*—when you try to figure these things out? You've been to college and you ought to know the answer—and I wish you'd tell me if you know.

My Lord, when I think sometimes of the way I used to be— the dreams I used to have. Playing the piano, practicing seven hours a day, thinking that some day I would be a great pianist. Taking singing lessons from Aunt Nell because I felt that some day I was going to have a great career in opera. . . . Can you beat it now? Can you imagine it? *Me!* In grand opera! . . . Now I want to ask you. I'd like to know.

My Lord! When I go uptown and walk down the street and see all these funny-looking little boys and girls hanging around the drug store—do you suppose any of them have ambitions the way we did? Do you suppose any of these funny-looking little girls are thinking about a big career in opera? . . . Didn't you ever see that picture of us? I was looking at it just the other day. It was made before the old house down on Woodson Street, with papa standing there in his swallow-tail, and mama there beside him—and Grover, and Ben, and Steve, and Daisy, and myself, with our feet upon our bicycles. Luke, poor kid, was only four or five. *He* didn't have a bicycle like us. But there he was. And there were all of us together.

Well, there I was, and my poor old skinny legs and long white dress, and two pigtails hanging down my back. And all the funny-looking clothes we wore, with the doo-lolley business on them. . . . But I guess you can't remember. You weren't born.

But, well, we were a right nice-looking set of people, if I do say so. And there was "86" the way it used to be, with the front porch, the grape vines, and the flower beds before the house— and "Miss Eliza" standing there by papa, with a watch charm pinned upon her waist. . . . I shouldn't laugh, but "Miss Eliza" —well, mama was a pretty woman then. Do you know what I mean? "Miss Eliza" was a right good-looking woman, and papa in his swallow-tail was a good-looking man. Do you remember how he used to get dressed up on Sunday? And how grand we thought he was? And how he let me take his money out and count it? And how rich we all thought he was? And how wonderful that dinkey little shop on the Square looked to us? . . . Can you beat it, now? Why we thought that papa was the biggest man in town and—oh, you can't tell me! You can't tell me! He had his faults, but papa was a wonderful man. You know he was!

And there was Steve and Ben and Grover, Daisy, Luke, and me lined up there before the house with one foot on our bicycles. And I got to thinking back about it all. It all came back.

Do you remember anything about St. Louis? You were only three or four years old then, but you must remember something. . . . Do you remember how you used to bawl when I would scrub you? How you'd bawl for Grover? Poor kid, you used to yell for Grover every time I'd get you in the tub. . . . He was a sweet kid and he was crazy about you—he almost brought you up.

That year Grover was working at the Inside Inn out on the Fair Grounds. Do you remember the old Inside Inn? That big old wooden thing inside the Fair? And how I used to take you there to wait for Grover when he got through working? And old fat Billy Pelham at the newsstand—how he always used to give you a stick of chewing gum?

They were all crazy about Grover. Everybody liked him. . . .

And how proud Grover was of you! Don't you remember how he used to show you off? How he used to take you around and make you talk to Billy Pelham? And Mr. Curtis at the desk? And how Grover would try to make you talk and get you to say "Grover"? And you couldn't say it—you couldn't pronounce the "r." You'd say "Gova." Have you forgotten that? You shouldn't forget *that*, because—you were a *cute* kid, then—Ho-ho-ho-ho-ho—I don't know where it's gone to, but you were a big hit in those days. . . . I tell you, boy, you were Somebody back in those days.

And I was thinking of it all the other day when I was looking at that photograph. How we used to go and meet Grover there, and how he'd take us to the Midway. Do you remember the Midway? The Snake-Eater and the Living Skeleton, the Fat Woman and the Chute-the-chute, the Scenic Railway and the Ferris Wheel? How you bawled the night we took you up on the Ferris Wheel? You yelled your head off—I tried to laugh it off, but I tell you, I was scared myself. Back in those days, that was Something. And how Grover laughed at us and told us there was no danger. . . . My lord! poor little Grover. He wasn't quite twelve years old at the time, but he seemed so grown up to us. I was two years older, but I thought he knew it all.

It was always that way with him. Looking back now, it sometimes seems that it was Grover who brought us up. He was always looking after us, telling us what to do, bringing us something—some ice cream or some candy, something he had bought out of the poor little money he'd gotten at the Inn.

Then I got to thinking of the afternoon we sneaked away from home. Mama had gone out somewhere. And Grover and I got on the street car and went downtown. And my Lord, we thought that we were going Somewhere. In those days, that was what we called a *trip*. A ride in the street car was something to write home about in those days. . . . I hear that it's all built up around there now.

So we got on the car and rode the whole way down into the business section of St. Louis. We got out on Washington Street and walked up and down. And I tell you, boy, we thought that that was Something. Grover took me into a drug store and set me up to soda water. Then we came out and walked around some more, down to the Union Station and clear over to the river. And both of us half scared to death at what we'd done and wondering what mama would say if she found out.

We stayed down there till it was getting dark, and we passed by a lunchroom—an old one-armed joint with one-armed chairs and people sitting on stools and eating at the counter. We read all the signs to see what they had to eat and how much it cost, and I guess nothing on the menu was more than fifteen cents, but it couldn't have looked grander to us if it had been Delmonico's. So we stood there with our noses pressed against the window, looking in. Two skinny little kids, both of us scared half to death, getting the thrill of a lifetime out of it. You know what I mean? And smelling everything with all our might and thinking how good it all smelled. . . . Then Grover turned to me and whispered: "Come on, Helen. Let's go in. It says fifteen cents for pork and beans. And I've got the money," Grover said. "I've got sixty cents."

I was so scared I couldn't speak. I'd never been in a place like that before. But I kept thinking, "Oh Lord, if mama should find out!" I felt as if we were committing some big crime. . . . Don't you know how it is when you're a kid? It was the thrill of a lifetime. . . . I couldn't resist. So we both went in and sat down on those high stools before the counter and ordered pork and beans and a cup of coffee. I suppose we were too frightened at what we'd done really to enjoy anything. We just gobbled it ail up in a hurry, and gulped our coffee down. And I don't know whether it was the excitement—I guess the poor kid was already sick when we came in there and didn't know it. But I turned and looked at him, and he was white as death. . . . And when I asked him what was the matter, he wouldn't tell me. He was too proud. He said he was all right, but I could see that he was sick as a dog. . . . So he paid the bill. It came to forty cents— I'll never forget *that* as long as I live. . . . And sure enough, we no more than got out the door—he hardly had time to reach the curb—before it all came up.

And the poor kid was so scared and so ashamed. And what scared him so was not that he had gotten sick, but that he had spent all that money and it had come to nothing. And mama would find out. . . . Poor kid, he just stood there looking at me and he whispered: "Oh Helen, don't tell mama. She'll be mad if she finds out." Then we hurried home, and he was still white as a sheet when we got there.

Mama was waiting for us. She looked at us—you know how "Miss Eliza" looks at you when she thinks you've been doing something that you shouldn't. Mama said, "Why, where on earth have you two children been?" I guess she was all set to lay us out. Then she took one look at Grover's face. That was enough for her. She said, "Why, child, what in the world!" She was white as a sheet herself. . . . And all that Grover said was— "Mama, I feel sick."

He was sick as a dog. He fell over on the bed, and we undressed him and mama put her hand upon his forehead and came out in the hall—she was so white you could have made a black mark on her face with chalk—and whispered to me, "Go get the doctor quick, he's burning up."

And I went chasing up the street, my pigtails flying, to Dr. Packer's house. I brought him back with me. When he came out

of Grover's room he told mama what to do but I don't know if
she even heard him.

Her face was white as a sheet. She looked at me and looked
right through me. She never saw me. And oh, my Lord, I'll
never forget the way she looked, the way my heart stopped and
came up in my throat. I was only a skinny little kid of fourteen.
But she looked as if she was dying right before my eyes. And I
knew that if anything happened to him, she'd never get over it
if she lived to be a hundred.

Poor old mama. You know, he always was her eyeballs—you
know that, don't you?—not the rest of us!—no, sir! I know what
I'm talking about. It always has been Grover—she always thought
more of him than she did of any of the others. And—poor kid!—
he was a sweet kid. I can still see him lying there, and remember
how sick he was, and how scared I was! I don't know why I was
so scared. All we'd done had been to sneak away from home
and go into a lunchroom—but I felt guilty about the whole thing,
as if it was my fault.

It all came back to me the other day when I was looking at
that picture, and I thought, my God, we were two kids together,
and I was only two years older than Grover was, and now I'm
forty-six. . . . Can you believe it? Can you figure it out—the way
we grow up and change and go away? . . . And my Lord,
Grover seemed so grown-up to me. He was such a quiet kid—I
guess that's why he seemed older than the rest of us.

I wonder what Grover would say now if he could see that
picture. All my hopes and dreams and big ambitions have come
to nothing, and it's all so long ago, as if it happened in another
world. Then it comes back, as if it happened yesterday. . . .
Sometimes I lie awake at night and think of all the people who
have come and gone, and how everything is different from the
way we thought that it would be. Then I go out on the street

next day and see the faces of the people that I pass. . . . Don't they look strange to you? Don't you see something funny in people's eyes, as if all of them were puzzled about something? As if they were wondering what had happened to them since they were kids? Wondering what it is that they have lost? . . . Now am I crazy, or do you know what I mean? You've been to college, Gene, and I want you to tell me if you know the answer. Now do they look that way to you? I never noticed that look in people's eyes when I was a kid—did you?

My God, I wish I knew the answer to these things. I'd like to find out what is wrong—what has changed since then—and if we have the same queer look in our eyes, too. Does it happen to us all, to everyone? . . . Grover and Ben, Steve, Daisy, Luke, and me—all standing there before that house on Woodson Street in Altamont—there we are, and you see the way we were—and how it all gets lost. What is it, anyway, that people lose?

How is it that nothing turns out the way we thought it would be? It all gets lost until it seems that it has never happened— that it is something we dreamed somewhere. . . . You see what I mean? . . . It seems that it must be something we heard some-where—that it happened to someone else. And then it all comes back again.

And suddenly you remember just how it was, and see again those two funny, frightened, skinny little kids with their noses pressed against the dirty window of that lunchroom thirty years ago. You remember the way it felt, the way it smelled, even the strange smell in the old pantry in that house we lived in then. And the steps before the house, the way the rooms looked. And those two little boys in sailor suits who used to ride up and down before the house on tricycles. . . . And the birthmark on Grover's neck. . . . The Inside Inn. . . . St. Louis, and the Fair.

It all comes back as if it happened yesterday. And then it goes away again, and seems farther off and stranger than if it happened in a dream.

IV—THE BROTHER

"*This* is King's Highway," the man said.

And then Eugene looked and saw that it was just a street. There were some big new buildings, a large hotel, some restaurants and "bar-grill" places of the modern kind, the livid monotone of neon lights, the ceaseless traffic of motor cars—all this was new, but it was just a street. And he knew that it had always been just a street, and nothing more—but somehow—well, he stood there looking at it, wondering what else he had expected to find.

The man kept looking at him with inquiry in his eyes, and Eugene asked him if the Fair had not been out this way.

"Sure, the Fair was out beyond here," the man said. "Out where the park is now. But this street you're looking for—don't you remember the name of it or nothing?" the man said.

Eugene said he thought the name of the street was Edgemont, but that he wasn't sure. Anyhow it was something like that. And he said the house was on the corner of that street and of another street.

Then the man said: "What was that other street?"

Eugene said he did not know, but that King's Highway was a block or so away, and that an interurban line ran past about half a block from where he once had lived.

"What line was this?" the man said, and stared at him.

"The interurban line," Eugene said.

Then the man stared at him again, and finally, "I don't know no interurban line," he said.

Eugene said it was a line that ran behind some houses, and that there were board fences there and grass beside the tracks.

But somehow he could not say that it was summer in those days and that you could smell the ties, a wooden, tarry smell, and feel a kind of absence in the afternoon after the car had gone. He only said the interurban line was back behind somewhere between the backyards of some houses and some old board fences, and that King's Highway was a block or two away.

He did not say that King's Highway had not been a street in those days but a kind of road that wound from magic out of some dim and haunted land, and that along the way it had got mixed in with Tom the Piper's son, with hot cross buns, with all the light that came and went, and with coming down through Indiana in the morning, and the smell of engine smoke, the Union Station, and most of all with voices lost and far and long ago that said "King's Highway."

He did not say these things about King's Highway because he looked about him and he saw what King's Highway was. All he could say was that the street was near King's Highway, and was on the corner, and that the interurban trolley line was close to there. He said it was a stone house, and that there were stone steps before it, and a strip of grass. He said he thought the house had had a turret at one corner, he could not be sure.

The man looked at him again, and said, "This is King's Highway, but I never heard of any street like that."

Eugene left him then, and went on till he found the place. And so at last he turned into the street, finding the place where the two corners met, the huddled block, the turret, and the steps, and paused a moment, looking back, as if the street were Time.

For a moment he stood there, waiting—for a word, and for a door to open, for the child to come. He waited, but no words were spoken; no one came.

Yet all of it was just as it had always been, except that the steps were lower, the porch less high, the strip of grass less wide, than he had thought. All the rest of it was as he had known it would be. A graystone front, three-storied, with a slant slate roof, the side red brick and windowed, still with the old arched entrance in the center for the doctor's use.

There was a tree in front, and a lamp post; and behind and to the side, more trees than he had known there would be. And all the slatey turret gables, all the slatey window gables, going into points, and the two arched windows, in strong stone, in the front room.

It was all so strong, so solid, and so ugly—and all so enduring and so good, the way he had remembered it, except he did not smell the tar, the hot and caulky dryness of the old cracked ties, the boards of backyard fences and the coarse and sultry grass, and absence in the afternoon when the street car had gone, and the twins, sharp-visaged in their sailor suits, pumping with furious shrillness on tricycles up and down before the house, and the feel of the hot afternoon, and the sense that everyone was absent at the Fair.

Except for this, it all was just the same; except for this and for King's Highway, which was now a street; except for this, and for the child that did not come.

It was a hot day. Darkness had come. The heat rose up and hung and sweltered like a sodden blanket in St. Louis. It was wet heat, and one knew that there would be no relief or coolness in the night. And when one tried to think of the time when the heat would go away, one said: "It cannot last. It's bound to go away," as we always say it in America. But one did not believe it when he said it. The heat soaked down and men sweltered in it; the faces of the people were pale and greasy with the heat. And in their faces was a patient wretchedness, and one felt the kind of desolation that one feels at the end of a hot day in a great city in America—when one's home is far away, across the continent, and he thinks of all that distance, all that heat, and feels, "Oh God! but it's a big country!"

And he feels nothing but absence, absence, and the desolation of America, the loneliness and sadness of the high, hot skies, and evening coming on across the Middle West, across the sweltering and heat-sunken land, across all the lonely little towns, the farms, the fields, the oven swelter of Ohio, Kansas, Iowa, and Indiana at the close of day, and voices, casual in the heat, voices at the little stations, quiet, casual, somehow faded into that enormous vacancy and weariness of heat, of space, and of the immense, the sorrowful, the most high and awful skies.

Then he hears the engine and the wheel again, the wailing whistle and the bell, the sound of shifting in the sweltering yard, and walks the street, and walks the street, beneath the clusters of hard lights, and by the people with sagged faces, and is drowned in desolation and in no belief.

He feels the way one feels when one comes back, and knows that he should not have come, and when he sees that, after all, King's Highway is—a street; and St. Louis—the enchanted name —a big, hot, common town upon the river, sweltering in wet, dreary heat, and not quite South, and nothing else enough to make it better.

It had not been like this before. He could remember how it would get hot, and how good the heat was, and how he would lie out in the backyard on an airing mattress, and how the mattress would get hot and dry and smell like a hot mattress full of sun, and how the sun would make him want to sleep, and how, sometimes, he would go down into the basement to feel coolness, and how the cellar smelled as cellars always smell—a cool, stale smell, the smell of cobwebs and of grimy bottles. And he could remember, when you opened the door upstairs, the smell of the cellar would come up to you—cool, musty, stale and dank and dark—and how the thought of the dark cellar always filled him with a kind of numb excitement, a kind of visceral expectancy.

He could remember how it got hot in the afternoons, and how he would feel a sense of absence and vague sadness in the afternoons, when everyone had gone away. The house would seem so lonely, and sometimes he would sit inside, on the second step of the hall stairs, and listen to the sound of silence and of absence in the afternoon. He could smell the oil upon the floor and on the stairs, and see the sliding doors with their brown varnish and the beady chains across the door, and thrust his hands among the beady chains, and gather them together in his arms, and let them clash, and swish with light beady swishings all around him. He could feel darkness, absence, varnished darkness, and stained light within the house, through the stained glass of the window on the stairs, through the small stained glasses by the door, stained light and absence, silence and the smell of floor oil and vague sadness in the house on a hot mid-afternoon. And all these things themselves would have a kind of life: would seem to wait attentively, to be most living and most still.

He would sit there and listen. He could hear the girl next door practice her piano lessons in the afternoon, and hear the street car coming by between the backyard fences, half a block away, and smell the dry and sultry smell of backyard fences, the smell of coarse hot grasses by the car tracks in the afternoon, the smell of tar, of dry caulked ties, the smell of bright worn flanges, and feel the loneliness of backyards in the afternoon and the sense of absence when the car was gone.

Then he would long for evening and return, the slant of light, and feet along the street, the sharp-faced twins in sailor suits upon their tricycles, the smell of supper and the sound of voices in the house again, and Grover coming from the Fair.

That is how it was when he came into the street, and found the place where the two corners met, and turned at last ᴜ see if Time was there. He passed the house: some lights were burning, the door was open, and a woman sat upon the porch. And presently he turned, came back, and stopped before the house again. The corner light fell blank upon the house. He stood looking at it, and put his foot upon the step.

Then he said to the woman who was sitting on the porch: "This house—excuse me—but could you tell me, please, who lives here in this house?"

He knew his words were strange and hollow, and he had not said what he wished to say. She stared at him a moment, puzzled.

Then she said: "I live here. Who are you looking for?"

He said, "Why, I am looking for——"

And then he stopped, because he knew he could not tell her what it was that he was looking for.

"There used to be a house—" he said.

The woman was now staring at him hard.

He said, "I think I used to live here."

She said nothing.

In a moment he continued, "I used to live here in this house," he said, "when I was a little boy."

She was silent, looking at him, then she said: "Oh. Are you sure this was the house? Do you remember the address?"

"I have forgotten the address," he said, "but it was Edgemont Street, and it was on the corner. And I know this is the house."

"This isn't Edgemont Street," the woman said. "The name is Bates."

"Well, then, they changed the name of the street," he said, "but this is the same house. It hasn't changed."

She was silent a moment, then she nodded: "Yes. They did change the name of the street. I remember when I was a child they called it something else," she said. "But that was a long time ago. When was it that you lived here?"

"In 1904."

Again she was silent, looking at him. Then presently: "Oh. That was the year of the Fair. You were here then?"

"Yes." He now spoke rapidly, with more confidence. "My mother had the house, and we were here for seven months. And the house belonged to Dr. Packer," he went on. "We rented it from him."

"Yes," the woman said, and nodded, "this was Dr. Packer's house. He's dead now, he's been dead for many years. But this was the Packer house, all right."

"That entrance on the side," he said, "where the steps go up, that was for Dr. Packer's patients. That was the entrance to his office."

"Oh," the woman said, "I didn't know that. I've often wondered what it was. I didn't know what it was for."

"And this big room in front here," he continued, "that was the office. And there were sliding doors, and next to it, a kind of alcove for his patients——"

"Yes, the alcove is still there, only all of it has been made into one room now—and I never knew just what the alcove was for."

"And there were sliding doors on this side, too, that opened on the hall—and a stairway going up upon this side. And halfway up the stairway, at the landing, a little window of colored glass—and across the sliding doors here in the hall, a kind of curtain made of strings of beads."

She nodded, smiling. "Yes, it's just the same—we still have the sliding doors and the stained glass window on the stairs. There's no bead curtain any more," she said, "but I remember when people had them. I know what you mean."

"When we were here," he said, "we used the doctor's office for a parlor—except later on—the last month or two—and then we used it for—a bedroom."

"It is a bedroom now," she said. "I run the house—I rent rooms —all of the rooms upstairs are rented—but I have two brothers and they sleep in this front room."

Both of them were silent for a moment, then Eugene said, "My brother stayed there too."

"In the front room?" the woman said.

He answered, "Yes."

She paused, then said: "Won't you come in? I don't believe it's changed much. Would you like to see?"

He thanked her and said he would, and he went up the steps. She opened the screen door to let him in.

Inside it was just the same—the stairs, the hallway, the sliding doors, the window of stained glass upon the stairs. And all of it was just the same, except for absence, the stained light of absence in the afternoon, and the child who once had sat there, waiting on the stairs.

It was all the same except that as a child he had sat there feeling things were *Somewhere*—and now he *knew*. He had sat there feeling that a vast and sultry river was somewhere—and now he knew! He had sat there wondering what King's Highway was, where it began, and where it ended—now he knew! He had sat there haunted by the magic word "downtown"— now he knew!—and by the street car, after it had gone—and by all things that came and went and came again, like the cloud shadows passing in a wood, that never could be captured.

And he felt that if he could only sit there on the stairs once

more, in solitude and absence in the afternoon, he would be able
to get it back again. Then would he be able to remember all
that he had seen and been—the brief sum of himself, the universe of his four years, with all the light of Time upon it—that
universe which was so short to measure, and yet so far, so endless, to remember. Then would he be able to see his own small
face again, pooled in the dark mirror of the hall, and peer once
more into the grave eyes of the child that he had been, and dis-
cover there in his quiet three-years' self the lone integrity of "I,"
knowing: "Here is the House, and here House listening; here
is Absence, Absence in the afternoon; and here in this House,
this Absence, is my core, my kernel—here am I!"

But as he thought it, he knew that even if he could sit here
alone and get it back again, it would be gone as soon as seized,
just as it had been then—first coming like the vast and drowsy
rumors of the distant and enchanted Fair, then fading like cloud
shadows on a hill, going like faces in a dream—coming, going,
coming, possessed and held but never captured, like lost voices
in the mountains long ago—and like the dark eyes and quiet
face of the dark, lost boy, his brother, who, in the mysterious
rhythms of his life and work, used to come into this house, then
go, and then return again.

The woman took Eugene back into the house and through the
hall. He told her of the pantry, told her where it was and pointed
to the place, but now it was no longer there. And he told her of
the backyard, and of the old board fence around the yard. But
the old board fence was gone. And he told her of the carriage
house, and told her it was painted red. But now there was a small
garage. And the backyard was still there, but smaller than he
thought, and now there was a tree.

"I did not know there was a tree," he said. "I do not remember any tree."

"Perhaps it was not there," she said. "A tree could grow in thirty years." And then they came back through the house again and paused at the sliding doors.

"And could I see this room?" he said.

She slid the doors back. They slid open smoothly, with a rolling heaviness, as they used to do. And then he saw the room again. It was the same. There was a window at the side, the two arched windows at the front, the alcove and the sliding doors, the fireplace with the tiles of mottled green, the mantle of dark mission wood, the mantel posts, a dresser and a bed, just where the dresser and the bed had been so long ago.

"Is this the room?" the woman said. "It hasn't changed?"

He told her that it was the same.

"And your brother slept here where my brothers sleep?"

"This is his room," he said.

They were silent. He turned to go, and said, "Well, thank you. I appreciate your showing me."

She said that she was glad and that it was no trouble. "And when you see your family, you can tell them that you saw the house," she said. "My name is Mrs. Bell. You can tell your mother that a Mrs. Bell has the house now. And when you see your brother, you can tell him that you saw the room he slept in, and that you found it just the same."

He told her then that his brother was dead.

The woman was silent for a moment. Then she looked at him and said: "He died here, didn't he? In this room?"

He told her that it was so.

"Well, then," she said, "I knew it. I don't know how. But when you told me he was here, I knew it."

He said nothing. In a moment the woman said, "What did he die of?"

"Typhoid."

She looked shocked and troubled, and said involuntarily, "My two brothers——"

"That was a long time ago," he said. "I don't think you need to worry now."

"Oh, I wasn't thinking about that," she said. "It was just hearing that a little boy—your brother—was—was in this room that my two brothers sleep in now——"

"Well, maybe I shouldn't have told you then. But he was a good boy—and if you'd known him you wouldn't mind."

She said nothing, and he added quickly: "Besides, he didn't stay here long. This wasn't really his room—but the night he came back with my sister he was so sick—they didn't move him."

"Oh," the woman said, "I see." And then: "Are you going to tell your mother you were here?"

"I don't think so."

"I—I wonder how she feels about this room."

"I don't know. She never speaks of it."

"Oh. . . . How old was he?"

"He was twelve."

"You must have been pretty young yourself."

"I was not quite four."

"And—you just wanted to see the room, didn't you? That's why you came back."

"Yes."

"Well—" indefinitely—"I guess you've seen it now."

"Yes, thank you."

"I guess you don't remember much about him, do you? I shouldn't think you would."

"No, not much."

The years dropped off like fallen leaves: the face came back again—the soft dark oval, the dark eyes, the soft brown berry on the neck, the raven hair, all bending down, approaching— the whole appearing to him ghost-wise, intent and instant.

"Now say it—*Grover!*"

"Gova."

"No—not Gova—*Grover!* . . . Say it!"

"Gova."

"Ah-h—you didn't say it. You said Gova. *Grover*—now say it!"

"Gova."

"Look, I tell you what I'll do if you say it right. Would you like to go down to King's Highway? Would you like Grover to set you up? All right, then. If you say Grover and say it right, I'll take you to King's Highway and set you up to ice cream. Now say it right—*Grover!*"

"Gova."

"Ah-h, you-u. You're the craziest little old boy I ever did see. Can't you even say Grover?"

"Gova."

"Ah-h, you-u. Old Tongue-Tie, that's what you are. . . . Well, come on, then, I'll set you up anyway."

It all came back, and faded, and was lost again. Eugene turned to go, and thanked the woman and said good-bye.

"Well, then, good-bye," the woman said, and they shook hands. "I'm glad if I could show you. I'm glad if—" She did not finish, and at length she said: "Well, then, that was a long time ago. You'll find everything changed now, I guess. It's all built up around here now—and way out beyond here, out beyond where the Fair Grounds used to be. I guess you'll find it changed."

They had nothing more to say. They just stood there for a moment on the steps, and then shook hands once more.

"Well, good-bye."

And again he was in the street, and found the place where the corners met, and for the last time turned to see where Time had gone.

And he knew that he would never come again, and that lost magic would not come again. Lost now was all of it—the street, the heat, King's Highway, and Tom the Piper's son, all mixed in with the vast and drowsy murmur of the Fair, and with the sense of absence in the afternoon, and the house that waited, and the child that dreamed. And out of the enchanted wood, that thicket of man's memory, Eugene knew that the dark eye and the quiet face of his friend and brother—poor child, life's stranger, and life's exile, lost like all of us, a cipher in blind mazes, long ago—the lost boy was gone forever, and would not return.

No Cure for It

S ON! SON! WHERE ARE YOU, BOY?"
He heard her call again, and listened plainly to her now,
and knew she would break in upon his life, his spell of time,
and wondered what it was she wanted of him. He could hear
her moving in the front of the house.

Suddenly he heard her open the front door and call out sharply:
"Oh, Doctor McGuire! . . . Will you stop in here a minute?
. . . There's something I want to ask you."

He heard the iron gate slam, and the doctor's slow, burly
tread, the gruff rumble of his voice, as he came up the steps.
Then he heard them talking in low voices at the front hall door.
He could not distinguish their words until, after a minute or
two, she raised her voice somewhat and he heard her say reflectively, "Why-y, no-o!"—and knew that she was pursing her
lips in a startled, yet thoughtful manner, as she said it. Then
she went on in her curiously fragmentary, desperate, and all-
inclusive fashion: "I don't think so. At least, he's always seemed
all right. Never complained of anything. . . . It's only the last
year or so. . . . I got to thinkin' about it—it worried me, you
know. . . . He seems strong an' healthy enough. . . . But the
way he's growin'! I was speakin' to his father about it the other
day—an' he agreed with me, you know. Says, 'Yes, you'd better
ask McGuire the next time you see him.' "

"Where is he?" McGuire said gruffly. "I'll take a look at him."

"Why, yes!" she said quickly. "That's the very thing! . . . Son!
. . . Where are you, boy?"

43

Then they came back along the hall, and into the sitting room. The gangling boy was still stretched out on the smooth, worn leather of his father's couch, listening to the time-strange tocking of the clock, and regarding his bare brown legs and sun-browned toes with a look of dreamy satisfaction as they entered.

"Why, boy!" his mother cried in a vexed tone. "What on earth do you mean? I've been callin' for you everywhere!"

He scrambled up sheepishly, unable to deny that he had heard her, yet knowing, somehow, that he had not willfully disobeyed her.

Doctor McGuire came over, looking like a large, tousled bear, smelling a little like his horse and buggy, and with a strong stench of cigar and corn whisky on his breath. He sat his burly figure down heavily on Gant's couch, took hold of the boy's arm in one large, meaty hand, and for a moment peered at him comically through his bleared, kindly, dark-yellow eyes.

"How old are you?" he grunted.

Eugene told him he was seven, going on eight, and McGuire grunted indecipherably again.

He opened the boy's shirt and skinned it up his back, and then felt carefully up and down his spinal column with thick, probing fingers. He wriggled the boy's neck back and forth a few times, held the skinny arm out and inspected it solemnly, and then peered with grave, owlish humor at the boy's enormous hands and feet. After that he commanded the boy to stoop over without bending his knees and touch the floor.

Eugene did so; and when the doctor asked him if he could bend no farther, the boy put his hands down flat upon the floor, and remained bent over, holding them that way, until the doctor told him to stand up and let his arms hang naturally. When he stood up and let his arms fall, his hands hung level with his knees, and for a moment McGuire peered at him very carefully. Then he turned and squinted comically at Eliza with his look of owlish gravity, and said nothing. She stood there, her hands clasped in their loose, powerful gesture at her apron strings, and when he looked at her she shook her puckered face rapidly in a movement of strong concern and apprehension.

"Hm! Hm! Hm! Hm! Hm!" she said. "I don't like it! It don't seem natural to me!"

McGuire made no comment, and did not answer her. After staring at her owlishly a moment longer, he turned to the boy again and told him to lie down upon the couch. Eugene did so. McGuire then told him to raise his legs and bend them back as far as they would go, and kept grunting, "Farther! Farther!" until the boy was bent double. Then McGuire grunted sarcastically:

"Go on! Is that the best you can do? I know a boy who can wrap his legs all the way around his neck."

When he said this, the boy stuck his right leg around his neck without any trouble at all, and remained in that posture for some time, happily wriggling his toes under his left ear. McGuire looked at him solemnly, and at last turned and squinted at his mother, saying nothing.

"Whew-w!" she shrieked with a puckered face of disapproval. "Get out of here! I don't like to look at anything like that! . . . Hm! Hm! Hm! Hm! Hm!" she muttered, shaking her head rapidly with an expression of strong concern, as the boy unwound his legs and straightened out again.

Eugene stood up. For a moment McGuire held him by the arm and squinted comically at him through his bleared eyes, without saying a word. Then his burly, bearlike shoulders began to heave slowly, a low, hoarse chuckle rose in his throat, and he said, poking the boy in the ribs with one fat thumb:

"Why, you little monkey!"

"Hah! What say? What is it?" cried his mother in a sharp, startled tone.

The doctor's huge shoulders heaved mountainously again, the hoarse sound rumbled in his throat, and, shaking his head slowly, he said:

"I've seen them when they were knock-kneed, bow-legged, cross-eyed, pigeon-toed, and rickety—but that's the damndest thing I ever saw! I never saw the beat of it!" he said—and the boy grinned back at him proudly.

"Hah! What say? What's wrong with him?" Eliza said sharply.

The burly shoulders heaved again:

"Nothing," McGuire said. "Nothing at all! He's all right! He's just a little monkey!"—and the rumbling noises came from his inner depths again.

He was silent for a moment, during which he squinted at Eliza as she stood there pursing her lips at him, then he went on:

"I've seen them when they shot up like weeds, and I've seen them when you couldn't make them grow at all," he said, "but I never saw one before who grew like a weed in one place while he was standing still in another! . . . Look at those arms and legs!" he cried. "And good God! Will you look at his hands and feet! Did you ever in your life see such hands and feet on a child his age?"

"Why, it's awful!" his mother agreed, nodding. "I know it is! We can't find anything in the stores to fit him now! What's it goin' to be like when he gets older? It's an awful thing!" she cried.

"Oh, he'll be all right," McGuire said, as he heaved slowly. "He'll get all of his parts together some day and grow out of it! . . . But God knows what he'll grow into!" he said, rumbling inside again and shaking his head as he peered at the boy. "A mountain or an elephant—I don't know which!" He paused, then added: "But at the present time he's just a little monkey. . . . That's what you are—a monkey!" and the tremendous shoulders heaved again.

Just then the iron gate slammed, and the boy heard his father lunge across the walk, take the front porch steps in bounds of three, and come striding around the porch into the sitting room. He was muttering madly to himself, but stopped short as he came upon the little group, and, with a startled look in his uneasy cold-gray eyes, he cried out—"Hey?" although no one had spoken to him.

Then, wetting his great thumb briefly on his lips, and slamming down the package he was carrying, he howled:

"Woman, this is your work! Unnatural female that you are, you have given birth to a monster who will not rest until he has ruined us all, eaten us out of house and home, and sent me to the poorhouse to perish in a pauper's grave! Nor man nor beast hath fallen so far! . . . Well, what's your opinion, hey?" he barked abruptly at McGuire, half bending toward him in a frenzied manner.

"He's all right," McGuire said, slowly heaving. "He's just a monkey."

For a moment Gant looked at his son with his restless, cold-gray eyes.

"Merciful God!" he said. "If he had hair on him, they couldn't tell him from a monkey now!" Then, wetting his great thumb, he grinned thinly and turned away. He strode rapidly about the room, his head thrown back, his eyes swinging in an arc about the ceiling; then he paused, grinned again, and came over to the boy. "Well, son," he said kindly, putting his great hand gently upon the boy's head, "I'm glad to know that it's all right. I guess it was the same with me. Now don't you worry. You'll grow up to be a big man some day."

They all stood looking at the boy—his mother with pursed, tremulous, bantering, proudly smiling lips, his father with a faint, thin grin, and McGuire with his owlish, bleared, half-drunken, kindly stare. The boy looked back at them, grinning proudly, worried about nothing. He thought his father was the grandest, finest person in the world, and as the three of them looked at him he could hear, in the hush of brooding noon, the time-strange tocking of his father's clock.

Gentlemen of the Press

Time: A hot night in June, 1916.

Scene: The city room of a small-town newspaper.

The room has three or four flat-topped desks, typewriters, green-shaded lights hanging from the ceiling by long cords, some filing cabinets. Upon the wall, a large map of the United States. Upon the desks, newspaper clippings, sheets of yellow flimsy, paste pots, pencils, etc. Over all, a warm smell of ink, a not unpleasant air of use and weariness.

To the right, a door opening to a small room which houses the A.P. man, his typewriter, and his instruments. To the left, a glass partition and a door into the compositors' room. This door stands open and compositors may be seen at work before the linotype machines, which make a quiet slotting sound. The A.P. man's door is also open and he can be seen within, typing rapidly, to the accompaniment of the clattering telegraph instrument on the table beside him.

In the outer room, Theodore Willis, a reporter, sits at his desk, banging away at a typewriter. He is about twenty-eight years old, consumptive, very dark of feature, with oval-shaped brown eyes, jet black hair, thin hands, and a face full of dark intelligence, quickness, humor, sensitivity. At another desk, his back toward Willis, sits another reporter—young, red-headed, red-necked, stocky—also typing. All the men wear green eyeshades. Theodore Willis is smoking a cigarette, which hangs from the corner of his mouth and which he inhales from time to time, narrowing his eyes to keep the smoke out.

49

THE A.P. WIRE (*clattering rapidly*): . . . Wash ¯une 18 Walter Johnson was invincible today held Athletics to four scattered hits Senators winning three to nothing batteries Washington Johnson and Ainsmith Philadelphia Bender Plank and Schang.

(*The telegraph instrument stops suddenly. The A.P. man gets up, pulls a sheet from the machine, comes out in the city room, and tosses it on Theodore Willis's desk.*)

THE A.P. MAN: Well, the big Swede was burning 'em in today.

WILLIS (*typing, without looking up*): Washington win?

THE A.P. MAN: Three-nothing.

WILLIS: How many did he fan?

A.P. MAN: Fourteen. (*He lights a cigarette and inhales.*) Christ! If he had a decent team behind him he'd never lose a game.

(*Far off across the town, the screeching noise of Pretty Polly is heard, coming from the roof of the Appalachicola Hotel. She is a local character who for years has earned her living by singing in public places, and nobody ever calls her anything but Pretty Polly.*)

PRETTY POLLY (*singing away in the distance, and plainly audible to the last syllable*): . . . threels—mee-uh—and stuh-heels—mee-uh—and luh-hulls—mee-uh—to r-r-r-rest . . .

(*Benjamin Gant passes through city room on way to compositors' room. Pauses a moment with lean fingers arched upon his hips, head cocked slightly in direction of the sound.*)

PRETTY POLLY (*as before, but fading away now*): . . . threels—mee-uh—and stuh-heels—mee-uh—and luh-hulls—mee-uh—to r-r-r-rest.

BEN GANT (*jerking his head up scornfully and speaking to some unknown auditor*): Oh for God's sake! Listen to that, won't you? (*He goes out into the compositors' room.*)

A.P. MAN: Christ, what a voice!

WILLIS: Voice! That's not a voice! It's a distress signal! They ought to take her out to sea and anchor her off Sandy Hook as a warning to in-coming liners.

(*Harry Tugman, the chief pressman, enters at this moment with a bundle tied in a newspaper under his arm. He is a powerful man, brutally built, with the neck, shoulders, and battered features of a prize fighter. His strong, pitted face is colorless, and pocked heavily with ink marks.*)

TUGMAN (*yelling as he enters*): Wow! Wouldn't that old battle-ax be somethin' in a fog! She's hot tonight! Boy, she's goin' good! (*These remarks are addressed to no one in particular, but now he pauses beside the little group of reporters and speaks to them with abusive good nature.*) Hello, you lousy reporters. Is that lousy rag of yours ready to be run off yet?

WILLIS (*quietly, and without looking up*): Hello, you gin-swizzling sot. Yes, the lousy rag is ready to be run off, and so are you if the Old Man ever gets a whiff of that breath of yours. You'd better beat it downstairs now and get your press to rolling before he comes in and takes you for a brewery.

TUGMAN (*with riotous good nature*): Whew! That's it, Ted— give 'em hell! (*Boisterously*) Boys, I've been in a crap game and I took 'em for a hundred and fifty bucks.

WILLIS: Which means you're a dollar and a quarter to the good, I suppose. (*Quietly, viciously*) A hundred and fifty bucks— why, God-damn your drunken soul, you never saw that much at one time in your whole life.

A.P. MAN: How much of it you got left, Tug?

TUGMAN: Not a lousy cent. They took me to the cleaners afterwards. Tell you how it was, boys. We was down at Chakales Pig. When I picked up the loot I looked around and counted up the house and decided it was safe to buy a round of drinks, seein' as there was only five guys there. (*His manner grows more riotously extravagant as with coarse but eloquent improvisation he builds up the farce.*) Well, I goes up to the bar, thinkin' I'm safe, and says: 'Step right up, gentlemen. This one's on me.' And you know what happens? (*He pauses a moment for dramatic effect.*) Well, boys, I ain't hardly got the words out of my mouth when there is a terrific crash of splintered glass and eighteen booze hounds bust in from the sidewalk, six more spring through the back windows, and the trap doors of the cellar come flyin' open and thirty-seven more swarm up like rats out of the lower depths. By that time the place is jammed. Then I hear the sireens goin' in the street, and before I know it the village fire department comes plungin' in, followed by two-thirds of the local constabulary. I tries to crawl out between the legs of One-eye McGloon and Silk McCarthy, but they have me cornered before I gets as far as the nearest spittoon. Well, to make a long story short, they rolled me for every nickel I had. Somebody got my socks and B.V.D.'s, and when I finally crawled to safety Chakales had my shirt and told me he was holdin' it as security until I came through with the six bits I still owed him for the drinks.

(*Ben Gant returns from the compositors' room, and, as he passes, Harry Tugman slaps him violently on his bony back.*)

TUGMAN (*yelling boisterously*): How's that, Ben? Is that gettin' 'em told, or not?

BEN (*arching his hands upon his hips, sniffing scornfully, and jerking his head toward his unknown auditor*): Oh for God's sake! Listen to this, won't you?

TUGMAN (*still boisterously*): Did I ever tell you boys about the time I came back from Scandinavia, where I'd been managin' Jack Johnson on a barn-stormin' tour?

WILLIS (*starting up suddenly, laughing, and seizing a paper weight*): Get out of here, you son-of-a-bitch. Scandinavia! You've never been north of Lynchburg. The last time you told that story it was South America.

TUGMAN (*laughing heartily*): That was another time. (*Loudly, immensely pleased with himself*) Whew! God-*damn*! Give 'em hell, boys!

WILLIS: On your way, bum. It's time to roll.

TUGMAN (*going out in high spirits, singing loudly a bawdy parody of Pretty Polly's song*): . . . sla-hays—mee-uh—and la-hays—me-uh—and luh-hulls—mee-uh—to r-r-r-rest.

WILLIS (*now standing at his desk and reading a sheet of yellow flimsy with an air of growing stupefaction*): Well I'll be— in the name of God, who wrote this anyway? (*Reads*) 'By this time the police had arrived and thrown a cordon around the blazing tenement in an effort to keep the milling throngs at a safe distance.' (*With an air of frank amazement*) Well, I'll be God-damned! (*Suddenly, irritably, in a rasping voice*) Who wrote this crap? 'Blazing tenement'—'milling throngs'—now ain't that nice? (*Reading again, slowly, deliberately*) 'By—this— time—the—police—had—arrived—and—thrown—a—cordon . . . a—*cordon* ——'

RED (*the young reporter, whose neck and face during this recital had become redder than ever*): We always said 'cordon' on the *Atlanta Constitution.*

WILLIS (*looking at him with an air of stunned disbelief*): Did you write this? Is this your story?

RED (*sulkily*): Who the hell do you think wrote it? The Angel Gabriel?

WILLIS (*with an air of frank defeat*): Well I'll be damned! If that's not the damndest description I ever read of a fire in Niggertown, I'll kiss a duck. (*With wicked insistence*) 'Blazing tenement.' What blazing tenement are you talking about—a two-roomed nigger shack in Valley Street? For Christ's sake, you'd think the whole East Side of New York was afire. And 'milling throngs.' Well, I'm a monkey's uncle if that ain't perfectly God-damned delightful! What do you mean by milling throngs—forty-two niggers and a couple of one-eyed mules? And 'cordon.' (*A trifle more emphatically*) Cordon! (*He holds the paper at arm's length and surveys it daintily, with a show of mincing reflection.*)

RED (*sulkily*): We always said 'cordon' on the *Constitution*.

WILLIS: *Constitution*, my—! If old man Matthews, John Ledbetter, and Captain Crane constitute a cordon, then I'm a whole God-damn regiment of the United States Marines!

RED (*angrily*): All right, then. If you don't like the way the story's written, why the hell don't you write it yourself?

WILLIS: Why the hell should I? That's your job, not mine. Christ Almighty, man! I've got enough to do on my own hook without having to rewrite your whole damned story every time I send you out to cover a lousy little fire in Niggertown.

RED: That story would have gone on the *Constitution*. (*Sarcastically*) But apparently it's not good enough for a one-horse paper in a hick town. (*He pulls off his eyeshade and tosses it down upon the desk; puts on his vest and coat and begins to button himself up viciously.*) To hell with it anyway! To hell with this whole damn outfit! I'm through with it! The trouble with you guys is that you're all a bunch of illiterate half-wits who don't know anything about style and don't appreciate a piece of writing when you see one!

WILLIS: Style, hell! What I'd appreciate from you is a simple declarative sentence in the English language. If you've got to get all that fancy palaver out of your system, write it in your memory book. But for God's sake, don't expect to get it published in a newspaper.

RED (*savagely, tugging at his vest*): I'll get it published all right, and it won't be in your lousy paper either!

WILLIS (*ironically, sitting down and adjusting his eyeshade*): No? Where are you going to get it published—in the *Woman's Home Companion*?

RED (*contemptuously*): You guys give me a pain. Wait till my book comes out. Wait till you read what the critics have to say about it.

WILLIS (*beginning to work on the unhappy story with a blue pencil*): Go on, go on. The suspense is awful. What are we going to do when we read it? Turn green with envy, I suppose?

RED (*wagging his head*): All right, all right. Have it your own way. Only you'll be laughing out of the other corner of your mouth some day. You wait and see.

WILLIS (*working rapidly with the blue pencil and still speaking ironically, but in a more kindly tone than before*): Don't make us wait too long, Red. I've got only one lung left, you know. (*He coughs suddenly into a wadded handkerchief, stares intently for an instant at the small stain of spreading red, then thrusts the crumpled handkerchief back into his pocket.*)

RED (*flushing uncomfortably, suddenly moved*): Oh, well— (*eagerly*) Jesus, Ted, I've got a whale of an idea! If I can come through on this one, it'll knock 'em loose!

WILLIS (*a trifle absently, still working busily on the story*): What is it this time, Red—something hot? The love affairs of a police court reporter, or something like that?

RED: Nah, nah. Nothing like that! It's a historical novel. It's about Lincoln.

WILLIS: Lincoln! You mean Abe?

RED (*nodding vigorously*): Sure! It's a romance—an adventure story. I've been working on the idea for years, and boy, it's a lulu if I can put it over! (*Looks around craftily toward the door to see if he is being overheard, lowers his voice carefully, with an insinuating tone*) Listen, Ted——

WILLIS (*absently*): Well?

RED (*in a tone of cunning secrecy*): If I let you in on the idea (*he peers around apprehensively again*), you won't tell anyone, will you?

WILLIS: You know me, Red. Did you ever hear of a newspaper reporter giving away a secret? All right, kid, spill it.

RED (*lowering his voice still more, to a confidential whisper*): The big idea is this. Lincoln—you know Lincoln——

WILLIS: Sure. You mean the guy that got shot.

RED: Sure. (*Then, cunningly, secretively*) Well, Ted, all the history books—all the big authorities and the wise guys—*they* tell you he was born out in Kentucky——

WILLIS: And you mean to tell me he wasn't?

RED (*scornfully*): You're God-damn right he wasn't! Nah! (*Coming closer and whispering earnestly*) Why, Ted, that guy was no more born in Kentucky than you and I were. (*Nodding vigorously*) Sure. I'm telling you. I've got the dope—and I know. (*Whispering impressively*) Why, Ted, that guy grew up right out here in Yancey County, not more than fifty miles from town.

WILLIS (*in a tone of mock astonishment*): Go on! You're kidding me!

RED (*very earnestly*): No I'm not. It's the truth, Ted! I know what I'm talking about. I've got all the dope now—I've been working on the thing for years. (*He looks around cautiously again, then whispers*) And say, Ted, you know what else I've got? I've got a little dress that Lincoln wore when he was a baby. And say (*his voice sinking now to an awed whisper*), do you know what I found?

WILLIS (*working, absently*): What was it, Red?

RED (*whispering*): They say, you know, that Lincoln's parents were poor—but that little baby dress is made of the finest lace! And Ted, it's all embroidered, too. It's got initials on it! (*His voice sinks to an almost inaudible whisper*) Ted, it's embroidered with the letter N. (*He pauses significantly to let this sink in, then repeats in a meaningful tone*) N, Ted. . . . N. . . . Do you get it?

WILLIS: Do I get what? N what?

RED (*impatiently*): N nothing. Just N, Ted. (*He pauses anxiously for this to sink in, but gets no response.*)

WILLIS (*after waiting a moment*): Well? What about it?

RED (*disappointedly, whispering*): Why, don't you see, Ted? Lincoln's name begins with L, and this little dress I got is embroidered with the letter N. (*Again he waits hopefully for a satisfactory response and gets none.*) N, Ted. . . . N. . . . Don't you see?

WILLIS (*looking up a trifle impatiently and slapping his blue pencil down on the desk*): What are you driving at, Red? Spill it, for Christ's sake!

RED: Why, Ted, Lincoln's name begins with L, and this little dress I got is embroidered with the letter ——

WILLIS (*nodding wearily*): The letter N. Sure, I get you, Red. (*Picks up his pencil and resumes work again*) Well, maybe the laundry got the tags mixed.

RED (*in a disgusted tone*): Nah, Ted. (*Slowly, significantly*) N . . . N . . . (*Slyly*) Can't you think of anyone, Ted, whose name begins with N?

WILLIS (*casually*): Napoleon Bonaparte.

RED (*patiently*): Not exactly, Ted. (*Looking around craftily again, then whispering cunningly*) But you're coming close You're getting warm.

WILLIS (*throwing down his pencil, pushing up his eyeshade,*

and settling back in his chair with an air of weary resignation):
Look here, what the hell are you trying to give me? Are you
trying to hint that Lincoln was related to Napoleon?

RED: You're on the scent, Ted. (*Looking around craftily, then
whispering*) You're getting warm, all right. (*A look of
triumphant satisfaction expands across his countenance, and he
nods his head in affirmation*) Sure! I'm telling you!

WILLIS (*staring at him with frank amazement*): You mean to
stand there and say that Abraham Lincoln was Napoleon's
nephew or something?

RED: No, Ted. Not his nephew. (*Craftily, in a hoarse whisper*)
His son.

WILLIS (*staring helplessly*): Well, I'll be——!

RED (*nodding vigorously*): Sure, sure, I'm telling you! You
see, Ted, Napoleon's son didn't die in Austria. That's what the
history books say, but it's the bunk. What really happened was
this. (*He looks slyly around the room before continuing in a
hoarse whisper.*) After the battle of Waterloo the Bourbons captured Napoleon's son, who was just a child then, and were going
to send him back with his mother to the Hapsburgs in Vienna.
But the Bonapartists got wind of the plan, and with Maria
Louisa's help they put another child of the same age in the young
prince's place. This imposter was the one that was sent back to
Austria, and he died there. Meanwhile a trusted officer of Napoleon's took the young prince and escaped with him. They got
away all right, but the curious thing is that they were never heard
of again. No one ever knew what became of them. No one, that
is (*lowering his voice confidingly*)—except me. But I found
out. I got the dope. I've been working on the thing for years,
and I got it all nailed down now. The officer and the young prince
escaped to this country—in a sailing ship.

WILLIS (*in a tone of ironic mockery*): Aw, go on, Red! You

know people like that never would have taken a common sailing ship. They'd at least have come over on the *Berengaria*.

RED (*disregarding the sarcasm and whispering earnestly*): Nah, Ted. It was a sailing ship. I've got all the dope—the name of the ship, the captain, everything. And the officer took an assumed name—he called himself Thomas Lincoln, and pretended that the young prince was his son.

WILLIS (*as before*): Go on, I don't believe you!

RED (*earnestly*): It's the truth, Ted. They landed at Baltimore, and then came south. They settled over here in Yancey County— and the officer lived to be an old, old man. (*Looking around again, and cautiously whispering*) Why hell, Ted! He only died about thirty years ago! He was way over a hundred when he died. And there are people out there in Yancey County who knew him! They talked to him. They remember stories about the child, and how he grew up and was sent to Illinois when he was a young man. And they say it was Napoleon's son, all right. Oh, I got all the dope. And what's more, this young man—this royal prince—(*pausing for effect and whispering dramatically*)—was also Abraham Lincoln.

WILLIS (*lying sprawled in his chair as though he had collapsed, with his thin hands upon the desk, his mouth slightly ajar, staring at his companion with paralyzed astonishment, and speaking very slowly*): Well—I'll—be—God—damned!

RED (*taking the words as tribute, beaming triumphantly*): Ain't it a lulu, boy? Ain't it a wham? Won't it knock 'em for a goal?

WILLIS (*waving his thin hand groggily before his face*): You win, kid. Pick up the marbles. You've got me licked.

RED (*exuberantly*): Boy, I've got the hit of the century here— the greatest story since *The Count of Monte Cristo*!

WILLIS (*feebly*): Don't stop at *Monte Cristo*, kid. You can go the whole way back to the Holy Bible as far as I'm concerned.

RED (*delighted, yet a trifle anxiously*): You won't say anything about it, Ted? You won't let it out?

WILLIS (*exhausted*): Not for the world and a cage of pet monkeys. (*He holds out a thin, limp hand.*) Put it there.

(*Red, his face crimson with happiness, seizes Theodore Willis's thin hand and wrings it heartily. And then, with a jubilant "Good night," he goes out. For a moment Willis sits quietly, in an exhausted attitude, then he opens his mouth and lets out a long sigh.*)

WILLIS: Whew-w!

THE A.P. MAN (*coming to his door and peering out*): What is it?

WILLIS (*slowly shaking his head*): That wins the gold-enameled mustache cup. That guy!

A.P. MAN: What is it now—a new idea for a book he's going to write?

WILLIS: Yep—and he's got the whole idea nailed down, trussed up, and hog-tied. It's going to paralyze the public, upset history, and make the faculty at Harvard look like a set of boobs.

A.P. MAN: What is it? What's the idea?

WILLIS (*shaking his head solemnly*): That, sir, I can nevermore divulge. He has my promise, my word of honor. And the word of a Willis is as good as his bond—in fact, a damn sight better. Wild horses could not drag his secret from me. But I'll tell you this, my friend. If you should suddenly read absolute historic proof that Shakespeare had come over on the *Mayflower* and was the grandfather of George Washington, you'd get some faint notion of what this book is going to do to us. (*He coughs suddenly, rackingly, spits carefully into his wadded handkerchief, looks intently at the small red stain. then, with an expres-*

sion of weariness and disgust, thrusts the wadded rag back in his pocket.) Christ! Maybe some day I'll write a book myself--about all the poor hams I've known in this game who were going to write a book—and never did. What a life!

(*The A.P. man shrugs and goes back into his little room. The telephone rings. With an expression of weariness Theodore Willis takes the receiver from the hook.*)

WILLIS: Hello. . . . Yes, this is the *Courier*. . . . (*In an agreeable tone that is belied by the expression of extreme boredom on his face*) Yes, Mrs. Purtle. Yes, of course. . . . Oh, yes, there's still time. . . . No, she's not here, but I'll see that it gets in. . . . Certainly, Mrs. Purtle. Oh, absolutely. . . . (*He rolls his dark eyes aloft with an expression of anguished entreaty to his Maker.*) Yes, indeed, I promise you. It will be in the morning edition. . . . Yes, I can well understand how important it is. (*He indicates his understanding of its importance by scratching himself languidly on the hind quarter.*) . . . Oh, absolutely without fail. You can depend on it. . . . Yes, Mrs. Purtle. . . . (*He sprawls forward on one elbow, takes the moist fag end of a cigarette from his mouth and puts it in a tray, picks up a pencil, and wearily begins to take notes.*) Mr. and Mrs. S. Frederick Purtle. . . . No, I won't forget the S. . . . Yes, I know we had it Fred last time. We had a new man on the job. . . . No, we'll get it right this time. Mr. and Mrs. S. Frederick Purtle . . . dinner and bridge . . . tomorrow night at eight . . . at their residence, 'Oaknook,' 169 Woodbine Drive . . . in honor of—Now just a moment, Mrs. Purtle. I want to be sure to get this straight. (*Then, very slowly, with an expression of fine concern*) In honor of their house guest . . . Mrs. J. Skidmore Pratt, of Paterson, New Jersey . . . the former Miss Annie Lou Bass of this city. (*Writing casually as he continues*) Those invited include Mr. and Mrs. Leroy Dingley . . . Mr. and Mrs. E. Seth Hooton . . . Mr. and

Mrs. Claude Belcher . . . Mr. Nemo McMurdie . . . all of this city . . . and Miss May Belle Buckmaster of Florence, South Carolina. . . . Now, just a moment, Mrs. Purtle, to see if I've got it all straight. (*He reads it over to her. The lady is apparently satisfied, for ct length he says*) Oh absolutely. No, I won't forget. . . . Not at all, Mrs. Purtle. (*He laughs falsely.*) Delighted, of course. . . . Good-bye.

(*He hangs up the receiver, lights a cigarette, inserts a fresh sheet in the typewriter, and begins to type it out. The A.P. man comes out chuckling with a piece of paper in his hand.*)

A.P. MAN: Here's a hot one. Fellow out in Kansas has made himself a pair of wings and sent word around to all the neighbors that tomorrow's going to be the last day of the world and he's going to take off for the Promised Land at four o'clock. Everyone's invited to be present. And what's more, all of them are coming.

WILLIS (*typing*): Not a bad idea at that. (*Pulls the paper from the machine viciously and looks at it*) Christ! If I could only be sure tomorrow was going to be the last day of the world, what a paper I'd get out! That's my idea of heaven—to have, just for once in my life, the chance to tell these bastards what they are.

A.P. MAN (*grinning*): Boy, you could sure go to town on that, couldn't you? Only, you couldn't get it in an ordinary edition. You'd need an extra-extra-extra feature edition with fourteen supplements.

WILLIS (*clutching the sheet he has just typed and shaking it viciously*): Listen to this, will you. (*Reads*) 'Mr. and Mrs. Fred Purtle' (*he coughs in an affected tone*)—I beg your pardon, 'Mr. and Mrs. S. Frederick Purtle'—and be sure to get in the Frederick, and don't leave out the S . . . 'Mr. and Mrs. Leroy Dingley' . . . 'Mr. and Mrs. E. Seth Hooton'—and don't leave out the E . . . 'in honor of Mrs. J. Skidmore Pratt'—now there's a good one!

(*Throws down the paper savagely*) Why, God-damn that bunch of mountaineers—half of 'em never owned an extra pair of pants until they were twenty-one. As for Fred Purtle, he was brought up out in Yancey County on hawg and hominy. His father used to go over him with a curry comb and horse clippers every Christmas, whether he needed it or not. Why, hell yes. They had to throw him down to hold him while they put shoes on him. And now, for Christ's sake, it's Mr. S. Frederick Purtle —and don't leave out the S. My God! What a world! And what a job I could do on all the bastards in this town if I only had the chance! To be able, just for once, to tell the truth, to spill the beans, to print the facts about every son-of-a-bitch of them. To tell where they came from, who they were, how they stole their money, who they cheated, who they robbed, whose wives they slept with, who they murdered and betrayed, how they got here, who they really are. My God, it would be like taking a trip down the sewer in a glass-bottomed boat! But it would be wonderful—if tomorrow were the last day of the world. Only it's not (*he coughs suddenly, chokingly, and spits carefully into his handkerchief*)—not for most of us.

(*In the little office the telegraph instrument begins to clatter and the A.P. man goes back, types rapidly for a moment, and returns with another paper in his hand.*)

A.P. MAN: Here's something, Ted. It might be a story for you. Did you know this guy?

WILLIS (*taking the paper and reading it*): 'In an official communiqué the French Air Ministry today confirmed the report that Flight Lieutenant Clifford McKinley Brownlow of the Lafayette Escadrille was killed in action Tuesday morning over the lines near Soissons. Lieut. Brownlow, who in point of service was one of the oldest pilots in the Escadrille, had previously brought down fourteen German planes and had been decorated with the Croix de Guerre. He was twenty-four years old, and a native of Altamont, Old Catawba.'

(*When he has finished reading, Theodore Willis is silent for a moment and stares straight ahead of him. Then:*)

WILLIS (*speaking very slowly, as if to himself*): Did I know him? . . . Clifford Brownlow . . . Mrs. Brownlow's darling boy . . . the one we used to call 'Miss Susie' . . . and chase home from school every day, calling (*changing his voice to a parody of throaty refinement*): 'Oh Clifford! Are you the-ah?' . . . His mother used to call him like that, and we all took it up. Poor little devil! He must have had a wretched life. Clifford seemed a perfect name for him—for his ice cream pants, his effeminate way of walking and of talking, and all the rest of him. And now? Lieutenant Clifford Brownlow . . . Lafayette Escadrille . . . killed in action. . . . Somehow that seems perfect, too. And not funny either. There'll be speeches now, and ceremonies for 'Miss Susie.' There'll be a statue, too, a park named after him, a Clifford Brownlow school, a Brownlow auditorium. And why? What makes a hero, anyway? . . . Was it because we used to call him 'Miss Susie' and run him home, calling after him: 'Oh Clifford! Are you the'ah?' Was it because we tormented the poor little bastard until we almost drove him mad? Was it because his mother wouldn't let him play with us, wouldn't let him mingle with the rough, rude boys? Is that the way a hero's made? . . . Poor kid, he used to have a game he had invented that he played all by himself. It was a sort of one-man football game. He had a dummy rigged up in the yard, something he had made himself, stuffed with straw and hung on a pulley and a wire. He had a football uniform, too, complete with jersey, shoulder pads, and cleated shoes—his mother always bought him the best of everything. And we used to go by in the afternoon and see him playing at his one-man game, running with his brand-new ball, tackling his home-made dummy, sprinting for a touchdown through an imaginary broken field. And we—may God have mercy on our souls—we used to stand by the fence and jeer at him! . . . Well, he's a hero now—about the only hero we have. And there'll be ceremonies, honors, letters to his mother from the President of the French Republic. He's a hero, and he's dead. And we? (*He coughs suddenly, chokingly, spits into his wadded handkerchief, and stares intently at the spreading blot.*) Well, Joe, (*huskily*) tomorrow may be the last day of the world. Is there any other war news?

A.P. MAN: Just the usual run. The French claim they've broken through and gained another hundred yards upon a half-mile front. The Germans say they killed six hundred Frenchmen.

WILLIS (*looking at his watch*): Twelve-two. Two minutes after five o'clock in France . . . and some bastard's getting his right at this moment. . . . Another day. . . . For how many will it be the last day of the world? God, if I only knew that it would be for me! (*Coughs, goes through the ritual with the handkerchief, then rises, takes off his eyeshade, throws it on the desk, and stretches slowly with an air of great weariness and disgust.*) Ah-h, Christ!

(*The scene fades out. Far off, in darkness, is heard the baying of a hound.*)

A Kinsman of His Blood

FROM TIME TO TIME, DURING HIS SUNDAY VISITS TO HIS UNCLE Bascom's house, Eugene would meet his cousin, Arnold Pentland. Arnold was the only one of Bascom's children who ever visited his father's house: the rest were studiously absent, saw their father only at Christmas or Thanksgiving, and then like soldiers who will make a kind of truce upon the morning of the Lord's nativity. And certainly the only reason that poor, tormented Arnold ever came to Bascom's house was not for any love he bore him—for their relation to each other was savage and hostile, as it had been since Arnold's childhood—but rather, he came through loneliness and terror, as a child comes home, to see his mother, to try to find some comfort with her if he could.

Even in the frequency of these visits, the dissonant quality of his life was evident. After months of absence he would appear suddenly, morosely, without a word of explanation, and then he would come back every Sunday for several weeks. Then he would disappear again, as suddenly as he came: for several months, sometimes for a year or more, none of them would see him. The dense and ancient web of Boston would repossess him— he would be engulfed in oblivion as completely as if the earth had swallowed him. Then after months of silence, he would again be heard from: his family would begin to receive postal cards from him, of which the meaning was often so confused that nothing was plain save that the furious resentment that sweltered in him against them was again at work.

Thus, in the same day, Bascom, his daughters, and his other son might all receive cards bearing a few splintered words that read somewhat as follows:

Have changed my name to Arthur Penn. *Do not try to find me, it is useless!* You have made an outcast out of me— now I want only to forget that I ever knew you, have the same blood in my veins. *You have brought this on yourselves —I hope 1 shall never see your faces again!*

Arthur Penn.

After this explosion they would hear nothing from him for months. Then one day he would reappear without a word of explanation, and for several weeks would put in a morose appearance every Sunday.

Eugene had met him first one Sunday afternoon in February at his uncle's house. Arnold was sprawled out on a sofa as he entered, and his mother, approaching him, spoke to him in the tender, almost pleading tone of a woman who is conscious of some past negligence in her treatment of her child and who is now, pitiably too late, trying to remedy it.

"Arnold," she said coaxingly, "Arnold—will you get up now, please, dear—this is your cousin—won't you say hello to him?"

The great fat obscenity of belly on the sofa stirred, the man got up abruptly and, blurting out something desperate and incoherent, thrust out a soft, grimy hand and turned away.

Arnold Pentland was a man of thirty-six. He could have been rather small of limb and figure had it not been for his great shapeless fatness—a fatness pale and grimy that suggested animal surfeits of unwholesome food. He had lank, greasy hair of black, carelessly parted in the middle, his face, like all the rest of him, was pale and soft, the features blurred by fatness and further disfigured by a greasy smudge of beard. And from this fat, pale face his eyes, brown and weak, looked out on the world with a hysterical shyness of retreat, his mouth trembled uncertainly with a movement that seemed always on the verge of laughter or hysteria, and his voice gagged, worked, stuttered incoherently, or wrenched out desperate, shocking phrases with an effort that was almost as painful as the speech of a paralytic.

His clothing was indescribably dirty. He wore a suit of old blue serge, completely shapeless, shiny with the use of years, and spotted with the droppings of a thousand meals. Half the buttons were burst off the vest, and between vest and trousers there was a six-inch hiatus of dirty shirt and mountainous fat belly. His shoes were so worn that his naked toes showed through, and his socks were barely more than rags, exposing his dirty heels every time he took a step. The whole creature was as grievously broken, dissonant, and exploded as it is possible for a human life to be, and all the time his soft brown eyes looked out with the startled, pleading look of a stricken animal.

It was impossible to remain with him without a painful feeling of embarrassment—a desire to turn away from this pitiable exposure of disintegration. Everyone felt this but his father; as for Bascom, he just dismissed the conduct of his son impatiently, snorting down his nose derisively, or turning away as one would turn away from the gibberings of an idiot.

Dinner that day—the Sunday of Eugene's first meeting with his cousin—was an agonizing experience for everyone save Bascom. Arnold's conduct of his food was a bestial performance; he fell upon it ravenously, tearing at it, drawing it in with a slobbering suction, panting, grunting over it like an animal until layers of perspiration stood out on his pale wide forehead. Meanwhile, his mother was making a pitiable effort to distract attention from this painful performance; with a mask of attempted gayety she tried to talk to her nephew about a dozen things—the news of the day, the latest researches in "psychology," the base conduct of the Senate "unreconcilables," or the researches of Professor Einstein, the wonder-working miracle of the human mind. At which Arnold, looking up and glaring defiantly at both of them, would suddenly explode into a jargon of startling noises that was even more shocking than his bestial ruminations over food:

"M-m-man at Harvard . . . fourteen languages. . . . A guh-guh-guh-guh-" he paused and glared at his mother with a look of desperate defiance while she smiled pitiable encouragement at him—"a gorilla," he marched it out at last triumphantly, "can't speak one!" and he paused again, his mouth trembling, his throat working convulsively, and then burst out again—"Put gorilla in cage with man . . . all over! . . . done for! . . . half a minute!" He snapped his fingers. "Gorilla make mince meat of him. . . . Homer . . . Dante . . . Milton . . . Newton . . . Laws of Gravity . . . Muh-muh-muh-muh-" again he gagged, craned his fat neck desperately along the edges of his dirty collar and burst out—"Mind of man! . . . Yet when dead—nothing! . . . No good! . . . Seven ten-penny nails worth more!" He paused, glaring, his throat working desperately again, and at length barked forth with triumphant concision: "Brisbane!" and was still.

"Ah-h!" Bascom muttered at this point, and, his features contorted in an expression of disgust, he pushed his chair back, and turned half away. "What is he talking about, anyway? . . . Gorillas—Harvard—fourteen languages!" Here he laughed sneeringly down his nose. "Phuh! Phuh! Phuh! Phuh! Phuh! . . . Homer—Dante—Newton—seven ten-penny nails—Brisbane! . . . Phuh! Phuh! Phuh! Phuh! Phuh! . . . Did anyone ever hear such stuff since time began!" And, contorting his powerful features, he laughed sneeringly down his nose again.

"Yes!" cried Arnold angrily, throwing down his napkin and

glaring at his father with wild, resentful eyes, shot suddenly with tears—"And you, too! . . . No match for guh-guh-guh-guh-*gorilla*!" he yelled. "Think you are! . . . Egotist! . . . Muh-muh-muh-" he paused, gagging, worked his neck along his greasy collar and burst out—"Megalomaniac! . . . Always were! . . . But no match for gorilla. . . . Get you!"

"Ah-h!" Bascom muttered, confiding his eloquent features into vacancy with an expression of powerful disgust—"You don't know what you're talking about! . . . He has no conception—oh, not the slightest!—not the faintest!—none whatever!" he howled, waving his great hand through the air with a gesture of scornful dismissal.

The next Sunday, when Eugene went again to Bascom's house, he was surprised when the old man himself came to the door and opened it. In response to the boy's quick inquiry about his aunt, Bascom, puckering his face in a gesture of disgust, and jerking his head toward the kitchen, muttered:

"Ah-h! She's in there talking to that—fool! . . . But come in, my boy!" he howled, with an instant change to cordiality. "Come in, come in!" he yelled enthusiastically. "We've been expecting you."

From the kitchen came the sound of voices—a woman's and a man's, at first low, urgent, blurred, then growing louder; and suddenly Eugene could hear Arnold's voice, the wrenched-out, desperate speech now passionately excited:

"Got to! . . . I tell you, mother, I've got to! . . . She needs me . . . and I've got to go!"

"But, Arnold, Arnold!" his mother's voice was tenderly persuasive and entreating. "Now quiet, dear, quiet! Can't you quiet yourself a moment while we talk about it?"

"Nothing to talk about!" his voice wrenched the words out

desperately. "You've seen the letters, mother. . . . You see what she says, don't you?" His voice rose to a hysterical scream.

"Yes, dear, but——"

"Then what is there to talk about?" he cried frantically. "Don't you see she wants me? . . . Don't you see she's in some terrible trouble with that—that brute . . . that she's begging me to come and take her away from him?"

"Oh, Arnold, Arnold!" his mother's voice was filled with pitiable entreaty, hushed with an infinite regret. "My poor boy, can't you see that all she says is that if you ever go out there she would be glad to see you." He made some blurted-out reply that was indecipherable, and then, speaking gently but incisively, she continued: "Arnold—listen to me, my dear. This woman is a married woman, twenty years older than yourself, with grown children of her own. Don't you understand, my dear, that those letters are just the friendly letters that a woman would write to a boy she once taught in school? Don't you see how much these letters you have written her have frightened her—how she is trying in a kind way to let you know——"

"It's a lie!" he said in a choking tone—"a dirty lie! You're against me like all the rest of them! I'll not listen to you any longer! I'll go and get her. . . . I'll bring her back with me, no matter what you say . . . and to hell with you!" he yelled. "To hell with all of you!"

There was a sound of scrambling confusion, and then he came flying through the swinging door that led from the kitchen, jamming his battered hat down on his head, his eyes wild with grief and anger, his lips trembling and convulsed, murmuring soundless imprecations as he fled. And his mother followed him, a small wrenlike figure of a woman, her face haggard, stamped with grief and pity, calling: "Arnold! Arnold!" desperately to that fat, untidy figure that went past like a creature whipped

with furies, never pausing to look or speak or say good-bye
to anyone, as he ran across the room, and left the house, slamming
the door behind him.

The story, with its wretched delusion, was pitiable enough.
Since his second year at high school, Arnold had cherished a deep
affection for a woman who had taught him at that time. She
was one of the few women who had ever shown a scrap of understanding for him, and her interest had been just the kindly
interest that a warm-hearted and intelligent woman might feel
for a wretched little boy. To her, as to everyone else, he had
been an ugly duckling, but this had wakened her protective
instinct, and actually made him dearer to her than the more
attractive children. And because of this she had taught him
more—done more for him—than any other person he had ever
known, and he had never forgotten her.

When Arnold had left school, this woman had married and
moved to California with her husband. But in the twenty years
that had elapsed since then her old friendship with the boy—
for "boy" he still was to her—had never been broken. During
all that time Arnold had written her several times a year—long,
rambling letters filled with his plans, despairs, ambitions, hopes,
and failures—the incoherent record of an incoherent personality
—and the woman had always answered him with short, brisk,
friendly letters of her own.

And during all these years, while he remained to her the
"boy" that she had taught, her own personality was undergoing
a fantastic transformation in his memory. Although she had been
a mature and rather spinsterly female when he had known her,
and was now a gray-haired woman in the upper fifties, it seemed
to him now that she had never been anything but young and
beautiful and fair.

And as that picture developed in his mind it seemed to him

that he had always loved her—as a man would love a woman—
and that the only possible meaning in these casual and friendly
letters that she wrote to him lay in the love she bore for him.

Nothing could be done to stop him. For months now he had
come to his mother with trembling haste each time that he
received one of the letters. He would read them in a trembly
voice, finding in the most casual phrases the declarations of a
buried love. And his own replies to these friendly notes had become steadily more ardent and intimate, until, at last, they had
become the passionate and hysterical professions of a man in
love. The effect of this correspondence on the woman was evident—evident to everyone but Arnold himself. At first, her replies
had been written in the same friendly tone that had always
characterized her notes to him, but a growing uneasiness was
apparent. It was evident that in a kindly way she was trying to
check this rising tide of passion, divert his emotion into the old
channel of fellowship. Then, as his letters increased in the urgent
ardor of their confessions, her own had grown steadily more im-
personal; the last, in answer to his declaration that he "must
see her and would come at once," was decidedly curt. It expressed her cold regret that such a visit as he proposed would be
impossible—that she and her family would be "away for the
summer"—told him that the journey to California would be long,
costly, and unpleasant, and advised him to seek his summer's
recreation in some more agreeable and less expensive way.

Even the chilling tenor of this letter failed to quench him. Instead, he "read between the lines," he insisted on finding in
these curt phrases the silent eloquence of love, and though months
had passed since this last letter, and he had written many ardent
times since then, he was even convinced that her protracted
silence was just another sign of her love—that she was being sup-
pressed through fear, that she was held in bitter constraint by

that tyrannical "brute," her husband—a man of whom he knew nothing, but for whom he had conceived a murderous hatred.

Thus, against all the persuasions of his mother, he had decided to go. And that day when he had fled out of his father's house with bitter imprecations on his lips had marked the final moment of decision. Nothing could be done to stop him, and he went.

He was gone perhaps a month; no one knew exactly how long he was away, for none of his family saw him for about a year. And what the result of that strange meeting may have been, they never heard—and yet never needed to be told.

From that moment on he was completely lost to them; the legend of that last defeat, the ruin of that final and impossible hope was written on him, inscribed on his heart and living in his eyes in letters of unspeakable terror, madness, and despair.

One night a year later, when Eugene had been prowling around the dark and grimy streets of the South Boston slums, he saw a familiar figure in lower Washington Street. It was his cousin, Arnold Pentland. A fine spring rain had been falling all night long, and below the elevated structure the pavements were wet and glistening. Arnold was standing at a corner, looking around with a quick, distracted glance, clutching a tattered bundle of old newspapers under one arm.

Eugene ran across the street, calling to him, "Arnold! Arnold!" The man did not seem to hear at first, then looked around him in a startled way, and at last, as Eugene approached him, calling him by name again, he shrank together and drew back, clutching his bundle of old papers before him with both hands and looking at his cousin with the terror-stricken eyes of a child who has suddenly been attacked.

"Arnold!" Eugene cried again. "*Arnold!* Don't you know

me? . . . I'm your cousin—Eugene!" And as he made another step toward the man, his hand outstretched in greeting, Arnold scrambled back with such violent terror that he almost fell, and then, still holding the bundle of old papers before him protectively, stammered:

"Duh-duh-duh-don't know you. . . . Some mistake!"

"Oh, there's no mistake!" the boy cried impatiently. "You know me! I've met you a dozen times at Uncle Bascom's house. . . . Look here, Arnold." He took off his hat so that the man could better see his face. "You know me now, don't you?"

"No!—No!" Arnold gasped, moving away all the time. "Wrong man. . . . Name's not Arnold!"

Eugene stared at him a moment in blank astonishment and then exploded:

"Not Arnold? Of course it's Arnold! Your name's Arnold Pentland, and you're my first cousin. Look here, Arnold—what the hell is this anyway? What are you trying to do?"

"No! . . . No! . . . Mistake, I tell you! . . . Don't know you! Name's not Arnold! . . . Name's Arthur Penn."

"I don't give a damn what you call yourself!" Eugene now cried angrily. "You're Arnold Pentland just the same, and you're not going to get away from me until you admit it! Look here! What kind of trick is this anyway? What are you trying to pull on me?"—and in his excitement he took the man by his arm and shook him.

Arnold uttered a long, wailing cry of terror and, wrenching free, struggled backward crying:

"You leave me alone now! . . . All of you leave me alone! . . . I never want to see any of you again!"

And, turning, he began to run blindly and heavily away, a grotesque and pitiable figure, clutching his bundle of sodden newspapers, bent over toward the rain.

Eugene watched him go with a feeling of nameless pity, lone-liness, and loss—the feeling of a man who for a moment in the huge unnumbered wilderness of life, the roaring jungle of America, sees a face he knows, a kinsman of his blood, and says farewell to him forever. For that moment's vision of that fat, stumbling figure running blindly away from him down a dark, wet street was the last he would ever have. He never saw the man again.

Chickamauga

O N THE SEVENTH DAY OF AUGUST, 1861, I WAS NINETEEN YEARS of age. If I live to the seventh day of August this year I'll be ninety-five years old. And the way I feel this mornin' I intend to live. Now I guess you'll have to admit that that's goin' a good ways back.

I was born up at the Forks of the Toe River in 1842. Your grandpaw, boy, was born at the same place in 1828. His father, and mine too, Bill Pentland—*your* great-grandfather, boy—moved into that region way back right after the Revolutionary War and settled at the Forks of Toe. The real Indian name fer hit was Estatoe, but the white men shortened hit to Toe, and hit's been known as Toe River ever since.

Of course hit was all Indian country in those days. I've heared that the Cherokees helped Bill Pentland's father build the first house he lived in, where some of us was born. I've heared, too, that Bill Pentland's grandfather came from Scotland back before the Revolution, and that thar was three brothers. That's all the Pentlands that I ever heared of in this country. If you ever meet a Pentland anywheres you can rest assured he's descended from one of those three.

Well, now, as I was tellin' you, upon the seventh day of August, 1861, I was nineteen years of age. At seven-thirty in the mornin' of that day I started out from home and walked the whole way in to Clingman. Jim Weaver had come over from Big Hickory where he lived the night before and stayed with me. And now he went along with me. He was the best friend I had. We had growed up alongside of each other: now we was to march alongside of each other fer many a long and weary mile—how many neither of us knowed that mornin' when we started out.

Hit was a good twenty mile away from where we lived to Clingman, and I reckon young folks nowadays would consider twenty mile a right smart walk. But fer people in those days hit wasn't anything at all. All of us was good walkers. Why Jim Weaver could keep goin' without stoppin' all day long.

Jim was big and I was little, about the way you see me now, except that I've shrunk up a bit, but I could keep up with him anywheres he went. We made hit into Clingman before twelve o'clock—hit was a hot day, too—and by three o'clock that afternoon we had both joined up with the Twenty-ninth. That was my regiment from then on, right on to the end of the war. Anyways, I was an enlisted man that night, the day that I was nineteen years of age, and I didn't see my home again fer four long years.

Your Uncle Bacchus, boy, was already in Virginny: we knowed he was thar because we'd had a letter from him. He joined up right at the start with the Fourteenth. He'd already been at First Manassas and I reckon from then on he didn't miss a big fight in Virginny fer the next four years, except after Antietam where he got wounded and was laid up fer four months.

Even way back in those days your Uncle Bacchus had those queer religious notions that you've heared about. The Pentlands are good people, but everyone who ever knowed 'em knows they can go queer on religion now and then. That's the reputation that they've always had. And that's the way Back was. He was a Russellite even in those days: accordin' to his notions the world was comin' to an end and he was goin' to be right in on hit when hit happened. That was the way he had hit figgered out. He was always prophesyin' and predictin' even back before the war, and when the war came, why Back just knowed that this was hit.

Why law! He wouldn't have missed that war fer anything. Back didn't go to war because he wanted to kill Yankees. He didn't want to kill nobody. He was as tender-hearted as a baby and as brave as a lion. Some fellers told hit on him later how they'd come on him at Gettysburg, shootin' over a stone wall, and his rifle bar'l had got so hot he had to put hit down and rub his hands on the seat of his pants because they got so blistered. He was singin' hymns, they said, with tears a-streamin' down his face—that's the way they told hit, anyway—and every time he fired he'd sing another verse. And I reckon he killed plenty because when Back had a rifle in his hands he didn't miss.

But he was a good man. He didn't want to hurt a fly. And I reckon the reason that he went to war was because he thought he'd be at Armageddon. That's the way he had hit figgered out, you know. When the war came, Back said: "Well, this is hit, and I'm a-goin' to be thar. The hour has come," he said, "when the Lord is goin' to set up His kingdom here on earth and separate the sheep upon the right hand and the goats upon the left—jest like hit was predicted long ago—and I'm a-goin' to be thar when hit happens."

Well, we didn't ask him which side *he* was goin' to be on, but we all knowed which side without havin' to ask. Back was goin' to be on the *sheep* side—that's the way *he* had hit figgered out. And that's the way he had hit figgered out right up to the day of his death ten years ago. He kept prophesyin' and predictin' right up to the end. No matter what happened, no matter what mistakes he made, he kept right on predictin'. First he said the war was goin' to be the Armageddon day. And when that didn't happen he said hit was goin' to come along in the eighties. And when hit didn't happen then he moved hit up to the nine-ties. And when the war broke out in 1914 and the whole world had to go, why Bacchus knowed that *that* was hit.

And no matter how hit all turned out, Back never would give in or own up he was wrong. He'd say he'd made a mistake in his figgers somers, but that he'd found out what hit was and that next time he'd be right. And that's the way he was up to the time he died.

I had to laugh when I heared the news of his death, because of course, accordin' to Back's belief, after you die nothin' hap-pens to you fer a thousand years. You jest lay in your grave and sleep until Christ comes and wakes you up. So that's why I had to laugh. I'd a-give anything to've been there the next mornin' when Back woke up and found himself in heaven. I'd've give anything just to've seen the expression on his face. I may have to wait a bit but I'm goin' to have some fun with him when I see him. But I'll bet you even then he won't give in. He'll have some reason fer hit, he'll try to argue he was right but that he made a little mistake about hit somers in his figgers.

But Back was a good man—a better man than Bacchus Pent-land never lived. His only failin' was the failin' that so many Pentlands have—he went and got queer religious notions and he wouldn't give them up.

Well, like I say then, Back was in the Fourteenth. Your Uncle Sam and Uncle George was with the Seventeenth, and all three of them was in Lee's army in Virginny. I never seed nor heared from either Back or Sam fer the next four years. I never knowed what had happened to them or whether they was dead or livin' until I got back home in '65. And of course I never heared from George again until they wrote me after Chancellorsville. And then I knowed that he was dead. They told hit later when I came back home that hit took seven men to take him. They asked him to surrender. And then they had to kill him because he wouldn't be taken. That's the way he was. He never would give up. When they got to his dead body they told how they had to crawl over a whole heap of dead Yankees before they found him. And then they knowed hit was George. That's the way he was, all right. He never would give in.

He is buried in the Confederate cemetery at Richmond, Virginny. Bacchus went through thar more than twenty years ago on his way to the big reunion up at Gettysburg. He hunted up his grave and found out where he was.

That's where Jim and me thought that we'd be too. I mean with Lee's men, in Virginny. That's where we thought that we was goin' when we joined. But, like I'm goin' to tell you now, hit turned out different from the way we thought.

Bob Saunders was our Captain; L. C. McIntyre our Major; and Leander Briggs the Colonel of our regiment. They kept us thar at Clingman fer two weeks. Then they marched us into Altamont and drilled us fer the next two months. Our drillin' ground was right up and down where Parker Street now is. In those days thar was nothing thar but open fields. Hit's all built up now. To look at hit today you'd never know thar'd ever been an open field thar. But that's where hit was, all right.

Late in October we was ready and they moved us on. The day they marched us out, Martha Patton came in all the way from Zebulon to see Jim Weaver before we went away. He'd known her fer jest two months; he'd met her the very week we joined up and I was with him when he met her. She came from out along Cane River. Thar was a camp revival meetin' goin' on outside of Clingman at the time, and she was visitin' this other gal in Clingman while the revival lasted; and that was how

Jim Weaver met her. We was walkin' along one evenin' toward sunset and we passed this house where she was stayin' with this other gal. And both of them was settin' on the porch as we went past. The other gal was fair, and she was dark: she had black hair and eyes, and she was plump and sort of little, and she had the pertiest complexion, and the pertiest white skin and teeth you ever seed; and when she smiled there was a dimple in her cheeks.

Well, neither of us knowed these gals, and so we couldn't stop and talk to them, but when Jim saw the little 'un he stopped short in his tracks like he was shot, and then he looked at her so hard she had to turn her face. Well, then, we walked on down the road a piece and then Jim stopped and turned and looked again, and when he did, why, sure enough, he caught *her* lookin' at him too. And then her face got red—she looked away again.

Well, that was where she landed him. He didn't say a word, but Lord! I felt him jerk there like a trout upon the line—and I knowed right then and thar she had him hooked. We turned and walked on down the road a ways, and then he stopped and looked at me and said:

"Did you see that gal back thar?"

"Do you mean the light one or the dark one?"

"You know damn good and well which one I mean," said Jim.

"Yes, I seed her—what about her?" I said.

"Well, nothin'—only I'm a-goin' to marry her," he said.

I knowed then that she had him hooked. And yet I never believed at first that hit would last. Fer Jim had had so many gals—I'd never had a gal in my whole life up to that time, but Lord! Jim would have him a new gal every other week. We had some fine-lookin' fellers in our company, but Jim Weaver was the handsomest feller that you ever seed. He was tall and lean and built just right, and he carried himself as straight as a rod: he had black hair and coal-black eyes, and when he looked at you he could burn a hole through you. And I reckon he'd burned a hole right through the heart of many a gal before he first saw Martha Patton. He could have had his pick of the whole lot—a born lady-killer if you ever seed one—and that was why I never thought that hit'd last.

And maybe hit was a pity that hit did. Fer Jim Weaver until the day that he met Martha Patton had been the most happy-go-lucky feller that you ever seed. He didn't have a care in the whole world—full of fun—ready fer anything and into every kind of devilment and foolishness. But from that moment on he was a different man. And I've always thought that maybe hit was a pity that hit hit him when hit did—that hit had to come jest at that time. If hit had only come a few years later—if hit could only have waited till the war was over! He'd wanted to go so much—he'd looked at the whole thing as a big lark—but now! Well she had him, and he had her: the day they marched us out of town he had her promise, and in his watch he had her picture and a little lock of her black hair, and as they marched us out, and him beside me, we passed her, and she looked at him, and I felt him jerk again and knowed the look she gave him had gone through him like a knife.

From that time on he was a different man; from that time on he was like a man in hell. Hit's funny how hit all turns out—how none of hit is like what we expect. Hit's funny how war and a little black-haired gal will change a man—but that's the story that I'm goin' to tell you now.

The nearest rail head in those days was eighty mile away at Locust Gap. They marched us out of town right up the Fairfield Road along the river up past Crestville, and right across the Blue Ridge there, and down the mountain. We made Old Stockade the first day's march and camped thar fer the night. Hit was twenty-four miles of marchin' right across the mountain, with the roads the way they was in those days, too. And let me tell you, fer new men with only two months' trainin' that was doin' good.

We made Locust Gap in three days and a half, and I wish you'd seed the welcome that they gave us! People were hollerin' and shoutin' the whole way. All the women folk and childern were lined up along the road, bands a-playin', boys runnin' along beside us, good shoes, new uniforms, the finest-lookin' set of fellers that you *ever* seed—Lord! you'd a-thought we was goin' to a picnic from the way hit looked. And I reckon that was the way most of us felt about hit, too. We thought we was goin' off to have a lot of fun. If anyone had knowed what he was in fer or could a-seed the passel o' scarecrows that came limpin' back barefoot and half naked four years later, I reckon he'd a-thought twice before he 'listed up.

Lord, when I think of hit! When I try to tell about hit thar jest ain't words enough to tell what hit was like. And when I think of the way I was when I joined up—and the way I was when I came back four years later! When I went away I was an ignorant country boy, so tender-hearted that I wouldn't harm a rabbit. And when I came back after the war was over I could a-stood by and seed a man murdered right before my eyes with no more feelin' than I'd have had fer a stuck hog. I had no more feelin' about human life than I had fer the life of a sparrer. I'd seed a ten-acre field so thick with dead men that you could have walked all over hit without steppin' on the ground a single time.

And that was where I made my big mistake. If I'd only knowed a little more, if I'd only waited jest a little longer after I got home, things would have been all right. That's been the big regret of my whole life. I never had no education. I never had a chance to git one before I went away. And when I came back I could a-had my schoolin' but I didn't take hit. The reason was I never knowed no better: I'd seed so much fightin' and killin' that I didn't care fer nothin'. I jest felt dead and numb like all the brains had been shot out of me. I jest wanted to git me a little patch of land somewheres and settle down and fergit about the world.

That's where I made my big mistake. I didn't wait long enough. I got married too soon, and after that the childern came and hit was root, hawg, or die: I had to grub fer hit. But if I'd only waited jest a little while hit would have been all right. In less'n a year hit all cleared up. I got my health back, pulled myself together and got my feet back on the ground, and had more mercy and understandin' in me, jest on account of all the sufferin' I'd seen, than I ever had. And as fer my head, why hit was better than hit ever was: with all I'd seen and knowed I could a-got a schoolin' in no time. But you see I wouldn't wait. I didn't think that hit'd ever come back. I was jest sick of livin'.

But as I say—they marched us down to Locust Gap in less'n four days' time, and then they put us on the cars fer Richmond. We got to Richmond on the mornin' of one day, and up to that very moment we had thought that they was sendin' us to join Lee's army in the north. But the next mornin' we got our orders —and they was sendin' us out west. They had been fightin' in Kentucky: we was in trouble thar; they sent us out to stop the Army of the Cumberland. And that was the last I ever saw of old Virginny. From that time on we fought it out thar in the west and south. That's where we was, the Twenty-ninth, from then on to the end.

We had no real big fights until the spring of '62. And hit takes a fight to make a soldier of a man. Before that, thar was skirmishin' and raids in Tennessee and in Kentucky. That winter we seed hard marchin' in the cold and wind and rain. We learned to know what hunger was, and what hit was to have to draw your belly in to fit your rations. I reckon by that time we knowed hit wasn't goin' to be a picnic like we thought that hit would be. We was a-learnin' all the time, but we wasn't soldiers yet. It takes a good big fight to make a soldier, and we hadn't had one yet. Early in '62 we almost had one. They marched us to the relief of Donelson—but law! They had taken her before we got thar—and I'm goin' to tell you a good story about that.

U. S. Grant was thar to take her, and we was marchin' to relieve her before old Butcher could git in. We was seven mile away, and hit was comin' on to sundown—we'd been marchin' hard. We got the order to fall out and rest. And that was when I heared the gun and knowed that Donelson had fallen. Thar was no sound of fightin'. Everything was still as Sunday. We was settin' thar aside the road and then I heared a cannon boom. Hit boomed five times, real slow like—Boom!—Boom!—Boom! —Boom!—Boom! And the moment that I heared hit, I had a premonition. I turned to Jim and I said: "Well, thar you are! That's Donelson—and she's surrendered!"

Cap'n Bob Saunders heared me, but he wouldn't believe me and he said: "You're wrong!"

"Well," said Jim, "I hope to God he's right. I wouldn't care if the whole damn war had fallen through. I'm ready to go home."

"Well, he's wrong," said Captain Bob, "and I'll bet money on hit that he is."

Well, I tell you, that jest suited me. That was the way I was in those days—right from the beginnin' of the war to the very end. If thar was any fun or devilment goin' on, any card playin' or gamblin', or any other kind of foolishness, I was right in on hit. I'd a-bet a man that red was green or that day was night, and if a gal had looked at me from a persimmon tree, why, law! I reckon I'd a-clumb the tree to git her. That's jest the way hit was with me all through the war. I never made a bet or played a game of cards in my life before the war or after hit was over, but while the war was goin' on I was ready fer anything.

"How much will you bet?" I said.

"I'll bet you a hundred dollars even money," said Bob Saunders, and no sooner got the words out of his mouth than the bet was on.

We planked the money down right thar and gave hit to Jim to hold the stakes. Well, sir, we didn't have to wait half an hour before a feller on a horse came ridin' up and told us hit was no use goin' any farther—Fort Donelson had fallen.

"What did I tell you?" I said to Cap'n Saunders, and I put the money in my pocket.

Well, the laugh was on him then. I wish you could a-seen the expression on his face—he looked mighty sheepish, I tell you. But he admitted hit, you know, he had to own up.

"You were right," he said. "You won the bet. But—I'll tell you what I'll do!" He put his hand into his pocket and pulled out a roll of bills. "I've got a hundred dollars left—and with me hit's all or nothin'! We'll draw cards fer this last hundred, mine against yorn—high card wins!"

Well, I was ready fer him. I pulled out my hundred, and I said, "Git out the deck!"

So they brought the deck out then and Jim Weaver shuffled hit and held hit while we drawed. Bob Saunders drawed first and he drawed the eight of spades. When I turned my card up I had one of the queens.

Well, sir, you should have seen the look upon Bob Saunders' face. I tell you what, the fellers whooped and hollered till he looked like he was ready to crawl through a hole in the floor. We all had some fun with him, and then, of course, I gave the money back. I never kept a penny in my life I made from gamblin'.

But that's the way hit was with me in those days—I was ready fer hit—fer anything. If any kind of devilment or foolishness came up I was right in on hit with the ringleaders.

Well then, Fort Donelson was the funniest fight that I was ever in because hit was all fun fer me without no fightin'. And that jest suited me. And Stone Mountain was the most peculiar fight that I was in because—well, I'll tell you a strange story and you can figger fer yourself if you ever heared about a fight like *that* before.

Did you ever hear of a battle in which one side never fired a shot and yet won the fight and did more damage and more destruction to the other side than all the guns and cannon in the world could do? Well, that was the battle of Stone Mountain. Now, I was in a lot of battles. But the battle of Stone Mountain was the queerest one of the whole war.

I'll tell you how hit was.

We was up on top of the Mountain and the Yankees was below us tryin' to drive us out and take the Mountain. We couldn't git our guns up thar, we didn't try to—we didn't *have* to git our guns up thar. The only gun I ever seed up thar was a little brass howitzer that we pulled up with ropes, but we never fired a shot with hit. We didn't git a chance to use hit. We no more'n got hit in position before a shell exploded right on top of hit and split that little howitzer plumb in two. Hit jest fell into two parts: you couldn't have made a neater job of hit if you'd cut hit down the middle with a saw. I'll never fergit that little howitzer and the way they split hit plumb in two.

As for the rest of the fightin' on our side, hit was done with rocks and stones. We gathered together a great pile of rocks and stones and boulders all along the top of the Mountain, and when they attacked we waited and let 'em have hit.

The Yankees attacked in three lines, one after the other. We waited until the first line was no more'n thirty feet below us—until we could see the whites of their eyes, as the sayin' goes—and then we let 'em have hit. We jest rolled those boulders down on 'em, and I tell you what, hit was an awful thing to watch. I never saw no worse destruction than *that* with guns and cannon during the whole war.

You could hear 'em screamin' and hollerin' until hit made your blood run cold. They kept comin' on and we mowed 'em down by the hundreds. We mowed 'em down without firin' a single shot. We crushed them, wiped them out—jest by rollin' those big rocks and boulders down on them.

There was bigger battles in the war, but Stone Mountain was the queerest one I ever seed.

Fort Donelson came early in the war, and Stone Mountain came later toward the end. And one was funny and the other was peculiar, but thar was fightin' in between that wasn't neither one. I'm goin' to tell you about that.

Fort Donelson was the first big fight that we was in—and as I say, we wasn't really in hit because we couldn't git to her in time. And after Donelson that spring, in April, thar was Shiloh. Well—all that I can tell you is, we was thar on time at Shiloh. Oh Lord, I reckon that we was! Perhaps we had been country boys before, perhaps some of us still made a joke of hit before—but after Shiloh we wasn't country boys no longer. We didn't make a joke about hit after Shiloh. They wiped the smile off of our faces at Shiloh. And after Shiloh we was boys no longer: we was vet'ran men.

From then on hit was fightin' to the end. That's where we learned what hit was like—at Shiloh. From then on we knowed what hit would be until the end.

Jim got wounded thar at Shiloh. Hit wasn't bad—not bad enough to suit him anyways—fer he wanted to go home fer good. Hit was a flesh wound in the leg, but hit was some time before they could git to him, and he was layin' out thar on the field and I reckon that he lost some blood. Anyways, he was unconscious when they picked him up. They carried him back and dressed his wound right thar upon the field. They cleaned hit out, I reckon, and they bandaged hit—thar was so many of 'em they couldn't do much more than that. Oh, I tell you what, in those days thar wasn't much that they could do. I've seed the surgeons workin' underneath an open shed with meat-saws, choppin' off the arms and legs and throwin' 'em out thar in a pile like they was sticks of wood, sometimes without no chloroform or nothin', and the screamin' and the hollerin' of the men was enough to make your head turn gray. And that was as much as anyone could do. Hit was live or die and take your chance—and thar was so many of 'em wounded so much worse than Jim that I reckon he was lucky they did anything fer him at all.

I heared 'em tell about hit later, how he come to, a-layin' stretched out thar on an old dirty blanket on the bare floor, and an army surgeon seed him lookin' at his leg all bandaged up and I reckon thought he'd cheer him up and said: "Oh, that ain't nothin'—you'll be up and fightin' Yanks again in two weeks' time."

Well, with that, they said, Jim got to cursin' and a-takin' on something terrible. They said the language he used was enough to make your hair stand up on end. They said he screamed and raved and reached down thar and jerked that bandage off and said—"Like hell I will!" They said the blood spouted up thar like a fountain, and they said that army doctor was so mad he throwed Jim down upon his back and sat on him and he took that bandage, all bloody as hit was, and he tied hit back around his leg again and he said: "Goddam you, if you pull that bandage off again, I'll let you bleed to death."

And Jim, they said, came ragin' back at him until you could have heared him fer a mile, and said: "Well, by God, I don't care if I do; I'd rather die than stay here any longer."

They say they had hit back and forth thar until Jim got so weak he couldn't talk no more. I know that when I come to see him a day or two later he was settin' up and I asked him: "Jim, how is your leg? Are you hurt bad?"

And he answered: "Not bad enough. They can take the whole damn leg off," he said, "as far as I'm concerned, and bury hit here at Shiloh if they'll only let me go back home and not come back again. Me and Martha will git along somehow," he said. "I'd rather be a cripple the rest of my life than have to come back and fight in this damn war."

Well, I knowed he meant hit too. I looked at him and seed how much he meant hit, and I knowed thar wasn't anything that I could do. When a man begins to talk that way, thar hain't much you can say to him. Well, sure enough, in a week or two, they let him go upon a two months' furlough and he went limpin' away upon a crutch. He was the happiest man I ever seed. "They gave me two months' leave," he said, "but if they jest let me git back home old Bragg'll have to send his whole damn army before he gits me out of thar again."

Well, he was gone two months or more, and I never knowed what happened—whether he got ashamed of himself when his wound healed up all right, or whether Martha talked him out of hit. But he was back with us again by late July—the grimmest, bitterest-lookin' man you ever seed. He wouldn't talk to me about hit, he wouldn't tell me what had happened, but I knowed from that time on he'd never draw his breath in peace until he left the army and got back home fer good.

Well, that was Shiloh, that was the time we didn't miss, that was where we lost our grin, where we knowed at last what hit would be until the end.

I've told you of three battles now, and one was funny, one was strange, and one was—well, one showed us what war and fightin' could be like. But I'll tell you of a fourth one now. And the fourth one was the greatest of the lot.

We seed some big fights in the war. And we was in some bloody battles. But the biggest fight we fought was Chickamauga. The bloodiest fight I ever seed was Chickamauga. Thar was big battles in the war, but thar never was a fight before, thar'll never be a fight again, like Chickamauga. I'm goin' to tell you how hit was at Chickamauga.

All through the spring and summer of that year Old Rosey follered us through Tennessee.

We had him stopped the year before, the time we whupped him at Stone's River at the end of '62. We tard him out so bad he had to wait. He waited thar six months at Murfreesboro. But we knowed he was a-comin' all the time. Old Rosey started at the end of June and drove us out of Shelbyville. We fell back on Tullahoma in rains the like of which you never seed. The rains that fell the last week in June that year was terrible. But Rosey kept a-comin' on.

He drove us out of Tullahoma too. We fell back across the Cumberland, we pulled back behind the mountain, but he follered us.

I reckon thar was fellers that was quicker when a fight was on, and when they'd seed just what hit was they had to do. But when it came to plannin' and a-figgerin', Old Rosey Rosecrans took the cake. Old Rosey was a fox. Fer sheer natural cunnin' I never knowed the beat of him.

While Bragg was watchin' him at Chattanooga to keep him from gittin' across the Tennessee, he sent some fellers forty mile up stream. And then he'd march 'em back and forth and round the hill and back in front of us again where we could look at 'em, until you'd a-thought that every Yankee in the world was there. But law! All that was just a dodge! He had fellers a-sawin' and a-hammerin', a-buildin' boats, a-blowin' bugles and a-beatin' drums, makin' all the noise they could—you could hear 'em over yonder gittin' ready—and all the time Old Rosey was fifty mile or more down stream, ten mile *past* Chattanooga, a-fixin' to git over way down thar. That was the kind of feller Rosey was.

We reached Chattanooga early in July and waited fer two months. Old Rosey hadn't caught up with us yet. He still had to cross the Cumberland, push his men and pull his trains across the ridges and through the gaps before he got to us. July went by, we had no news of him. "Oh Lord!" said Jim, "perhaps he ain't a-comin'!" I knowed he was a-comin', but I let Jim have his way.

Some of the fellers would git used to hit. A feller'd git into a frame of mind where he wouldn't let hit worry him. He'd let termorrer look out fer hitself. That was the way hit was with me.

With Jim hit was the other way around. Now that he knowed Martha Patton he was a different man. I think he hated the war and army life from the moment that he met her. From that time he was livin' only fer one thing—to go back home and marry that gal. When mail would come and some of us was gittin' letters he'd be the first in line; and if she wrote him why he'd walk away like someone in a dream. And if she failed to write he'd jest go off somers and set down by himself: he'd be in such a state of misery he didn't want to talk to no one. He got the reputation with the fellers fer bein' queer—unsociable—always a-broodin' and a-frettin' about somethin' and a-wantin' to be left alone. And so, after a time, they let him be. He wasn't popular with most of them—but they never knowed what was wrong, they never knowed that he wasn't really the way they thought he was at all. Hit was jest that he was hit so desperate hard, the worst-in-love man that I ever seed. But law! I knowed! I knowed what was the trouble from the start.

Hit's funny how war took a feller. Before the war I was the serious one, and Jim had been the one to play.

I reckon that I'd had to work too hard. We was so poor. Before the war hit almost seemed I never knowed the time I didn't have to work. And when the war came, why I only thought of all the fun and frolic I was goin' to have; and then at last, when I knowed what hit was like, why I was used to hit and didn't care.

I always could git used to things. And I reckon maybe that's the reason that I'm here. I wasn't one to worry much, and no matter how rough the goin' got I always figgered I could hold out if the others could. I let termorrer look out fer hitself. I reckon that you'd have to say I was an optimist. If things got bad, well, I always figgered that they could be worse; and if they got so bad they couldn't be no worse, why then I'd figger that they couldn't last this way ferever, they'd have to git some better sometime later on.

I reckon toward the end thar, when they got so bad we didn't think they'd ever git no better, I'd reached the place where I jest didn't care. I could still lay down and go to sleep and not worry over what was goin' to come termorrer, because I never *knowed* what was to come and so I didn't let hit worry me. I reckon you'd have to say that was the Pentland in me— our belief in what we call predestination.

Now, Jim was jest the other way. Before the war he was happy as a lark and thought of nothin' except havin' fun. But then the war came and hit changed him so you wouldn't a-knowed he was the same man.

And, as I say, hit didn't happen all at once. Jim was the happiest man I ever seed that mornin' that we started out from home. I reckon he thought of the war as we all did, as a big frolic. We gave hit jest about six months. We figgered we'd be back by then, and of course all that jest suited Jim. I reckon that suited all of us. It would give us all a chance to wear a uniform and to see the world, to shoot some Yankees and to run 'em north, and then to come back home and lord it over those who hadn't been and be a hero and court the gals.

That was the way hit looked to us when we set out from Zebulon. We never thought about the winter. We never thought about the mud and cold and rain. We never knowed what hit would be to have to march on an empty belly, to have to march barefoot with frozen feet and with no coat upon your back, to have to lay down on bare ground and try to sleep with no coverin' above you, and thankful half the time if you could find dry ground to sleep upon, and too tard the rest of hit to care. We never knowed or thought about such things as these. We never knowed how hit would be there in the cedar thickets beside Chickamauga Creek. And if we had a-knowed, if someone had a-told us, why I reckon that none of us would a-cared. We was too young and ignorant to care. And as fer *knowin'*—law! The only trouble about *knowin'* is that you've got to know what knowin's *like* before you know what knowin' *is*. Thar's no one that can tell you. You've got to know hit fer yourself.

Well, like I say, we'd been fightin' all this time and still thar was no sign of the war endin'. Old Rosey jest kept a-follerin' us and— "Lord!" Jim would say, "will it never end?"

I never knowed myself. We'd been fightin' fer two years, and I'd given over knowin' long ago. With Jim hit was different.

He'd been a-prayin' and a-hopin' from the first that soon hit would be over and that he could go back and get that gal. And at first, fer a year or more, I tried to cheer him up. I told him that it couldn't last ferever. But after a while hit wasn't no use to tell him that. He wouldn't believe me any longer.

Because Old Rosey kept a-comin' on. We'd whup him and we'd stop him fer a while, but then he'd git his wind, he'd be on our trail again, he'd drive us back.—"Oh Lord!" said Jim, "will hit never stop?"

That summer I been tellin' you about, he drove us down through Tennessee. He drove us out of Shelbyville, and we fell back on Tullahoma, to the passes of the hills. When we pulled back across the Cumberland I said to Jim: "Now we've got him. He'll have to cross the mountains now to git at us. And when he does, we'll have him. That's all that Bragg's been waitin' fer. We'll whup the daylights out of him this time," I said, "and after that thar'll be nothin' left of him. We'll be home by Christmas, Jim—you wait and see."

And Jim just looked at me and shook his head and said: "Lord, Lord, I don't believe this war'll ever end!"

Hit wasn't that he was afraid—or, if he was, hit made a wild-cat of him in the fightin'. Jim could get fightin' mad like no one else I ever seed. He could do things, take chances no one else I ever knowed would take. But I reckon hit was jest because he was so desperate. He hated hit so much. He couldn't git used to hit the way the others could. He couldn't take hit as hit came. Hit wasn't so much that he was afraid to die. I guess hit was that he was still so full of livin'. He didn't want to die because he wanted to live so much. And he wanted to live so much because he was in love.

. . . So, like I say, Old Rosey finally pushed us back across the Cumberland. We was in Chattanooga in July, and fer a few weeks hit was quiet thar. But all the time I knowed that Rosev would keep comin' on. We got wind of him again along in August. He had started after us again. He pushed his trains across the Cumberland, with the roads so bad, what with the rains, his wagons sunk down to the axle hubs. But he got 'em over, came down in the valley, then across the ridge, and early in September he was on our heels again.

We cleared out of Chattanooga on the eighth. And our tail end was pullin' out at one end of the town as Rosey came in through the other. We dropped down around the mountain south of town and Rosey thought he had us on the run again.

But this time he was fooled. We was ready fer him now, a-pickin' out our spot and layin' low. Old Rosey follered us. He sent McCook around down toward the south to head us off. He thought he had us in retreat but when McCook got thar we wasn't thar at all. We'd come down south of town and taken our positions along Chickamauga Creek. McCook had gone too far. Thomas was follerin' us from the north and when McCook tried to git back to join Thomas, he couldn't pass us, fer we blocked the way. They had to fight us or be cut in two.

We was in position on the Chickamauga on the seventeenth. The Yankees streamed in on the eighteenth, and took their position in the woods a-facin' us. We had our backs to Lookout Mountain and the Chickamauga Creek. The Yankees had their line thar in the woods before us on a rise, with Missionary Ridge behind them to the east.

The Battle of Chickamauga was fought in a cedar thicket. That cedar thicket, from what I knowed of hit, was about three miles long and one mile wide. We fought fer two days all up and down that thicket and to and fro across hit. When the fight started that cedar thicket was so thick and dense you could a-took a butcher knife and drove hit in thar anywheres and hit would a-stuck. And when that fight was over that cedar thicket had been so destroyed by shot and shell you could a-looked in thar anywheres with your naked eye and seed a black snake run a hundred yards away. If you'd a-looked at that cedar thicket the day after that fight was over you'd a-wondered how a hummin' bird the size of your thumbnail could a-flown through thar without bein' torn into pieces by the fire. And yet more than half of us who went into that thicket came out of hit alive and told the tale. You wouldn't have thought that hit was possible. But I was thar and seed hit, and hit was.

A little after midnight—hit may have been about two o'clock that mornin', while we lay there waitin' for the fight we knowed was bound to come next day—Jim woke me up. I woke up like a flash—you got used to hit in those days—and though hit was so dark you could hardly see your hand a foot away, I knowed his face at once. He was white as a ghost and he had got thin as a rail in that last year's campaign. In the dark his face looked white as paper. He dug his hand into my arm so hard hit hurt. I roused up sharp-like; then I seed him and knowed who hit was.

"John!" he said—"John!"—and he dug his fingers in my arm so hard he made hit ache—"John! I've seed him! He was here again!"

I tell you what, the way he said hit made my blood run cold. They say we Pentlands are a superstitious people, and perhaps we are. They told hit how they saw my brother George a-comin' up the hill one day at sunset, how they all went out upon the porch and waited fer him, how everyone, the childern and the grown-ups alike, all seed him as he clumb the hill, and how he passed behind a tree and disappeared as if the ground had swallered him—and how they got the news ten days later that he'd been killed at Chancellorsville on that very day and hour.

I've heared these stories and I know the others all believe them, but I never put no stock in them myself. And yet, I tell you what! The sight of that white face and those black eyes a-burnin' at me in the dark—the way he said hit and the way hit was—fer I could feel the men around me and hear somethin' movin' in the wood—I heared a trace chain rattle and hit was enough to make your blood run cold! I grabbed hold of him—I shook him by the arm—I didn't want the rest of 'em to hear—I told him to hush up——

"John, he was here!" he said.

I never asked him what he meant—I knowed too well to ask. It was the third time he'd seed hit in a month—a man upon a horse. I didn't want to hear no more—I told him that hit was a dream and I told him to go back to sleep.

"I tell you, John, hit was no dream!" he said. "Oh John, I heared hit—and I heared his horse—and I seed him sittin' thar as plain as day—and he never said a word to me—he jest sat thar lookin' down, and then he turned and rode away into the woods. . . . John, John, I heared him and I don't know what hit means!"

Well, whether he seed hit or imagined hit or dreamed hit, I don't know. But the sight of his black eyes a-burnin' holes through me in the dark made me feel almost as if I'd seed hit too. I told him to lay down by me—and still I seed his eyes a-blazin' thar. I know he didn't sleep a wink the rest of that whole night. I closed my eyes and tried to make him think that I was sleepin' but hit was no use—we lay thar wide awake. And both of us was glad when mornin' came.

The fight began upon our right at ten o'clock. We couldn't find out what was happenin': the woods thar was so close and thick we never knowed fer two days what had happened, and we didn't know fer certain then. We never knowed how many we was fightin' or how many we had lost. I've heared them say that even Old Rosey himself didn't know jest what had happened when he rode back into town next day, and didn't know that Thomas was still standin' like a rock. And if Old Rosey didn't know no more than this about hit, what could a common soldier know? We fought back and forth across that cedar thicket fer two days, and thar was times when you would be right up on top of them before you even knowed that they was thar. And that's the way the fightin' went—the bloodiest fightin' that was ever knowed, until that cedar thicket was soaked red with blood, and thar was hardly a place left in thar where a sparrer could have perched.

And as I say, we heared 'em fightin' out upon our right at ten o'clock, and then the fightin' came our way. I heared later that this fightin' started when the Yanks come down to the Creek and run into a bunch of Forrest's men and drove 'em back. And then they had hit back and forth until they got drove back themselves, and that's the way we had hit all day long. We'd attack and then they'd throw us back, then they'd attack and we'd beat them off. And that was the way hit went from mornin' till night. We piled up there upon their left: they mowed us down with canister and grape until the very grass was soakin' with our blood, but we kept comin' on. We must have charged a dozen times that day—I was in four of 'em myself. We fought back and forth across that wood until there wasn't a piece of hit as big as the palm of your hand we hadn't fought on. We busted through their right at two-thirty in the afternoon and got way over past the Widder Glenn's, where Rosey had his quarters, and beat 'em back until we got the whole way cross the Lafayette Road and took possession of the road. And then they drove us out again. And we kept comin' on, and both sides were still at hit after darkness fell.

We fought back and forth across that road all day with first one side and then the tother holdin' hit until that road hitself was soaked in blood. They called that road the Bloody Lane, and that was jest the name fer hit.

We kept fightin' fer an hour or more after hit had gotten dark, and you could see the rifles flashin' in the woods, but then hit all died down. I tell you what, that night was somethin' to remember and to marvel at as long as you live. The fight had set the wood afire in places, and you could see the smoke and flames and hear the screamin' and the hollerin' of the wounded until hit made your blood run cold. We got as many as we could —but some we didn't even try to git—we jest let 'em lay. It was an awful thing to hear. I reckon many a wounded man was jest left to die or burn to death because we couldn't git 'em out.

You could see the nurses and the stretcher-bearers movin' through the woods, and each side huntin' fer hits dead. You could see them movin' in the smoke an' flames, an' you could see the dead men layin' there as thick as wheat, with their corpse-like faces an' black powder on their lips, an' a little bit of moonlight comin' through the trees, and all of hit more like a nightmare out of hell than anything I ever knowed before.

But we had other work to do. All through the night we could hear the Yanks a-choppin' and a-thrashin' round, and we knowed that they was fellin' trees to block us when we went fer them next mornin'. Fer we knowed the fight was only jest begun. We figgered that we'd had the best of hit, but we knowed no one had won the battle yet. We knowed the second day would beat the first.

Jim knowed hit too. Poor Jim, he didn't sleep that night—he never seed the man upon the horse that night—he jest sat there, a-grippin' his knees and starin', and a-sayin': "Lord God, Lord God, when will hit ever end?"

Then mornin' came at last. This time we knowed jest where we was and what hit was we had to do. Our line was fixed by that time. Bragg knowed at last where Rosey had his line, and Rosey knowed where we was. So we waited there, both sides, till mornin' came. Hit was a foggy mornin' with mist upon the ground. Around ten o'clock when the mist began to rise, we got the order and we went chargin' through the wood again.

We knowed the fight was goin' to be upon the right—upon our right, that is—on Rosey's left. And we knowed that Thomas was in charge of Rosey's left. And we all knowed that hit was easier to crack a flint rock with your teeth than to make old Thomas budge. But we went after him, and I tell you what, that was a fight! The first day's fight had been like playin' marbles when compared to this.

We hit old Thomas on his left at half-past ten, and Breckenridge came sweepin' round and turned old Thomas's flank and came in at his back, and then we had hit hot and heavy. Old Thomas whupped his men around like he would crack a rawhide whup and drove Breckenridge back around the flank again, but we was back on top of him before you knowed the first attack was over.

The fight went ragin' down the flank, down to the center of Old Rosey's army and back and forth across the left, and all up and down old Thomas's line. We'd hit him right and left and in the middle, and he'd come back at us and throw us back again. And we went ragin' back and forth thar like two bloody lions with that cedar thicket so tore up, so bloody and so thick with dead by that time, that hit looked as if all hell had broken loose in thar.

Rosey kept a-whuppin' men around off of his right, to help old Thomas on the left to stave us off. And then we'd hit old Thomas left of center and we'd bang him in the middle and we'd hit him on his left again, and he'd whup those Yankees back and forth off of the right into his flanks and middle as we went fer him, until we run those Yankees ragged. We had them gallopin' back and forth like kangaroos, and in the end that was the thing that cooked their goose.

The worst fightin' had been on the left, on Thomas's line, but to hold us thar they'd thinned their right out and had failed to close in on the center of their line. And at two o'clock that afternoon when Longstreet seed the gap in Wood's position on the right, he took five brigades of us and poured us through. That whupped them. That broke their line and smashed their whole right all to smithereens. We went after them like a pack of ragin' devils. We killed 'em and we took 'em by the thousands, and those we didn't kill and take right thar went streamin' back across the Ridge as if all hell was at their heels.

That was a rout if ever I heared tell of one! They went streamin' back across the Ridge—hit was each man fer himself and the devil take the hindmost. They caught Rosey comin' up—he rode into them—he tried to check 'em, face 'em round, and get 'em to come on again—hit was like tryin' to swim the Mississippi upstream on a boneyard mule! They swept him back with them as if he'd been a wooden chip. They went streamin' into Rossville like the rag-tag of creation—the worst whupped army that you ever seed, and Old Rosey was along with all the rest!

He knowed hit was all up with him, or thought he knowed hit, for everybody told him the Army of the Cumberland had been blowed to smithereens and that hit was a general rout. And Old Rosey turned and rode to Chattanooga, and he was a beaten man. I've heared tell that when he rode up to his headquarters thar in Chattanooga they had to help him from his horse, and that he walked into the house all dazed and fuddled-like, like

he never knowed what had happened to him—and that he jest
sat thar struck dumb and never spoke.

This was at four o'clock of that same afternoon. And then the
news was brought to him that Thomas was still thar upon the
field and wouldn't budge. Old Thomas stayed thar like a rock.
We'd smashed the right, we'd sent it flyin' back across the Ridge,
the whole Yankee right was broken into bits and streamin' back
to Rossville for dear life. Then we bent old Thomas back upon
his left. We thought we had him, he'd have to leave the field or
else surrender. But old Thomas turned and fell back along the
Ridge and put his back against the wall thar, and he wouldn't
budge.

Longstreet pulled us back at three o'clock when we had broken
up the right and sent them streamin' back across the Ridge. We
thought that hit was over then. We moved back stumblin' like
men walkin' in a dream. And I turned to Jim—I put my arm
around him, and I said: "Jim, what did I say? I knowed hit,
we've licked 'em and this is the end!" I never even knowed if
he heard me. He went stumblin' on beside me with his face as
white as paper and his lips black with the powder of the cartridge-
bite, mumblin' and mutterin' to himself like someone talkin' in
a dream. And we fell back to position, and they told us all to
rest. And we leaned thar on our rifles like men who hardly
knowed if they had come out of that hell alive or dead.

"Oh Jim, we've got 'em and this is the end!" I said.

He leaned thar swayin' on his rifle, starin' through the wood.
He jest leaned and swayed thar, and he never said a word, and
those great eyes of his a-burnin' through the wood.

"Jim, don't you hear me?"—and I shook him by the arm.
"Hit's over, man! We've licked 'em and the fight is over!—Can't
you understand?"

And then I heared them shoutin' on the right, the word came

down the line again, and Jim—poor Jim!—he raised his head and listened, and "Oh God!" he said, "we've got to go again!"

Well, hit was true. The word had come that Thomas had lined up upon the Ridge, and we had to go fer him again. After that I never exactly knowed what happened. Hit was like fightin' in a bloody dream—like doin' somethin' in a nightmare—only the nightmare was like death and hell. Longstreet threw us up that hill five times, I think, before darkness came. We'd charge up to the very muzzles of their guns, and they'd mow us down like grass, and we'd come stumblin' back—or what was left of us—and form again at the foot of the hill, and then come on again. We'd charge right up the Ridge and drive 'em through the gap and fight 'em with cold steel, and they'd come back again and we'd brain each other with the butt end of our guns. Then they'd throw us back and we'd re-form and come on after 'em again.

The last charge happened jest at dark. We came along and stripped the ammunition off the dead—we took hit from the wounded—we had nothin' left ourselves. Then we hit the first line—and we drove them back. We hit the second and swept over them. We were goin' up to take the third and last—they waited till they saw the color of our eyes before they let us have hit. Hit was like a river of red-hot lead had poured down on us: the line melted thar like snow. Jim stumbled and spun round as if somethin' had whupped him like a top. He fell right toward me, with his eyes wide open and the blood a-pourin' from his mouth. I took one look at him and then stepped over him like he was a log. Thar was no more to see or think of now—no more to reach—except that line. We reached hit and they let us have hit—and we stumbled back.

And yet we knowed that we had won a victory. That's what they told us later—and we knowed hit must be so because when daybreak came next mornin' the Yankees was all gone. They had all retreated into town, and we was left there by the Creek at Chickamauga in possession of the field.

I don't know how many men got killed. I don't know which side lost the most. I only know you could have walked across the dead men without settin' foot upon the ground. I only know that cedar thicket which had been so dense and thick two days before you could've drove a knife into hit and hit would of stuck, had been so shot to pieces that you could've looked in thar on Monday mornin' with your naked eye and seed a black snake run a hundred yards away.

I don't know how many men we lost or how many of the Yankees we may have killed. The Generals on both sides can figger all that out to suit themselves. But I know that when that fight was over you could have looked in thar and wondered how a hummin' bird could've flown through that cedar thicket and come out alive. And yet that happened, yes, and something more than hummin' birds—fer men came out, alive.

And on that Monday mornin', when I went back up the Ridge to where Jim lay, thar just beside him on a little torn piece of bough, I heard a redbird sing. I turned Jim over and got his watch, his pocket-knife, and what few papers and belongin's that he had, and some letters that he'd had from Martha Patton. And I put them in my pocket.

And then I got up and looked around. It all seemed funny after hit had happened, like something that had happened in a dream. Fer Jim had wanted so desperate hard to live, and hit had never mattered half so much to me, and now I was a-standin' thar with Jim's watch and Martha Patton's letters in my pocket and a-listenin' to that little redbird sing.

And I would go all through the war and go back home and

marry Martha later on, and fellers like poor Jim was layin' thar at Chickamauga Creek.

Hit's all so strange now when you think of hit. Hit all turned out so different from the way we thought. And that was long ago, and I'll be ninety-five years old if I am livin' on the seventh day of August, of this present year. Now that's goin' back a long ways, hain't hit? And yet hit all comes back to me as clear as if hit happened yesterday. And then hit all will go away and be as strange as if hit happened in a dream.

But I have been in some big battles I can tell you. I've seen strange things and been in bloody fights. But the biggest fight that I was ever in—the bloodiest battle anyone has ever fought— was at Chickamauga in that cedar thicket—at Chickamauga Creek in that great war.

The Return of the Prodigal

1. The Thing Imagined

EUGENE GANT WAS A WRITER, AND IN THE GREAT WORLD HE HAD attained some little fame with his books. After a while, indeed, he became quite a famous person. His work was known, and everywhere he went he found that his name had preceded him. Everywhere, that is, except where he would most have wished it—at home.

The reason for this anomaly was not far to seek. His first novel had been based in large measure upon a knowledge of people derived from his boyhood in a little town. When the book came out, the townsfolk read it and thought they recognized themselves in the portraits he had drawn, and almost to a man the town rose up against him. He received threatening letters. He was warned never to show his face again in the precincts from which his very life had sprung.

He had not expected anything like this, and the shock of it had a profound effect upon him. He took it hard. And for seven years thereafter he did not go home again. He became an exile and a wanderer.

And through all these seven years when he did not go back, his thoughts went back forever. At night as he walked the streets of distant cities or tossed sleepless in his bed in foreign lands, he would think of home, recalling every feature of the little town's familiar visage, and wondering what reception he would get at home if he should decide at last to visit it again.

He thought of this so often with the intensity of nostalgic longing that in the end his feelings built up in his mind an image which seemed to him more true than anything that he had ever actually experienced. After that it became an image that never varied. It came back to haunt him a thousand times—this image of what it would be like if he did go home again:

One blustery night toward the end of October a man was walking swiftly down a street in the little town of Altamont in the hill district of Old Catawba. The hour was late, and a small, cold rain was falling, swept by occasional gusts of wind. Save for this solitary pedestrian, the street was bare of life.

The street itself was one of those shabby and nondescript streets whereon the passage of swift change and departed grandeur is strikingly apparent. Even at this dreary season and hour it was possible to see that the street had known a time of greater prosperity than it now enjoyed and that it had once been a pleasant place in which to live. The houses were for the most part frame structures in the style of that ugly, confused, and rather pretentious architecture which flourished forty or fifty years ago, and, so late at night, they were darkened and deserted looking. Many of them were set back in yards spacious enough to give an illusion of moderate opulence and security, and they stood beneath ancient trees, through the bare branches of which the wind howled mournfully. But even in the darkness one could see on what hard times the houses and the street had fallen. The gaunt and many-gabled structures, beaten and swept by the cold rain, seemed to sag and to be warped by age and disrepair, and to confer there dismally like a congress of old crones in the bleak nakedness of night and storm that surrounded them. In the dreary concealments of the dark, one knew by certain instinct that the old houses had fallen upon grievous times and had been unpainted for many years, and even if one's intuition had not conveyed this, the strangely mixed and broken character of the street would have afforded telling evidence of the fate which had befallen it. Here and there the old design of pleasant lawns had been brutally deformed by the intrusion of small, cheap, raw, and ugly structures of brick and cement blocks. These represented a variety of enterprises: one or two were grocery stores, one was a garage, some were small shops which dealt in automobile accessories, and one, the most pretentious of the lot, was a salesroom for a motor car agency. In the harsh light of a corner lamp, broken by the stiff shadows of bare, tangled boughs, the powerful and perfect shapes of the new automobiles glittered splendidly, but in this splendor there was, curiously, a kind of terrible, cold, and desolate bleakness which was even more cruel, lonely, and forbidding than all the other dismal bleakness of the dark old street.

The man, who was the only evidence of life the street provided at this hour, seemed to take only a casual and indifferent interest in his surroundings. He was carrying a small suitcase. and from his appearance he might have been taken for a stranger, but his manner—the certain purpose in his stride, and the swift, rather detached glances he took from time to time at objects along the way—indicated that the scene was by no means an unfamiliar one but had at some period in his life been well known to him.

Arrived at length before an old house set midway down the street, he paused, set down his suitcase on the pavement, and for the first time showed signs of doubt and indecision. For some moments he stood looking with nervous and distracted intentness at the dark house as if trying to read upon its blank and gloomy visage some portent of the life within, or to decipher in one of its gaunt and ugly lineaments some answer to the question in his mind. For some time he stood this way, but at length, with an impatient movement, he picked up his suitcase, mounted the brief flight of concrete steps that went up to the yard, advanced swiftly along the walk and up the steps onto the porch, set down his suitcase at the door, and after a final instant of disturbed hesitancy shook his head, impatiently and almost angrily, and rang the bell.

The bell sent through the old dark hall within, lit dimly at the farther end by one small light, a sharp and vital thring of sound that drew from the man a shocked and involuntary movement, almost of protest and surprise. For a moment his jaw muscles knotted grimly; then, thrusting his hands doggedly into the pockets of his raincoat, he lowered his head and waited.

—They flee us, who beforetime did us seek, with desolate pauses sounding between our chambers, in old chapters of the night that sag and creak and pass and stir and come again. They flee us who beforetime did us seek. And now, in an old house of life, forever in the dark mid-pause and watches of the night, we sit alone and wait.

What things are these, what shells and curios of outworn custom, what relics here of old, forgotten time? Festoons of gathered string and twines of thread, and boxes filled with many buttons, and bundles of old letters covered with scrawled and faded writings of the dead, and on a warped old cupboard, shelved with broken and mended crockery, an old wooden clock where Time his fatal, unperturbed measure keeps, while through the night the rats of time and silence gnaw the timbers of the old house of life.

A woman sits here among such things as these, a woman old in years, and binded to the past, remembering while storm shakes the house and all the festoons of hung string sway gently and the glasses rattle, the way the dust rose on a certain day, and the way the sun was shining, and the sound of many voices that are dead, and how sometimes in these mid-watches of the night a word will come, and how she hears a step that comes and goes forever, and old doors that sag and creak, and something passing in the old house of life and time in which she waits alone.

The naked, sudden shock of the bell broke with explosive force against her reverie. The old woman started as if someone had spoken suddenly across her shoulder. Her swollen, misshapen feet were drawn quickly from the edge of the open oven door where she had been holding them for warmth, and, glancing around and upward sharply with the sudden attentiveness of a startled bird, she cried out instinctively, although no one was there: "Hah? What say?"

Then, peering through her glasses at the wooden clock, she got up slowly, stood for a moment holding her broad, work-roughened hands clasped loosely at the waist, and after a few seconds' troubled indecision went out into the hall and toward the closed front door, peering uncertainly and with a puzzled, troubled look upon her face as she approached. Arrived at the door, she paused again and, still holding her hands in their loose clasp across her waist, she waited a moment in uncertain and troubled meditation. Then, grasping the heavy brass knob of the door, she opened it cautiously a few inches and, prying out into the dark with curious, startled face, she repeated to the man she saw standing there the same words that she had spoken to herself in solitude a minute or two before: "Hah? What say?"—and immediately, with a note of sharp suspicion in her voice: "What do you want?"

He made no answer for a moment, but had there been light enough for her to observe the look upon his face she might have seen him start and change expression, and be about to speak, and check himself with an almost convulsive movement of control. Finally he said quietly:

"A room."

"What's that?" she said, peering at him suspiciously and almost accusingly. "A room, you say?" Then, sharply, after a brief pause: "Who sent you?"

The man hesitated, then said: "Someone I met in town. A man in the lunchroom. I told him I had to put up somewhere overnight, and he gave me your address."

She answered him as before, repeating his words in the same suspicious manner, yet her tone also had in it now a certain quality of swift reflection, as if she were not so much questioning him as considering his words. "A man—lunchroom—say he told you?" she said quickly. And then instantly, as if for the first time recognizing and accepting the purpose of this nocturnal visit, she added: "Oh, yes! MacDonald! He often sends me people. . . . Well, come in," she said, and opened the door and stood aside for him to enter. "You say you want a room?" she went on now more tolerantly. "How long do you intend to stay?"

"Just overnight," he said. "I've got to go on in the morning."

Something in his tone awoke a quick and troubled recollection in her. In the dim light of the hall she peered sharply and rather painfully at him with a troubled expression on her face, and, speaking with the same abrupt and almost challenging inquiry that had characterized her former speech but now with an added tinge of doubt, she said: "Say you're a stranger here?"— although he had said nothing of the sort. "I guess you're here on business, then?"

"Well—not exactly," he answered hesitantly. "I guess you could almost call me a stranger, though. I've been away from here so long. But I came from this part of the country."

"Well, I was thinkin'," she began in a doubtful but somewhat

more assured tone, "there was somethin' about your voice. I
don't know what it was, but—" she smiled a tremulous yet
somewhat friendly smile—"it seemed like I must have heard it
somewhere. I knew you must have come from somewheres
around here. I knew you couldn't be a Northern man—you don't
have that way of talkin'. . . . Well, then, come in," she said
conciliatingly, as if satisfied with the result of her investigation,
"if it's only a room for the night you want, I guess I can fix
you up. You'll have to take things as you find them," she said
bluntly. "I used to be in the roomin'-house business, but I'm not
young enough or strong enough to take the interest in it I once
did. This house is gettin' old and run-down. It's got too big for
me. I can't look after it like I used to. But I try to keep everything clean, and if you're satisfied with things the way they are,
why—" she folded her hands across her waist in a loose, reflective
gesture and considered judicially for a moment—"why," she said,
"I reckon you can have the room for fifty cents."

"It's little enough," she thought, "but still it looks as if that's
about all he's able to pay, an' things have got to such a state
nowadays it's either take what you can get an' get somethin', or
take nothin' at all an' lose everything. Yes, he's a pretty seedy-
lookin' customer, all right," she went on thinking. "A fly-by-
night sort of feller if I ever saw one. But then I reckon Mac-
Donald had a chance to size him up, an' if MacDonald sent him
I guess it's all right. An', anyway, that's the only kind that ever
comes here nowadays. The better class all have their automobiles
an' want to get out in the mountains. And besides, no one wants
to come to an old, cold, run-down sort of place like this if they
can afford to go to a hotel. So I'd better let him in, I guess, an'
take what little he can pay. It's better than nothin' at all."

During the course of this reflection she was peering through
her glasses at him sharply and intently, and with a somewhat

puzzled and troubled expression on her face. The figure that her old, worn, and enfeebled eyes made out in the dim, bleak light of the hall was certainly far from prepossessing. It was that of an uncommonly tall man, heavily built, and shabbily dressed in garments which were badly in need of pressing, and which, as she phrased it to herself, "looked as if he'd come the whole way across the country in a day coach." His face was covered with the heavy black furze of a week-old beard, and, although the features were neither large nor coarse, they had, somewhere in life, suffered a severe battering. The nose, which was short, tilted, and pugnacious-looking, had been broken across the ridge and was badly set, and there was a scar which ran slant-wise across the base of the nose. This disfigurement gave the man's face a somewhat savage appearance, an impression which was rein-·forced by the look in his eyes. His eyes, which were brown, had a curiously harsh and dark and hurt look in them, as though the man had been deeply wounded by life and was trying to hide the fact with a show of fierce and naked truculence as challenging as an angry word.

Nevertheless, it was the cold anger in his eyes that somehow finally reassured the old woman. As he returned her prying stare with his direct and angry look she felt vaguely comforted, and reflected: "Well, he's a rough-lookin' customer, sure enough, but then he looks honest—nothin' hang-dog about him—an' I reckon it's all right."

And, aloud, she repeated: "Well, then, come on. If you're satis-fied with things the way they are, I guess I can let you have this room here."

Then turning, she led the way into a room which opened from the hall to the right and switched on the dingy light. It was a large front room, gaunt in proportions like the house, high-ceilinged, cheerless, bare and clean and cold, with whitewashed walls. There was a black old fireplace, fresh-painted and unused, which gave a bleak enhancement to the cold white bareness of the room. A clean but threadbare carpet covered the worn planking of the floor. In one corner there was a cheap dresser with an oval mirror, in another a small washstand with a bowl and pitcher and a rack of towels, and in the ugly bay window which fronted the street side of the house there was a nondescript small table covered with a white cloth. Opposite the door stood a clean but uninviting white iron bed.

The old woman stood for a moment with her hands clasped loosely at her waist as she surveyed the room with a reflective stare.

"Well," she remarked at last with an air of tranquil and indifferent concession, "I reckon you'll find it pretty cold in here, but then there's no one in the house but one roomer and myself, an' I can't afford to keep fires burnin' in a house like this when there's nothin' comin' in. But you'll find things clean enough," she added quietly, "an' there's lots of good, warm covers on the bed. You'll sleep warm enough, an' if you're gettin' up to make an early start tomorrow, I don't guess you'll want to sit up late anyway."

"No, ma'am," he answered, in a tone that was at once harsh and hurt. "I'll get along all right. And I'll pay you now," he said, "in case I don't see you in the morning when I leave."

He fished into his pockets for a coin and gave it to her. She accepted it with the calm indifference of old, patient, unperturbed people, and then remained standing there in a reflective pause while she gave the room a final meditative look before leaving him.

"Well, then," she said, "I guess you've got all you need. You'll find clean towels on the washstand rack, and the bathroom's upstairs at the end of the first hallway to the left."

"Thank you, ma'am," he answered in the same tone as before. "I'll try not to disturb anyone."

"There's no one to disturb," she said quietly. "I sleep at the back of the house away from everything, an' as for Mr. Gilmer—he's the only steady roomer I've got left—he's been here for years, an' he's so quiet I hardly know when he's in the house. Besides, he sleeps so sound he won't even know you're here. He's still out, but he ought to be comin' in any minute now. So you needn't worry about disturbin' us. An' no one will disturb you either," she said, looking straight at him suddenly and smiling the pale, tremulous smile of an old woman with false teeth. "For there's one thing sure—this is as quiet a house as you could find. So if you hear anyone comin' in, you needn't worry; it's only Mr. Gilmer goin' to his room."

"Thank you," the man said coldly. "Everything's all right. And now," he added, turning away as if anxious to terminate a more protracted conversation, "I'm going to turn in. It's past your bedtime, too, and I won't keep you up, ma'am, any longer."

"Yes," she said hastily, turning to go, yet still regarding him with a puzzled, indecisive look. "Well, then, if there's anything else you need——"

"No, ma'am," he said. "I'll be all right. Good night to you."

"Good night," she answered, and, after one more parting glance around the cold walls of the room, she went out quietly and closed the door behind her.

For a moment after she was gone, the man stood motionless and made no sound. Then he looked about him slowly, rubbing his hand reflectively across the rough furze-stubble of his beard. His traveling gaze at length rested on his reflected image in the dresser mirror, and for a brief instant he regarded himself intently, with a kind of stupid and surprised wonder. And suddenly his features were contorted by a grimace as anguished and instinctive as a cornered animal's.

Almost instantly, however, it was gone. He ran his hands through his disheveled hair and shook his head angrily as though throwing off a hurt. Then quickly and impatiently he took off his coat, flung it down across a chair, sat down upon the bed, bent and swiftly untied his muddy shoes and removed them, and then sat there numbly in a stupor for some minutes, staring before him blindly at the wall. The cold, white bareness of the room stole over him and seemed to hold his spirit in a spell.

At length he stirred. For a moment his lips moved suddenly. Slowly he looked around the bare white walls with an expression of dawning recognition and disbelief. Then, shaking his head and shrugging his thick shoulders with an involuntary and convulsive shudder, he got up abruptly, switched off the light, and, without removing the rest of his clothes, lay down upon the bed and drew a quilt across his body.

And then, while storm beat against the house and cold silence filled it, he lay there, flat and rigid on his back, staring up with fixed eyes into blackness. But at last the drug of cold, dark silence possessed him, his eyes closed, and he slept.

In the old house of time and silence there is something that creaks forever in the night, something that moves and creaks forever, and that never can be still.

The man awoke instantly, and instantly it was as if he had never slept at all. Instantly it was as if he had never been absent from the house, had never been away from home.

Strong, unreasoning terror gripped him, numb horror clove his breath, the cold, still silence laid its hand upon his heart. For in his brain it seemed a long-forgotten voice had just re-echoed, in his heart a word, and in his ear it seemed a footfall, soft and instant, had just passed.

"Is anybody there?" he said.

Storm beat about the house, and darkness filled it. There was nothing but cold silence and the million drumming hoof-beats of small rain.

"But I heard it!" his mind repeated. "I heard a voice now lost, belonging to a name now seldom spoken. I heard a step that passed here—that of a phantom stranger and a friend—and with it was a voice that spoke to me, saying the one word, 'Brother!'

"Is it the storm," he said to himself, "that has a million voices? Is it the rain? Is it the darkness that fills an old house of life and gives a tongue to silence, a voice to something that moves and creaks forever in the night? Or is it the terror of cold silence that makes of my returning no return, and of me an alien in this house, where my very mother has forgotten me? Oh, is it the cold and living silence of strong terror moving in the house at night that stabs into the living heart of man the phantom daggers of old time and memory? Is there a tongue to silence and the dark? ——"

Light and instant as the rain a footfall passed above him.

"Who's there?" he said.

Storm beat upon the house, and silence filled it. Strong darkness prowled there and the bare boughs creaked, and something viewless as the dark had come into the house, and suddenly he heard it again and knew that it was there.

Above his head, in Ben's old room—the room of his brother, Ben, now dead these many years, and, like himself, forgotten too—he heard a light, odd step, as nimble as a bird's, as soft as ashes, and as quick as rain.

And with the step he heard once more the old familiar voice, saying softly:

"Brother! Brother! . . . What did you come home for? . . . You know now that you can't go home again!"

2. The Real Thing

Eugene Gant had been seven years from home, and many times in those long years of absence he had debated with himself, saying: "I will go home again. I shall lay bare my purposes about the book, say my piece, speak so that no man living in the world can doubt me. Oh, I shall tell them till the thing is crystal clear when I go home again."

Concerning the town's bitter and ancient quarrel with him, he knew that there was much to say that could be said. He also knew that there was much to say that never could be spoken. But time passes, and puts halters to debate. And one day, when his seven years were up, he packed his bag and started out for home.

Each man of us has his own America, his own stretch, from which, here outward, the patterns are familiar as his mother's face and the prospect is all his. Eugene's began at Gettysburg, his father's earth; then southward through Hagerstown, and down the Valley of Virginia.

First, the great barns, the wide sweep and noble roll of Pennsylvania fields, the neat-kept houses. Lower down, still wide fields, still neat-kept houses, white fences and painted barns, a grace and sweetness that still lingers in the Valley of Virginia. But now, for the first time, the hodden drab of nigger gray also appears—gray barns, gray sheds, gray shacks and lean-tos sturdy to the weather that had given them this patina to make up for the lack of paint. Now, too, the gashed and familiar red of common clay. To Eugene Gant returning home it was all most beautiful, seen so with the eyes of absence.

The rains of spring were heavy through Virginia, the land was sodden and everywhere was spotted with wet pools of light. It was almost the time of apple blossoms, and faintly there was the smell of rain and apple blossoms on the air.

Through the Valley of Virginia he went down very slowly. And slowly the rains lifted, and one day, in sun and light, the blue veil round the shouldering ramparts of the great Blue Ridge appeared.

Quickly, now, the hills drew in out of wide valleydom, and signs of old kept spaciousness vanished into the blue immediate. Here was another life, another language of its own—the life and language of creek, hill, and hollow, of gulch and notch and ridge and knob, and of cabins nestling in their little patches of bottom land.

And suddenly Eugene was back in space and color and in time, the weather of his youth was round him, he was home again.

Following some deep, unreasoning urge that sought to delay the moment and put off the final impact of his return, he took a circuitous course that carried him southwestward from Virginia into Tennessee, then south again, beyond the high wall of the mountains, to Knoxville. From there the road to Altamont is long and roundabout. Almost at once it starts to mount the ramparts of the Great Smokies. It winds in and out, and goes by rocky waters boiling at the bottom of steep knolls, then climbs, climbs, winds and climbs. May is late and cold among the upper timber. Torn filaments of mist wash slowly round the shoulders of the hills. Here the chestnut blight is evident: ruined, in the blasted sweeps, the great sentries of the heights appear.

Very steep, now, the road went up across the final crest of the mountains. The ruined hulks of the enormous chestnut trees stood bleakly on the slopes. High up on the eroded hillsides, denuded of their growth, were the raw scars of mica pits. Beyond, stretching into limitless vistas, were the blue and rugged undulations of a lost and forgotten world. And suddenly a roadside sign—Eugene was back in Old Catawba, and the road started down again, to Zebulon.

Zebulon—the lost world. Zebulon—the syllables that shaped the very clay of his mother's ancestral earth.

And all at once he heard his mother's voice echo across the years: "Son! Son! . . . Where are you, boy? I'll vow—where has he gone?" And with it came faint echoes of the bell that came and went like cloud shadows passing on a hill, and like the lost voices of his kinsmen in the mountains long ago. With it returned old memories of his mother's endless stories about her people, stories of Marches long ago, of bleak dusk and rutted clay, of things that happened at sunset in the mountains when the westering red was pale, ragged, cold, and desolate, and winter was howling in the oak.

And with the echo of his mother's voice, that had seemed to fill all the days of his childhood with its unending monotone, there returned to him an immediate sense of everything that he had ever known: the front porch of the old house in Altamont where he had lived, the coarse and cool sound of Black's cow munching grass in the alleyway, along the edges of the backyard fence, the mid-morning sound of sawn ice out in the hot street of summer, the turbaned slatterns of good housewives awaiting noon, the smell of turnip greens, and, upon the corner up above, the screeching halt of the street car, and the sound of absence after it had gone, then the liquid smack of leather on the pavement as the men came home at noon for dinner, and the slam of screen doors and the quiet greetings; and, inside the house, the cool, stale smell of the old parlor, and the coffined, rich piano smell, the tinkling glasspoints of the chandelier, the stereopticon of Gettysburg, the wax fruit on the mantel underneath its glass hood, and he himself reclining on his father's couch, buried in a book, his imagination soaring with Hans Grimm, and with thoughts of witches, a fair princess, fairies, elves, and gnomes, and of a magic castle on a rock.

Then a memory of one particular day, and his mother's voice again:

"Child! Child! . . . I'll vow—where is that boy? . . . Son! Son! Where are you? . . . Oh, here! Boy, here's your Uncle Bacchus. He comes from Zebulon, where all your folks—*my* folks —were from. Father lived for years in Zebulon, where he was born a hundred years ago—an' Uncle Bacchus, he was my father's brother."

And then the voice of Uncle Bacchus, drawling, quiet as the sifting of the winter ash, impregnant with all time and memory, and in it suggestive overtones of the voices of lost kinsmen long ago: "I knowed the minute that I seed him, 'Liza—fer he looks like you." The voice was benevolent, all-sure, triumphant, unforgettable—as hateful as the sound of good and unctuous voices that speak softly while men drown. It was the very death-watch of a voice, the voice of one who waits and watches, all-triumphant, while others die, and then keeps vigil by the dead in a cabin in the hills, and drawls the death-watch out to the accompaniment of crackling pine-knots on the hearth and the slow crumbling of the ash.

"Your Uncle Bacchus, child, from Zebulon ——"

So memory returned with Eugene Gant's return. And this was Zebulon. Now down the stretch of road he went his own way home. The tallest hills in all the eastern part of North America soared on every side. The way wound steeply down by blighted chestnut trees and brawling waters into the mountain fastnesses of old Zebulon.

And the voice of Uncle Bacchus came back again:

"Yore grandpaw, son, was my own brother. He was born, like all of us, on the South Toe out in Zebulon. He married yore grandmaw thar and settled down and raised a family. His paw before him—my paw, too—he come in thar long years before. I've heerd him tell it was wild country then. Thar was Cherokees when yore great-grandpaw first come in thar. Yes, sir. And he hunted, fished, and laid traps fer bear. He growed or trapped everything he et. He was a great hunter, and one time they say he run the hounds the whole way over into Tennessee."

Then his mother's voice again:

"That's the way it was, all right. I've heard father tell about it a thousand times. . . . You must go out there some day, son. It's many years since I was there, but dozens of my people are still livin' out in Zebulon. There's Uncle John, an' Thad an' Sid, an' Bern, Luke, an' James—they're all there with the families they have raised. . . . Well, now, I tell you what— Uncle Bacchus is right about it. It was a wild place back in those days. Why, father used to tell us how much wild life there was even in his time. But look here—why, wasn't I readin' about it just the other day?—an article, you know—says the wild life has all gone now."

The county seat of Zebulon is a little town. Eugene decided to stay overnight and see if he could hunt out any of his mother's people. There was no hotel, but he found a boarding house. And the moment he began to make inquiries about the Pentlands, his mother's family, he seemed to run into people everywhere who said they were relatives of his. Most of them he had never seen before, or even heard of, but as soon as he identified himself they all appeared to know who he was, and the first show of suspicion and mountain aloofness with which they had greeted him when they thought him a stranger quickly melted into friendly interest when they placed him as "Eliza Pentland's boy." One man in particular proved most obliging.

"Why, hell," he said, "we've all heard of you from your cousin Thad. He lives a mile from town. And your Uncle Johnny and Bern and Sid—the whole crowd of them are out upon the Toe. They'll want to see you. I can drive you out tomorrow. My name is Joe Pentland, and we're fifth cousins. Everybody's kinfolks here. There are only fifteen thousand people in Zebulon County, and we're all related somehow. . . . So you're goin' home again? Well, it's all blown over now. The people who were mad about the book have forgotten it. They'll be glad to see you. . . . Well, you won't find this much of a town after the cities you have seen. Six hundred people, a main street, a few stores and a bank, a church or two—that's all there is. . . . Yes, you can get cigarettes in the drug store. It's still open— this is Saturday night. You'd better wear your coat. We're thirty-seven hundred feet up here—we've got a thousand feet on Altamont—you'll find it cooler than it is down there. . . . I'll go with you."

The night had the chill cool of mountain May, and as the two men walked along, a nerve, half ecstasy, was set atremble in Eugene's blood. The country street was fronted by a few brick stores, their monotony broken only by the harsh rawness of the Baptist Church. A light was burning inside the church, and the single squat and ugly window that faced the street depicted Christ giving mercy in the bleak colors of raw glass. The drug store was on the corner at the crossroads. Next door was a lunchroom. Three or four ancient and very muddy Fords were parked slanting at the curb before the drug store. A few feet away, outside the lunchroom, there was a huddled group of men in overalls, attentive, watching, like men looking at a game of cards. From the center of the group came a few low words—drawling, mountain-quiet, somehow ominous. Eugene's companion spoke casually to one of the men:

"What is it, Bob?"

The answer came evasive, easy, mountain-quiet again:

"Oh, I don't know. A little argument, I guess."

"Who was that?" asked Eugene as they entered the drug store.

"That was Bob Creasman. Said there was some argument going on. Ted Reed's there—he's my cousin—and he's drunk again. It happens every Saturday night. A bunch of 'em was at the quarry this afternoon, and they've been drinkin' corn. I guess they're arguin' a bit. . . . What's yours? A Coca-Cola? . . . Make it two cokes and a couple of packs of Chesterfields."

Five minutes later, as the two men emerged from the drug store, there was a just-perceptible stir in the attentive group of men outside.

"Wait a minute," said Joe Pentland. "Let's see what's goin' on."

There was the same quietness as before, but the waiting men were now drawn back against the lunchroom window, and in front of them two others stood and faced each other. One of them was in overalls, and he was saying:

"Now, Ted. . . ."

The other was more urbanely clothed in dark trousers and a white shirt without a collar. His hat was pushed to the back of his head, and he just stood there staring heavily, his sullen face, sleepy-eyed, thrust forward, silent, waiting.

"Now, Ted," the one in overalls repeated. "I'm warnin' ye. ... You're goin' too fer now. ... Now leave me be."

Drowsy-eyed, swart-visaged, and unspeaking, a little sagging at the jowls, a little petulant like a plump child, darkly and coarsely handsome, with his head thrust forward, the other listens sullenly, while the men, attentive, feeding, wait.

"You leave me be now, Ted. ... I'm not lookin' fer no trouble, so you leave me be."

Still sullen and unspeaking, the swart visage waits.

"Ted, now, I'm tellin' ye. ... When ye cut me up six years ago, yore family an' yore kindfolks begged you out of hit. ... Now you leave me be. ... I'm not lookin' fer no trouble with ye, Ted, but you're goin' too fer now. ... You leave me be."

"It's Ted Reed and Emmet Rogers," Joe whispers hoarsely in Eugene's ear, "and they've started in again. They had a fight six years ago. Ted cut Emmet up, and now they always get this way on Saturday night. Ted, he gets to drinkin' and acts big—but pshaw! he wouldn't hurt a fly. He ain't got the kind of guts it takes to be *real* mean. Besides, Will Saggs is here—the one there in the white shirt—he's the cop. Will's scared—you can see that. Not scared of Ted, though. See that big man standin' back of Will—that's Lewis Blake, Ted's cousin. That's who Will's afraid of. Lewis is the kind that won't take nothin' off of nobody, and if it wasn't for him Will Saggs would break this up. ... *Wait* a minute! Something's happening!"

A quick flurry, and——

"Now, goddam you, Ted, you leave me be!"

The two men are apart now, Ted circling the other, and slowly his hand goes back upon his hip.

"Look out!"—shouted from the crowd. "He's got his gun!"

There is the dull wink of blue metal at Ted Reed's hips, the overalled line fades back, and every waiting man now jumps for cover. The two principals are left alone.

"Go on and shoot, goddam you! I'm not afraid of you!"

To Eugene, who has dodged back into the recessed entrance of the drug store, someone calls out sharply: "Better git behind a car there at the curb, man! You ain't got no protection in that doorway!"

Moving with the urgency of instant fear, Eugene dives across the expanse of open pavement just as the explosion of the first shot blasts the air. The bullet whistles right past his nose as he ducks behind a car. Cautiously he peers around the side to see Emmet moving slowly with a strange grin on his face, circling slowly to the shot, mocking his antagonist with the gun, his big hands spread palms outward in a gesture of invitation.

"Go on, goddam you, shoot! You bastard, I'm not scared of you!"

The second shot blows out a tire on the car Eugene has retreated to. He crouches lower—another shot—the sharp hiss of escaping air from another tire, and Emmet's whine, derisive, scornful:

"Why, go on and shoot, goddam you!"

A fourth shot——

"Go on! Go on! Goddam you, I'm not——"

A fifth—and silence.

Then Ted Reed comes walking slowly past the row of cars. Men step out from behind them and say quietly:

"What's wrong, Ted?"

Sullenly, the gun held straight downward at his thigh: "Oh, he tried to git smart with me."

Other voices now, calling to each other:

"Where'd he git 'im?"

"Right underneath the eye. He never knowed what hit 'im."

"You'd better go on, Ted. They'll be lookin' fer you now."

Still sullen: "The bastard wasn't goin' to git smart with me.
. . . Who's this?"—stopping to look Eugene up and down.

Joe Pentland, quickly: "Must be a cousin of yours, Ted. Least-
ways, he's a cousin of mine. You know—the feller who wrote
that book."

With a slow and sullen grin Ted shifts the gun and offers
his hand. The hand of murder is thick flesh, strong, a little
sticky, cool and moist.

"Why, sure, I know about you. I know your folks. But, by
God, you'd better never put *this* in a book! Because if you do ——"

Other voices, coaxingly: "You better go along now, Ted, before the sheriff gits here. . . . Go on, you fool, go on."

"because if you do—" with a shake of the head and a throaty
laugh—"you and me's goin' to git together!"

The voices breaking in again: "You're in fer it this time, Ted.
You carried it too fer this time."

"Hell, you couldn't git a jury here in Zebulon to convict a
Reed!"

"Go on, now. They'll be lookin' fer ye."

"They don't make jails that can hold a Reed!"

"Go on. Go on."

And he was gone, alone, and with his gun still in his hand—
gone right down the middle of the quiet street, still sullen-
jowled and sleepy-eyed—leaving a circle of blue-denimed men,
and a thing there on the pavement which, two minutes before,
had been one of their native kind.

Eugene saw it all, and turned away with a leaden sickness in
his heart. And once again he heard the echoes of his mother's
voice, saying:

"The wild life has all gone now."

At last Eugene was home again in Altamont, and at first it
was good to be home again. How many times in those seven

years had he dreamed and thought of going home and wondered what it would be like! Now he was back, and saw, felt, knew it as it really was—and nothing was the way he had imagined it. Indeed, there was very little that was even as he remembered it.

Of course there were some things that had not changed, some things that were still the same. He heard again all the small familiar sounds of his boyhood: the sounds of night, of voices raised in final greetings, saying "Good night" as screen doors slammed—"Good night," far off, and the receding thunder-drone of a racing motor—"Good night," and the last street car going—"Good night," and the rustle of the maple leaves around the street light on the corner. Again he heard in the still-night distance the barking of a dog, the shifting of the engines in the yards, the heavy thunder of the wheels along the river's edge, the clanking rumble of the long freights, and far off, wind-broken, mournful, the faint tolling of the bell. He saw again the first blue light of morning break against the rim of eastern hills, and heard the first cock's crow just as he had heard it a thousand times in childhood.

Niggertown was also still the same, with the branch-mire running in the nigger depths, yellow, rank with nigger sewage. And the smells were just the same—the sour reek from the iron laundry pots mixed in with the branchmire smell and the acrid tang of woodsmoke from the nigger shacks. So, too, no doubt, were the smells the same inside of nigger-shackdom—the smells of pork, urine, nigger funk, and darkness. He remembered all of this with the acid etchings of a thousand wintry mornings, when, twenty-five years ago, with the canvas strap around his neck and the galling weight of the bag forever pulling at him, he had gone down to Niggertown upon his paper route and had heard, a hundred times repeated every morning, the level smack of ink-fresh news against the shanty doors and the drowsy moan of funky wenches in the sleeping jungle depths.

These things were still the same. They would never change. But for the rest, well ——

"Hello, there, Gene! I see you've put on weight! How are you, boy?"

"Oh, fine. Glad to see you. *You* haven't changed much."

"Have you seen Jim yet?"

"No. He came by the house last night, but I wasn't there."

"Well, Jim Orton's been looking for you—he and Ed Sladen, Hershel Brye, Holmes Benson, Brady Chalmers, Erwin Hines. . . . Why, say! Here's Jim now, and all the rest of them."

A chorus of voices, laughing and calling out greetings as they all piled out of the car that had pulled up at the curb:

"Here he is! . . . All right, we've got him now! . . . So you decided to come home again? . . . What was it you said about me in the book—that I concealed the essential vulgarity of my nature behind a hearty laugh?"

"Now look here, Jim—I—I ——"

"I—I—hell!"

"I didn't mean ——"

"The hell you didn't!"

"Let me explain ——"

"Explain nothing! Why hell, man, what is there to explain? You didn't even get started in that book. If you were going to write *that* kind of book, why didn't you let me know? I could have told you dirt on some of the people in this town that you never even heard about. . . . Look at his face! . . . We've got him now! . . . Hell, son, don't look so backed. It's all forgotten now. A lot of them around here were pretty hot about it for a while. Two or three of them were out to get you—or said they were."

Laughter, then a sly voice:

"Have you seen Dan Fagan yet?"

"No, I haven't. Why?"

"Oh, nothing. I just wondered. Only——"

"Hell, he won't do nothing! No one will. The only ones who are mad today are those you left out!"

More laughter.

"Hell, it's true! The rest of 'em are proud of it! . . . We're all proud of you, son. We're glad that you came home. You've been away too long. Stay with us now."

"Why, hello, son! Glad to see you back! . . . You'll find many changes. The town has improved a lot since you were here. I guess the new Courthouse and the County Hall were put up since you left. Cost four million dollars. Have you seen the tunnel they bored under the mountain for that new roadway out of town? Cost two million more. And the High School and the Junior College, and the new streets, and all the new improvements? . . . And look at the Square here. I think it's pretty now the way they've laid it out, with flower beds and benches for the people. That's the thing this town needs most—some parks, some new amusements. If we hope to bring tourists here and make this a tourist town, we've got to give them some amuse- ments. I've always said that. But you get a bunch of messheads in at City Hall and they can't see it. . . . Fact is, tourists don't stay here any more. They used to come and stay a month. You ought to know—you wrote about them sitting on the porches of the boarding houses. They'd come and sit and rock upon the porches, and they'd stay a month, people from all over— Memphis, Jacksonville, Atlanta, New Orleans. But we don't get them any more. They've all got cars now, and there are good roads everywhere, so they just stay overnight and then hit it for the mountains. You can't blame them—we've got no amusements. . . . Why, I can remember when this was a *sporting* center. The big swells all came here, the millionaires and racing men. And we had seventeen saloons—Malone's, and Creasman's, and Tim O'Connell's, and Blake's, and Carlton Leathergood's— your father used to go in there, he was a friend of Leathergood's. Do you remember Leathergood's tall, pock-marked, yellow nigger and his spotted dog? All gone now—dead, forgotten. . . . Here's where your father's shop used to stand. Do you remember the angel on the porch, the draymen sitting on the wooden steps, your father standing in the door, and the old calaboose across the street? It's pretty now, the way they've got all the grass and flower beds where the old calaboose used to be, but somehow the whole Square looks funny, empty at one end. And it's strange to see this sixteen-story building where your father's old marble shop once stood. But, say what you will, they've certainly improved things a lot. . . . Well, good-bye. The whole town wants to see you. I won't keep you. Come to see me sometime. My office is on the eleventh floor—right over where your father's workbench used to be. I'll show you a view you never dreamed of when your father's shop was here."

The return of the prodigal, and the whole town broken into greetings, while the on-coming, never-ceasing younger generation just gaped, curiously a-stare:

"He's back. . . . Have you seen him yet? . . . Which one is he?"

"Don't you see him there, talking to all those people? . . . There—over *there*—before the shoe-shine shop."

A girl's voice, disappointed: "Oh-h! Is that him? . . . Why, he's *old*!"

"Oh, Eugene's not so *very* old. He's thirty-six. He only seems old to you, honey. . . . Why I remember him when he was a snotty-nosed little kid, running around the street selling *Saturday Evening Posts*, and delivering a route in Niggertown for the *Courier*."

"But—why, he's fat around the waist. . . . And look! He just took his hat off. Why, he's getting bald on top! . . . Oh-h, I never thought——"

"What did you think? He's thirty-six years old, and he never was very much to look at, anyway. He's just Eugene Gant, a snot-nosed kid who used to carry a paper route in Niggertown, and whose mother ran a boarding house, and whose father had a tombstone shop upon the Square. . . . And now just look at him! The snot-nosed kid who went away and wrote a book or two—and look there, will you!—look at all those people crowding round him! They called him every name they could think of, and now they're crawling over one another just to shake his hand."

And across the street:

"Hello, Gene!"

"Oh hello—ah—hello—ah ——"

"Come on, now: hello-ah what?"

"Why, hello—ah——"

"Boy, I'll beat your head in if you don't call me by my name. Look at me. Now, what is it? Hello-ah *what*?"

"Why, ah—ah ——"

"Come on, now! . . . Well, tell me this: who was it that called you 'Jocko' in that book?"

"Why—ah—ah—Sid! Sidney Purtle!"

"By God, you better *had*!"

"Why Sid, how are you? Hell, I knew you the minute you spoke to me!"

"The hell you did!"

"Only I couldn't quite . . . Oh, hello, Carl. Hello, Vic. Hello, Harry, Doc, Ike——"

He felt someone plucking at his sleeve and turned:

"Yes, ma'am?"

The lady spoke through artificial teeth, close-lipped, prim, and very hurriedly:

"Eugene I know you don't remember me I'm Long Wilson's mother who used to be in school with you at Plum Street School Miss Lizzy Moody was your teacher and——"

"Oh yes, Mrs. Wilson. How is Long?"

"He's very well thank you I won't keep you now I see you're busy with your friends I know everyone wants to see you you must be rushed to death but sometime when you aren't busy I'd like to talk to you my daughter-in-law is very talented she paints sculptures and writes plays she's dying to meet you she's written a book and she says the experience of her life is so much like yours that she's sure you'd both have a lot in common if you could only get together to talk about it——"

"Oh, I'd love to. I'd love to, Mrs. Wilson."

"She's sure if she could talk to you you'd be able to give her some suggestions about her book and help her to find a publisher I know you're bothered with so many people that you've hardly any time to call your own but if you could only talk to her——"

"Oh, I'd be glad to."

"She's a very in-ter-est-ing person and if you'd only let us see you sometime I know——"

"Oh, I will. I will. Thank you so much, Mrs. Wilson. I will. I will. I will."

And at home:

"Mama, have there been any calls?"

"Why, child, the telephone's been goin' *all* day long. I've never known the like of it. Sue Black called up an' says for you to ring her back—an' Roy Hitchebrand, an' Howard Bartlett, an'—oh yes, that's so—a lady from out along Big Homing. Says she's written a book an' she's comin' in to see you. Says she wants you to read it an' criticize it for her an' tell her how to make it good so it will sell. . . . An' yes—that's so now—Fred Patton called up for the Rotary Club an' wants to know if you will speak to them at lunch next Tuesday. I think you ought to do that, son. They're good, substantial men, all of them, with a high standin' in the community. That's the kind of people you ought to be in with if you're goin' to keep on writin' books. . . . An'—oh yes!—someone called up from the Veterans' Hospital— a girl named Lake, or Lape, or somethin' like that—says she used to be in the same class with you at Plum Street School, an' she's in charge of the Recreation Center for the veterans—says a lot of 'em have read your books an' want to see you an' won't you be the guest of honor on Saturday night. I wish you'd do that, child. I reckon the poor fellers, most of 'em, are far from home, an' many of 'em will never go back again to where they came from—it might cheer 'em up. . . . An' yes, that's so!— Sam Colton called up for the alumni committee of the university, an' they want you to speak to 'em at the big alumni rally next week at the Country Club. You ought to go, child. They're your old friends an' classmates, an' they want to see you. An' yes!—what about it, now!—why, you're to speak on the same program with "Our Dick"—Senator Richard L. Williams of the United States Senate, if you please! As Sam said, you and him are the two most famous alumni of the university that the town has yet produced. Hm-m! . . . Then there was Jimmy Stevenson, he called up and wanted you to come to a steak dinner to be given by the Business Men's Convention out at Sharpe's Cabin on the Beetree Creek, nine miles from Gudgerton. I'd certainly go if I were you. I've never seen the place, but they say Ed Sharpe certainly has a beautiful cabin, the best one around here—an' as the feller says, right in the heart of Nature's Wonderland, in the center of these glorious hills. I know the section well, for that's where father an' mother went to live ninety years ago, just after they were married—they moved there from Zebulon—didn't stay, of course—I reckon the pull of Zebulon an' all their kinfolks there was too much for 'em—but you couldn't pick a prettier spot if you hunted all over for it, right out in the heart of nature, with old Craggy Tavern in the background. That's the place I'd go, boy, if I was a writer an' wanted to get inspiration. Get close to Nature, as the feller says, an' you'll get close to God. . . . An', yes—two young fellers called up from over in Tennessee—said they're the Blakely boys. You've heard of the famous Blakely Canners. Why, I hear that they own almost every farm in three counties there, an' they've got factories everywhere, through Tennessee, an' way down South, an' all out through the Middle West—why, they're worth millions. Says—oh, just a boy, you know—but says, real slylike, 'Is this Miss Delia?'—givin' me the name you gave me in the book. Well, I just played right along with him—'Well, now,' I says, 'I don't know about that. My name's Eliza. Now I've heard that I've been called Delia, but you mustn't believe all that you read,' I says. 'For all you know, I may be human just like everybody else. Now,' I says, 'I looked real good and hard at myself this mornin' in the mirror, an' if there are any

horns stickin' out of my head, why I must've missed 'em, I didn't
see any. Of course I'm growin' old, an' maybe my eyesight's
failin' me,' I says, 'but you're young an' ought to have good
eyes, so why don't you come an' have a look an' tell me what
you think.' Well, sir, he laughed right out across the phone as
big as you please, an' says, 'Well, you're all right! I think you're
wonderful! An' I'm tryin' to be a writer—even if my father
does put up tomatoes—an' I think your son's one of the best
writers that we have.' Well, I didn't let on, of course. Father
always taught us that it was vulgar an' unrefined to brag about
your own, so I just said, 'Well, now, I don't know about that.
But you come on an' look at him. Up to the time he was twelve
years old,' I says, 'he was a good, normal sort of boy like everybody else. Now what happened to him after that,' I says—you
see, I thought I'd have a little fun with him—'what happened
after that I don't know—I'm not responsible. But you come
an' take a look at him. Maybe you'll get surprised. Maybe you'll
find he doesn't have horns, either.' Well, he laughed right out
an' said, 'You're all right! An' I'm goin' to take you up on that.
My brother an' I are drivin' over tomorrow afternoon—an'
we're goin' to bring him back with us,' he says. 'If he wants a
cabin like I hear he does, I've got one here that I can give him,
so we're goin' to bring him back,' he says. Well, you can't do
that, of course, child, but be nice to them. He spoke like a very
well-brought-up sort of boy—an' the Blakelys are the kind of
people that you ought to know. . . . An' after that a lot of girls
called up an' said they heard you needed someone to type for
you—said they'd like to do it, and knew how to type good. One
of 'em said she'd be willin' to do it for nothin'—says she wants
to be a writer, an' knew she'd learn so much from you an'
what an inspiration it would he. Hm! pshaw!—I cut her off
mighty quick, I can tell you! Sounded funny to me—wantin'

to work for nothin', an' all that gushy talk about inspiration. I knew what *she* was after, all right. You watch out, son—don't let any of these silly women rope you in. . . . Yes, that's so. Cash Hopkins was here askin' about you. Of course he's just a plain, workin' sort of man. He used to do jobs for your father, but your father liked him, an' he's always been our friend, interested in all of you. . . . Mr. Higginson was here, too. He's an Episcopal minister that came to town several years ago for his health—an' what about it!—he's been your friend right from the start. When all the preachers were denouncin' you, an' sayin' you'd disgraced us all, an' everyone was down on you an' said if you ever came back here they'd kill you—he *defended* you, sir! He stood right up for you! He read everything you wrote an' he said, 'That boy should have been a preacher. He's got more of the true gospel in his books than all of us preachers put together!' Oh, he came right out for you, you know. 'It's we who have failed,' he said, 'not him!' Child, I hope you'll be nice to Mr. Higginson. He's been your friend from the first, an', as the sayin' goes, he's a scholar an' a Christian gentleman. . . . An', law, what about it! I'm sorry you were not here to see it. I'll vow, I had to turn my head away to keep from laughin'. Why, Ernest Pegram, if you please, in his big car—all rared back there in a brand-new Cadillac as fat as a pig, an' with a big cigar stickin' out of his mouth. Why, of course; he's *rich* now! He's well-fixed—every last one of the Pegrams is! You see, when Will Pegram died two years ago up there in the North somewhere, he was a wealthy man, a big official in some large corporation. You see, he was the only one of the Pegrams who got away. But, poor Will! I can remember just as well the day he left here more than forty years ago—this corporation had given him a job down in the eastern part of the state, an', as the sayin' goes, he didn't have an extra shirt to put on his back. An' here he dies two years ago an' leaves close to a million dollars. So they're well-fixed! Of course, Will had no childern, an' his brothers an' sisters got it all. He left Ernest a flat hundred thousand—that's what it was, all right, because I read it in the papers, an' Ernest told me so himself. The others came in for their share, too. Here the rest of us are broke, the whole town ruined, everyone has lost everything they had—as the Bible says, 'How have the mighty fallen!'—but the Pegrams don't have to worry from now on. So Ernest drives up an' stops before the house this afternoon in his big, new car, smokin' his fine cigar. 'Why, Ernest,' I says, 'I don't think I ever saw you lookin' better. Are you still workin' at your plumbin' trade?' I says. Of course I knew he wasn't—I just wanted to hear what he would say. 'No, Eliza,' he says—oh, the biggest thing you ever saw, puffin' away at his cigar. 'No,' he says. 'I've reached the age,' he says, 'when I figgered it was about time to retire.' Pshaw! *Retire!* I had to turn my head away to keep from laughin'. Who ever heard of a plumber retirin'? What did *he* ever have to retire *on*—that's what *I'd* like to know—if it hadn't been for Will? But—oh yes, see here, now—says: 'You tell Gene,' he says, 'that I haven't got a thing to do. My time is free,' he says, 'an' if there's any place he wants to go, any place where I can take him, why, my car is here,' he says, 'an' it's at his disposal.' You know how goodhearted he's always been. I reckon he was thinkin' of the days when he used to live next to us on Woodson Street, an' how he watched all you childern grow up. The Pegrams have always been our friends an' taken a great interest in your career. I wish, son, that you'd go to see them all while you're here. They'll be glad to see you. But when I saw Ernest there in his big car, puffin' away on his cigar, an' lookin' fat enough, as the sayin' goes, to pop right out of his britches, an' tellin' me he had retired—well, I just had to turn my head away an' laugh. . . .

Well, in all my life I've never seen the beat of it! There's been a steady string of them here all day long, an' the telephone has just rung constantly. I'll vow—it seems to me that everyone in town has either been here or called up today. . . . An', oh yes! There are two of 'em out in the sun parlor now—old Cap'n Fitzgerald and a Miss Morgan, a trained nurse. I don't know what they want. They've been waitin' for an hour, so I wish you'd just step out an' say hello to 'em. . . . An' yes! There's three more in the front parlor—a lady who says she's from Charleston an' had read your books an' was just passin' through town an' heard you were here an' wanted to shake hands with you, an' that young Tipton that you used to know, an'—oh yes! that's so!—the reporter from the paper, he's there, too. I guess he wants to write you up, so you'd better go right in. . . . I'll vow! There goes that phone again! Just a minute, son—I'll answer it."

On Leprechauns

A N ARMENIAN FRIEND OF OURS, A MR. VLADIMIR ADZIGIAN OF SOUTH Brooklyn, has mentioned among the defects of our literary style a certain coldness and economy of tone and manner, which, while it makes for precision and temperance, is likely to err too much on the side of understatement. This critic feels—and rightly, too, we think—that our work would profit if it had a little more exuberance, a more impulsive warmth, even a little exaggeration here and there. "For," says he, "exaggeration is in itself a form of enthusiasm, and enthusiasm, in my opinion, is the quality that your work, together with almost all American writing, lacks." This cultivated gentleman then goes on to say that here in America we have never overcome the repressive influences of our Puritan ancestry, and he thinks we will never completely realize ourselves until we do.

While admitting the truth of our friend's observations and conceding regretfully that our own style does suffer from a kind of puritanic sparseness, an almost frigid restraint, we think we might interpose a few mild, although apologetic, reservations to the general tenor of his remarks. In the first place, if our style does suffer from a puritanic frigidity, it is because we, in our own person, suffer from the same defect. And however much we may regret it, however much we may want to burst through the barriers of our reserve to a warm and free communication with the universe, it is probably better to reflect the color of our soul—even though that color be cold and hard—than to assume a false, unwarranted spontaneity that we do not have. More-over, even if we could overcome the constrained reserve of our nature and break through to a more impulsive spontaneity, we should hesitate to attempt it, because we have so many friends and readers whose own sense of propriety and personal modesty would be affronted if we did.

Chief among these people are our Irish friends, whom we number by the hundreds. Our admiration and affection for the Irish is, we believe, well known. In addition to the traditional affection for the race in which every American boy is brought up, and which is as natural to him as a sore toe, we have had the privilege time and again in our written works of expressing—as soberly and temperately as any man could, it seemed to us, and certainly far too soberly and temperately to suit the tastes of Mr. Adzigian—what seemed to us to be the shining and distinguishing qualities of the race, its great and lasting contribu-tions to our nation's life.

We have found frequent occasion to pay tribute to their sterling honesty, the devotion of their public service, their brilliant skill in politics and government, which have given them a record of unselfish and incorruptible administration that is, we be-lieve, unequaled by any other people in the world. Where else in the world may a people be found who will so cheerfully and uncomplainingly take over the onerous and thankless burden of running the government, and whose devotion to the principles of law and order, sobriety, reasonable conciliation, and selfless and unseeking consecration to the common weal are as high, loyal, and untarnished in their idealism as are those of the Irish? Where else, among all the peoples who make up the vast polyglot of American life, will another people be found whose patriotism is not only one hundred per cent American, but maintains a con-stant average of one hundred and thirty-seven per cent?

We have considered it not only a duty but an agreeable privilege to refer to these well-known facts on several occasions, and if we finally desisted, it was largely because of the quiet protests of our Irish friends themselves.

For, said they, the only reward they ever desired or hoped for was the knowledge of public duty modestly done and honorably completed. Virtue was its own exceeding great reward. There were, it was true, among other peoples, certain odious demagogues who were always making public speeches in their own behalf, and slapping themselves proudly on their own breasts; there were even those contemptible characters who regarded politics as a means of feathering their own nests out of the common funds. As for themselves, however, all they asked was the joyful privilege of serving their state or their city as well as they could, giving to their country the last full measure of devotion. That was reward enough, and the knowledge that one had given his *all* for his country should be sufficient for any man. Certainly the thought of public acknowledgment for such a noble and idealistic service was odious, and would we please not affront their deepest and most sacred feelings by speaking of it further?

Since the matter was presented to us in this way by many of our dear Irish friends, we consented reluctantly to refrain from a further public display of our enthusiasm rather than incur the quiet reproaches of a people who, as is well known, are among the shyest and most modest races in the world. In matters of literary judgment, however, we trust we may be allowed a more full and free expression of our emotions, since every race, no matter how innately modest, how consecrated to a public trust, may be justly proud of its artistic achievements, and justly boastful of all its men of genius.

We take it as a matter of general consent that Ireland has always swarmed with geniuses. Old Erin has been for centuries running over with them—has, in fact, had so many of this glorious type that it has been necessary to establish a kind of emigration service for the exportation of Irish geniuses to other nations which, though bigger, are lamentably deficient in their genius supply.

The leading customer for the importation of Irish geniuses has been our own fair land. In fact, we do not believe it any extravagant exaggeration to say that where genius is concerned the Irish brand tops the list with us. Here in America we'd rather have one good, bona-fide, Irish genius than a half-dozen Polish, Swedish, Czecho-Slovakian, or Hungarian specimens, no matter what their reputations.

It is true that visiting Englishmen are still in considerable demand, and ply a thriving trade before the Culture Clubs and Female Forums of the Corn Belt. Almost any ninth-rate scribbler from Great Britain can still come over here and insult the country with the choicest and most indecipherable sneers in his whole Oxford vocabulary, and command prices from his adoring audiences that no American could dream of asking.

Yes, there is still a good market for the English genius, but among the *haut ton*, so to say, the true sophisticates of culture, the Irish bards and story tellers come first. A bad English writer may still put in a profitable six or eight months and eat and drink his way across the pampas from Portland, Maine to Tacoma, Washington, at the expense of this great, benevolent, and culture-loving people. But to do so requires considerable traveling, and the English genius cannot always pick his spots; he must occasionally prepare himself for the uncomfortable exigencies of one-night stands, bad accommodations, and poor food.

An Irish genius is faced with none of these embarrassing possibilities. He can pick his spots and do as he damn pleases. He can remain in New York in the perfumed salons of the art-loving

plutocracy, and can always have the very best of everything at
no cost to himself, provided he exercises only a very small degree
of caution and has sense enough to know upon which side his
cake is caviared. An Englishman may have to stand an occasional
round of drinks, or stay with the second-best family in Ham-
tramck, Michigan, but a visiting Irishman—never! A visiting
Englishman may have to have at least the vestige of a reputation
—to have received the endorsement of Hugh Walpole, or to have
in his pocket a letter of introduction from J. B. Priestley—but a
visiting Irishman needs nothing. It is naturally preferable if
someone has heard of him before, but it is by no means essential.
The main thing is that he be a visiting Irish writer, and, of course,
all visiting Irish writers are geniuses, and not only geniuses, but
the most Extra-Special, A-Number-1, Eighteen-Carat Geniuses
in existence.

After that, no introduction is necessary. He can just call himself Sean O'Mulligan or Seamus O'Toole or some other whimsical
appellative of this nature, and everything will be all right. He
needs only to get off the boat and announce to the reporters that
he is the author of an untranslated and untranslatable epic,
written in pure Gaelic (he disdains, of course, to use the English
speech, unless it be to cash a check; otherwise he abhors the
race that has cruelly, bloodily, and damnably oppressed Old
Erin for a thousand years, etc., etc., etc.), and from that time
on his path is smooth, his bed is roses.

If, in addition, he will only come down the gangplank muttering through his whiskers something about "a green leprechaun
which they do be sayin' an old man in the west was afther seein'
on the hill behint his house, year afther year, bedad," or some
other elfin talk of this nature, by which the bearded adults of
this race strive to convince themselves and other people that
they are really just a lot of little boys, the whole thing will be

!apped up greedily, will travel the round of the salons, and be hailed as a perfect masterpiece of whimsey, just too Irish, quaint, and delightful for words. Many a visiting Irish bard has established a reputation, achieved celebrity, and eaten and drunk his way into the Great American Heart on no better grounds than this.

It may be perfectly true, of course, that while all this is going on—while the Irish genius is muttering through his whiskers about the fairies and the leprechauns, and is being coddled in the silken laps of the adoring plutocracy as a reward for his whimsical caprice—some poor, benighted bastard of a native son, some gaunt-eyed yokel from Nebraska, Texas, Tennessee, or Minnesota, may be eating his heart out in a Greenwich Village garret, opening canned beans at midnight, and wreaking out the vision of his life here in America with all the passion, fury, terror, suffering, poverty, cruelty, and neglect which a young man in this abundant land may know. It may be true, we say, that while the visiting Seans and Seamuses are chirping on Park Avenue about their leprechauns to an adoring audience of silken wenches, some wild-eyed native youth may be pounding at the wall of his garret with bloody knuckles, wondering where, when, and how in God's name, in a swarming city of eight millions, he can find a woman, or even slake his hunger for a moment with the bought and bitter briefness of a whore.

Yes, while the lovely legs cross slowly, and slide the silken thighs, while the fragrant bellies heave in unction to the elfin blandishments of Sean, a boy may be burning in the night, burning in the lone, stern watches of darkness, and giving a tongue to silence that will shape a new language long after silken thighs and Sean and Seamus are no more.

But have no perturbations, gentle reader. When the boy has won through from the agony of silence to an uttered fame, when his toiling and imperiled soul has beat its way to shore, when by his own unaided effort he stands safe on land, you may depend on it that he will be at once encumbered with the help he no longer needs. Lovely legs and silken thighs and fragrant bellies will then heave amorously for *him*, as they do now for Sean, and every little whore of wealth and fashion will contend for the honors of the bed that poverty had bachelored and that fame has filled. The youth, once left to rot and starve, will now be fawned upon and honeyed over by the very apes of fashion who previously ignored him, and who now seek to make him their ape. And the treachery of their adoration will be more odious than the treachery of their neglect, for it stands written in Fame's lexicon that he who lets himself he whored by fashion will be whored by time.

Perhaps the reader may detect in these grave lines a color of some bitterness. Perhaps he may be shocked to realize that there is some slight neglect among the people of this present age, in this enlightened and art-loving nation, toward the young native artist. It is conceivable that the reader may espy here, in this true picture of our native customs, some tincture of injustice, some snobbery of fashion, some conceit of taste. But there are high authorities on these matters who will quickly inform the reader that if he thinks any of these things he is seriously mistaken.

It is necessary to look at what George Webber learned in college to call "The Deeper and More Significant Aspects of the Situation." Seen in this light, things which may have seemed a little difficult and puzzling become beautifully clear. Elsewhere I have told the story of George Webber's life in considerable detail, and in that chronicle I have shown that the usual reception of our young native artist during the years of his apprenticeship is a good, swift kick in the teeth, followed by a good, swift kick in the seat of the pants that will send him flying out of doors onto the pavement. The reason why this happens to the poor, young, native son, while Sean and Seamus eat and drink and wench it to their heart's content, is not because anyone means to be cruel or indifferent, but because great men and lovely women of the Cultured Classes have found out long since that the best thing that could possibly happen to a poor young man of native stock and talent is to get a few good kicks in the face. They know that he can come to his full maturity only through adversity, so they kick him out of doors just to help him along.

In this way he is prevented from getting soft. People who live in luxury, on assured incomes, have very stern and Spartan notions about getting soft. To be sure, everyone is willing to sympathize with a young man's early struggles after he has had them, but, obviously, there can be no sympathy unless he *has* had them.

Any enlightened millionaire can explain "The Deeper and More Significant Aspects of the Situation." It is really a part of what we call "The American Dream." It belongs to our ideal of rugged individualism. The more often one gets kicked in the teeth, the more rugged he becomes. It is our method of doing things, and such a simple and direct expression of our life that we have even invented a name for it. We speak of it proudly as "The American Way."

Portrait of a Literary Critic

THE PERSONALITY OF THE CELEBRATED DR. TURNER—OR DR. HUGO
Twelvetrees Turner as he was generally known to the reading public—was not an unfamiliar one to George Webber, the novelist. Dr. Turner's wider reputation had been well known to the public for fifteen years or more. And for ten years he had been the guiding spirit of the splendid journal he had himself established, the *Fortnightly Cycle of Reading, Writing, and the Allied Arts.*

The establishment of the *Fortnightly Cycle* marked, as one critic says, "one of the most important literary events of our time," and life without it, another offered, would have been "simply unthinkable." *The Cycle* came into being at the time when the critical field was more or less divided between the somewhat prosaic conservatism of the *Saturday Review of Literature* and the rather mannered preciosity of *The Dial*. Between the two, Dr. Turner and *The Cycle* struck a happy medium; the position of *The Cycle* might be best classified as middle-of-the-road, and Dr. Turner himself might be described as the nation's leading critical practitioner of middle-of-the-roadism. Here, really, lay his greatest contribution.

It is true that there were certain skeptics who stubbornly disputed Dr. Turner's right to such a title. These critics, instead of being reassured by the broad yet sane liberalism of the Doctor's views, were seriously alarmed by it: they professed to see in Dr. Turner's critical opinions a tendency toward a disturbing—nay dangerous!—radicalism. Such a judgment was simply ridiculous. Dr. Turner's position was neither too far to the right nor too far to the left, but "a little left of center." With this definition he would himself have instantly agreed; the phrasing would have pleased him.

True, there had been a period in Dr. Turner's rich career when his position had been much more conservative than it now was. But to his everlasting credit let it be said that his views had grown broader as the years went on; the years had brought increase of tolerance, depth of knowledge, width of understanding; ripeness with this valiant soul was all.

There had been a time when Dr. Turner had dismissed the works of some of the more modern writers as being the productions of "a group of dirty little boys." Indeed the first use of this delightfully homely and pungent phrase may be safely accredited to Dr. Turner himself. People on Beacon Hill read it with appreciative chuckles, gentlemen in clubs slapped the *Fortnightly Cycle* on their thighs and cried out "Capital!" It was just the way they themselves had always felt about these moderns, except that they had never found quite the words to put it so; but this man now, this What's-His-Name, this Turner—oh, Capital! Capital! It was evident that a fearless, new, and salutary force had come into the Nation's Letters.

A little later on, however, Dr. Turner's "dirty little boy" had been qualified somewhat by the adjectival words, "who scrawls bad words which he hopes may shock his elders upon the walls of privies."

This was even better! A pleasing image was thus conveyed to the readers of Dr. Turner's *Fortnightly Cycle* that brought much unction to their souls. For what could be more comforting to a devoted reader of the *Fortnightly Cycle* than the reassuring sense that just as he was settling down to attend to one of the most inevitable of the natural functions, he might look up and read with an amused and tolerating eye certain words that various dirty little boys like Anatole France, George Bernard Shaw, Theodore Dreiser, Sherwood Anderson, and D. H. Lawrence had scrawled up there with the intention of shocking him.

If Dr. Turner had made no further contribution to literature, his position would have been secure. But more, much more, was yet to come. For even at this early stage one of the salient qualities of Dr. Turner's talent had revealed itself. He was always able to keep at least two jumps ahead, not only of his own critics, but of his own admirers. Thus it was Dr. Turner who first made the astonishing discovery that Sex is Dull. The news at first stunned the readers of the *Fortnightly Cycle*, who had begun to be seriously alarmed about the whole matter, shocked, appalled, and finally reduced to a state of sputtering indignation by "This—this Sort of Thing, now; Sort of Thing they're writing nowadays; this, this—why, this Filth! This fellow Lawrence, now!"

Dr. Turner put these perturbed spirits to rest. Dr. Turner was neither appalled, shocked, nor incensed by anything he read about sex. He didn't get indignant. He knew a trick worth six of these. Dr. Turner was amused. Or would have been amused, that is, if he had not found the whole business so excessively boring. Even as early as 1924, he was writing the following in comment on a recent book of D. H. Lawrence:

"This preoccupation with Sex—really not unlike the preoccupation of a naughty little boy with certain four-letter words which he surreptitiously scrawls upon the sides of barns—(observe how the earlier exuberances of the Doctor are here subtly modified)—would on the whole be mildly amusing to an adult intelligence who had presumed that these were things that one had lived through and forgotten in one's salad days, if it were not for the fact that the author contrives to make the whole business so appallingly dull."

The readers of the *Fortnightly Cycle* were at first amazed, then simply enchanted by this information. They had been dismayed and sore perplexed—but now! Why, hah-hah-hah, the whole thing was very funny, wasn't it? The extreme seriousness of the fellow about the Kind of Thing they had themselves forgotten since their sophomore days—would really be quite amusing if he had not contrived to make it so abysmally Dull!

There was more, much more, to come. The whole tormented complex of the 'twenties was upon good Dr. Turner. People everywhere were bewildered by the kaleidoscopic swiftness with which things changed. It was a trial that might well have floored a less valiant spirit than that of Dr. Turner. Hardly a week went by without its discovery of a new great poet. Scarcely an issue of the *Fortnightly Cycle* appeared without proclaiming to the world some new novel to equal *War and Peace*. And not a month passed without producing some new and sensational movement in the bewildering flux of fashion. Charlie Chaplin was discovered to be, not primarily a comedian at all, but the greatest tragic actor of the time (learned adepts of the arts assured the nation that his proper role was Hamlet). The true art-expression of America was the comic strip (the productions of the Copleys, Whistlers, Sargents, Bellowses, and Lies could never hold a candle to it). The only theater that was truly native and worth preserving was the burlesque show. The only music that was real was Jazz. There had been only one writer in America: his name was Twain, and he had been defeated just because he was— American; he was so good just because he was—American; but if he had not been American he could have been—*so* good! Aside from this, the only worthwhile writing in the land was what the advertising writers wrote; this was the true expression of the Yankee clime—all else had failed us, all was dross.

The madness grew from week to week. With every revolution of the clock the Chaos of the Cultures grew. But through it all the soul of Dr. Turner kept its feet. Turner hewed true and took the Middle Way. To all things in their course, in their true proportion, he was just.

True, he had lapses. In culture's armies he was not always foremost to the front. But he caught up. He always caught up. If there were sometimes errors in his calculations, he always rectified them before it was too late. If he made mistakes—like the man he was, he gallantly forgot them.

It was inspiring just to watch his growth. In 1923, for instance, he referred to the *Ulysses* of James Joyce as "that encyclopædia of filth which has become the bible of our younger intellectuals"; in 1925, more tolerantly, as "that bible of our younger intellectuals which differs from the real one in that it manages to be so consistently dull"; in 1929 (behold this man!) as "that amazing *tour de force* which has had more influence on our young writers than any other work of our generation"; and in 1933, when Justice Woolsey handed down the famous decision that made the sale of *Ulysses* legally permissible throughout these United States (in a notable editorial that covered the entire front page of the *Fortnightly Cycle*), as "a magnificent vindication of artistic integrity . . . the most notable triumph over the forces of bigotry and intolerance that has been scored in the Republic of Letters in our time."

Similarly, when one of the earlier books of William Faulkner appeared, Dr. Turner greeted it with an editorial that was entitled, "The School of Bad Taste." He wrote:

"One wonders what our bright young men will do for material now that the supply of four-letter words and putrescent situations has been so exhausted that further efforts in this direction can only rouse the jaded reader to a state of apathy. Is it too much to hope that our young writers may grow tired of their own monsters and turn their talents to a possible investigation of— dare we hope it?—normal life?"

A few years later, however, when Mr. Faulkner's *Sanctuary* appeared, the Doctor had so altered his views that, after likening the author to Poe in "the quality of his brooding imagination . . . his sense of the macabre . . . his power to evoke stark fear, sheer horror, as no other writer of his time has done," he concluded his article by saying darkly to his readers, "This man may go far."

Thus, although Dr. Turner was occasionally out of step, he always fell in again before the Top Sergeant perceived his fault. Moreover, once he got into the fore, he had a very brave and thrilling way of announcing his position to his readers as if he had been in the crow's nest all along and had cried "Land Ho!" at the very moment when the faint shore of some new and brave America was first visible.

These, then, were among the Doctor's more daring discoveries. Some of the more conservative of his following were made uneasy by such risky venturesomeness, but they should not have been alarmed. For, if the Doctor ever stuck his neck out, it was only when he had it safely armor-plated: his bolder sorties out among the new and strange were always well-hedged round by flanking guards of reservations. Upon more familiar ground, however, the Doctor would go the whole hog in a way that warmed the soul. His praises of the Joyces, Faulkners, Eliots, and Lawrences were always fenced in by parentheses of safe reserve; even the Dreisers and the Lewises had their moderating checks; but when the Millays, Glasgows, Cabells, Nathans, and Morleys were his meat, he spoke out of the fullness of his heart—then it was, in vulgar phrase, that the Doctor really went to town.

And, curiously enough, it was just here, when Dr. Turner was on what he himself was fond of classifying as "safe ground," that his judgment was likely to grow giddy and was prone to err. This exuberance later caused him some embarrassment. Thus, at various stages of his editorial career, he had described Christopher Morley as being the possessor of "the most delightful prose style that the familiar essay has known since the days of his true contemporary and, may I say, *almost* his equal, Charles Lamb. Aside from Lamb there is no other essayist since Montaigne's time to match him." Of Ellen Glasgow he wrote: "She is not only our greatest living novelist, but one of the greatest novelists that ever lived," and that lady's many works he characterized as ". . . in their entirety comprising a picture of a whole society that, for variety and scope, has no parallel in literature except the *Comédie Humaine*, and that, in the perfection of their form and style, achieve a faultless artistry that Balzac's cruder talent never reached." The whimsy-whamsy of Robert Nathan he pronounced "sheer genius. There's no other word for it; it's sheer elfin genius of a kind that not even Barrie has attained, and that has no rival in our language unless perchance it be the elfin loveliness of the Titania-Oberon scenes in *A Midsummer Night's Dream*." Of the baroque pilgrimage of Mr. Cabell in his Province of Cockaigne he wrote: "He is our greatest ironist, with the greatest prose style in the language—perhaps the only Pure Artist that we have." And of a young gentleman who wrote a book about a bridge in South America he said: "A great writer—certainly the greatest writer that the Younger Generation has produced. And the book! Ah, what a book! A book to be treasured, cherished, and re-read; a book to put upon your shelves beside *War and Peace, Don Quixote, Moby Dick, Candide*

. . . and withal a book, that, without one touch of the dreary and degrading realism that disfigures the work of most of our younger writers, is so essentially, splendidly American . . . as American as Washington, Lincoln, or the Rocky Mountains, since in its story are implicit the two qualities that are most characteristic of our folk: Democracy through Love; Love through Democracy."

The world being the grim place it sometimes is, it is sorrowful but not surprising to relate that there were a few wicked spirits who took a cruel delight in unearthing these lush phrases years after they had first been uttered, and after they had lain decently interred in old copies of the *Fortnightly Cycle* for so long that presumably they were as dead as most of the books that had evoked them. Then the worthy Doctor had to pretend he did not know that they were there, or else eat them, and of all the forms of diet this is the toughest and least palatable.

But on the whole the Doctor came through nobly. The sea at times was stormy and the waves ran very high, but the staunch ship that was Turner weathered through.

Among his followers, it is true, there were some whose tendencies were so conservative that they deplored the catholicity of the Doctor's tastes. And among his enemies there were some who were cruel enough to suggest that he wanted to be all things to all men, that Turner was not only the proper, but the inevitable, name for him, that the corkscrew shaped his course, and that if he went around the corner he would run into himself on the way back. Dr. Turner's answer to both these groups was simple, dignified, and complete: "In the Republic of Letters," said he, "of which I am a humble citizen, there are, I am glad to say, no factions, groups, or class distinctions. It is a true Democracy, perhaps the only one that now exists. And as long as I am privileged to belong to it, in however modest a capacity, I hope I shall be worthy of it, too, and broad enough to see all sides."

In appearance, Dr. Turner was scarcely prepossessing. He was so much below the middle height that at first sight it seemed that one of Singer's Midgets had enjoyed a run of extra growth. His little bread-crumb of a body (for in appearance he suggested nothing so much as a piece of well-done toast) was surmounted by a head of normal size which appeared too large for the meager figure that supported it. His face resembled somewhat that of the little man one so often sees in political cartoons, and which bears the caption "The Common People." It was such a face as one might see upon the streets a hundred times a day, and never think of later: it might have belonged to a bank clerk, a bookkeeper, an insurance agent, or someone going home to Plainfield on the 5:15.

George Webber was himself one of the good Doctor's more belated discoveries. When the author's first book, *Home to Our Mountains*, appeared, Dr. Turner had not been favorably impressed. The review in the *Fortnightly Cycle* had been a very gem of bland dismissal: "No doubt the thing is well enough," said Dr. Turner, "but after all, old Rabelais is really so much better"—a conclusion which the unhappy author was by no means minded to dispute.

Six years later, upon the eve of publication of Webber's second book, the good Doctor was still undecided just what he was going to do about it or him. Three weeks before the book was released for general sale, the Doctor met Webber's publisher and, after confessing that he had read an advance copy of the new work, he added grimly: "I haven't yet made up my mind about Webber. But," said he bodingly, "I'll make it up within a week or two." Between then and the time the book came out,

Dr. Turner apparently felt the telepathy of moderating influences —"You can always tell," as he was wont to say, "when Things are in the Air"—so that when his critique ultimately appeared, it was much more favorable than Webber or his publisher had dared to hope. Not that the Doctor was thoroughly persuaded, but he took a more conciliating tone. The book, he averred, "could hardly be called a novel"—he did not trouble to explain what could—it was really "a Spiritual Autobiography." Then, having arrived at this sounding definition, he discussed the volume freely in spiritual-autobiographical terms, and on the whole was pretty favorable about it, too, having neatly furnished forth a special little nest for Webber without in any way impinging on the jealous precincts of more splendid birds on more important boughs.

The way for a rapprochement was thus opened gracefully and when George Webber first met the Doctor some months later their greetings were of a friendly kind. Indeed the good Doctor was so very friendly that he insisted forthwith on taking Webber home with him, and would accept no refusal. So they went, and the manner of their going was very much like that of an ocean liner being warped from its berth and down the river and out to sea by a busy little tug.

"Darling," said Dr. Turner to his wife when at last they reached the house, "I want you to meet Mr. Webber. Oh, pshaw, now! I can't get used to all this Mister stuff. I'm going to call you George!" cried Dr. Turner with an air of bluff heartiness that was simply irresistible. "I know so many people that you know, and have heard them call you George for so many years, that no other name seems possible."

Webber murmured that he was enchanted to be thus addressed, meanwhile feeling a little helpless and confused under the hypnotic influence of Mrs. Turner, who, holding him by the hand, was looking steadily into his eyes with a slow, strange smile.

"You!" she said at length. *"You!"* she repeated slowly and deliberately, and then concluded simply, "You wrote the book."

Webber felt vague, not knowing just how to answer this, but managed to mumble that he had. The lady's reply was to continue to hold him by the hand and to regard him steadily with a fixed smile that seemed to harbor some dawning mirth to which no one else was a party.

"You!" she said presently again. "I don't know, but somehow you make me laugh. You amuse me. There is something about you that is like—is like—an Elf!"

"Yes," said Dr. Turner quickly, and, meeting Webber's bewildered eye, he went on with an air of hasty explanation in the manner of people steering away from well-known reefs: "My wife was *awfully* interested in that book of yours. *Awfully.* Of course, we *all* were," he went on rapidly. "Matter of fact, I wrote three full columns on it," he went on with just a tinge of nervous constraint, as if he hoped this fact would make everything all right. "I believe it was the longest review I have done since *An American Tragedy.* I was *awfully* interested in it. Did you see my review by any chance?" he asked, and then quickly, before Webber could answer: "I was really *awfully* interested. I called your book a kind of Spiritual Autobiography. I mean," he added quickly as Webber opened his mouth as if to speak, "it really made me think of *Wilhelm Meister.* Not—" the Doctor instantly cried, as Webber started to open his mouth again—"not that that was all of it. Of course there were passages in it that were *very* much like *War and Peace.* I remember saying to Mrs. Turner at the time, 'You know, there are times when he is very much like Tolstoi.'"

"And like—an Elf," said Mrs. Turner at this point, never for a moment relinquishing her grasp on Webber's hand, and continuing to smile steadily at him in a slow, strange way. "So like an Elf," she said, and laughed merrily.

"And, of course," said Dr. Turner rapidly, "there's the *Moby Dick* influence, too. I know I told my wife at the time that there were passages, magnificent passages," cried Dr. Turner, "that were much like Herman Melville."

"And like an Elf!" the wife said.

"But *more* like *Moby Dick*!" the Doctor said decidedly.

"And still *more*," thought Webber, whose mind was at last beginning to work slowly, "oh, much, *much* more like a whale!"

In this way, after so long and perilous a voyage, the storm-tossed mariner, George Webber, was brought to port by the good Dr. Turner. And if he was not berthed among the mighty liners, at least he now had anchorage in the slips where some of the smaller vessels in the Turnerian haven were.

The Lion at Morning

I T WAS MORNING, SHINING MORNING, BRIGHT MOTES OF MORNING
in the month of May, when James awoke. An old man in
a big room in a great house in the East Seventies near Central
Park. A little, wiry, bright-eyed man in the great master's chamber
of one of those lavish, fatly sumptuous, limestone-and-marble,
mansard-roof, bastard-French-chateau atrocities which rich men
were forever building for their wives some forty or fifty years
ago. But this was 1929, and shining morning in the month of
May, when James awoke.

He awoke as he did everything, very cleanly, abruptly, and
aggressively, with a kind of grim pugnacity. He would not *fool*
with slumber: once he was done with sleep, he was *done* with
it. He liked comfort and the best of everything, but he hated
softness, sloth, and feeble indecision. There was a proper time
and place for everything—a time for work; a time for sport,
travel, pleasure, and society; a time for a good dinner, brandy,
and a good cigar; and last of all, a time for sleep. James knew
when the time for everything should be.

For when a thing was finished it was finished. This applied
to sleep as well as to every other useful, pleasant thing in life.
He had discharged his debt to sleep and darkness for eight hours,
now he was done with it. He paid sleep off as he would sign a
check—cleanly, sharply, vigorously, with a final flourish of the
pen—

"Pay to the order of—*Sleep*—Eight - - - - - - and $\frac{no}{100}$ hrs.

—James Wyman, Sr."

There you are, sir! You are satisfied, I hope? Good! The matter's settled! But, come now! No silly business, if you please, of yawning sleepily, stretching out luxuriously, rolling over on your other side, and mumbling some damned nonsense about "just five minutes more," or some such stuff as that! And none of this business of pulling cobwebs from your brain, getting your eyes unglued, brushing the filaments of sleep away, trying to wake up, come out of it, remember where you are! No! Wake up at once! Come out of it cleanly! Be done with it the moment your eyes are open! Get up and go about your work—day's beginning, night is over, sleep-time's done!

James awoke like this. He was a small and wiry figure of a man, aged seventy-four, with a cold fighter's face. It was not a hard face, in no respect a brutal, savage, or distempered face— no, on the whole it was a rather pleasant face, certainly a very decisive face, and just as certainly a fighting face.

The face was very bright, and had a brisk, sharp, and rather frosty look. The eyes were very blue, frosty-looking, and as cold and straight as steel. The hair was white and close-cropped, likewise the mustache. The nose was long and cold and definite, the whole structure of the face slightly concave, the straight, grim mouth touched faintly at the edges with the eternal suggestion of a grin—a grin that was good-humored enough, but also straight, hard, cold, naturally truculent. It was the face of a man who hated fear and despised those who were afraid, which could respect another face that looked right back at it and told it to go to hell, and feel contempt for the face that trembled and the eye that shifted from its own cold steel; a face which could be savage, ruthless, merciless to what it hated and despised, and gravely generous, loyal, and devoted to what it liked; a face which could be intolerant, arrogant, insensitive, and occasionally unjust; but a face which could not be mean.

James lay still for a moment with his cold blue eyes wide

awake and staring at the ceiling. Then he looked at his watch. It lacked only a few minutes of eight o'clock, his invariable time for rising every morning in the city for the past fifty years. In the country, save for Sundays, he rose one hour and fifteen minutes earlier. He fumbled in the bosom of his nightshirt and scratched himself hairily and reflectively. He had worn a nightshirt all his life, as his father had before him, and as any sensible man would do. He had enough of the discomforts of clothing during the business day. When he went to bed he wasn't going to put on a damned monkey suit with bright green stripes all over it, rope himself in around the belly like a sack of meal, and incase his legs in trousers. No! The place to wear pants was on the street and in the office. When he went to bed he wanted all the free space he could get for his legs and belly.

He swung to a sitting posture, worked his toes into his bedroom slippers, got up, walked across the room, and stood looking out the window at the street. For a moment he felt giddy: the clear mind reeled a little, the knees felt weak, he shook his head impatiently, and breathed deep; pushed the heavy, corded curtains as far back as they would go, opened the window wider. His heart was pumping hard; the thin, grim smile around the firm mouth deepened. Seventy-four! Well, then—what? And for a moment, still holding to the heavy curtain with the veined old hand, he stood looking out into the street. Few people were about and stirring. Across the street, in a big limestone-and-marble mansion similar to his own, a housemaid on her knees was mopping marble steps. A rickety-looking wagon drawn by a shaggy little horse went rattling by. Six doors away a taxi drilled past in the early morning of Fifth Avenue; and, beyond, old James could see the trees and shrubs of Central Park just greening into May. Here in his own street, before the ugly, lavish houses, there were a few trees, all spangled with young green.

Bright, shining morning slanted on the house fronts of the street, and from the tender, living green of the young trees the bird song rose.

A fine morning, then, and, from Nature, May, and sunlight it borrowed a too pleasant coloring, James thought, for such a damned ugly street. It was a typical street of the rich in the East Seventies—a hodgepodge of pretentious architectures. The starkly bleak and solid ugliness of brownstone fronts was interrupted here and there by lavish bastard-French chateaux like his, and in the middle of the block by the pale salmon brick façade, the fashionable flat front, and the green canopy of a new apartment house.

He turned, still smiling grimly. Out in the hall the deep-toned grandfather clock was striking eight through morning's quietness, and on the last stroke the handle of the great walnut door was turned, his valet entered.

The man said, "Good morning, sir," in a quiet tone. James grunted "Morning" in reply, and without another word walked across the room into the bathroom, and after a moment flushed the toilet noisily, then washed his hands in the old streaked-marble basin, turned the tumbling water on full blast into the big old-fashioned ivory-yellow tub, and, while the tub filled, surveyed himself in the mirror, craning his neck, and rubbing his hand reflectively across the wiry gray stubble of his beard. He got his shaving things out of the cabinet and set them up in readiness, stropped his old straight razor vigorously, and with an air of satisfaction tested its deadly whetted blade, laid his razor down beside the other shaving things, turned off the water, stripped the nightshirt off over his head, stepped into the tub, and let himself down gingerly and with an easeful grunt into the water.

It took him four minutes to bathe and dry himself, and just

six more to lather his face, crane cautiously, and shave the tough gray stubble of his beard as smooth as a grained wood. By the time he had finished, cleaned his old, worn razor with tender pride, and put his shaving things away again, it was eight-ten.

As he re-entered his bedroom in his dressing gown, the servant had just finished laying out his clothes. From the old walnut dresser or bureau, the man had taken socks, fresh underwear, a clean shirt, cufflinks, and a collar; and from the huge old walnut wardrobe a suit of dark clothes, a black necktie, and a pair of shoes. James would have none of "this new-fangled furniture" in his room. By this he meant that he would have neither the modern style of recent years, nor the passionately revived Colonial. His bedroom was furnished with massive Victorian pieces that had come from his father's bedroom many years before. The high and hideous old dresser, or bureau, had a tall mirror with a carved, towering, cornice-like frame of wood, and a slab of gray-streaked marble, indented and sunk between some little boxlike drawers (God knows what these were for, but probably for collar buttons, shirt studs, cufflinks, collars, and what he called "thing-ma-jigs"); below were some ponderous walnut drawers with brass knobs, which held his shirts, socks, underwear and nightshirts. The huge walnut wardrobe was at least ten feet tall; and there was a monstrous walnut table with thick curved legs and a top of the same hideous gray-streaked marble that the bureau had.

James crossed the room to the chair beside the bed, threw off his dressing gown, and, grunting a little and holding on to the man with one hand for support, thrust first one wiry shank, and then the other, into a pair of long half-weight flannel drawers, buttoned a light flannel undershirt across his hairy chest, put on his white starched shirt and buttoned it, got the starched cuffs linked together, and looked around for his trousers, which the man was holding for him, when he changed his mind suddenly, and said:

"Wait a minute! Where's that gray suit—the one I got last year? I think I'll wear it to-day."

The valet's eyes were startled, his quiet voice touched just traceably with surprise:

"The *gray*, sir?"

"I said gray, didn't I?" said James grimly, and looked at him with a naked challenge of the cold blue eyes.

"Very well, sir," the man answered quietly; but for a moment their eyes met, and although the face of each was grave, and that of James a trifle grim and truculent, there was also a sharp enkindled twinkle in the eyes of each, a kind of "tickled" quality that would not speak, because there was no need to speak.

Gravely, imperturbably, the man went to the doors of the great walnut wardrobe, opened them, and took out a neat, double-breasted suit of light gray—a decidedly gay and skittish suit for James, whose apparel was habitually dark and sober. Still imperturbable, the man came back, laid out the coat, held out the trousers to his master, and gravely held the trouser ends as James grunted and thrust gingerly into them. The servant did not speak again until James had hitched his braces over his square shoulders and was buttoning up the neat buttons of the vest.

"And the necktie, sir?" the man inquired. "You will not be wearing the dark one now, I suppose."

"No," said James, hesitated for a moment, then looked the man pugnaciously in the eye and said: "Give me a light one— something that goes with this suit of clothes—something gay."

"Yes, sir," the man answered calmly; and again their eyes met, their faces grave and stern, but in their eyes again the sly, enkindled twinkle of their recognition.

It was not until James was carefully knotting under his wing collar a distinctly fashionable cravat of light spring gray, slashed smartly with black stripes, that the man found occasion to say smoothly:

"It's a fine morning, isn't it, sir?"

"It is! Yes, sir!" said James firmly and grimly, and looked at his servant truculently again; but again there was the enkindled sparkle in their eyes, and the man was smiling quietly behind his master's back as James marched sprucely from his chamber.

Outside the master's door the hall was dark and heavy, cushioned to the tread, still with silence, sleep, and morning, filled with walnut light and the slow tocking of the clock.

James glanced toward the door of his wife's chamber. The huge walnut door was also eloquent with silence, steep, inviolable repose. He smiled grimly and went down lavish marble stairs. They swept down with magnificence: the ghostly feet of memory and old event thronged on them—the rustle of silk and satin and the gleam of naked shoulders, proud tiaras, bustles, dog-collars of hard diamonds, ropes of pearls.

He smiled grimly to himself and with displeasure. *Damned old barn!* From the great reception hall at the bottom he looked in at the lush magnificence of the huge salon: at the red carpet, velvet to the tread; at the fat red-plush chairs with gold backs and gilded arms; at the straight, flimsy, ugly, brutally uncomfortable little chairs of gold, with faded coverings of silk; at the huge mirrors with gilt frames, also a little faded; at the French clock, a mass of fat gilt cupids, gew-gaws, thing-ma-jigs; at the damned ugly tables, cabinets, glass cases, all loaded down with more thing-ma-jigs, gew-gaws, china figures, vases, fat gilt cupids. *Junk!*

Well, this was what they wanted forty years ago—what they

thought they wanted, anyway—what the *women* wanted—what *she* wanted. He had let her have it! He had always hated it. He had said often and grimly that the only comfortable room in the whole damned place was his bathroom; the only easy chair, the stool. They had tried to change *that* a year ago: he wouldn't let them!

As for the rest of it, it was no home. It was a kind of frigid mausoleum for what people used to call "Society." It had been built for that purpose forty years ago, when people went in for that kind of thing, and when everyone was trying to outdo his neighbor in ugliness, vulgarity, lavish pretentiousness—in strident costliness, blind waste, and arrogant expense.

As such, no doubt, it had served its purpose well! It had cost him a quarter of a million dollars, but he doubted if he'd get a hundred thousand if he put it on the block tomorrow. You couldn't even keep the damned barn warm! And now? And for the future? Well, *she* would outlive him. The Parrotts always lived longer than the Wymans. What would happen? He didn't have to die and go to heaven to find out the answer to that one! She'd try to swing it for a while, then she'd find out! It'd be *her* money then—she'd run the show, and she'd find out! She'd give a reception or two, attempt a party in the old grand manner, try to revive dog-collardom—and find out dog-collardom was dead forever!

She'd get a few old hags, their skinny necks and bony arms encrusted with their jewelry; a few doddering old fools, creaking at the joints and lisping through their artificial teeth—all trying to revive the ghostly pomps of Mrs. Astor! She'd get a few furiously bored young people, there at grandma's imperative command, wondering when in God's name the ghastly business would be over, when they could decently escape from the Morgue and flee to glittering spots of music, dancing, noise, and alcohol —and she'd find out!

Grimly, he fancied he could already hear her anguished screech when bills came in and she discovered what it cost, discovered further that it was *her* money she was spending now, and that money didn't grow on trees—or if it did, it was her *own* tree now, the *Parrott* tree.

That made a difference, didn't it? For the Parrotts, he reflected grimly, were known for their tender solicitude where their *own* tree was concerned—whether it was a family tree or a money tree. Her father—damned old fool!—had spent the last twenty years of his life writing a single book. And what a book! *The Beginnings of the New England Tradition: A History of the Parrott Family.* Great God, had anyone ever heard of such conceited bilge as that since time began! And he—James Wyman, Sr.—had had to persuade one of his publishing acquaintances to print the damned thing; and then he had had to endure the gibes, the digs, the witticisms of all his friends at the club—or else listen to the Parrott screech. Of the two evils he had taken, he thought, the lesser one. Swift ridicule, he had concluded, was better than slow torture; a silly book is soon forgotten, but a woman's tongue cannot be stilled.

Well, *she'd* find out, he thought, and grimly paused upon the marble flags of the reception hall, and grimly stared into the faded splendors of the great salon. He thought he foresaw the anguished progress of events already: The screech of pained astonishment when she saw the bills—the bills for coal alone— those ten-ton truck loads, car loads, barge loads, train loads of black coal required just to keep the grave-damp chill of this damned tomb reduced to a degree of semi-frigidness from October until May. And the caretakers, the nightwatchmen, the housekeepers, and so on, required to keep it guarded, watched and mended, dusted off—from May until October—when the family was away! As if anyone was going to walk off with the damned thing! Oh, if someone only would!—if a parliament of public-spirited second-story men, yeggmen, dynamiters, roof-and-cellar men, elegant silk-hatted Raffleses, and plain common-garden burglars in secret session assembled would only, in their large benevolence of soul, agree to enter, search, seize, and take away everything they could lay their hands on while the family was out of town: if they would only turn up before the barn at night in five-ton trucks, armored motor cars, swift sedans: if they would only come with any vehicle they had—wheelbarrows, furniture vans, or covered wagons—and walk out with every bit of junk in sight—all of the damned plush chairs, and gilt French clocks; all of the vases, statuettes, and figurines; all of the painted china, crimson carpets, agonizing chairs and hideous tables; all of the gew-gaws and thing-ma-jigs, the imposing sets of unread books and the bad portraits of the ancestors, including the atrocious one of Parrott, Sr., author of *The Beginnings of the New England Tradition*—the old fool!—and while they were about it, also overpower, gag, chloroform, and spirit away into oblivion all of the caretakers, housekeepers, nightwatchmen, and——

"Breakfast is served, sir!"

At the soft, the whispered, the oh-most-elegant, refined, and sugared tones, James started. As if shocked with an electric current, he turned and stared grimly into the unctuous, oily visage of his butler, Mr. Warren.

—and yes! above all, and by all means, if some kind-hearted gang of kidnappers would only remove out of his hearing, sight, and memory forever the pompous person and the odious presence of Old Sugarlips——

"Coming," James said curtly.

"Very good, sir," Sugarlips replied with maddening unctuous-

ness. Then the butler turned solemnly and departed down the
hall—departed with the pompous waddle of his big, fat buttocks,
his bulging and obscenely sensual calves; departed like the disgusting fat old woman that he was, with his oily face and his fat
lips set in an expression of simpering propriety——

—Oh, if only Sugarlips would depart for good! If only noble-
hearted kidnappers would do their merciful work! If only he—
James Wyman, Sr.—could somehow free himself from Sugarlips, somehow detach this fat Old Woman of the Sea from his
life, so that he could enjoy a moment's peace and privacy in
his own house without being told that something was "Very
good, sir," enjoy a moment's rest and relaxation without Sugarlips "Begging your pardon, Sir," sit down at his own table to
feed himself in his own way without feeling Sugarlips' damned
moist breath upon his neck, eat as he chose and what he chose
and help himself the way he chose without having every movement censured by the interrogation of that fishy eye, the infuriating assurance of "Allow me, sir."

If only he—James Wyman, Sr.—free, white, and—seventy-
four!—a free American citizen, by God!—could come and go
the way he chose to come and go, sit where he wanted, eat as
he wished to eat, do as he pleased and as a free man had a right
to do—without having all the acts, engagements, and arrange-
ments of his personal and most private life subjected to the
constant supervision of a fool! He was tired; he was ill, he knew;
he was getting sour and crotchety—yes, he knew all this—but,
Great God! Great God!—he was an old man and he wanted to
be left alone! He'd seen and known it all, now—he'd tried all
the arguments, found all the answers, done all the things he
should have done—that the world of his time, his wife, his family,
and Society, had expected of him—even *this*—and Great God!
why had he done them? Was it worth it? He stared in again

among the faded splendors of the great salon, and for a moment his cold blue eyes were clouded by the shade of baffled doubt. He had wanted a home to live in, hadn't he?—a place of warmth, of light, a dwelling place of love and deep security—he had had all the means of getting it, hadn't he?—wealth, courage, character, and intelligence—and he had come to this? Somewhere, somehow, he had missed out in life, something had been put over on him. But where? And how? How and where had he failed?

He had been one of the conspicuous men of his time and generation—conspicuous not alone for his material achievements, but conspicuous for character, honesty, integrity, and fair-dealing in the world of money-getting, pirate-hearted, and red-handed Yankeedom. Of all the men of that time and generation, he was among the first. There were great names in America today— names great for wealth, for power, for ruthlessness, for their stupendous aggrandizements. And he knew the way most of those names were tainted with dishonor, those names of men who had so ruthlessly exploited life, destroyed their fellows, betrayed mankind and their own country. Those names, he knew, would be a stench in the nostrils of future generations, a shame and a disgrace to the unfortunate children and grandchildren who would have to acknowledge them; and from this shameful taint he knew that his own name was triumphantly secure. And yet something had gone wrong! Where? How?

He was no whiner; he was a brave man and a fighter; and he knew that wherever lay the fault, the fault, dear Brutus, lay not in his stars, but in himself! But—(James stared grimly in among the faded splendors of the great salon)—his life had come to *this*! And why? Why? Why?

Had all gone ill then? By no means! There had been high effort, great accomplishment. There had been true friendship;

rooted, deep affection; the confident regard of Kings and Presi-
dents, statesmen, men of letters, great industrialists, other leading
bankers and financiers like himself.

He had yielded to no man to his own dishonor; he had yielded
to many with fair-dealing, generous concession, unresentful pardon. He had fought hardest when the odds were all against him,
but had eased pressure when he was on top; he had not with-
held the stroke in battle, but he had not exulted over a fallen foe.

No, the slate was clean, the mirror was unclouded—yet, he
had come to *this*. An old man, living with an old wife, in an
old dead graveyard of a house—alone.

Old James looked in upon the faded gilt of morning with a
baffled eye. Where had it gone to, then—all of the passion and
the fire of youth, and the proud singing; all of the faith, the
hope, the clean belief of fifty years ago? Where had it gone to,
then—the strength, the faith, the wisdom, the sound health and
substance of his lost America? Had it been only a dream, then?
No, it was no dream—"for he lay broad awaking"—or, if dream,
then such a dream as men have lived a million years to dream—
to hope for—to achieve. But where now?

Gone—all gone—gone like phantasmal images of smoke, the
shining bright reality of that deathless dream submerged in ruin.
In the great world all around him now he saw black chaos exploding into unpurposeful and blatant power; confusion swarming through the earth, the howling jargons of a million tongues,
each one dissimilar, none speaking to another; brute corruption
crowned with glory, privilege enthroned. Where once there had
been the patient hard confusion of honest doubt, the worried
perturbation of strong faith, was now the vile smirk of a passive
acceptance, the cheap sneer of the weakling lip, the feeble gibe
of the ignoble vanquished, gibing their own treason and their
lack of faith, the fattied heart no longer sound enough for battle,

the clouded and beclamored mind no longer clear enough for truth, the bleared eye murked with rotten mockeries. The thin venom of the tongues just sneered and said—"Well, what are you going to do about it?"—and so were lost, all joined together in the corrupt defenses of their shame and cowardice—all kneeling basely at the feet of their own traitors, all bent in obscene reverence before their own monsters, all yielding, all submissive to the gods of money-getting and of mockery, all bent forward to kiss the dyer's bloody hand subdued to its own dye. So was his lost America rotted out. Gone, now, the faith, the youth, the morning, and the passion: the gold, the singing, and the dream —all vanished like phantasmal smoke, and come to *this!*

And *from* this, too! For had he not sold out somewhere along the line? But where? Where? Where? The *hour*, the *moment*, and the actual point of *crisis*—where?

Had not he who was James Wyman fifty years ago—young and brave and an American who had the faith, and felt the strength and heard the singing, who had seen the plains, the rivers, and the mountains, the quiet blueness in a farmhand's eyes, and had heard the voices in the darkness talking, known how the land went, and the shapes of things, and known, too, that the dream was something more than dream, the great hope something more than hope—had not he, James Wyman, who had seen and heard and felt and known all these things, as all men in this land have known them—had he not sold out somewhere down the line?—taken what the others had to give?— believed what others had to say?—accepted what they had to offer? And what was that? Dog-collardom, vulgarity, and empty show, the hypocrisies and shrill pretenses of a clownlike aristocracy, the swinish gluttonies of last year's hog all varnished over with his this-year's coat-of-arms, the no-questions-asked philosophy of money-sewerdom, proud noses lifted with refined disdain at uncouth table manners, but not too nice or dainty to appraise with charity the full, rich droppings of a scoundrel's bank account.

Yes, he had so accepted, he had been so persuaded, he had so believed; or, so believing that he so believed, had so sold out somewhere, being young along the line—and so had come to *this*: an old man, living with an old wife, in an old graveyard of a house—alone.

And, looking grimly in upon the faded gilt of morning in the great salon, James reflected that not even morning entered here. No, nothing young and sweet and fresh and alive and shining could exist here. Even light, the crystal shining light of spring, of morning, and of May, was staled and deadened here. It forced its way in dustily, it thrust in through the reluctant folds of the plush curtains, it came in in mote-filled beams of dusty light, it was old and dead before it got here— like the plush, the gilt, the carpets, the chairs and tables, the gew-gaws, bric-a-brac, and thing-ma-jigs—as musty, stale, and full of death as all the things it fell upon.

No, it was not like Morning, really, by the time it had forced its painful entrance in that room. Rather, James reflected grimly, it was like the Morning After—it was—it was—well, it was like After the Ball Is Over.

The whole house, he thought, was like After the Ball Is Over. It had always been like that. "After the Ball," he thought, would be an excellent name for the damned thing: that had always been the effect it had produced on him. It had never been a home, never a place to come back to at night, and find rest and peace and warmth and homeliness and comfort. No, it had always been the cold mausoleum of departed guests; a great, frigid, splendid, and completely lifeless temple to the memory of the glittering and fashionable parties which should have been given here last night, but which probably had not occurred. Thus, the great house was haunted constantly by the haughty ghosts of stuffed-shirtdom and dog-collardom; but by the presences of living warmth, familiar usage, genial homeliness—never! The great marble steps with their magnificent sweep, the marble entrance hall, the great salon, always seemed to be congealing mournfully, fading again into a melancholy staleness, mustiness, and frigid loneliness after the rustling silks and satins, the blazing chandeliers, the refined and cultivated voices, the silvery laughter and the champagne bubbles, the dog-collars, ropes of pearls, bare backs, stiff shirts, and glowing shoulders of last night's splendid gathering had departed.

All that was needed to complete the illusion was a corps of caterer's men—twenty or thirty swarthy little fellows in monkey suits marching in to clear up the litter of the party—the empty champagne glasses, salad dishes, the cigar butts; the ashes on the carpet, and the filaments of colored paper hanging from the chandeliers—tattered remnants of the ball.

James sighed a little, then turned brusquely and marched down the hall into the great dining room.

The dining room, too, was splendid and magnificent—cold, cold, cold—like eating in a tomb. The room was on the west side of the house: the morning sun had not yet entered here. The great table was a somber polished slab, the large buffet, resplendent as a coffin, set with massive plate. At one end of the enormous table, a great high-backed chair, of carved and somber darkness, a big plate, a great heavy knife and fork and spoon, the slender elegance of a silver coffee pot, a fragile purity of cups and saucers, another plate domed richly with an enormous silver warming-cover, a glass of orange juice, and stiff, heavy, spotless napery.

James seated himself down there, a lonely little figure at the end of the enormous table—and surveyed the feast. First he looked at the glass of orange juice, raised it to his lips, shuddered, and set it down. Then, gingerly, he lifted the great silver warming-lid and peered beneath the cover: three thin brown slices of dry toast lay chastely on a big white plate. James let the silver cover fall with a large clatter. Sugarlips appeared. James poured black fluid from the coffee pot into his cup and tasted it: a slight convulsion twisted his firm mouth, he said:

"What is this stuff?"

"Coffee, sir," said Sugarlips.

"Coffee?" said James coldly.

"A new coffee, sir," breathed Sugarlips, "that has no caffein in it."

James made no answer, but his cold blue eyes were bright and hard, and, nodding toward the covered dish, he spoke coldly, tonelessly, as before:

"And this?"

"Your toast, sir," breathed Sugarlips moistly.

"*My* toast?" James inquired, in the same cold and unpersuaded tone.

"Yes, sir," breathed Sugarlips. "*Your* toast—dry toast, sir."

"Oh, no," said James grimly, "you're wrong there. It's not *my* toast—dry toast has never been *my* toast! . . . What's this?" he said with brutal suddenness, jerking his head toward the glass of orange juice.

"Your fruit juice, sir," breathed Sugarlips.

"Oh, no," said James, more cold and grim than ever. "It's not *my* fruit juice. You're wrong again! You never saw me drink it yet." For a moment he surveyed the butler with blue blazing eyes. Cold fury choked him. "Look here," he rasped suddenly, "what the hell's the meaning of all this? Where's my breakfast? You told me it was ready!"

"Begging your pardon, sir—" Sugarlips began, dilating his full lips moistly.

"Begging my pardon, hell!" cried James, and threw his napkin to the floor. "I don't want my pardon begged—I want my breakfast! Where is it?"

"Yes, sir," Sugarlips began, and moistened his full lips nervously—"but the doctor, sir—the diet he prescribed, sir! . . . It was the mistress's orders that you get it, sir."

"Whose breakfast is this, anyway?" said James, "Mine or your mistress's?"

"Why, *yours,* sir," Sugarlips hastily agreed.

"Who's *eating* it?" James went on brusquely. "Your mistress or me?"

"Why, you are, sir," said Sugarlips. "Of course, sir!"

"Then bring it to me!" shouted James. "At once! When I need anyone's help to tell me what I have to eat, I'll let you know!"

"Yes sir, yes sir," Sugarlips breathed, all of a twitter now. "Then you desire——"

"You know what I desire," James yelled. "I desire my breakfast! At once! Now! Right away! . . . The same breakfast that I always have! The breakfast that I've had for forty years! The breakfast that my father had before me! The breakfast that a working man has *got* to have—as it was in the beginning, is now, and ever shall be! Amen!" James shouted. "Namely, a dish of oatmeal, four slices of buttered toast, a plate of ham and eggs, and a pot of coffee—strong black coffee—*real* coffee!" James shouted. "Do you understand?"

"Y-y-yes, sir," stammered Sugarlips. "P-p-perfectly, sir."

"Then go and get it! . . . Have you got any real coffee in the house?" he demanded sharply.

"Of course, sir."

"Then bring it!" James cried, and struck the table. "At once!

Now! . . . And hurry up with it! I'll be late to the bank as it is!" He picked up the folded pages of *The Times* beside his plate and opened it with a vicious rattle— "And take this slop away!" he barked, as an afterthought, indicating the rejected breakfast with a curt nod. "Do what you like with it—throw it down the sink—but take it away!" And he went back savagely to the crisp pages of *The Times* again.

The coffee came in, Sugarlips poured it, and James was just on the point of drinking it when something happened. He bent forward sharply, ready with the cup of real right coffee almost to his lips, grunted suddenly with surprise, put the cup down sharply, and leaned forward with the paper tightly gripped in his two hands, reading intently. What he read—what caught and held his startled interest—ran as follows:

ACTRESS SUES SUNDAY SCHOOL SUPERINTENDENT, CLAIMING HEART BALM

Notice of suit was filed yesterday before Mr. Justice Mc-Gonigle in an action for breach of promise brought by Mrs. Margaret Hall Davis, 37, against W. Wainwright Parsons, 58. Mr. Parsons is well known as the author of many books on religious subjects, and for the past fifteen years he has been Superintendent of the Church School at the fashionable Episcopal Church of St. Balthazar, whose vestrymen include such leading citizens of New York as Mr. James Wyman, Sr., the banker, and . . . .

Old James swore softly to himself at this linking of his own name with such a scandal. He skimmed swiftly through the list of his fellow vestrymen and read on avidly:

Mr. Parsons could not be found last night at the University Club, where he lives. Officials at the club said he had occupied his rooms there until three days ago, when he departed, leaving no address. Members of the club, when questioned, expressed surprise when informed of Mrs. Davis's suit. Mr. Parsons, they said, was a bachelor of quiet habits, and no one had ever heard of his alleged connection with the actress.

Mrs. Davis, interviewed at her Riverside Drive apartment, answered questions willingly. She is a comely blonde of mature charms, and was formerly, she said, a member of the Ziegfeld Follies, and later a performer on the musical comedy stage. She said that she met the elderly Mr. Parsons two years ago, during a week-end at Atlantic City. Their friendship, she asserted, developed rapidly. Mr. Parsons proposed marriage to her, she claims, a year ago, but requested a postponement until New Year's Day, pleading business and financial difficulties and the illness of a member of his family as reasons for the delay. To this the pretty divorcee agreed, she says, and as a result of his ardent persuasions consented to a temporary alliance prior to their marriage. Since the first of last October, she asserted, they have occupied the Riverside Drive apartment jointly, and were known to the landlord and the other tenants of the building as "Mr. and Mrs. Parsons."

As the time for their marriage approached, the woman alleges, Mr. Parsons pleaded further complications in his personal affairs, and asked for another postponement until Easter. To this she also agreed, still confident of the sincerity of his intentions. Early in March, however, he left the apartment, telling her he had been called to Boston on business, but would return in a few days. Since that time, she says, she has not seen him, and all efforts to communicate with him have been fruitless. The woman further asserts that, in reply to repeated letters from her, Mr. Parsons finally wrote her three weeks ago, stating it would now be impossible for him to fulfill his promise of marriage and suggesting that "for the good of all concerned, we call the whole thing off."

This, Mrs. Davis asserted, she is unwilling to do.

"I loved Willy," she declared, with tears in her eyes. "God is my witness that I loved him with the deepest, purest love a woman ever had to give a man. And Willy loved me, loves

me still. I know he does. I am *sure* of it! If you could only
see the letters that he wrote me—I have dozens of them
here"—she indicated a thick packet of letters on the table,
tied with a pink ribbon—"the most passionate and romantic
letters any lover ever wrote," she declared. "Willy was a wonderful lover—so gentle, so tender, so poetic—and always such
a perfect gentleman! I can not give him up!" she passionately declared. "I *will* not! I love him still in spite of everything that has happened. I am willing to forgive all, forget
all—if only he will come back to me."

The actress is suing for damages of one hundred thousand
dollars. The firm of Hoggenheimer, Blaustein, Glutz, and Levy,
of 111 Broadway, are her legal representatives.

Mr. Parsons is well known for his books in the religious
field. According to *Who's Who*, he was born in Lima, Ohio,
April 19, 1871, the son of the Reverend Samuel Abner Parsons,
and the late Martha Elizabeth Bushmiller Parsons. Educated
at De Pauw University, and later at the Union Theological
Seminary, he was himself ordained to the ministry in 1897,
and during the next ten years filled successive pulpits in
Fort Wayne, Indiana, Pottstown, Pennsylvania, and Elizabeth,
New Jersey. In 1907, he retired from the ministry to devote
his entire time to literary activity. Always a prolific writer,
and gifted with a facile pen, his success in this field was rapid.
He is the author of more than a score of books on devotional
subjects, several of which have run through repeated editions,
and one of which, a travel book, *Afoot In The Holy Land,*
enjoyed a tremendous sale not only in this country but abroad.
Some of his other works, according to *Who's Who*, are as
follows:

Following After the Master (1907); *Almost Thou Persuadest Me* (1908); *Job's Comforters* (1909); *Who Follows in
His Train* (1910); *For They Shall See God* (1912); *Jordan
and the Marne* (1915); *Armageddon and Verdun* (1917);
Christianity and the Fuller Life (1921); *The Way of Temptation* (1927); *The Song of Solomon* (1927); *Behold, He Cometh*
(1928).

James saw the item just as he had been bending forward to sip his coffee. The name of W. Wainwright Parsons leaped out at him and hit him in the eye. Down went the coffee cup with a bang. James read on. It was not reading so much as a kind of lightninglike absorption. He tore through the column, ripping splintered fragments from the thing—all he needed!—until he had it clear and blazing in his mind. Then for a moment, after he had finished, he sat completely motionless, with a look of utter stupefaction on his face. Finally he raised the outspread paper in both hands, banged it down emphatically on the table, leaned back in his great chair, stared straight and far and viewlessly across the enormous polished vista of the table, and said slowly and with emphasis:

"I'll—be—God—damned!"

Just then Sugarlips came in with the oatmeal, smoking hot, and slid it unctuously before him. James slashed thick cream all over it, spread sugar with a copious spoon, and dug in savagely. At the third mouthful he paused again, picked up the paper in one old hand and stared at it, flung it down with an impatient growl, took another mouthful of hot oatmeal, couldn't keep away from the accursed paper—took it finally and propped it up against the coffee pot with the accusing article staring blank and square in his cold eye, and then re-read it slowly, carefully, precisely, word for word and comma for comma, and between mouthfuls of hot oatmeal let out a running commentary of low-muttered growls:

" 'I loved Willy——' "

"Why, the damned——!"

" 'Willy was a wonderful lover—so gentle, so tender, so poetic——' "

"Why—that damned mealy-mouthed, butter-lipped, two-faced——!"

"Mr. Parsons is well known as the author of many books on religious subjects ——"

James dug savagely into the oatmeal and swallowed. *"Religious subjects! Bah!"*

"Superintendent . . . Church School . . . fashionable Episcopal Church of St. Balthazar . . . whose vestrymen include . . . Mr. James Wyman, Sr. ——"

James groaned, picked up the offending paper, folded it, and banged it down with the story out of sight. The ham and eggs had come and he ate savagely, in a preoccupied silence, broken by an occasional angry growl. When he got up to go, he had composed himself, but his bright blue eyes were as hard and cold as glacial ice and the suggestion of a faint grim grin about the edges of his mouth was sharper, finer, more deadly than it had ever been before.

He looked at the paper, growled impatiently, started for the door, paused, turned round, looked back, came back growling, picked up the paper, thrust it angrily into his pocket, and marched down the enormous hall. He paused at the entrance, took a derby hat and placed it firmly, a trifle jauntily, and at an angle on his well-shaped head, stepped down and opened the enormous front door, went out and down the street at a brisk pace, turned left, and so into Fifth Avenue.

To one side, the Park and young greening trees; in the roadway, the traffic beginning to thicken and drill past; everywhere, people thronging and hurrying; directly ahead, the frontal blaze and cliff of the terrific city, and morning, shining morning, on the tall towers—while an old man with cold-blazing eyes went sprucely swinging through the canyoned slant, muttering to himself:

—Following After the Master—*Bah!*

—Almost Thou Persuadest Me—*Bah!*

—The Way of Temptation ——

Suddenly he whipped the folded newspaper out of his pocket, turned it over, and peered intently at the story again, comparing dates. The faint grim grin around the edges of his mouth relaxed a little.

—The Song of Solomon ——

The grin spread over his face, suffusing it with color, and his old eyes twinkled as, still peering intently, he re-read the last iine of the story.

—Behold, He Cometh ——

With a jaunty motion he slapped the folded paper against his thigh, and, chuckling to himself with a full return of his good humor, he muttered:

"By God! I didn't know he had it in him!"

God's Lonely Man

MY LIFE, MORE THAN THAT OF ANYONE I KNOW, HAS BEEN SPENT in solitude and wandering. Why this is true, or how it happened, I cannot say; yet it is so. From my fifteenth year— save for a single interval—I have lived about as solitary a life as a modern man can have. I mean by this that the number of hours, days, months, and years that I have spent alone has been immense and extraordinary. I propose, therefore, to describe the experience of human loneliness exactly as I have known it.

The reason that impels me to do this is not that I think my knowledge of loneliness different in kind from that of other men. Quite the contrary. The whole conviction of my life now rests upon the belief that loneliness, far from being a rare and curious phenomenon, peculiar to myself and to a few other solitary men, is the central and inevitable fact of human existence. When we examine the moments, acts, and statements of all kinds of people—not only the grief and ecstasy of the greatest poets, but also the huge unhappiness of the average soul, as evidenced by the innumerable strident words of abuse, hatred, contempt, mistrust, and scorn that forever grate upon our ears as the manswarm passes us in the streets—we find, I think, that they are all suffering from the same thing. The final cause of their complaint is loneliness.

But if my experience of loneliness has not been different in kind from that of other men, I suspect it has been sharper in intensity. This gives me the best authority in the world to write of this, our general complaint, for I believe I know more about it than anyone of my generation. In saying this, I am merely stating a fact as I see it, though I realize that it may sound like arrogance or vanity. But before anyone jumps to that conclusion, let him consider how strange it would be to meet with arrogance in one who has lived alone as much as I. The surest cure for vanity is loneliness. For, more than other men, we who dwell in the heart of solitude are always the victims of self-doubt. For-ever and forever in our loneliness, shameful feelings of inferiority will rise up suddenly to overwhelm us in a poisonous flood of horror, disbelief, and desolation, to sicken and corrupt our health and confidence, to spread pollution at the very root of strong, exultant joy. And the eternal paradox of it is that if a man is to know the triumphant labor of creation, he must for long periods resign himself to loneliness, and suffer loneliness to rob him of the health, the confidence, the belief and joy which are essential to creative work.

To live alone as I have lived, a man should have the confidence of God, the tranquil faith of a monastic saint, the stern im-pregnability of Gibraltar. Lacking these, there are times when anything, everything, all or nothing, the most trivial incidents, the most casual words, can in an instant strip me of my armor, palsy my hand, constrict my heart with frozen horror, and fill my bowels with the gray substance of shuddering impotence. Sometimes it is nothing but a shadow passing on the sun; some-times nothing but the torrid milky light of August, or the naked, sprawling ugliness and squalid decencies of streets in Brooklyn fading in the weary vistas of that milky light and evoking the intolerable misery of countless drab and nameless lives. Sometimes it is just the barren horror of raw concrete, or the heat blazing on a million beetles of machinery darting through the torrid streets, or the cindered weariness of parking spaces, or the slamming smash and racket of the El, or the driven manswarm of the earth, thrusting on forever in exacerbated fury, going nowhere in a hurry.

Again, it may be just a phrase, a look, a gesture. It may be the cold, disdainful inclination of the head with which a precious, kept, exquisite princeling of Park Avenue acknowledges an introduction, as if to say: "You are nothing." Or it may be a sneering reference and dismissal by a critic in a high-class weekly magazine. Or a letter from a woman saying I am lost and ruined, my talent vanished, all my efforts false and worthless—since I have forsaken the truth, vision, and reality which are so beautifully her own.

And sometimes it is less than these—nothing I can touch or see or hear or definitely remember. It may be so vague as to be a kind of hideous weather of the soul, subtly compounded of all the hunger, fury, and impossible desire my life has ever known. Or, again, it may be a half-forgotten memory of the cold wintry red of waning Sunday afternoons in Cambridge, and of a pallid, sensitive, æsthetic face that held me once in earnest discourse on such a Sunday afternoon in Cambridge, telling me that all my youthful hopes were pitiful delusions and that all my life would come to naught, and the red and waning light of March was reflected on the pallid face with a desolate impotence that instantly quenched all the young ardors of my blood.

Beneath the evocations of these lights and weathers, and the cold, disdainful words of precious, sneering, and contemptuous people, all of the joy and singing of the day goes out like an extinguished candle, hope seems lost to me forever, and every truth that I have ever found and known seems false. At such a time the lonely man will feel that all the evidence of his own senses has betrayed him, and that nothing really lives and moves on earth but creatures of the death-in-life—those of the cold, constricted heart and the sterile loins, who exist forever in the red waning light of March and Sunday afternoon.

All this hideous doubt, despair, and dark confusion of the soul a lonely man must know, for he is united to no image save that which he creates himself, he is bolstered by no other knowledge save that which he can gather for himself with the vision of his own eyes and brain. He is sustained and cheered and aided by no party, he is given comfort by no creed, he has no faith in him except his own. And often that faith deserts him, leaving him shaken and filled with impotence. And then it seems to him that his life has come to nothing, that he is ruined, lost, and broken past redemption, and that morning—bright, shining morning, with its promise of new beginnings—will never come upon the earth again as it did once.

He knows that dark time is flowing by him like a river. The huge, dark wall of loneliness is around him now. It encloses and presses in upon him, and he cannot escape. And the cancerous plant of memory is feeding at his entrails, recalling hundreds of forgotten faces and ten thousand vanished days, until all life seems as strange and insubstantial as a dream. Time flows by him like a river, and he waits in his little room like a creature held captive by an evil spell. And he will hear, far off, the murmurous drone of the great earth, and feel that he has been forgotten, that his powers are wasting from him while the river flows, and that all his life has come to nothing. He feels that his strength is gone, his power withered, while he sits there drugged and fettered in the prison of his loneliness.

Then suddenly, one day, for no apparent reason, his faith and his belief in life will come back to him in a tidal flood. It will rise up in him with a jubilant and invincible power, bursting a window in the world's great wall and restoring everything to shapes of deathless brightness. Made miraculously whole and secure in himself, he will plunge once more into the triumphant labor of creation. All his old strength is his again: he knows what he knows, he is what he is, he has found what he has found. And he will say the truth that is in him, speak it even though the whole world deny it, affirm it though a million men cry out that it is false.

At such a moment of triumphant confidence, with this feeling in me, I dare now assert that I have known Loneliness as well as any man, and will now write of him as if he were my very brother, which he is. I will paint him for you with such fidelity to his true figure that no man who reads will ever doubt his visage when Loneliness comes to him hereafter.

The most tragic, sublime, and beautiful expression of human loneliness which I have ever read is the Book of Job; the grandest and most philosophical, Ecclesiastes. Here I must point out a fact which is so much at variance with everything I was told as a child concerning loneliness and the tragic underweft of life that, when I first discovered it, I was astounded and incredulous, doubting the overwhelming weight of evidence that had revealed it to me. But there it was, as solid as a rock, not to be shaken or denied; and as the years passed, the truth of this discovery became part of the structure of my life.

The fact is this: the lonely man, who is also the tragic man, is invariably the man who loves life dearly—which is to say, the joyful man. In these statements there is no paradox whatever. The one condition implies the other, and makes it necessary. The essence of human tragedy is in loneliness, not in conflict, no matter what the arguments of the theater may assert. And just as the great tragic writer (I say, "the tragic writer" as distinguished from "the writer of tragedies," for certain nations, the Roman and French among them, have had no great tragic writers, for Vergil and Racine were none, but rather great writers of tragedy): just as the great tragic writer—Job, Sophocles, Dante, Milton, Swift, Dostoevski—has always been the lonely man, so has he also been the man who loved life best and had the deepest sense of joy. The real quality and substance of human joy is to be found in the works of these great tragic writers as nowhere else in all the records of man's life upon the earth. In proof of this, I can give here one conclusive illustration:

In my childhood, any mention of the Book of Job evoked instantly in my mind a long train of gloomy, gray, and unbrokenly dismal associations. This has been true, I suspect, with most of us. Such phrases as "Job's comforter," and "the patience of Job," and "the afflictions of Job," have become part of our common idiom and are used to refer to people whose woes seem uncountable and unceasing, who have suffered long and silently, and whose gloom has never been interrupted by a ray of hope or joy. All these associations had united to make for me a picture of the Book of Job that was grim, bleak, and constant in its misery. When I first read it as a child, it seemed to me that the record of Job's tribulations was relieved only by a kind of gloomy and unwilling humor—a humor not intended by the author, but supplied by my own exasperation, for my childish sense of proportion and justice was at length so put upon by this dreary tidal flood of calamities that I had to laugh in protest.

But any reader of intelligence and experience who has reaa that great book in his mature years will realize how false such a picture is. For the Book of Job, far from being dreary, gray, and dismal, is woven entire, more than any single piece of writing I can recall, from the sensuous, flashing, infinitely various, and gloriously palpable material of great poetry; and it wears at the heart of its tremendous chant of everlasting sorrow the exulting song of everlasting joy.

In this there is nothing strange or curious, but only what is inevitable and right. For the tragic writer knows that joy is rooted at the heart of sorrow, that ecstasy is shot through with the sudden crimson thread of pain, that the knife-thrust of intolerable desire and the wild, brief glory of possession are pierced most bitterly, at the very instant of man's greatest victory, by the premonitory sense of loss and death. So seen and so felt, the best and worst that the human heart can know are merely different aspects of the same thing, and are interwoven, both together, into the tragic web of life.

It is the sense of death and loneliness, the knowledge of the brevity of his days, and the huge impending burden of his sorrow, growing always, never lessening, that makes joy glorious, tragic, and unutterably precious to a man like Job. Beauty comes and passes, is lost the moment that we touch it, can no more be stayed or held than one can stay the flowing of a river. Out of this pain of loss, this bitter ecstasy of brief having, this fatal glory of the single moment, the tragic writer will therefore make a song for joy. That, at least, he may keep and treasure always. And his song is full of grief, because he knows that joy is fleeting, gone the instant that we have it, and that is why it is so precious, gaining its full glory from the very things that limit and destroy it.

He knows that joy gains its glory out of sorrow, bitter sorrow, and man's loneliness, and that it is haunted always with the certainty of death, dark death, which stops our tongues, our eyes, our living breath, with the twin oblivions of dust and nothingness. Therefore a man like Job will make a chant for sorrow, too, but it will still be a song for joy as well, and one more strange and beautiful than any other that man has ever sung:

> Hast thou given the horse strength? hast thou clothed his neck with thunder?
> Canst thou make him afraid as a grasshopper? the glory of his nostrils is terrible.
> He paweth in the valley, and rejoiceth in his strength: he goeth on to meet the armed men.
> He mocketh at fear, and is not affrighted; neither turneth he back from the sword.
> The quiver rattleth against him, the glittering spear and the shield.
> He swalloweth the ground with fierceness and rage; neither believeth he that it is the sound of the trumpet.
> He saith among the trumpets, Ha, ha; and he smelleth the battle afar off, the thunder of the captains, and the shouting.

That is joy—joy solemn and triumphant; stern, lonely, everlasting joy, which has in it the full depth and humility of man's wonder, his sense of glory, and his feeling of awe before the mystery of the universe. An exultant cry is torn from our lips as we read the lines about that glorious horse, and the joy we feel is wild and strange, lonely and dark like death, and grander than the delicate and lovely joy that men like Herrick and Theocritus described, great poets though they were.

Just as the Book of Job and the sermon of Ecclesiastes are, each in its own way, supreme histories of man's loneliness, so do all the books of the Old Testament, in their entirety, provide the most final and profound literature of human loneliness that the world has known. It is astonishing with what a coherent unity of spirit and belief the life of loneliness is recorded in those many books—how it finds its full expression in the chants, songs, prophecies, and chronicles of so many men, all so various, and each so individual, each revealing some new image of man's secret and most lonely heart, and all combining to produce a single image of his loneliness that is matchless in its grandeur and magnificence.

Thus, in a dozen books of the Old Testament—in Job, Ecclesiastes, and the Song of Solomon; in Psalms, Proverbs, and Isaiah; in words of praise and words of lamentation; in songs of triumph and in chants of sorrow, bondage, and despair; in boasts of pride and arrogant assertion, and in stricken confessions of humility and fear; in warning, promise, and in prophecy; in love, hate, grief, death, loss, revenge, and resignation; in wild, singing jubilation and in bitter sorrow—the lonely man has wrought out in a swelling and tremendous chorus the final vision of his life.

The total, all-contributary unity of this conception of man's loneliness in the books of the Old Testament becomes even more astonishing when we begin to read the New. For, just as the Old Testament becomes the chronicle of the life of loneliness, the gospels of the New Testament, with the same miraculous and unswerving unity, become the chronicle of the life of love. What Christ is saying always, what he never swerves from saying, what he says a thousand times and in a thousand different ways, but always with a central unity of belief, is this: "I am my Father's son, and you are my brothers." And the unity that binds us all together, that makes this earth a family, and all men brothers and the sons of God, is love.

The central purpose of Christ's life, therefore, is to destroy the life of loneliness and to establish here on earth the life of love. The evidence to support this is clear and overwhelming. It should be obvious to everyone that when Christ says: "Blessed are the poor in spirit: for theirs is the kingdom of heaven," "Blessed are they that mourn: for they shall be comforted," "Blessed are the meek: for they shall inherit the earth," "Blessed are they which do hunger and thirst after righteousness: for they shall be filled," "Blessed are the merciful: for they shall obtain mercy," and "Blessed are the pure in heart: for they shall see God"—Christ is not here extolling the qualities of humility, sorrow, meekness, righteousness, mercy, and purity as virtues sufficient in themselves, but he promises to men who have these virtues the richest reward that men were ever offered.

And what is that reward? It is a reward that promises not only the inheritance of the earth, but the kingdom of heaven as well. It tells men that they shall not live and die in loneliness, that their sorrow will not go unassuaged, their prayers unheard, their hunger and thirst unfed, their love unrequited: but that, through love, they shall destroy the walls of loneliness forever; and even if the evil and unrighteous of this earth shall grind them down into the dust, yet if they bear all things meekly and with love, they will enter into a fellowship of joy, a brotherhood of love, such as no men on earth ever knew before.

Such was the final intention of Christ's life, the purpose of his teaching. And its total import was that the life of loneliness could be destroyed forever by the life of love. Or such, at least, has been the meaning which I read into his life. For in these recent years when I have lived alone so much, and known loneliness so well, I have gone back many times and read the story of this man's words and life to see if I could find in them a meaning for myself, a way of life that would be better than the one I had. I read what he had said, not in a mood of piety or holiness, not from a sense of sin, a feeling of contrition, or because his promise of a heavenly reward meant very much to me. But I tried to read his bare words nakedly and simply, as it seems to me he must have uttered them, and as I have read the words of other men—of Homer, Donne, and Whitman, and the writer of Ecclesiastes—and if the meaning I have put upon his words seems foolish or extravagant, childishly simple or banal, mine alone or not different from what ten million other men have thought, I have only set it down here as I saw it, felt it, found it for myself, and have tried to add, subtract, and alter nothing.

And now I know that though the way and meaning of Christ's life is a far, far better way and meaning than my own, yet I can never make it mine; and I think that this is true of all the other lonely men that I have seen or known about—the nameless, voiceless, faceless atoms of this earth as well as Job and Everyman and Swift. And Christ himself, who preached the life of love, was yet as lonely as any man that ever lived. Yet I could not say that he was mistaken because he preached the life of love and fellowship, and lived and died in loneliness; nor would I dare assert his way was wrong because a billion men have since professed his way and never followed it.

I can only say that I could not make his way my own. For I have found the constant, everlasting weather of man's life to be, not love, but loneliness. Love itself is not the weather of our lives. It is the rare, the precious flower. Sometimes it is the flower that gives us life, that breaches the dark walls of all our loneliness and restores us to the fellowship of life, the family of the earth, the brotherhood of man. But sometimes love is the flower that brings us death; and from it we get pain and darkness; and the mutilations of the soul, the maddening of the brain, may be in it.

How or why or in what way the flower of love will come to us, whether with life or death, triumph or defeat, joy or madness, no man on this earth can say. But I know that at the end, forever at the end for us—the houseless, homeless, doorless, driven wanderers of life, the lonely men—there waits forever the dark visage of our comrade, Loneliness.

But the old refusals drop away, the old avowals stand—and we who were dead have risen, we who were lost are found again, and we who sold the talent, the passion, and belief of youth into the keeping of the fleshless dead, until our hearts were corrupted, our talent wasted, and our hope gone, have won our lives back bloodily, in solitude and darkness; and we know that things will be for us as they have been, and we see again, as we saw once, the image of the shining city. Far flung, and blazing into tiers of jeweled light, it burns forever in our vision as we walk the Bridge, and strong tides are bound round it, and the great ships call. And we walk the Bridge, always we walk the Bridge alone with you, stern friend, the one to whom we speak, who never failed us. Hear:

"Loneliness forever and the earth again! Dark brother and stern friend, immortal face of darkness and of night, with whom the half part of my life was spent, and with whom I shall abide now till my death forever—what is there for me to fear as long as you are with me? Heroic friend, blood-brother of my life, dark face—have we not gone together down a million ways, have we not coursed together the great and furious avenues of night, have we not crossed the stormy seas alone, and known strange lands, and come again to walk the continent of night and listen to the silence of the earth? Have we not been brave and glorious when we were together, friend? Have we not known triumph, joy, and glory on this earth—and will it not be again with me as it was then, if you come back to me? Come to me, brother, in the watches of the night. Come to me in the secret and most silent heart of darkness. Come to me as you always came, bringing to me again the old invincible strength, the deathless hope, the triumphant joy and confidence that will storm the earth again."

The Hills Beyond

Chapter 1

THE QUICK AND THE DEAD

ABOUT MIDWAY ALONG THE ATLANTIC SEABOARD OF THE NORTH American continent lies a strip of land which is known today as the State of Old Catawba. It is an ancient part of the everlasting earth, but its history is quite young. One of the earliest references to it occurs in the chronicle of old Hugh Fortescue. His narrative is so well known that it would hardly bear recounting, were it not for the curious legend which has grown out of it.

In the month of September, 1593, Fortescue, one of the hardiest and most celebrated sea adventurers of the time, set sail from Plymouth harbor with a full cargo of provisions and material, and, in addition to his crew, a company of one hundred and seven men, women, and children, whom he proposed to land upon the shores of Old Catawba to establish a colony there. The colony, as everyone knows, was founded four months later, in January, 1594. According to Fortescue's account, he remained for two months, helping the colonists build huts and log houses; then Fortescue sailed for England, leaving the colony apparently well established, with everything going briskly.

It was the old sea dog's intention, as he tells us in his lusty chronicle, to return again early the following year with additional supplies for the settlers, and with the further purpose, of course, of collecting and taking home the first fruits of their crops or findings in the New World. Troubles at home, however, delayed him far beyond his reckoning, and it was August, 1595, before he stood in past the shifting dunes again, into the pearl gray waters of the Great Sound. He was a good six months late. And everyone knows what he found.

The settlement was still there, but all the people had disappeared. The natural supposition was that they had been massacred by the Indians. Curiously, however, the rude huts and cabins were intact. Fortescue says that they had been stripped of every utensil, ornament, and stick of furniture that might conceivably be of use to anyone, but there was no evidence of violence. The whole place was just empty and deserted. And, nailed to a tree at the edge of the clearing, was a kind of rude sign on which had been crudely painted the word "here"—or "heare," as it was actually spelled. Below, an arrowhead, blazed in the bark, pointed toward the wilderness. This was all.

Fortescue and his men, taking this clue for what it was worth, or what it might imply, explored the wilderness of the whole region for weeks. They found nothing—not even a footprint—that could give any hint of what had happened to the people in the settlement. So, after exhausting every hope and every possibility of search, Fortescue set sail again and headed back for England.

That's the story—all that was ever known. No new light has since been shed upon the mystery. But the human mind is so constructed that it cannot abide an unresolved mystery. From Fortescue's day onward, people wondered what became of the Lost Colony, and since history gave no answer, they were free to invent an answer of their own. This, as we shall shortly see, is exactly what they did.

Time passed, and other settlers came to Old Catawba. The

manner of their coming was very much like that by which all the colonies of the British Crown were eventually peopled. And like the nation of which it was to be a part, Old Catawba grew from east to west. Its expansion followed the inevitable direction prescribed by geography and economic pressure. The earliest settlements were in the tide-water regions along the coast. In the 1660's the population of the colony did not exceed ten thousand persons, and they were distributed in a thin belt of settlements that penetrated no more than seventy-five or a hundred miles inland.

One hundred years later, just before the outbreak of the Revolutionary War, the population had grown to two hundred thousand, and had pushed westward to the foothills of the upper Piedmont, at the base of the great mountain wall, three hundred and fifty miles from the ocean. Intrepid pioneers and daring huntsmen had actually surmounted the last barrier of the West, had blazed their way through the wilderness, had lived for months alone in what was then Indian country, and had returned at length laden with furs and skins and other trophies of the hunt, as token of the fact that they had been there. The first settlements behind the mountain wall, in the great wilderness of western Catawba, occurred in the years immediately following the Revolution, and as a direct result of the war: the settlers were men who had been soldiers in the Continental Army, and had been induced to go there through land grants given them as a reward for their services.

Slowly but surely the movement to the West continued, until by the first quarter of the nineteenth century the western regions of the state had so grown in numbers that they threatened to wrest control of the government from the East, which had hitherto maintained its supremacy unchallenged. The West demanded its rightful representation in the legislature. The East, stiffnecked with pride, refused, and since the East still had the edge in population, as well as most of the wealth, the refusal stood. Thus began the first in the long series of conflicts between East and West that were to disturb the life of the state for years.

But it was an unequal struggle, and time was with the West. The East fought back desperately against this giant stripling, this obscure country cousin, this uncouth hillbilly, but the West, with gangling stride and dangling arms and gap-toothed grin, refused to know when it was licked, and instead just wiped the lank hair from its eyes, spat briefly through its bloody lips, and kept coming on again after every knockdown. The East used every weapon at its command, and when fair means failed, it did not scruple to use foul. One of the foulest and most specious weapons that it used was the arrogant claim that the East was superior to the West in birth and breeding, and therefore born to rule.

Now the history of genealogies is very significant and curious. In America, as in most young countries, people are much less likely to be snobs over the thing they have than over the thing they lack. Thus, Americans are seldom snobs about money, but they are often snobs about "family." The amount of time spent by certain people in New England and the South in talking about their "families" is appalling. In the South, particularly, this preoccupation seems to absorb most of the spare energies of the female population, for it is an axiom of Southern life that a woman without "family" is nothing. A woman may be poor; she may be abysmally ignorant (and usually is); she may have read nothing, seen nothing, gone nowhere; she may be lazy, nasty, vain, arrogant, venomous, and dishonest; her standards of morality, government, justice may not differ one whit from that of the lynching mob: but if she can assert, loudly and without challenge, that her "family" is older (and therefore better) than other families, then her position in the community is un-questioned, she is the delicate flower of "Southern culture," she must not be "talked back to"—she is, in short, "a lady."

So it was in this final phase of the war between the East and the West. As a last resort, the East claimed the right to rule the West on grounds of "family." In a state which had hitherto been singularly free of aristocratic pretensions this was a most peculiar development. But the reasons for it are not far to seek.

The East now knew that its cause was hopeless. It had grown fat on power, and now it saw that it must yield before the new men of the West. It read the signs of its declining influence, and hated to think of the future. So, as nearly always happens under such circumstances, the East took refuge in the glories of an imagined past as compensation for the threatened loss of its future.

What happened was this:

The bare facts of the Lost Colony, as old Hugh Fortescue recorded them, had been known for years to the more literate people in the eastern part of the state. The mystery surrounding the disappearance of those first colonists had always been a sub-ject of speculation, and a body of legend had grown up about it. According to this legend, the people of that colony were not killed, but were taken captive and carried off into the wilderness by an Indian tribe. In the course of time they adopted the language and customs of their captors; they intermarried with the Indians and bore children; and these children, in turn, intermarried with colonists of a still later date. Thus the Lost Colony was not really lost at all. And it followed from the legend that the de-scendants of this colony were not only still living, but could lay claim to the oldest English ancestry of any people in the New World—dating thirteen years before Jamestown, and twenty-six before Plymouth.

For years, this legend had existed as folklore, kept alive by idle curiosity and gossip. No one believed it. It was not until about a decade before the Civil War, at a time when the legends of Massachusetts and Virginia were already venerable with tradition, that the Catawba legend began to congeal into a form imposing enough for anyone to take it seriously.

Then it was that a professor of history at one of the local colleges published a book entitled *The History of the Lost Colony*. It achieved some passing notice in the world at large, being generally received in learned circles as a fairly interesting experiment in conjectural possibility. The author himself did not make any greater claim for it. He was too conservative and cautious a historian to try to prove that the legend of the colonists' survival through intermarriage with the Indians was anything more than a theory of what *might* have happened. Still, in a manner that is distressingly familiar to the local historian everywhere, he sometimes let his patriotic ardor get the better of his scholarly judgment, and, in modern parlance, was inclined "to give himself the breaks."

No doubt it was for this reason that the book produced a considerable sensation at home. Its sales in Old Catawba were phenomenal, and its effect was both profound and startling, in a way that the worthy professor had never intended or foreseen. The time was ripe for it, and people in the eastern part of the state fell upon the book eagerly, and began straightway to embroider and to weave, as composers do, with what are called "improvisations on a theme." The ladies proved themselves especially proficient in this form of intellectual exercise. Starting from scratch—indeed, from the most scratchy sort of scratch—they began to erect a glittering edifice of pure fantasy, all of it proceeding, of course, out of something which started merely as a titillating thought, grew rapidly to a rosy hope, and ended in an unshakable conviction that *they themselves* were descended from the presumptive survivors of the Lost Colony.

In almost no time at all a new and highly exclusive social organization came into being, calling itself The Society of the Sons and Daughters of the Aborigines. The aristocratic pretensions of its members threatened overnight to eclipse even the haughty claims of the F. F. V.'s and the Mayflower descendants. The Sons and Daughters of the Aborigines had just discovered who they were, and from this point on they would play second fiddle to no one. No doubt it was all well enough, they said patronizingly, to talk about royal grants and tide-water plantations and the early days of Plymouth, but such trifling originalities as these could not be expected to matter very greatly to people who were *aboriginally* descended from the *first* English colonists *and* from Indian chieftains. It was quite surprising to see how proudly the Aborigines laid claim to this tinge of savage color in their veins. Ladies whose husbands would have reached for their dueling pistols at any imputation of a *recent* tinge of color in their blood telt no hesitation whatever in proclaiming their dusky ancestors of some two and a half centuries before.

There have been critics unkind enough to suggest that throughout this whole extraordinary performance necessity was the mother of invention, and that the ready acceptance of the Catawba legend as historic fact was no more than might have been expected of a people who had too long been irked by their own obscurity and too long been indifferent to the claims of "family." Thus, "a lady of family" in Virginia is known to have remarked one time, when informed that her nephew had married a mere nobody for no other reason than because he loved her: "Well, what else can you expect? He was brought up in Johnsville, and that's *practically* a Catawba town." This shrewd observation reflects pretty much the estimation in which Old Catawba has been commonly held by outsiders. And certainly it is true that the history of the state has always been more distinguished for its homespun ruggedness than for its aristocratic splendor.

In spite of all gibes and taunts, The Society of the Sons and Daughters of the Aborigines grew strong and flourished throughout the eastern part of the state. And what had begun as a social organization quickly became the chief ally of entrenched power in the state's politics. The Sons and Daughters brought up their heaviest artillery of "family" to stem the rising tide of the West, and in the pivotal campaign of 1858 they nominated one of their own number to run for Governor against a country lawyer from the wilds of Zebulon County.

The country lawyer stumped the state, pleading the cause of democracy, and telling his audiences that the ruling caste in the East, with its money and privileges and humbug aristocracy, was dead and didn't know it. Like Swift when he announced the death of Partridge, the almanac maker, his logic was irrefutable: for, as Swift retorted, when Partridge came forward to assert that he was still alive, *if Partridge was not dead, he should have been*—so the country lawyer held to the proposition that the East was dead, or should be; and his delighted followers called the fight that ensued "The Battle of the Quick and the Dead."

Under that banner the East was beaten. The West had won at last. And the leader and hero of that victory became from that time on the symbol of the West.

His name was Zachariah Joyner—a name famous to everyone who since that time has lived upon Catawba earth and breathed Catawba air. Throughout his life he was a vigorous and undaunted champion of the common people. The pretensions of the Aborigines disgusted him, and he let no opportunity go by to flail them with the brutal lash of his coarse but devastating ridicule.

Joyner's opponent in the campaign for the governorship was himself a Son of the Aborigines, his right to this distinction being founded upon the aristocratic claims of his mother, a charming lady who had inherited money and idleness, both together, and with this endowment had thus been one of the first to trace her ancestry back to the Lost Colony. Her son had campaigned vigorously to save what he called "our precious heritage" and "the Catawba way of life" from the raw crudeness of a Western victory. In the end he was even rash enough to accept Joyner's challenge to appear on the same platform and debate the issues face to face. On this occasion the gentleman-champion of the East gave everything he had. He was not only eloquent in his show of filial devotion to his mother—"that delicate flower of Southern womanhood, etc. . . . . to whom I owe, etc. . . . . at whose knees I learned, etc."—but he also sought to endear himself to the masses by condescension: he went so far as to admit that he made no claims to aristocratic lineage on his father's side, his father's people being descended, so he said, "from good old yeoman stock."

"Good old yeoman stock, my ——!" bellowed Zachariah Joyner in rebuttal. "They came here because the jails in England were crowded, and to keep from being hanged"—this was an exaggerated reference to the settlement of a group of exiled convicts on the eastern coast in 1683—"and the only yeomen they ever saw were the yoemen of the guard!"

So Zachariah Joyner won, and his victory was a great deal more than the triumph of one half of the state over the other half. It was the triumph of the common man—of all the obscure and unknown lives that somewhere had turned a wheel, or swung an ax, or plowed a furrow, or blazed a trail and made a clearing in the wilderness. His was the voice, the tongue, the language of every one of these who had lived and died and gone unrecorded to the earth—and who now arose again, incarnate in one living man, to say to all proud hearts, stiff necks, and Aborigines soever that in the final reckoning the representatives of privilege must bow before the insistent rights of universal humanity.

Old Catawba had found its man.

Chapter 2

OLD MAN OF THE TRIBE

ZACHARIAH JOYNER WAS NEVER ONE TO INDULGE IN THE REVERENT pruning of family trees. When he was Governor of Old Catawba he often said that if people in the eastern part of the state would spend less time in thinking about where they came from, and more in thinking about where they were going, they would be a lot easier to get along with.

He was also impatient of all attempts to dignify himself and his own family genealogically. In the heyday of his later fame, the Aborigines made some conciliating overtures to bring Catawba's most distinguished citizen into the fold. They did not quite dare hint that Zack had as good a right as anybody else to claim an ancestor in the Lost Colony, for they knew too well what he would say to that; but they did draw up quite a formidable account of the doings of the Joyners in the annals of history. They traced the name back to the Middle Ages. They even had one of the Joyners doing valiant service in defense of King Richard of the Lion Heart, when that great sovereign was surrounded by a murderous host of Saracens before the walls of old Jerusalem. They dug out others with baronial titles, and found some of them contending back and forth in the Wars of the Roses. There were Joyners who had fought loyally under the banners of King Charles, and others just as doggedly with Cromwell's men. From that point the earliest migrations of the family were traced to Virginia, thence to the coastal regions of Catawba, and finally to their stronghold in the mountain districts of the West. By dint of much contriving, the whole thing had been linked together in a kind of chain.

But Zachariah was not impressed. His comment on the document, when it was presented for his inspection and approval, was characteristically blunt and to the point:

"I don't know where we came from, and, what's more, I don't give a damn. The point is, we're here now."

There was not only good democracy in this, but the ring of sound truth, too. For the essential trait of the Joyner tribe was in those words. They were "here now," and Catawba would have been inconceivable without them. They were, in fact, a kind of native dragon seed. They may have had some other and more ancient antecedents, but in their magnificent quality of Now-ness —the quality of being what they were because they were where they were—they were so naturally a part of western Catawba, its life, its speech, its history, even the clay of its soil, that any other previous existence for them seemed fantastically detached, ghostly, and unreal.

Since every mother's son of us has got to come from somewhere, their lineage, no doubt, went back like everyone's to Father Adam, or to the origins of primeval man. So perhaps their ancestor was some prehistoric anthropoid. But if anyone wants to know who the founder of the family was, the answer is that it was old William Joyner, the father of Zack, and the sire of the whole clan. Even today the memory of old William is still kept alive in the hills, for in his own way he attained a legendary repute which almost equals that of his more celebrated son.

There is some doubt about William Joyner's antecedents, and no certainty whatever about where he came from. It is known that he came to Zebulon County because of a Revolutionary land grant. And the date of his coming is established. It was in 1793 when he took up his grant upon the south fork of what is now known as the Thumb Toe River. If he was not actually the first settler in that region, he was among the first. From this time on, people began to come in rapidly, and when William Joyner married, in 1798, the wife he took was the daughter of another settler who had recently arrived in the mountains.

Her name was Martha Creasman, and by her he had a family of seven. She died at the birth of her last child. Later, William married a second time. By this wife he had fourteen or sixteen children—for there were so many of them, and their destinies were so diverse, that even their number has been disputed. But of these matters, with all the ramifications of kinship and heredity they imply, it is our purpose to speak later. Here we shall tell a little more of William Joyner.

There were, in the earlier years of the present century, old men alive who could remember him; for he lived to a great old age, and there were people who were children in the 1840's who had seen him and had heard the stories men told of him. Even at that time, a hundred years ago, he was an almost legendary figure. The stories of his great physical strength, for example, were prodigious, and yet apparently were founded in substantial fact.

He was said to have been, particularly in his earlier years, a man of a hot temper, who liked a fight. There is a story of his fight with a big blacksmith: a quarrel having broken out between them over the shoeing of a horse, the blacksmith brained him with an iron shoe and knocked him flat. As William started to get up again, bleeding and half conscious, the blacksmith came at him again, and Joyner hit him while still resting on one knee. The blow broke the blacksmith's ribs and caved in his side as one would crack a shell.

He was known in his own day to be a mighty hunter; and old men who remembered him used to tell of the time he "chased the dogs the whole way over into Tennessee, and was gone four days and nights, and never knowed how fer from home he was."

There is also the story of his fight with a grizzly bear: the bear charged him at close quarters and there was nothing left for him to do but fight. A searching party found him two days later, more dead than living—as they told it, "all chawed up," but with the carcass of the bear: "and in the fight he had bit the nose off that big b'ar and chawed off both his years, and that b'ar was so tored up hit was a caution."

Then there is the story of the time when he walked off with enough leather on his back to shoe a regiment. The brother of Joyner's first wife owned a kind of trading post or country store, and had besides a pound of savage and ferocious dogs. It was the storekeeper's boast that no one but himself could manage these fierce animals, and certainly no one else had ever attempted to. People generally were afraid of them, and gave them a wide berth. Their owner was so proud of their untamed ferocity that on one occasion, when he was talking of his dogs to a group of men who were in his store, he offered any man who could subdue them "as much leather as he can tote out of here upon his back."

William Joyner was present and instantly accepted the challenge. In spite of the efforts of his friends to dissuade him, he went out to the pound, and, while the others watched, opened the gate and went in. The great dogs sprang snarling at him with bared fangs. According to the story, "he jest snapped his fingers once or twice," and the dogs whimpered and came crawling to him like a pack of curs. To add insult to injury, he is said to have stooped down and picked up two of the largest and most savage of the dogs and held them under his arms, "a-hangin' thar real foolish-like, like a couple of pigs." After walking about the pen with them a time or two, he tossed them down, snapped his fingers again, opened the gate, and walked out unscathed.

The storekeeper, although beaten and dumbfounded, was as good as his word. He pointed to the pile of leather in his store and told William he could take as much as he could carry. Joyner stood there while his companions heaped the leather on, and finally staggered out the door with eight hundred pounds of it on his shoulders.

There are many other stories about him, but these suffice to indicate the unusual qualities of his person, his great strength, and his undaunted courage. He was said by everyone who ever saw him to have been a person of remarkable gifts. Indeed, one does not have to probe a mystery to find an explanation for the amazing family he produced: the seed of all their talents was aware in him. Although he came to Zebulon with nothing but his rifle and his grant of land, within twenty years, through his ability as a shrewd trader, he had accumulated what was, in his time and place, a substantial property. He was the owner of a mill, to which his neighbors brought their corn for grinding. He increased his holdings until he owned and had under cultivation hundreds of acres of the most fertile land in the beautiful valley that now bears the name of Joyner's Creek. And eventually he became the owner of the largest and most flourishing trading post in the whole district.

From these beginnings came the start of the whole clan. It is true that Zachariah, in the later years of his political career, made frequent and eloquent reference, in the phrases of the orotund rhetoric of which he was a master, to "the little log cabin where I was born." It is further true that the little log cabin where

Zachariah so often and so advantageously asserted he was born, still exists, kept piously by the State Historical Commission, in a condition of trimmed, sodded, planted, and be-flowered snugness that it assuredly did not know at the time when William Joyner lived in it. The State Highway Commission has likewise memorialized the sanctuary in a system of neat signs, which notify the modern pilgrim that he is now approaching "the birthplace of Zachariah Joyner—four miles."

It is unfortunate, perhaps, both for the lovers of sentiment and the believers in historic fact, that Zachariah was not born here at all. William Joyner did live here for years, and built the cabin with his own hands, with the assistance of some friendly Cherokees; but by the time of Zachariah's birth, his father was already a person of considerable substance, and in accordance not only with his new position, but with the expansive needs of his growing family, he had built the larger and much more substantial dwelling that adjoins it, and which also still exists. "The little log cabin where I was born," existed in Zachariah's childhood as a kind of outside kitchen; it was certainly in such a capacity that Zachariah himself must have known it, no matter how he remembered it later in the more imaginative flights of political oratory by which he gave it fame.

In his later years, William Joyner having now become a man of weight and standing in the community, his wife tried, as wives of successful citizens are apt to do, to ameliorate some of his social imperfections. The story goes that she tried to get him to wear shoes in summertime—for apparently he was a man who liked bare feet, and when he went out to the fields to work, the weather and the season permitting, he always worked so.

Failing to win this really formidable concession, the worthy woman then attempted to persuade him "at least to put your shoes on when you come into the house." Her efforts even in this direction were not successful, for although he made some effort to please her, he "kept forgittin'." Failing in all this, she finally tried to prevail on him "for pity's sake, at least to put your shoes on when company comes." But this also proved too much, for she used to say despairingly: "I don't know what to do with him. I've begged an' I've pled an' he promises to try, but the minute we have company—even when the preacher's there—here he comes without his shoes, trampin' along out of the fields in his big feet."

As for "Bear" Joyner—for, after his famous encounter with the grizzly, he was known by this name—he would often say: "I thought I was marryin' me a wife, but I reckon what I done was to go an' git myself hitched to a blacksmith. My advice to you young'uns is, if you ever go and git yourself married, make sure first whether you're marryin' a woman who is goin' to cook fer you, or one who is goin' to try to throw you down an' shoe you every time you come into the house."

He was a man of keen wit, and everyone who ever knew him said that he would have "gone far" if he had had the advantages of formal education. He was unable to read or write his own name until he was more than forty years old; but he learned how to do both in his later years. Indeed, he developed quite a taste for reading, and, limited as his facilities were, he managed to acquire a surprising store of bookish information.

Bear Joyner, like his famous son, was increate with myth, because the very nature of the man persuaded it. Such myths, then —*facts* most probably, indeed—as his bear-fighting, hunting, blacksmith-crushing, dog-mastering, and his instinctive shoelessness we have adduced to give the flavor of the man.

These things get into the story, make the picture. Yet it is not the Myth that falsifies the true identity of man (our debunking truth-tellers of the present notwithstanding—would to God they were themselves debunked!) The Myth is true. Let those who doubt it deny that Lincoln liked a joke, and had a gift for making one; split rails; was very strong; said h—l and d—n; so far as we can guess, was not averse to—; was pungent in his speech, and said his legs were long enough to reach the ground (which certainly was high sense); picked up the dirty pig; was chased out of doors by his wife—yes, and even when embarrassed by the presence of surrounding ladies on a railroad platform, told a little boy who pointed to a certain word scrawled upon the wall by other little boys, that the thing it stood for was "a station, son . . . the name, son, of a certain station . . . a most important station . . . the station where more men get on and off than any other station in the world."

A myth, then, to like food and women, and to take a drink? . . . A myth to know the use of corncobs in the country? . . . To be able to say ——, and make a joke about it? . . . To be a lawyer, and have "a high and squeaky voice," and yet be able to speak *Gettysburg*?

O, little men, come, come!

Then why the Myth?

The Myth is founded on *extorted* fact: wrenched from the context of ten thousand days, and rutted roads, the desolations of lost voices long ago, the rheumy nostrils in the month of March, the winter howling in the oak, the superfetation of the dreary wait, the vacancy of unremembered hours.

For it is not a question of having faith, or lack of it. It is a simple fact of seeing. Seeing, we are saved. Half-seeing, we are worse than blind. And wrong.

It is important, then, to know that William Joyner "chawed the b'ar." But it is even more important to know that William Joyner was a man who learned to read a book.

It may be that some later period in the human history will dispense with the whole necessity of print, and that book-reading, book-writing, book-publishing, all the ramified accessories that have accumulated since old Gutenberg, will (through some system of psychophones, printoscopes, empathic waves, or type telepathies; or what more of the strange and unbelievable we can wot not of) be as prehistoric as the dinosaur. But in William Joyner's day the thing was known—not only known, but, aside from speech, the swiftest and most common way of all communication; and the point is that, illiterate as he was until his fortieth year, unread, unlettered, not even knowing the look of his own name in common script—he learned it!

Why?

We do not know; and cannot guess the reason except that men sought India once, and braved inhuman seas beyond the world's edge, in their scallop shells; and looked at one another with "a wild surmise." As for all other antecedents—possible Joyners in the Middle Ages, with the Roses, or King Charles—let others search them: all things must have their precincts, and our own are there, in Old Catawba, with Bear Joyner, in the hills of home.

Whatever seed produced him, or what kernel of his own unknown heritage, the man was "there"—and not only "chawed the b'ar," but learned to read a book. And of all the facts that can be evidenced, of all the traits that bind the clan of William Joyner's seed together, none is more strange than its respect for learning.

Where did it come from?

In the century since old Bear Joyner's time, there have been some thousands of his name who have been dwellers in these hills. Some have been mountain folk, bowed down by poverty, who never learned to write, or to construe in print, their names. Others have been half-literate. Others have had the rudiments of education. Still others have risen in the world to places of commercial eminence: some have been lawyers, doctors, business men; there has been a preacher here and there; there has been more, much more, than an average sprinkling of "radical thinkers"—"atheists and agnostics" (that is to say, people who would openly debate the divinity of Jesus Christ, or the existence of "the after-life"); others who had "radical notions" (people who would challenge the accepted standards of law and property: there was one such who ran for Congress on the ticket of Eugene Debs, and got eight votes—it was said, however, that his sons and brothers did not vote for him). In the mountain districts to this day the Joyners have the reputation of being "queer." The word is not used scornfully, for generally, no matter what their station, the Joyners are respected folk. But any variation from the norm in them does not astonish anyone: people have come to accept it casually and as a matter of expected fact. If a Joyner is an "atheist," an "agnostic," a "socialist," a "radical," it has come to be accepted because the Joyners are "queer" folk.

But again—why?

Boiled down to their essential element, all of these "eccentric" qualities which have, for a hundred years or more, caused their neighbors to accept the Joyners as belonging to their special type, and "queer," are nothing but the marks of an intensely heightened curiosity, a questioning, probing, debating, and examining intelligence that their neighbors did not have. There's the mystery—if mystery it be; indeed, the only mystery there is.

The Joyners have always been "individualists." But so are all mountain folk. Yet other mountain folk are individualistic more convenably. Most mountain folk are individuals within the narrow frame of a convention. True, they will go their own way, make their own law, "take nothing off of any man"—but all of this follows a close code. They are clannish, suspicious of the strange, world-lost, mistrustful of the outer world—conformant, really, in their non-conforming. For even when they go their way and kill their man, they are unquestioning of the special law of their own world.

In this respect the Joyners were all different from their neighbors, and the pattern of divergence was set by the founder of the clan. At a time when it was the convention for all men in the wilderness to be illiterate, in a place where the knowledge contained in books was of no earthly use, nothing would suit old Bear Joyner but that he must learn to read.

At a later time, as has already been stated, the genealogists of the Aborigines tried to account for Zachariah Joyner's distinction by tracing his line back to the Middle Ages. It was no use. The answer lay closer home. For no one ever really knew where his father came from. And it did not matter. Old Bear Joyner came from the same place, and was of the same kind, as all the other people in the mountains. But he was a man who learned to read. And there is the core of the whole mystery.

Chapter 3

THE GREAT SCHISM

I F, AS CARLYLE SAYS, THE HISTORY OF THE WORLD IS RECORDED IN the lives of its great men, so, too, the spirit of a people is recorded in the heroes it picks. No better illustration of this fact could be found than in the life of Zachariah Joyner. Historically, his position is secure enough. True, his greatest fame is where he would himself have wished it to be—at home. His name has not attained the national celebrity of a Webster or Calhoun; no doubt most people outside Catawba would have difficulty in placing him. But historians will remember him as a leader in the affairs of his own state for almost fifty years; as an able and resourceful Governor; later, as one of the more forceful and colorful leaders of debate in the affairs of the United States Senate; and all in all, when the whole record of his life is weighed and estimated, as a man of great natural ability and intelligence, considering his place and time and situation.

He directed the affairs of his state through the Civil War, and he directed them courageously and ably. In periods of stress he was unmoved by threat and unswayed by the hysterias of popular feeling. In the closing days of the Confederacy, when the armies were in desperate need, he curtly refused a demand from Jefferson Davis for almost seventy thousand suits of uniforms, shoes, and coats which the state owned and had in its possession. He refused bluntly and without apology, saying that the equipment would be used first of all for the rehabilitation of his own people; and although this act of rebellion brought down upon him bitter denunciation from all quarters, he stuck to his decision and refused to budge.

Later, in the darker days of Reconstruction, military occupation, black legislatures, and night riders, he rendered even greater service to his state. And he concluded a long life, full of honors and accomplishment, as a member of the nation's Senate, in which capacity he died, during Cleveland's last administration, in 1893.

All these facts are sufficiently well known to make his position in the nation's chronicle secure. But to people in Catawba his name means a great deal more than this. They are well acquainted with the story of his life, and the record of his offices as it has been outlined here. But these honors and accomplishments, splendid as they are, do not in themselves explain the place he holds in Catawba's heart. For he is their hero: in the most local and particular sense, they feel that he belongs to them, is of them, could in no conceivable way belong to anything else, is theirs and theirs alone. Therefore, they love him.

He was not only their own native Lincoln—their backwoods son who marched to glory by the log-rail route—he was their Crockett and Paul Bunyan rolled in one. He was not alone their hero; he was their legend and their myth. He was, and has remained so to this day, a kind of living prophecy of all that they themselves might wish to be; a native divinity, shaped out of their own clay, and breathing their own air; a tongue that spoke the words, a voice that understood and spoke the language, they would have him speak.

They tell a thousand stories about him today. What does it matter if many of the things which they describe never happened? They are true because they are the kind of things he would have said, the kind of things that would have happened to him. Thus, to what degree, and in what complex ways, he was created so in their imaginations, no one can say. How much the man shaped the myth, how much the myth shaped the man, how much Zack Joyner created his own folk, or how much his people created him —no one can know, and it does not matter.

For he was of them, and the rib; and they of him the body and the flesh. He was indigenous to them as their own clay, as much a part of all their lives as the geography of their native earth, the climate of their special weather. No other place on earth but Old Catawba could have produced him. And the people know this: therefore, again, they love him.

In examining the history of that great man, we have collected more than eight hundred stories, anecdotes, and jokes that are told of him, and of this number at least six hundred have the unmistakable ring—or *smack*—of truth. If they did not happen— they *should* have! They belong to him: they fit him like an old shoe.

"But," the pedants cunningly inquire, "*did* they happen? Now, really, *did* they? Ah, yes, they *sound* like him—he *might* have said them—but that's not the point! *Did* he?"

Well, we are not wholly unprepared for these objections. Of the six hundred stories which have the smack of truth, we have actually verified three hundred as authentic beyond the shadow of a doubt, and are ready to cite them by the book—place, time, occasion, evidence—to anyone who may inquire. In these stories there is a strength, a humor, a coarseness, and a native originality that belonged to the man and marked his every utterance. They come straight out of his own earth.

As a result of our researches, we can state unequivocally that there is no foundation in fact for the story that one time, in answer to a lady's wish, he called out to a Negro urchin at a station curb, who had a donkey wagon and a load of peanuts:

"Boy! Back your —— over here and show this lady your ——!"

But he certainly did make the speech in the United States Senate (in rejoinder to the Honorable Barnaby Bulwinkle) that is generally accredited to him, even though there is no account of it in the *Congressional Record*:

"Mr. President, sir, we are asked by the honorable gentleman to appropriate two hundred thousand dollars of the taxpayer's money for the purpose of building a bridge across Coon Creek in the honorable gentleman's district—a stream, sir, which I have seen, and which, sir, I assure you, I could —— halfway across."

The Vice-President (pounding with his gavel): "The Senator is out of order."

Senator Joyner: "Mr. President, sir, you are right. If I was *in* order, sir, I could —— the whole way across it!"

The last story that is told of Zachariah Joyner is that in his final days of illness (and, like King Charles, in dying, he was "an unconscionable time") he was aroused from coma one afternoon by the sound of rapid hoofs and wheels, and, looking wearily out of the window of his room, he saw the spare figure of his brother Rufus hastening toward the house. Even in his last extremity his humor did not forsake him, for he is said to have smiled wanly and feebly croaked:

"My God! I reckon it's all up with me! For here comes Rufe!"

People told the story later and, despite the grimness of the joke, they laughed at it; for the family trait to which it pointed was well known.

Bear Joyner, in his later years, after he had moved to Libya Hill, when told of the death of one of his sons in Zebulon by his second marriage, is known to have said:

"Well, I reckon some of the childern will attend the funeral."

Here he considered seriously a moment, then nodded his head with an air of confirmation. "Hit's—hit's no more than right!" And after another pause he added virtuously: "If I was thar, *I'd go myself!*" And with these words, he wagged his head quite solemnly, in such a way as to leave no doubt about the seriousness of his intent.

Zachariah is reported, when asked the number of his kin, to have replied: "Hell, I don't know! You can't throw a rock in Zebulon without hitting one of them!" He reflected on his metaphor a moment, and then said: "However, let him that is without sin among you throw the first stone. I can't!" And with these words he turned virtuously away, scratching himself vigorously in the behind.

Again, when he responded to the greeting of a member of the audience after a political rally at which he had made a speech, he is reported to have said:

"My friend, your face looks familiar to me. Haven't I seen you somewhere before?"

To which the person so addressed replied: "Yes, sir. I think you have. I was yore pappy's ninth child by his second marriage, and you was his fourth 'un by his first. So I reckon you might say that you and me was both half-brothers, distantly removed."

The grimmest story in the whole Joyner catalogue, perhaps, is that old Bear Joyner, when reproached one time for a seeming neglect of his own brood, is reputed to have said to his inquisitor:

"My God Almighty! A man can plant the seed, but he cain't make the weather! I sowed 'em—now, goddamn 'em, let 'em grow!"

There is no reason to believe that either William or his children were as neglectful of each other as these stories indicate, yet they really do denote a trait—or failing—of the clan. The fault —if fault it be—has long been known in Catawba, where it is said that "the only thing that will bring 'em all together is a wedding or a funeral; and it has to be a good one to do that." And yet, this trait has been too easily interpreted. Many people have taken such stories as evidence that the Joyners were lacking in a sense of family feeling; but nothing could be further from the truth.

The truth is that no family ever lived that had a stronger sense of their identity. It is hard to describe the thing in more familiar terms, for the whole tribe violates the standards by which such things are commonly appraised. Of "affection," "love," "devotion," even "clannishness"—as these terms are generally ac, cepted—the family seems to have had little. It is perfectly true that years have gone by when brothers have not seen or spoken to each other, even when they lived in the same town. It is also true that some have grown rich, indifferent to others who have struggled on in obscure poverty; that children have been born, and grown up, and gone away, scarcely familiar with the look of a cousin's face, the identity of a cousin's name.

Many people have observed these things and wondered at them, and then accepted them as further proof that the tribe was "queer." And yet, paradoxically, out of this very indifference came the family unity. From this very separateness came the deep and lasting sense of their identity. In a way, they reversed completely the old adage that if men refuse to hang together, they will all hang separately: of the Joyners it could rather be said that they hang separately because they know they hang together.

To find what produced their sense of "separateness" one must look into the history of the family.

The many children of Bear Joyner by his two marriages—there were more than twenty by the lowest count—grew up in a community where every man had to look out for himself. As for old Bill himself, nothing in his earlier life had prepared him for the exacting duties of parenthood. Whatever his career had been before he came into the hill-bound fastnesses of Zebulon, it had been very hard. He is known to have said: "If a young'un don't learn to root afore fourteen, he never will. A hen'll scrabble for young chicks, but before they're fryin' size they've got to scratch for themselves."

Although he was a man of substance for his time and place, his means were not enough to give two dozen children an easy start in life. Moreover, it must be owned that, like so many men who have been widowed in first marriage, he ventured into a second because it was the best expedient to meet his need. And the fourteen or sixteen children who came later—well, it is a brutal fact, but it was a sowing of blind seed. They came. They just came. And that was all.

Perhaps it is unjust to emphasize the schism of this second marriage. And yet, a separation did exist. It is inevitable that this should have been. For one thing, the older children of Bear Joyner's first marriage were fairly well grown when he married for the second time, and when the children of the second brood began to come along. Again, the surviving children of the first— Zack, Robert, Hattie, Theodore, and Rufe—were, if not a different breed, yet of a separate clan. And they knew it. From the first, instinctively, they seemed to know it. It was not that, consciously, they felt themselves to be "superior"—a bitter accusation that was later made—and yet they seemed to feel they were. And—since the blunt truth must be spoken—in the light of their accomplishment, and in the world's esteem, they were.

Another fact—the Joyners, first to last, were a vainglorious folk. Even old William had his share of this defect, perhaps even more than the rest of them, for old men thirty years ago who could remember him, and who would pay due tribute to his prowess and his extraordinary gifts, would often add: "Well, he *knowed* that he was good. . . . He was remarkable, but he *knowed* that he was good. And he was bigoted. He could be bigoted; and he was overbearing, too. . . . And as for Zack," old men would smile when they said his name, "Well, there was Zack, too. He knowed that *he* was good. Zack was a wonder . . . but no one ever said he was a blushing violet."

The Joyners of this early flowering not only "knowed that they was good," but they made little effort to conceal it. Apparently, none of them—unless it was Robert—hid his light under a bushel. And the truth is, each of them, in his own way—even Theodore! —had a light to show.

The reasons? Well, the reasons were complex, but perhaps the first one was the consciousness they had of special heritage. Bear Joyner's first wife was a "special woman": she was a Creasman, and the Creasmans were "good people." The Joyners of the first lot were all proud of their Creasman ancestry. Of Martha Creasman herself there is little to be told except that she was a good wife, a quiet and hard-working mother, and a Presbyterian. This last fact, trifling as it seems, was all important: for it bespeaks a kind of denominational snobbishness which is still more prevalent than the world may know, and which the Joyners of the first lot never lost.

As to Bear Joyner's second wife, she was a Baptist. The first Joyners—Zack, and all the rest of them—were always careful to speak of her respectfully, but with a touch of unconscious patronage that was infuriating to "the country cousins" of the lesser breed:

"Well now, she was a mighty good woman, and all of that. . . . Of course"—with a kind of hesitant and regretful concessiveness—"she was a Baptist. . . . I reckon you might call her a kind of religious fanatic. . . . She had queer religious notions. . . . But she was a good woman. . . . She had some queer ideas, but she was a good mother to those children. . . . Now everyone will have to give her *that*!"

Here then, obviously, were the roots of the great schism. Bear Joyner himself seems to have shared unconsciously in this prejudice of his elder children. He had apparently always been somewhat in awe of his first wife: her family was well known, and there is reason to believe he felt he was making a considerable step forward in the world when he married her. Toward his second wife he had no such feeling: she was one of a hard-shell Baptist tribe, and there is a story that he met her at camp meeting. However that may be, he was "looking for a woman to keep house"; and it was pretty much in this capacity that he married her.

That she worked long and faithfully there can be no doubt; or that she was a patient, strong, enduring woman—"a good mother," as the elder Joyners always willingly admitted, to the numerous family that she now began to bring into the world.

As for Bear Joyner's older children by his previous marriage—Zack, Hattie, Robert, Theodore, and Rufe (Martha and George, the two remaining of the seven, had died in childhood)—they seem from the beginning to have been outside the sphere of their stepmother's control. Their strongly marked individualities had already been defined and shaped by the time their father married again. They had inherited, in liberal measure, his own strong character, his arrogant confidence in his own powers, a good measure of his color, his independence, his intelligence, his coarse and swingeing humor, his quick wit.

There is no evidence that they were consciously contemptuous of their new mother, but there is no doubt they felt superior to her. Even in a backwoods community theirs was a larger, bolder, more tolerant and experienced view of life than she had ever known; and her narrow prejudice, her cramped vision, her rigid small moralities (all products of an inheritance she couldn't help) simply amused them, aroused their ridicule and mirth.

Zachariah, especially, although in later years he always spoke feelingly of her excellent qualities, was particularly active in his humorous analysis of her. Her superstitions and prejudices amused him; the operations of her mind, and the narrow cells of her morality seemed grotesque and ludicrous to him; and he questioned, teased, examined her rather cruelly in order, as he said, "to see what made her tick."

Hers, indeed, poor woman, was a strange and contradictory code, and yet, because it was the only one she knew, she thought it was the only one there was: it seemed natural to her, and it never occurred to her to question it.

That harsh code to which she adhered was indigenous to America. It has not only done much to shape our lives and histories, but it persists to this day, and is at the root of much of the sickness, the moral complex of America. For example, she believed it was wrong to take a life "in cold blood," but it was not nearly so wrong as to take a drink. She was always warning her children against evil ways and loose living, and speaking of people who committed "all kinds of immorality and licentiousness"; but it would have come strangely to her ears to hear murder referred to as an immoral act. True, it was "an awful crime"—she could understand it in these terms because the Bible told about Cain and Abel, and taught that it was wicked to take life. But, privately, she did not consider it half as bad for a man to take a life as to take a drink, or—what was the most immoral act of all—to sleep with a woman who was not his wife.

Life-taking, the shedding of man's blood, was so much a part of the life of a pioneer community that it occasioned no surprise. To be sure, she would not openly defend the practice of killing, although in a surprising number of individual cases she was willing to defend it, becoming quite aroused, in fact, when Zachariah, with deceptive gravity, would point out that her own brother—whose life in other ways she esteemed as a model of the Christian virtues—had been quite handy with his gun in his hot youth, and was known to have killed three men:

"Now, Zack," she would cry angrily, "don't you go a-diggin' into that. Reese had his faults, like everyone, and I reckon maybe in his young days he may have been hot-tempered. But he's always led a good Christian and God-fearin' sort of life. He never drank or smoked or used bad language or ran around with women —like *some* people I know about." Here she glared accusingly at her erring stepson, who returned her look with an expression of bland innocence. "So don't you start on him: he's always been an upright, moral sort of man."

All of this amused Zachariah no end: he did not mean to be cruel to her, but, as she said, he was "always tormenting" her, rummaging gravely about in the confusing rag-bag of her moral consciousness to see what further mysteries would be revealed.

He is known to have spoken of the physical sharpness of her sense of smell, which really was amazing, and which all of her children inherited (she is said one time to have "smelled burning leaves five miles away upon the mountain, long before anyone else knowed there was a fire"):

"Well, she can smell fire and brimstone farther off than that. And Hell! If I took a drink in Libya Hill, she'd smell it on my breath before I crossed the county line!"

On another occasion, she is said to have called out to him the moment that he came into the house: "Zack Joyner! You've been drinkin' that bad, old, rotten, vile corn licker again. I can smell it on your breath!"

"Now, mother," he answered temperately, "there is no bad, old, rotten, vile corn licker. Some is good—" he went on in a tone of

judicious appraisal that she must have found very hard to take—
"and some is better. But there is no bad!"

Again, when Bear Joyner returned from Libya Hill one day
with this announcement:

"Well, Thad Burton's gone and done it again!"

"Gone and done what?" said Zachariah, looking up.

"Gone and killed a man," Bear Joyner answered.

"Oh!" said Zachariah with a relieved air, casting a sly look toward his stepmother, "I was afraid you were goin' to tell me he'd
done something really bad, like gettin' drunk."

Bear Joyner was no less adept than his sons in this sport of
teasing his bewildered wife. It is said that having driven in with
her one day from Zebulon, to see the boys who at that time were
"keeping store" for him in Libya Hill, he went into the store and,
finding Zack on duty there, the following conversation then
took place between them:

"You boys been leadin' the Christ-life like your mother told you
to?"

"Yes, sir," Zachariah said.

"Have you done your chores this mornin'?"

"Yes, sir."

"Watered the milk?"

"Yes, sir."

"Sanded the sugar?"

"Yes, sir."

"*Fixed* the scales?"

"Yes, sir."

"Well," said Bear, "you'd better call in Ted and Bob. Your
mother's here, an' we're goin' to have prayers."

Finally, there was the case of Harriet—the "Miss Hattie" of
later years, for she never married—to add to the confusion and
distress of William Joyner's second wife. Of all Bear Joyner's

children, Hattie was the favorite. In her, perhaps, more than in any of the others he saw the qualities—the quick wit, the humor, the independence and intelligence—that in himself he most esteemed. It has been said she was his "love child"—a euphemism maybe for the fact that she was illegitimate—and that this accounted for her father's deeper care. At any rate, although her birth was hidden in an obscurity that was never cleared—for old Bear Joyner never spoke of it, and no one dared to speak of it to him—she was brought up as a member of his elder brood. The story goes that he was gone one time for several weeks upon a journey to the south, and that when he returned he brought the child with him. She was almost eight years old then, and Martha, the first wife, was still alive. The story goes that Joyner brought the child into the house—the family was at dinner, and the faces of the other children wonderingly turned—and sat her down beside them at the table.

"This," he said, "is your new sister. From this time on, she'll be one of the family, and you'll treat her so."

And this is all that was ever spoken. It is said that Martha, Joyner's first wife, took the child as one of her own; and in justice to the second wife, no matter what additional distress and confusion this new proof of Joyner wickedness may have caused that bewildered woman's soul, it was always freely acknowledged, most loyally of all by Harriet herself, as a further tribute to the woman's qualities, that she was a good mother, and brought the girl up as if she were "one of her own."

Historically, time-periods are most curiously defined: the world does not grow up together. The footpads that made Johnson carry his stick at night when he went out alone in London in the Eighteenth Century have been quite actively abroad in recent years in our own land. And as for "human life," a commodity which our editorial writers tell us they most jealously esteem, the security of human life in our own broad land—whether from murder, violence, or sudden death of every kind soever—is perhaps *almost* as great in America at the present time as it was in England at the period of Elizabeth, although our figures are by far the more bloody of the two.

And as for our own Dick Whittingtons—our country boys who went to town—there, too, we ape the European pattern; but we have been late.

The history of human celebrity for the most part is an urban one. In our own land, although children are taught that most of their great men "came from the country," it is not sufficiently emphasized that most of them also "went to town." Certainly, this has been true in America: the national history could almost be written in the lives of men who went to town.

Zachariah Joyner, in his later years, was very fond of using the log-cabin theme for politics, but if he had been more true to fact, he would have admitted that the turning point in his own career had come when he abandoned finally the world-lost fastnesses of Zebulon for the more urban settlement of Libya Hill. There, truly, was *his* starting point, his threshold, the step from which he gained his vantage, took off for the larger community of public life and general notice in which for fifty years he was to play so large a role.

And, in various ways, the same transitional experience was true of his more immediate family—his three brothers, who came with him. In one sense the whole history of the many Joyners, their divided lot and the boundary that separated the lowly from the great, might be stated in one phrase. It was the history of those who stayed at home, and of those who went to town.

As the years passed, the division of each group became more widely marked, the sense of unity more faint and far. Hill-bound, world-lost, locked in the narrow valleys and the mountain walls of Zebulon, the Joyners who remained at home became almost as strange and far away to those who lived in Libya Hill as if their home had been the Mountains of the Moon. True, they lived only fifty miles away, but as Bear Joyner had himself said so many years before, it was "the wrong way." It really was this sense of two directions that divided them. The Libya Hill Joyners were facing ever toward the world, and those in Zebulon away from it; and as years went by, it seemed that this directiveness became more marked than ever—the town Joyners ever more the world's men; those in Zebulon more withdrawn from the world.

By 1900, a whole century since William Joyner crossed the Blue Ridge and came down into the wilderness with his rifle and his grant of land, if some curious historian, gifted with immortality, could have returned there, he would have observed a change as startling as it was profound. He would have found the lives of the town Joyners (for by this time Libya Hill had grown to twelve thousand people) so greatly altered as to be scarcely recognizable; but he would have found the lives of the country Joyners scarcely changed at all.

True, some changes had occurred in Zebulon in those hundred years, but for the most part these were tragic ones. The great mountain slopes and forests of the section had been ruinously detimbered; the farm-soil on hill sides had eroded and washed down; high up, upon the hills, one saw the raw scars of old mica pits, the dump heaps of deserted mines. Some vast destructive "Suck" had been at work here; and a visitor, had he returned after one hundred years, would have been compelled to note the ruin of the change. It was evident that a huge compulsive greed had been at work: the whole region had been sucked and gutted, milked dry, denuded of its rich primeval treasures: something blind and ruthless had been here, grasped, and gone. The blind scars on the hills, the denuded slopes, the empty mica pits were what was left.

And true, the hills were left—with these deteriorations; and all around, far-flung in their great barricades, the immense wild grandeur of the mountain wall, the great Blue Ridge across which they had come long, long ago; and which had held them from the world.

And the old formations of the earth were left: the boiling clamor of the rocky streams, the cool slant darkness of the mountain hollows. Something wild, world-lost, and lyrical, and special to the place called Zebulon was somehow left: the sound of rock-bright waters, birds calls, and something swift and fleeting in a wood; the way light comes and goes; cloud shadows passing on a hill; the wind through the hill grasses, and the quality of light— something world-lost, far, and haunting (special to the place as is the very climate of the soil) in the quality of light; and little shacks and cabins stuck to hill or hollow, sunken, tiny, in the gap; the small, heart-piercing wisps of smoke that coiled into the clear immensity of weather from some mountain shack, with its poignant evidence that men fasten to a ledge, and draw their living from a patch of earth—because they have been here so long and love it and cannot be made to leave; together with lost voices of one's kinsmen long ago—all this was left, but their inheritance was bare. Something had come into the wilderness, and had left the barren land.

And the people—ah, the people!—yes, the people! ——

They were left! They were left "singing the same songs" (as college Doctors of Philosophy so gloatingly assure us) "their Elizabethan forebears sang"—which is a falsehood; and no glory— they should have made new and better ones for themselves.

"Speaking the same tongue" their Elizabethan forebears spoke—which also is a falsehood; and they should have made a new one for themselves. "Living the same lives" their forebears lived a hundred years ago—which further is a falsehood. The lives their forebears lived were harsh and new, still seeking and explorative; their own lives often were just squalid, which should have been better.

What remained? It has been said, "The earth remains." But this was wrong. The earth had changed, the earth had eroded, the earth had washed down the gulleys in a billion runnels of red clay; the earth was gone.

But the people—ah, the people!—yes, the people! The people were still there!

Turned backwards now, world-lost, in what was once new land! Unseeking now, in what their forebears with blue vistas in their eyes, alone, in Indian country, sought! Turned in upon themselves, congruent as a tribe, all intermarried (so each man now was cousin to the very blood he took: each Cain among them brother to his very deed!) ——

The people!—aye, the people! The people of Zack Joyner, and old Bear, who sought a world, and *found* it, that such as these might lose it; had wandered so that such as these should *stay*; had sought great vistas to the West, so that such as these remain ——

The people! To be gloated over by exultant Ph.D's (who find in mountain shacks the accents of Elizabeth); to be gawked at by tourists (now the roads are good) in search of the rare picturesque; to be yearned over by consecrated school-marms "from the North"; have their "standards" "improved" by social service workers, who dote upon the squalor, ignorance, and poverty; lasciviously regret the degradations of the people's lot, and who do valiantly their little bit (God bless their little, little souls!)

ro help the people, teach the people, prop the people, *heal* the people, with their little salves (not too completely, else what are little salves and social service work about?)—and who therefore (in spite of dirt, filth, rickets, murder, lean-tos, children, syphilis, hunger, incest, and pellagra) love the people, adore the people, see underneath their "drawbacks" and their "lack of opportunities" all "the good" in people—because the people, at the bottom, "are so fine."

It is a lie! . . . Dear God! . . . Dear Jesus God, protect us, all men living, and the people, from such stuff as this!

The people are not "fine"—the people are not picturesque—the people——

Well, after a hundred years of it—denudings, minings, lootings, intermarryings, killings, dyings, bornings, livings, all the rest of it—the people—in spite of Smike, the lumber thief, who stole their hills; and Snead, his son, who stole their balladry; in spite of Gripe, who took their mica and their ore, and gave them "the lung-sickness" in exchange for it; despite Grace, Gripe's daughter, who now brings rubber condoms and tuberculin; and his wife, Gertrude, who schools them in hand-weaving—despite Gripe, Smike, and Grace, and all lovers of the picturesque soever—despite rickets, incest, syphilis, and sham—the people!—ah, the people!—well, the *peuple*——

"Why, goddamn it!" Zachariah Joyner roared— "I'll tell you what the people are! . . . The people . . . the *people*! . . . Why, goddamn it, sir, the people are the *people*!"

And so they are!—Smike, Gripe, rickets, Grace, and Snead— all forces to the contrary notwithstanding.

The people are the people.

And the Joyners—second Joyners; the humble, world-lost Joyners out in Zebulon—they're the people!

Chapter 4

HOW CERTAIN JOYNERS WENT TO TOWN

BEAR JOYNER WAS WHAT WOULD BE CALLED TODAY "A forward-looking man." He had not been settled down in Zebulon very long before he began to regret the choice that had brought him there, saying: "Hit's too *fer back*! Hit's purty, but you can't git *out*!"

Here was the spirit of the empire-builder. He was not, in his own phrase, a man to "crawl into a hole and pull it in after him." If there was an "in," there must also be an "out"—and soon after he came to Zebulon he began to look for it.

During the next twenty years his life was punctuated by his explorations, which, comparatively short though they were, were most significant. Throughout those two decades, restless, seeking, forever unsatisfied, he was still "looking for the place." In this period of his early manhood he seems to have been regarded with misgivings by his neighbors in Zebulon, especially by the older and more conservative element. His good qualities—his energy, his skill, his strength, and his intelligence—were recognized and esteemed, but there was a strong suspicion that he was by temperament a rolling stone, and that his worldly fortunes would never flourish because he would not stay at home long enough to allow them to take root.

At first, his life was that of the woodsman and trapper. He fished, he hunted, and he had his little patch of land where he

could grow such food as he needed. Wild game, including bear
and venison, was plentiful. Even after his first marriage, this is
the way he continued to live, in the cabin on the south fork
of the Toe.

But in those early years, as people told it later, he was forever
"up and gone." He would go off on long hunting trips, or on
mysterious expeditions into the surrounding country. Sometimes
these journeys took him into Tennessee, or down to South Carolina, or eastward across the Blue Ridge to the Piedmont, or even
far north into Virginia. He would be gone for days, sometimes
for weeks, "leavin' that woman out thar all alone." There were
forebodings and grave shakings of the head; but while the
others stayed at home, Bear Joyner saw new lands.

People admitted freely that he "knew more about this country"
than any other person living there. And his restless explorations
were to bear fruit in unsuspected ways. Gradually he acquired
a kind of gigantic mental blueprint of the whole region for a
hundred miles around, until there was scarcely a stream, a creek,
a valley, or a hollow in that vast wilderness which he did not
know. Little by little, his knowledge began to define itself more
clearly and to shape his moves, until at last it led him to Libya
Hill.

Libya Hill is a sort of great encampment in the hills, the tenting
ground of the Blue Ridge. It is on a high plateau, close-held
against the east, and again in semi-circles to the north and south,
by a border of low hills, but opening to the west, and the soaring
vistas of the western ranges forty miles away. The great ranges
come down to the rolling slopes of Libya Hill like lions to a
water-hole; and westward, northward, southward, eastward, in
smoky vistas the great ranges soar away. When Bear Joyner

first saw it he said, as Brigham Young was to say a little later of another spot: "This is the place."

It was, indeed, of all that mountain district of the west, "the place." It was a natural confluence of the hills, the junction of the four directions of the map—the appointed, the inevitable, place. A river, broader than any of the small streams of Zebulon, wound through the passes of the hills into the West. Along the narrow valley of another winding stream another road was open to the East. Here was the place, not only where the world got out, but also where the world got in.

Bear Joyner saw this; and here at last, for him, was journey's end. From this time on, the story of his life is the story of his withdrawings out of Zebulon toward this chosen place. In the end he took the four sons of his first marriage with him; and he left the rest behind. The Joyners at last had come to town. Thence dates the final schism of the clan, as well as the beginning of its greater history.

By 1828 Bear Joyner owned the country store in Libya Hill— the largest one in the whole section—and thenceforth his fortunes were secure. In the years that followed, before the end of his long life, he bought up various tracts of land, and these were ultimately dispersed among the "four town Joyners" who became his heirs.

Indeed, as recently as sixty years ago, when Libya Hill had grown to perhaps two thousand people, the Joyner heirs still held large tracts of land. And even in this present century children were familiar with the regretful recollections of their elders, who could recall when "Rufus Joyner offered me that whole block— from where the Palais Royal now stands all the way down to the Post Office corner—for *two hundred dollars*! And I was such a fool I didn't take it! If I had, I'd have been a rich man today. You couldn't buy it now for a million dollars! But then—why, I just laughed at him. It was nothing but an old field, with a pig pen in the hollow, and the hogs used to wallow in the mud where Main Street is today. Two hundred dollars for that hole? I thought Rufe Joyner must be crazy; or else he took me for a fool. 'All right,' he said. 'You wait and see.' Well, I waited, and I did!"

By the time the Civil War broke out the Joyners were accounted wealthy folk. It was "the big family" of the whole community. Even long before that their position was so generally acknowledged throughout the western mountains that when the boys began to "make their mark," it occasioned no surprise.

When Zack Joyner was Governor of the state, and later United States Senator, he was fond of saying, for purposes political, that he had been "raised on hawg and hominy."

"I have known what it was," he would say, warming up to his subject, and dropping into the mountain idiom for the benefit of his delighted followers—"I've known what it was, boys, to go to bed on bacon and awake on grits. Yes, and I've known what it was to go to bed and to git up without either of 'em. I have clumb the persimmon tree many's the time to shrink my belly up to fit my rations, so don't talk to me of no hard times. I can go right out into the cornfield or the tobacco patch today and spit on my hands and keep up with any man that's settin' here tonight. If I was twenty years younger, I'd give ye all a head start and beat ye."

Like so many other specimens of political autobiography, this was a good deal less than accurate. Far from being the barefoot and half-starved infant born in a humble cabin—the image which he was fondest of evoking—Zack had been brought up under circumstances which were amazingly comfortable for the time and place. Before he was half grown, his father was already considered well off and was one of the leading citizens of the town. Zack's public statements about himself were simply part of the legend which he created, and which helped to create him—the legend of the backwoods savior, the country Moses, schooled by poverty, hardship, solitude, and the precepts of a stern and homely virtue, until at last he had been ready to come out of the wilderness and lead his people into the promised land.

In elaboration of the log-cabin theme, Zack would say that "all the schoolin' I ever had would not amount to three months put together, and even then I had to walk six miles for what I got." This, too, was part of the myth on which great Zachariah's life was founded. Privately, he would confess that he knew how to "read and write and cipher" before he came to Libya Hill. And there is proof that he, along with Theodore and Robert, attended school in Libya Hill for some time under the tutelage of a pedagogue who was always referred to later by the Joyners with considerable respect as "Old Professor Coleman." Zack managed to learn, among other things, a smattering of Latin, for even in his old age he could quote from *Caesar's Gallic Wars*.

In talking with his closer friends, he would admit something of the truth and say good-naturedly: "Well, it wasn't a great deal, but it was something. Bob, Ted, and I learned how to read and write and cipher. And *Uriah!*"—this was his familiar name for Rufus when his older brother was not present (an indication that he knew his Dickens, too)—"Uriah," chuckled Zack, "he never took the time to read or write, but, by God!"—here his shoulders would begin to heave—"*Uriah* always did know how to cipher!"

Rufus, the oldest of the four, was, by general consent and his own choice, the storekeeper of the crowd. Of his career, all that need be set forth here are the bare facts. And the bare facts in Rufe's case are peculiarly appropriate, for his was a bare life, a grooved life, a hard-bitten, steady, quiet life which from first to last, with one exception, was to run on a single track. The great exception, of course, was the Civil War. When the call came he went to war, he lived through the war, he came back from the war, and that was the only interruption that his purpose suffered. And his purpose was business. His purpose was money. That was all he ever did or thought about. He never married. He carried on his father's business, he built it into a really great enterprise, and he became a rich man. Of any man, perhaps all that can be truly said when his life is done is that "he lived, he suffered, and he died." With the same succinct finality it would later be said of Rufus: "He made money, and he died."

Meanwhile he lived in his father's old house on College Street. Eventually his lusty, gusty, old-maid sister, Hattie, came from Zebulon to keep house for him. But not all the wit and savor, the irrepressible spirits and joy of living that animated the sprightly figure of Miss Hattie Joyner could ever deflect Rufus from his grim purpose. Even in his youth his stinginess was proverbial, and in his old age his brother, Zachariah, then also hale and sere, had no hesitation in proclaiming it:

"Why, he's so mean," Zack roared, "he wouldn't —— down a preacher's throat if his guts were on fire! If you fell down and broke your leg he wouldn't come across the street to help you because of the shoe leather he'd use up. He stops the clocks at night to keep the cogs from wearing out, and when he goes to church he puts a two-cent stamp in the collection plate and takes back a penny's change!"

Hattie, who was more like Zachariah in her ribald humor than any of the others, and who outlived all of them, would cackle gleefully and say: "Just wait till that old skinflint dies! I'll beat him yet—even if I have to live to be a hundred. When he's gone I'm goin' to open up the purse strings and let the moths fly out! I tell you, I'm just waitin' till he dies *to cut loose and raise hell!*"

In the course of this chronicle we have mentioned the fact that old Bear Joyner had some fourteen or sixteen children by his second wife, all of whom were left behind in Zebulon when their father came to Libya Hill. He did not exactly leave them, for he was always going back for visits—the point is that he did not bring them with him, and they did not have gumption enough to insist on coming. We have not yet had occasion to tell about these members of the lesser breed, although they all had Christian names like other folk. Of those who survived the rigors of infancy and childhood there were, among the girls, Betsy, Alice, Melissa, and Florabelle, and, among the boys, Lafayette, Sam, John, Claudius, Sid, and Rance. Insofar as they get into our story, each of these shall have his due in time. For the present they will have to look after themselves. We have left them behind in the fastnesses of Zebulon County where they made their bed, and there they will have to lie in it. They would not come along with us. They did not have it in them to push on with the Joyners of the great will, the great spirit, the great determination. Therefore we shall now leave them to the honorable but mute oblivion of unrecorded history, and shall forget about them until the turn of events compels us to seek them out again.

Suffice it to say that they grew up and married and had children and grandchildren. They tilled the soil, they grew much corn and tobacco, they timbered the rugged slopes of Zebulon for Smike, the lumber thief, and mined for feldspar and for mica in the wretched pay of Gripe, Smike's brother, until the very wilderness which had been their sole inheritance became scarred and barren. They despoiled the land, and were in turn themselves despoiled. But still they were very worthy and honest people. There were few horse thieves among them, and only two or three of them got hanged. Just the same, it must be owned that they were small potatoes. They did not join the Joyners of the greater breed. They never went to town—none of them, that is, except for Lafayette, and he came late, and the reasons for his coming were of quite another order from those which had moved his half-brothers years before. But of that, more anon. To everything its season, and our story now concerns the Joyners of the first coming.

To be sure, it was not very much of a town that these first Joyners came to—unless "a hole in the road," a log courthouse of one room, a log church, a general store, a hitching post, and a ramshackle tavern for itinerant drovers could be called a town. But the fact remains that town it was—town in the core, in the making, in the process of becoming. Libya Hill was at that time the only semblance of a town that the whole mountain district could boast of.

When Bear Joyner became the owner of the general store and his fortunes began to flourish, he gave to his four favorite sons the education that each was fitted for. While Rufus settled down to keeping store like one who had been born for it, Zachariah, Robert, and Theodore were sent away, in turn, to college.

At just what time in Zachariah's formative years the idea of the law as a career first came to him, it is impossible to say; but it came early, and the choice was inevitable. As a boy of eighteen, when he was helping Rufe to "tend store" for their father, he was already noted for his ready wit, his coarse humor, and his gift of repartee. People would come into the store "just to hear Zack Joyner talk."

And even in that backwoods community there was a pretty shrewd appraisal of him from the first. Already people suspected, or observed, more than a trace of charlatanism in his make-up. It was said: "He can talk you *out* or talk you *in* to anything."

Among other tendencies that many noticed in him was a certain indisposition to hard work. Bear Joyner himself was well aware of this, because he said: "Well, I don't know what to do with him unless I make a lawyer of him. He won't *work*—that's certain." Here he paused a moment; then he grinned and added: "But he won't starve, neither. Not Zack."

It may be that there is wisdom in the observation of the showman that "the people like to be fooled." Anyhow, the experience of Zack Joyner's life would seem to bear this out. For the very basis of his amazing political success lay in the people's *awareness* of him: not only the fact that they knew him so well, but also that he was so much *of* them, as if they felt him to be, in some special way, their own. And among the qualities which people seemed most to admire in Zack, and to be proud of rather than otherwise, was his tincture of charlatanism and smooth dealing. They loved to tell stories to illustrate Zack's smartness, his adeptness, his superior adroitness and cunning, and men would wag their heads and laugh with envious approval, as though they wished they could do such things themselves, but knew, being merely average men, that they could not make the grade.

So Zack was sent away for a year of legal training at Pine Rock College (a year was considered ample in those days). Bob followed him there and also had his year of training for the law. Then both boys returned home again, were admitted to the bar, and hung out their shingle as the firm of Joyner and Joyner. By 1840 they were enjoying a thriving practice. For in that day the fact that the two Joyner boys had become full-fledged lawyers —this very same Zack and Bob whom everybody in town had known and liked and watched grow up—was quite a thing to marvel at and feel a sense of personal pride in.

Lawyers, of course—that articulate tribe which was to breed and multiply with such astonishing proliferation during the next century—were not utterly foreign to the little town. From its beginnings Libya Hill had been the county seat, and had had its courthouse, its circuit judges, and its trials for thirty years or more. But the Joyners were the first lawyers to come of local stock. The others heretofore had been imported.

These other lawyers had come in to the sessions of the court from older and more populous communities beyond the Blue Ridge—from Old Stockade, from Millerton, from Locust Gap— and occasionally from still larger towns farther east, down in the Piedmont. They had come in by stage, by coach, by horse and saddle. They had ccme in with their frocktails parted across the cruppers of their horses, with long and spindly legs hung loosely down around the shining flanks. They had come in with their jaws lank and learned, their thin lips closed, their cold eyes ruminant and speculative, narrowed into slits, their saddlebags stuffed with all the cunning of their accursed and incessant papers. They had come in and dismounted and tied up at the hitching post before the log courthouse, had swung their bony hands beneath their coattails and carried in the saddlebags and unpacked their papers, and then had spoke strange words— strange words of depth and learning no one else could understand. While all the helpless natives looked on and gaped their wonderment, the great men cleared their throats and uttered strange and mystic words and shuffled their accursed papers in their parchment fingers. And, so speaking and so doing, they had then departed, leaving native awe behind them, taking with them native fees.

Now this was changed. The Joyner boys had gone away beyond the Blue Ridge, farther off than anyone else had ever been, had seen strange peoples and strange cities, and had got much learning—deep learning, lawyer learning—and now could speak and write the mystic words that no one else could read, that no one but the Joyners or another lawyer could even make out the sense of. Zack and Bob, as everybody owned, were smart—had always been—and now that they had learned nearly everything there was to know, they had come back to town and could hold their own with any other of the lawyer crew—in fact, could say words as big and deep and dark as any other lawyer in the world. And people marveled that the Joyners were their very own. They themselves had produced the Joyners. Accordingly they felt, not only the humility of awe, but the pride of ownership and the ecstasy of submission. Everyone had the satisfaction of knowing that hereafter if he was going to be eaten by a shark, it would be one of his own choosing that had grown in native waters.

Zack and Bob, therefore, were now in clover. They had the inestimable advantage, not only of belonging, but of being in at the beginning. Before very long they were enjoying what was practically a monopoly of their chosen profession and were doing most of the legal work of the entire mountain region.

It was a curious paradox, though, that these two brothers, sprung from the same seed, brought up in exactly the same way, educated to the same degree as far as formal training went, and set upon the parallel courses of their lives at precisely the same point, were to have such widely divergent careers. From the first, their natures inclined them to seek different objectives.

It was the primary fact of Robert's nature, once he became interested in the law, to study it profoundly, to pierce beyond the letter to the spirit of the thing, and to see it as an adaptive instrument of the common good. Once he had made up his mind to be a lawyer, he concentrated all his fine qualities of character and intellect upon the single goal of making himself into the very best lawyer it was in him to be. From that point on, it never entered his head to want to be anything else.

Zack, however, was never seriously interested in the law. Oh, he wanted to be a lawyer right enough, and as a trial lawyer he became one of the best, with a courtroom manner that could sweep a jury completely off its feet even when the weight of evidence was against him. Yes, he wanted to be a lawyer, but he wanted it not because he loved the law, but because he loved something else a great deal more and saw in the law the surest means of getting it. And what Zack really wanted more than anything in life was to be a politician. That was the role he had been born for. All his talents fitted him for it as for nothing else. The law, therefore, was just a stepping stone for Zack, and a very handy one it proved to be.

In the general estimation, even back in the days of their earliest practice together, Robert was always the most respected, the most trusted; but Zachariah was by all odds the most popular, the most loved. And already Zack's feet were firmly planted on the rungs of the political ladder. It did not hurt his chances of success for people to say, as they were now saying: "The man that beats Zack Joyner'll have to git up early and stay up late." He was, throughout his life, the hero of the crowd.

Robert, on the other hand, never played up to an audience. Quiet, blunt, plain-spoken whenever there was need for plain speaking, he was first and last a forthright and an honest man. His purposes he kept forever single, and already those few who knew him well were predicting for him a useful, and indeed a noble, career. How useful and how noble, not even they could have foretold, but it was written in the stars that such a man as Robert, in a profession which is so frequently besmirched by base and shady uses, could not fail to distinguish himself upon the bench. And so, in time, he did, as we shall see.

Meanwhile both brothers married, and chose their mates well. Robert married rather late in life and had an only son, who in-

herited both his father's character and the delicate sensitivity of
his mother. Zachariah, despite a robust predilection for pretty
women, married young, and he surprised some people by remaining constant to his wife until the end of her days. He became the
devoted father of three lovely daughters, and of a son in whom he
took great pride.

The difference between these two brothers became more and
more marked with the passage of time. And strange to say, it
never brought them into conflict. Their talents were complemen-
tary, and each man respected the other for what he was. For
Zack, in spite of the deliberate charlatanism of speech and manner
which so endeared him to the people, had a solid inner core of
sincerity which even such a completely upright man as Robert
could respect. Thus each was equipped to fulfill his destiny,
but in their later years, even after Zachariah had risen to the
place of highest eminence in the state, people would still say:

"Zack Joyner will promise you the moon, and you'll be lucky
if you get green cheese. Bob Joyner won't even promise cheese;
but you're likely to get *something* in the end."

Often those communities which are most ruthless in their
violation of the law are also the most devout in their respect for
it. Of no section has this been truer than of the South. Almost
from the beginning, among rich and poor alike, the profession
of the law has been esteemed above all others. With people of
the wealthier class, it represented the most approved and honorable alternative to the other career of plantation agriculture; and;
of course, an incomparable advance over the almost ignominious
last resort of trade. To the sons of poorer people, the hardy products of small tenantry and the descendants of the mountain white,
it represented an even higher goal—the highest goal they could
attain. For, to such people as Zack Joyner, to such people as

the more able, fortunate, and intelligent children of old Bear, the law represented almost the only possible means of escape from an environment and from a life that could promise nothing more than the narrow world of backwoods isolation, and the reward of a bare living, hardly gained.

In this way, it came to be accepted almost without question among mountain folk that the most gifted of their sons would, if possible, get into the profession of the law. The lawyer was a kind of medicine man to the community. To his ruder, simpler, and less talented contemporaries, he was the man of learning and of argument, the man of reason and of fluent speech. He was the man to wear good clothes, to have white hands, to live in a good house, and to be vested with the honors and rewards of high authority by his less fortunate fellows, because his talents and accomplishments entitled him to them.

The evil of this system—an evil that has become widespread, rooted in the very structure of the nation's life—is instantly apparent. It offered to many unscrupulous men, under the protections of a high authority, the opportunity to prey upon their neighbors—neighbors who were not endowed with their own shrewdness, smoothness, gift of gab, and formal training, and who, by the conditions of the system, were forced to seek recourse for their troubles from the very men who preyed on them. Not that the lawyers themselves were inevitably and invariably dishonest men. But the system put a high premium on dishonesty, and those lawyers who had integrity enough to resist the ever-present temptation to prey upon their neighbors were, at best, left in the unhappy position of being themselves a part of one of the basic functions of society that had been tainted at its source.

It was very unfortunate that from the beginnings of American life the profession of the law was commonly considered, not so much an end in itself, as a means to an end. And the end to which the law supplied the means was, in the final analysis, almost identical with the end of business—namely, personal advantage and private profit. With business, it did not matter so much, because, until recently, no one had ever supposed that business had a social purpose as well as a private one; and this was why, through all human history, business and trade had been looked down upon, and the business man condemned by lofty minds as the stinking, swinking fellow that he usually was. But the law, in theory at least, was supposed to be different from this. It represented one of the most elemental of social functions, and if private profit entered into its operations, this was supposed to be only incidental, in order that lawyers might eat. Actually, matters worked out quite otherwise in practice. Too often the end to which the law supplied the means was private profit, and the avenue by which one arrived at that end was politics, party conflict, candidacy, and election to public office.

In Zachariah Joyner's day, and in his own community, this process was considered so right and so inevitable that any variation from it seemed extraordinary. A lawyer who did not also "get into politics," or at least show a partisan and active interest in it, was a queer fish. So when Robert Joyner decided to stick to the law and refused to have any truck or traffic with politicians, people began to wonder about it; and when they could find no satisfactory explanation of his extraordinary conduct, they shook their heads and said he was a fine man, of course, but a little queer. There was nothing queer about Zack. When he began to get into politics he was doing exactly what everyone naturally expected him to do. People not only understood, they enthusiastically approved, and showed their approval by voting for him the first chance they got.

The course which Zack followed was the accepted procedure throughout the greater part of the nation. It is still the standard procedure. And the social implications of this fact are enormous. For, from the very beginnings of American life, there seems to have been a general assumption among the majority of the population that the functions of the law and of justice were divergent, and perhaps quite incompatible and hostile to each other. This accounted for the grotesque paradox that in such communities as that from which Zachariah Joyner came, where lawlessness, personal violence, and the taking of human life flourished in their most extreme and savage forms, respect for "the law" was curiously deep-seated and profound. People in such communities felt instinctively that justice was a personal matter, and that the ends of justice could only be individually secured; but that the law was a political and public matter, and that its purposes and concerns had better be left as far as possible to the unpredictable operation of its mysterious machinery.

Thus a man would kill another man to get justice for himself; but he would go to court to keep from being hanged for it. Anyone who has ever attended a murder trial in a mountain community—such a trial as Zack Joyner attended hundreds of times, and took part in as counsel for prosecution or defense; such a trial, indeed, as is still being enacted in Zebulon today—must have observed the astonishing illustration of this paradox.

A man has killed another man, with whom there has been "bad blood" for years; and now he is on trial for his life, and the entire community has come to witness and take part. On one side, at a rude table, are seated the attorneys for the state, and the private counsel which the family of the murdered man has employed to help the state in prosecuting of its case. On the other side, at another similar table, are marshaled the battery of attorneys which the family of the accused man has engaged to defend him, and to secure, if possible, a verdict of acquittal.

Behind these two batteries of embattled legal talent, separated from them only by a low wooden barrier, upon the front rows of battered seats, are clustered the many witnesses whom both the prosecution and the defense have summonsed in support of their own arguments—the wives, friends, brothers, children, relatives, and neighbors who have some evidence to contribute. And behind them, crowding the rows of battered seats, packed in the dusty aisles, pressed into the rear four-deep, jammed so thick and dense that they are not able to move in the suffocating atmosphere of mid-July, is as much of the blue-shirted, faded-overalled, and gingham-bonneted community as the dingy whitewashed room will hold.

In the center, upon a small raised platform, the presiding judge sits at his desk—sometimes a table. To his left is the witness box and the clerk of the court. To his right, the court stenographer. Behind him, tacked to the whitewashed wall, are the Stars and Stripes. And to his left again, upon two rows of chairs, are the twelve men selected for a jury after a three days' inquisition by the contending forces of attorneys: selected from a whole army of veniremen, one hundred in all, such men as these in Zebulon— be-whiskered, overalled, blue-shirted—summonsed and brought in from another county, because everyone in Zebulon, in one fashion or another, is related. In some distant way, even the murdered man is a cousin of the man who sits here now accused of killing him. And the feeling is too high, the passions too fierce—the skein of prejudice, family loyalties, and clannishness; the dense web of more than a hundred years of intermarrying, of conflicts gone but not forgotten, of feuds long past but never dead—it is all too complex and too dangerous to find here a jury that could pass impartial judgment.

The whole thing is as deadly and as thrilling in the naked impact of its social forces as anything on earth can be. The air is electric with its tension; one feels that if a match were struck, the whole place might explode. For everything is here—not only the whole present life of the community, packed, tense, and crowded, stripped down at length to the naked trial of this hour—but the whole history of man is here: his own life, and the life of all his neighbors, the lives of his fathers and his kinsmen and of all who have gone before him.

And with it all, at the very peak and crest of this desperate and final hour, one feels upon all sides, from both groups, among all parties and all partisans, a curious impassivity. Passion leashed there is, the unforgiving will to kill, and kill again, to get full measure of reprisal—an eye for an eye, a tooth for a tooth, a brother for a brother, and a friend for a friend—and yet, with it all, a curious, fatal, deadly impassivity of judgment. For passion belongs to justice, passion shall come later on—and there shall be again a time for justice and vengeance and for blood of murdered men.

But now it is a question of "the law." The law has spoken, the law must have now its full day in court, according to all the devices of its operations, and according to the schedule of its own particular machinery. And these people, every woman, man, and child of them, in this way, in this astounding way, understand, respect, and make a separate place in their own judgment for the law and for its judgments. And in such ways as these, no other folk on earth so deeply understand the law; for, in such ways as these, it has been rooted in their lives, as much a part of them as the very air they breathe, the very speech they speak— yes! the very justice that they take upon themselves and execute, the very vengeance that they so secure.

The trial begins, in such a scene as this—a scene that has not changed an atom since the days when Zachariah Joyner knew it, and took his part in it—a scene which, with all its strange and terrible contradictions, is somehow as memorable and as moving as it is thrilling; for in it, somehow, is the whole enigma of our violent and tormented life—the huge complex of America, with all its innocence and guilt, its justice and its cruelty, its lawlessness and its law.

There at his table sits the judge, a white-haired man, with his string necktie, his boiled shirt, his dark clothes—the quiet vestments of his high authority. Blood of their blood, bone of their bone, kin of their kin—the whole story of their thousand feuds, the knowledge of all their passions and their guilts, together with the very names of each of them, are as familiar to him as the names of his own sons. And he sits in judgment there above the raging furnace of that packed and very quiet hell—not only a man of their own people, but, as the trial proceeds, a man of wisdom and of courage, a splendid and impartial embodiment of law. Here, too, the years have not changed man—for this judge is the same kind of man as Robert Joyner, who sat here, in such trials as these, sixty years ago.

And now the charge is read, the fatal question asked and answered. From the left side of the court, the state rises, and the trial begins. The state's witnesses are called forward. Uneasy, awkward, they shuffle in around the wooden rail—a snag-toothed mountain woman, with a harelip and a bewildered look; a stupid shag-haired fellow with a blunted face; another, small, compact, contained, soft-voiced, with furtive eyes; another, with an uneasy look of divided loyalties; another, grim, determined-looking; some others of this kind; then the murdered man's pregnant wife, large, oily-eyed, and swollen featured—they are all sworn in together, with their right hands dividing three battered books. The first is called into the box; the state Solicitor arises, and the trial is on.

"Where were you on the night of May 14, a little before eight o'clock?" The very words and phrases since Zack Joyner's day have not changed a jot. In kind, not even the Solicitor has changed. This was Zack Joyner's job before him: it's how they begin.

The Solicitor is a young man now, in his mid-thirties, well-made, of something more than middle height—five feet eleven, we should guess—one hundred and eighty pounds of him, abundant, curly hair, by nature crisp, tinged reddish brown. It is a strong face, too, the angles well-defined, high-boned; the jaw strong, competent, jutting out a little; the long lip touched with humor and belligerency—the whole Scotch-Irish, long upper lip more Irish than Scotch. He is already schooled in the manner of the country lawyer, the country politician, still bearing with him traces of high school debate, and subsequent experiments in commencement oratory. He is already able to refer to "the little log cabin where I was born"—or, in somewhat more modern phrase, to "the farm where I grew up."

He's out to get "a good conviction." He admits it. The talk of justice doesn't enter in. A murder has been done—he knows that, so does the other side, and so does everyone. There's no debate in that; it is agreed. The only question now is: "How much?"

The first degree is "out." No one wastes time in talking of the first degree in Zebulon. There hasn't been a conviction in the first degree in Zebulon since before the Civil War. Zack Joyner got that one when he was Solicitor; and it was for rape. There's no first degree for murder out in Zebulon—the only question is: "How much?"

The Solicitor admits he has "a strong side" against him. The murderer is prominent, his family are "big people" in the county; his father back before him killed his man in youth, and his father was a highly respected citizen. The family has stood high, has great connections; to get a conviction will be hard.

Moreover, they have lined up the best murder lawyers that the western districts can provide—the killer's uncle, old man Martin, a good lawyer and a Baptist and a pillar of the church— he "knows the law"; Zeb Pendergraft, the best defense lawyer in the county; Whit Gardiner of Millerton; and several others.

But the long lip, and the smile, good-humored but belligerent, show the Solicitor's belief that he has a chance. It's going to be a hard fight, but he believes he has a chance to get a conviction in the second degree—from twelve to twenty years—and if he does, another feather in his cap. Twelve years for murder out in Zebulon, added to a mounting record. The pattern of his plan is set: a little later on he'll try the legislature; and after that, we'll see.

It hasn't changed a bit. The man could be Zack Joyner's twin. Even the degrees and stages, the necessary steps, haven't changed a bit since Joyner's day.

And now, the question asked—and from the other side, like an electric flash, the crackle of "Objection!" up and down the line. The leading forward of the witness step by step, the turning over of the witness to the thirsty jackals of the other side. Eyes turn: there is Zeb Pendergraft rocking back and forth in tilted chair, the red eyes and the alcoholic face inflamed and ready now. He tilts back and through his widened knees spits through discolored teeth a dribble of tobacco juice, rocks forward again and comes to rest, and, suddenly, the inflamed face thrust forward, the voice harsh and rasping as a saw, the bully of the murder courts is at his work—the work for which he gets his pay—the work for which he is invariably employed—the work that is his noted specialty.

"*You* know—" compacted equally of tearing rasp and overbearing sneer— "You *know* why you were there! Tell this court why you were there! Tell this court *why* you heard him! . . .

Isn't it true that you were there in jail yourself because you'd been arrested for being drunk? . . . You wouldn't *say* that? . . . Well then, what *would* you say? . . . And you don't even know how drunk you were—now, do you? You couldn't even tell this court where you got arrested, could you? . . . You were so drunk you don't even remember where it was now, do you? . . .

"How many times have you been on the chain gang? *Tell* this court how many times you've been on the chain gang. . . . You don't even *know* how many times, do you? . . . You wouldn't *say* that? . . . Well, come on then, and tell this court how many times you *think* it was. . . . Was it four? . . . Or six? . . . You wouldn't *say*? . . . Well, I'll tell the court. You've been on the chain gang six times, haven't you? . . . All told, you've served twenty months upon the gang—and *you're* here to testify against a man who is on trial for his life! . . . Why, your honor. . . ."

"Objection!" . . . "Objection sustained!" Or "Objection overruled!" . . . The duel crackles back and forth like flashes of artillery, the Solicitor tenacious, truculent, half-grinning; Pendergraft, a series of explosive flashes, a snarling rasp of scalding words, the inflamed cockerel of the out-thrust head, broken by deliberate tiltings back at interrupted intervals to shift his quid and spit deliberately downwards, between widened knees, his dribble of tobacco juice . . . while the currents of excitement, whispers, and taut interest, broken by the judge's warning gavel, flash through the crowd—and while the poor dumb creature, with stunned face and matted hair, squirms helplessly in his chair like a hooked fish.

The game goes on; the duel flashes back and forth—the Solicitor now alert to save the testimony of his challenged witness:

"Yes, and *tell* the court . . . tell the court just *why* you were on the chain gang all those times."

And at last, the poor tormented witling has his day:

"Fer gittin' drunk—" and quickly, with an out-jerked thumb toward Pendergraft—"just like *he* does all the time."

Then, instant and explosive, an approving roar, a guffaw of applause, hand-clapping, and the shout of sympathetic laughter from that overalled, blue-shirted crowd, as if the heart of simple and tormented man has found support—the warmth of its own kind against the thrusts and shrewd outwittings of the law. But the old judge is on his feet now, his gavel pounding on the table, his face red beneath his silver shock, with righteous wrath:

"If that occurs again, I'll clear the court! . . . If I knew who was responsible for this, I'd arrest you all for contempt of court. . . . Mr. Sheriff, I shall hold you responsible for any further outbreak or disturbance! . . . I order you to arrest anyone you see guilty of such disturbance, and if you have not enough men, I empower you to appoint deputies!" Sternly, more quietly, after a moment's pause, almost like a schoolmaster speaking to a classroom of unruly boys: "This is a court of law, and a man is on trial here for his life today! . . . This is a solemn occasion. . . . It is disgraceful that any of you should come here to treat it as if it were a circus!"

The court room is as silent as a tomb now: those overalled and blue-shirted men almost seem to hold their breath as the old man with the white hair looks at them. In a moment, when he sees that they are properly chastened and subdued, he resumes his seat, adjusts his spectacles, and says quietly:

"Mr. Solicitor, you may proceed with your examination."

It is all the same—the same great and thrilling drama of violence, crime, and human passion; the same drama of the human community, the great spectacle of "the law," in the process of its orderly enfoldment—the rapier duel of embattled wits, the rough-and-ready school of quick rejoinder, the school of hammer-and-tongs debate, fighting it out on the dusty floor of a country court room, in the rough and tumble of a battle for a man's life and liberty—while the whole concerted life of the community looks on.

It is the same today as it was in Zachariah Joyner's time. And this is the way he began, the school that taught him.

Chapter 5

THE PLUMED KNIGHT

THEODORE JOYNER WAS OLD BEAR'S YOUNGEST SON BY HIS FIRST marriage. As so often happens with the younger children of a self-made man, he got more education than the others. "And," said Zachariah whenever the fact was mentioned, "just *look* at him!" For, mingled with the Joyner reverence for learning, there was an equally hearty contempt among them for those who could not use it for some practical end.

Like his two more able brothers, Theodore had been destined for the law. He followed them to Pine Rock College and had his year of legal training. Then he "took the bar," and failed ingloriously; tried and failed again; and ——

"Hell!" old Bear said disgustedly—"hit looked like he wa'nt fit fer nothin' else, so I jest sent him back to school!"

The result was that Theodore returned to Pine Rock for three years more, and finally succeeded in taking his diploma and bachelor's degree. Hence his eventual reputation as the scholar of the family.

Schoolmastering was the trade he turned to now, and, Libya Hill having grown and there being some demand for higher learning, he set up for a "Professor." He "scratched about" among the people he knew—which was everyone, of course—and got twenty or thirty pupils at the start. The tuition was fifteen dollars for the term, which was five months; and he taught them in a frame church.

After a while " 'Fessor Joyner's School," as it was called, grew to such enlargement that Theodore had to move to bigger quarters. His father let him have the hill he owned across the river two miles west of town, and here Theodore built a frame house to live in and another wooden building to serve as a dormitory and classroom. The eminence on which the new school stood had always been known as Hogwart Heights. Theodore did not like the inelegant sound of that, so he rechristened it Joyner Heights, and the school, as befitted its new grandeur, was now named "The Joyner Heights Academy." The people in the town, however, just went on calling the hill Hogwart as they had always done, and to Theodore's intense chagrin they even dubbed the academy Hogwart, too.

In spite of this handicap the school prospered in its modest way. It was by no means a flourishing institution, but as people said, it was a good thing for Theodore. He could not have earned his living at anything else, and the school at least gave him a livelihood. The years passed uneventfully, and Theodore seemed settled forever in the comfortable little groove he had worn for himself.

Then, three years before the outbreak of the Civil War, a startling change occurred. By that time the fever of the approaching conflict was already sweeping through the South, and that fact gave Theodore his great opportunity. He seized it eagerly, and overnight transformed his school into "The Joyner Heights *Military* Academy." By this simple expedient he jumped his enrollment from sixty boys to eighty, and—more important—transmogrified himself from a rustic pedagogue into a military man.

So much is true, so cannot be denied—although Zachariah, in his ribald way, was forever belittling Theodore and his accomplishments. On Zachariah's side it must be admitted that Theodore loved a uniform a good deal better than he wore one; and that he, as Master, with the help of the single instructor who completed the school's faculty, undertook the work of military training, drill, and discipline with an easy confidence which, if not sublime, was rather staggering. But Zachariah *was* unjust.

"I have heard," Zachariah would say in later years, warming up to his subject and assuming the ponderously solemn air that always filled his circle of cronies with delighted anticipation of what was to come—"I have heard that fools rush in where angels fear to tread, but in the case of my brother Theodore, it would be more accurate to say that he *leaps* in where God Almighty crawls! . . . I have seen a good many remarkable examples of military chaos," he continued, "particularly at the outset of the war, when they were trying to teach farm hands and mountain boys the rudiments of the soldier's art in two weeks' time. But I have never seen anything so remarkable as the spectacle of Theodore, assisted by a knock-kneed fellow with the itch, tripping over his sword and falling on his belly every time he tried to instruct twenty-seven pimply boys in the intricacies of squads right."

That was unfair. Not *all*, assuredly, were pimply, and there were more than twenty-seven.

"Theodore," Zack went on with the extravagance that characterized these lapses into humorous loquacity—"Theodore was so short that every time he —— he blew dust in his eyes; and the knock-kneed fellow with the itch was so tall that he had to lay down on his belly to let the moon go by. And somehow they had got their uniforms mixed up, so that Theodore had the one that was meant for the knock-kneed tall fellow, and the knock-kneed tall fellow had on Theodore's. The trousers Theodore was wearing were so baggy at the knees they looked as if a nest of kangaroos had spent the last six months in them, and the knock-kneed fellow's pants were stretched so tight that he looked like a couple of long sausages. In addition to all this, Theodore had a head shaped like a balloon—and about the size of one. The knock-kneed fellow had a peanut for a head. And whoever had mixed up their uniforms had also got their hats exchanged. So every time Theodore reared back and bawled out a command, that small hat he was wearing would pop right off his head into the air, as if it had been shot out of a gun. And when the knock-kneed fellow would repeat the order, the big hat he had on would fall down over his ears and eyes as if someone had thrown a bushel basket over his head, and he would come clawing his way out of it with a bewildered expression on his face, as if to say, 'Where the hell am I, anyway?' . . . They had a devil of a time getting those twenty-seven pimply boys straightened up as straight as they could get—which is to say, about as straight as a row of crooked radishes. Then, when they were all lined up at attention, ready to go, the knock-kneed fellow would be taken with the itch. He'd shudder up and down, and all over, as if someone had dropped a cold worm down his back; he'd twitch and wiggle, and suddenly he'd begin to scratch himself in the behind."

These flights on Zachariah's part were famous. Once launched, his inventive power was enormous. Every fresh extravagance would suggest half a dozen new ones. He was not cruel, but his treatment of his brother bordered on brutality.

The truth of the matter is that the "pimply boys" drilled so hard and earnestly that the grass was beaten bare on the peaceful summit of Hogwart Heights. Uniforms and muskets of a haphazard sort had been provided for them, and all that could be accomplished by a pious reading of the drill manual and a dry history of Napoleonic strategy was done for them by Theodore and his knock-kneed brother in arms. And when war was declared, in

April 1861, the entire enrollment of the academy marched away to battle with Theodore at their head.

The trouble between Zachariah and Theodore afterwards was that the war proved to be the great event in Theodore's life, and he never got over it. His existence had been empty and pointless enough before the war, and afterwards, knowing there was nothing left to live for that could possibly match the glories he had seen, he developed rather quickly into the professional warrior, the garrulous hero forever talking of past exploits. This is what annoyed Zachariah more and more as time went on, and he never let a chance go by to puncture Theodore's illusions of grandeur and to take him down a peg or two.

Separate volumes could be written about each member of this remarkable family. A noble biography for Robert, done with a Plutarchian pen—that is what he deserves. A lusty, gusty Rabelaisian chronicle to do justice to the virtues of old Miss Hattie. A stern portrait of Rufus in the Balsac manner. For Zachariah, his own salty memoirs would be the best thing, if he had only thought to write them, for he saw through everybody, himself included; and if he could have been assured that not a word would leak out till his death, so that no political harm could come of it, he would have shamed the devil and told the naked and uproarious truth. As for Theodore—well, we'll try to do our best in the pages of this book, but we know full well beforehand that it won't be good enough for Theodore. No book, no single pen, could ever do for Theodore what should be done for him.

Theodore should have had a group photograph taken of himself. He should have been blocked out by Rubens, painted in his elemental colors by fourteen of Rubens's young men, had his whiskers done by Van Dyke, his light and shade by Rembrandt, his uniform by Velasquez; then if the whole thing might have beer, gone over by Daumier, and touched up here and there with the satiric pencil of George Belcher, perhaps in the end you might have got a portrait that would reveal, in the colors of life itself, the august personage of Colonel Theodore Joyner, C.S.A.

Theodore rapidly became almost the stock type of the "Southern Colonel-plumed knight" kind of man. By 1870, he had developed a complete vocabulary and mythology of the war—"The Battle of the Clouds," Zachariah termed it. Nothing could be called by its right name. Theodore would never dream of using a plain or common word if he could find a fancy one. The Southern side of the war was always spoken of in a solemn whisper, mixed of phlegm and reverent hoarseness, as "Our Cause." The Confederate flag became "Our Holy Oriflamme—dyed in the royal purple of the heroes' blood." To listen to Theodore tell about the war, one would have thought it had been conducted by several hundred thousand knighted Galahads upon one side, engaged in a struggle to the death against several hundred million villainous and black-hearted rascals, the purpose of said war being the protection "of all that we hold most sacred—the purity of Southern womanhood."

The more completely Theodore emerged as the romantic embodiment of Southern Colonelcy, the more he also came to look the part. He had the great mane of warrior hair, getting grayer and more distinguished-looking as the years went by; he had the bushy eyebrows, the grizzled mustache, and all the rest of it. In speech and tone and manner he was leonine. He moved his head exactly like an old lion, and growled like one, whenever he uttered such proud sentiments as these:

"Little did I dream, sir," he would begin—"little did I *dream*, when I marched out at the head of the Joyner Military Academy —of which the entire enrollment, sir—the *entire* enrollment, had volunteered to a man—all boys in years, yet each breast beating with a hero's heart—one hundred and thirty-seven fine young men, sir—the flower of the South—all under nineteen years of age—think of it, sir!" he growled impressively—"one hundred and thirty-seven under nineteen!——"

"Now wait a minute, Theodore," Zachariah would interpose with a deceptive mildness. "I'm not questioning your veracity, but if my memory is not playing tricks, your facts and figures are a little off."

"What do you mean, sir?" growled Theodore, and peered at him suspiciously. "In what way?"

"Well," said Zachariah calmly, "I don't remember that the enrollment of the academy had risen to any such substantial proportions as you mention by the time the war broke out. One hundred and thirty-seven under nineteen?" he repeated. "Wouldn't you come closer to the truth if you said there were nineteen under one hundred and thirty-seven?"

"Sir—Sir—" said Theodore, breathing heavily and leaning forward in his chair. "Why you—Sir!" he spluttered, and then glared fiercely at his brother and could say no more.

Is it any wonder that fraternal relations between Zack and Theodore were sometimes strained?

To the credit of Theodore's lads, and to the honor of the times and Colonel Joyner's own veracity, let it be admitted here and now that whether there were nineteen or fifty or a hundred and thirty-seven of them, they did march out "to a man," and many of them did not return. For four years and more the grass grew thick and deep on Hogwart Heights: the school was closed, the doors were barred, the windows shuttered.

When the war was over and Theodore came home again, the hill, with its little cluster of buildings, was a desolate sight. The place just hung there stogged in weeds. A few stray cows jangled their melancholy bells and wrenched the coarse, cool grass beneath the oak trees, before the bolted doors. And so the old place stood and stayed for three years more, settling a little deeper into the forgetfulness of dilapidation.

The South was stunned and prostrate now, and Theodore himself was more stunned and prostrate than most of the men who came back from the war. The one bit of purpose he had found in life was swallowed up in the great defeat, and he had no other that could take its place. He did not know what to do with himself. Half-heartedly, he "took the bar" again, and for the third time failed. Then, in 1869, he pulled himself together, and, using money that his brothers loaned him, he repaired the school and opened it anew.

It was a gesture of futility, really—and a symptom of something that was happening all over the South in that bleak decade of poverty and reconstruction. The South lacked money for all the vital things, yet somehow, like other war-struck and war-ravaged communities before it, the South found funds to lay out in tin-soldierism. Pigmy West Points sprang up everywhere, with their attendant claptrap of "Send us the boy, and we'll return you the man." It was a pitiable spectacle to see a great region and a valiant people bedaubing itself with such gimcrack frills and tin-horn fopperies after it had been exhausted and laid waste by the very demon it was making obeisance to. It was as if a group of exhausted farmers with blackened faces, singed whiskers, and lack-luster eyes had come staggering back from some tremendous conflagration that had burned their homes and barns and crops right to the ground, and then had bedecked themselves in outlandish garments and started banging on the village gong and crying out: "At last, brothers, we're all members of the fire department!"

Theodore took a new lease on life with the reopening of The

Joyner Military Academy. When he first decided to restore the place he thought he could resume his career at the point where the war had broken in upon it, and things would go on as though the war had never been. Then, as his plans took shape and he got more and more into the spirit of the enterprise, his attitude and feelings underwent a subtle change. As the great day for the re-opening approached, he knew that it would not be just a resuming of his interrupted career. It would be much better than that. For the war was a heroic fact that could not be denied, and it now seemed to Theodore that in some strange and transcendental way the South had been gloriously triumphant even in defeat, and that he himself had played a decisive part in bringing about this transcendental victory.

Theodore was no more consciously aware of the psychic processes by which he had arrived at this conclusion than were thousands of others all over the South who, at this same time, were coming to the same conclusion themselves. But once the attitude had crystallized and become accepted, it became the point of departure for a whole new rationale of life. Out of it grew a vast mythology of the war—a mythology so universally believed that to doubt its truth was worse than treason. In a curious way, the war became no longer a thing finished and done with, a thing to be put aside and forgotten as belonging to the buried past, but a dead fact recharged with new vitality, and one to be cherished more dearly than life itself. The mythology which this gave rise to acquired in time the force of an almost supernatural sanction. It became a kind of folk-religion. And under its soothing, other-worldly spell, the South began to turn its face away from the hard and ugly realities of daily living that confronted it on every hand, and escaped into the soft dream of vanished glories—imagined glories—glories that had never been.

The first concrete manifestation of all this in Theodore was an inspiration that came to him as he lay in bed the night before the great day when the Joyner Military Academy was to reopen its doors. As he lay there, neither quite awake nor yet asleep, letting his mind shuttle back and forth between remembered exploits on the field of battle and the exciting event scheduled for the morrow, the two objects of his interest became fused: he felt that they were really one, and he saw the military school as belonging to the war, a part of it, a continuation and extension of it into the present, and on down through the long, dim vista of the future. Out of this there flowed instantly into his consciousness a sequence of ringing phrases that brought him as wide awake as the clanging of a bell, and he saw at once that he had invented a perfect slogan for his school. The next day he announced it at the formal convocation.

It is true that Theodore's slogan occasioned a good deal of mirth at his expense when it was repeated all over town with Zachariah's running commentary upon it. The father of a student at the school was one of Zack's most intimate friends; this man had attended the convocation, and he told Zack all about it afterwards.

"Theodore," this friend reported, "gave the boys a rousing new motto to live up to—earned, he said, by their predecessors on the glorious field of battle. Theodore made such a moving speech about it that he had all the mothers in tears. You never heard such a blubbering in your life. The chorus of snifflings and chokings and blowing of noses almost drowned Theodore out. It was most impressive."

"I don't doubt it," said Zack. "Theodore always did have an impressive manner. If he only had the gray matter that ought to go with it, he'd be a wonder. But what did he say? What was the motto?"

"*First at Manassas——*"

"First to eat, he means!" said Zachariah.

"*—fightingest at Antietam Creek——*"

"Yes, fightingest to see who could get back first across the creek!"

"*—and by far the farthest in the Wilderness.*"

"By God, he's right!" shouted Zachariah. "Too far, in fact, to be of any use to anyone! They thrashed around all night long, bawling like a herd of cattle and taking pot-shots at one another in the belief that they had come upon a company of Grant's infantry. They had to be gathered together and withdrawn from the line in order to prevent their total self-destruction. My brother Theodore," Zachariah went on with obvious relish, "is the only officer of my acquaintance who performed the remarkable feat of getting completely lost in an open field, and ordering an attack upon his own position. . . . His wounds, of course, are honorable, as he himself will tell you on the slightest provocation—but he was shot in the behind. So far as I know, he is the only officer in the history of the Confederacy who possesses the distinction of having been shot in the seat of the pants by one of his own sharp-shooters, while stealthily and craftily reconnoitering his own breastworks in search of any enemy who was at that time nine miles away and marching in the opposite direction!"

From this time on, the best description of Theodore is to say that he "grew" with his academy. The institution thrived in the nostalgic atmosphere that had made its resurrection possible in the first place, and Theodore himself became the personal embodiment of the post-war tradition, a kind of romantic vindication of rebellion, a whole regiment of plumed knights in his own person. And there can be no doubt whatever that he grew to believe it all himself.

According to contemporary accounts, he had been anything but a prepossessing figure when he went off to war, and, if any part of Zachariah's extravagant stories can be believed, anything but a master strategist of arms on the actual field of battle. But with the passage of the years he grew into his role, until at last, in his old age, he looked a perfect specimen of the grizzled warrior.

Long before that, people had stopped laughing at him. No one but Zachariah now dared to question publicly any of Theodore's pronouncements, and Zachariah's irreverence was tolerated only because he was considered to be a privileged person, above the common *mores*. Theodore was now held in universal respect. Thus the youngest of "the Joyner boys"—the one from whom least had been expected—finally came into his own as a kind of sacred symbol.

In Libya Hill during those later years it was to be a familiar spectacle every Monday—the day when the "cadets" enjoyed their holiday in town—to see old Colonel Joyner being conveyed through the streets in an old victoria, driven by an aged Negro in white gloves and a silk hat. The Colonel was always dressed in his old uniform of Confederate gray; he wore his battered old Confederate service hat, and, winter or summer, he was never seen without an old gray cape about his shoulders. He did not loll back among the faded leather cushions of the victoria: he sat bolt upright—and when he got too old to sit bolt upright under his own power, he used a cane to help him.

He would ride through the streets, always sitting soldierly erect, gripping the head of his supporting cane with palsied hands, brown with the blotches of old age, and glowering out to left and right beneath bushy eyebrows of coarse white with kindling glances of his fierce old eyes, at the same time clinching his jaw grimly and working sternly at his lips beneath his close-cropped grizzled mustache. This may have been just the effect of his false teeth, but it suggested to awed little boys that he was muttering warlike epithets. That is what every inch of him seemed to imply, but actually he was only growling out such commands as "Go on, you scoundrel! Go on!" to his aged charioteer, or muttering with fierce scorn as he saw the slovenly postures of his own cadets lounging in drugstore doors:

"Not a whole man among 'em! Look at 'em now! A race of weaklings, hollow-chested and hump-backed—not made of the same stuff their fathers were—not like the crowd we were the day we all marched out to a man—the bravest of the brave, the flower of our youth and our young manhood! One hundred and thirty-seven under nineteen!—Hrumph! Hrumph!—Get along, you scoundrel! Get along!"

Chapter 6

THE BATTLE OF HOGWART HEIGHTS

THEODORE HAD MARRIED THE YEAR AFTER HE REOPENED THE JOYNER Military Academy, and everyone agreed at the time that he had made an exceedingly good match. He went to Virginia for his wife. She was Miss Emily Drumgoole, daughter of a Confederate officer, another plumed veteran of the war who, like Theodore, ran a military school, near Winchester. Thus she was also a daughter of the Shenandoah Valley, which had boasted stately houses, courtly manors, and green acres in the days of powdered hair and periwigs, when the wild fastnesses of Zebulon County had been broken only by the moccasin of the Cherokee.

Yes, decidedly, Theodore had done well. His wife was not only a Drumgoole of the Virginia Drumgooles, she was also a lady of quite considerable beauty, flawed only a little by the unfriendly hauteur of a long, cold nose. She came to Catawba in the role of a disdainful invader, and she never dropped the role throughout the remainder of her life.

Being a person of considerable confidence and force, however, she did not spend too much time bemoaning the vanished splendors of her past. Her vision was dominated not so much by the thought of what she had lost as by the calculation of what she was willing now to accept. In her cold, sure way, it was never so much a question of what she was going to take as of what she was going to reject. It was in this frigid frame of mind that she came as Theodore's bride to Hogwart Heights, and settled down there as the glacial monarch of all that she was willing to survey.

And what was she willing to survey? Well, very little, certainly, from the small precincts of Libya Hill.

Robert Joyner and his family she was pleased to welcome among the picked circle of her intimates, for he had been a Brigade Commander in the Civil War and the bosom friend of General Jubel Early—and Jubel Early, like herself, came from Virginia. So when Jubel Early or other great ones came to visit Robert Joyner, she would always invite him to call and bring his guests.

Zachariah was too strong meat for her. She tried to stomach him, but could not, so she coldly turned away. She could not stand his ribaldry and his coarseness. She suspected very shrewdly that in her presence he literally outdid himself in these respects for her special benefit. True, he was a famous man—but in Catawba. He had been Governor of the state—but the state was Catawba. He was now a member of the nation's Senate—but from Catawba. He chewed tobacco and he spat tobacco juice, he made coarse jokes and uttered words that no gentleman would ever utter—all in the presence of a lady. And although he knew much better, and could speak with elegance and beauty when he would, he often deliberately used the language of a backwoods yokel, mentioning with disgusting relish such revolting foods as "hawg and hominy," and delighting in crude anecdotes about how his father had gone barefoot and had never learned to read and write until he was forty years old—this, too, before a lady and her friends.

Miss Hattie Joyner was too much like her celebrated brother in character and plain speaking to find a cordial welcome on the hill. And Rufus, so the lady felt, smelt strongly of his store—a kind of compost of general merchandise, her proud, cold nose informed her, mixed of dry goods and of groceries, and dominated, it seemed to her, by the especial commonness of cheese and calico.

The Joyner clan being thus disposed of, the survivors of her choice were few. She admitted the existence of Dr. Burleigh and his wife and their three mannish and unmarried daughters. He was a dentist, it is true, and dull as dust, but he had come from Charleston and had good connections. The Randolphs also were accepted in her graces. They were Virginia people, and their family was a good one even there.

Her standards of selection were as rigid as the law of the Medes and the Persians, and just as incomprehensible to most of her neighbors; but she knew well enough what they were, and she adhered to them to the end of her days. Wit did not count with her, nor did wisdom, charm, grace, intelligence, character, or any other happy faculty with which men are endowed by nature. The only standard that she had, really, was "family." To her credit be it said that money counted with her not at all. Old Dr. Burleigh was as poor as he was dull. The Randolph fortune was a very meager one. But both of them had "family"—in her own quite definite and restricted meaning of the word. So she received them.

Mrs. Theodore Joyner presented her warlike mate with three offspring, and their arrivals occurred in a sequence almost as rapid as nature would allow. The daughter, Emmaline, was born the year after her parents' marriage. Eleven months later the lady rewarded her delighted spouse with a male heir, who was promptly named Drumgoole to perpetuate the proud accents of his mother's line. The next year she gave birth to her third child, also a boy. The Colonel was secretly a little resentful of the fact that his wife had named the first son, and he claimed for himself the right to name this one; so, after great cogitation and much thumbing of military histories—the only books he ever read—he finally ruled out Hannibal and Quintus Fabius and settled upon Gustavus Adolphus. Mrs. Joyner objected that the boys would call him Gus, but Theodore stood his ground. He pointed out that Dolph had a pleasant sound and was just as easy to say as Gus, and that Dolph would likely stick if the family used it, so that is what they called him. And it became apparent fairly soon that whatever brains and physical attractions these children were to possess would be held in almost exclusive monopoly by the last and youngest of them.

Emmaline grew up under her mother's exacting tutelage, a gawky and unlovely girl, preserved from God-knows-what contaminations by the proud isolation of Hogwart Heights. Of her mother's beauty, character, and personality she inherited nothing except the extravagant snobbishness, as evidenced by the same long, cold nose. In the course of time she was sent off to the approved girls' finishing school in Virginia, which, then as now, was a kind of elegant country club for Southern maidens—a sanctuary where they could wait till marriage or early spinsterhood claimed them, and meanwhile could fill their empty heads, not with any smattering of conceivably useful knowledge, but with vicious triviality, gossip, and the accepted rituals and mannerisms of their own grotesque, aborted little world. The school was attended by none but born snobs like Emmaline herself, but most of the others were much more personable and far more adept than she in the dreary drivel that has always been held in such high esteem by the professional representatives of "Southern charm."

After four years of this, Emmaline was pronounced "finished" and she returned home again, having learned all the accents and vocabularies of the approved mode, but without having found wholly adequate substitutes for a long nose, a flat bosom, and a small, dull mind. At twenty-two she was already confirmed, though by no means reconciled, to a life of unsullied virginity.

Young Drumgoole, or Drum as they called him, was brought up with the same narrowness of view which his mother had so painstakingly implanted in his sister. From the beginning his father had fondly hoped that the youth would carry on the war-like strain and had envisioned the proud day when he should be a candidate for West Point. And eventually the proud day came, and Drum was sent away into the very heart of the enemy's country with many fond flourishes of fatherly advice and admonition. But it was all to no purpose. He never saw the conclusion of his first term at the great academy on the Hudson. He was a casualty to the rapid fire of trigonometry. He was cut down the first charge. He never even heard the booming of the heavy guns upon the distant front of calculus.

After this, of course, there was nothing left for him to do except to go to Charlottesville and enroll himself among the princelings of the blood at the University of Virginia. Any other alternative was clearly impossible. A gentleman could still attend the United States Military Academy without dishonor, for Lee himself had been a West Point man, but to submit his person to the Yankee degradations of Harvard, Yale, or Princeton was, in the eyes of the Colonel and his wife, unthinkable.

So Drum was sent to Charlottesville as the next-best thing to West Point. Of his life there, there is little to record save that he finally scraped through and learned "to hold his liquor like a gentleman"—which apparently has always been one of the stiffest requirements of the curriculum at that famous university. At length Drum came home again wearing a small blond mustache, and was instantly appointed a Major in his father's celebrated corps, and second in command, the appointment also carrying with it an instructorship in mathematics, trigonometry and calculus included.

If the life of Drum Joyner was the inner seal and signing of his mother's purpose, stamped in wax, then molded outwardly to fit the pattern of his father's wishes, the life of his younger brother, Dolph, was from the outset governed by a purpose of its own. Dolph was one who could have gained and held the coveted honors of West Point training had he so willed, but he would have none of it. He elected to follow Drum to Charlottesville, and his college years showed unmistakable evidence of those qualities which were later to distinguish his whole career.

It is true, he did not shine in scholarship. It is also true, he made no effort to. He was content to pass acceptably, which he had no difficulty in doing, and to leave accomplishments of profounder learning to his more earnest brethren. It was not that Dolph was lacking in earnestness: he possessed it to a degree and in a way that would have astonished his more solemn-seeming contemporaries had they suspected what lay in his mind and heart. It was merely that he already knew of other laurels which seemed to him far more worth winning than any to be found in the academic groves. He had his vision fixed on larger ends. The world, and nothing less, was the oyster of this young Gustavus Adolphus —this young American with the medieval name—and the world had been the mollusk of his desire since childhood.

The geography of western Catawba is especially conducive to the stimulation of visions of the earth. Many writers have spoken of the isolation of these magic hills, the provincial insularity of the mountain man, his remoteness and his consequent asylumage from the affairs and doings of the great and distant world. All of this is true. But the effect of early imprisonment in these hills may lead, in some men, to quite another ending. In the little coves and hollows of the mountain fastnesses of Zebulon County, in the narrow valleys along the rocky creeks that boil down from Clingmans Dome, there may still be found in shack and cabin whole families of people who have never been as far from home as Libya Hill, and for whom the ranging earth beyond the abutment of the mountain at their back is as strange, as alien to all their thoughts and dreams, as Timbuktu. But let the acorn fall on proper earth, or let the lightning strike a chosen rock, and the oak will flourish there, the rock burst forth abundantly with water as it did in Moses' day, and there will be a prophet there to glimpse a Promised Land as golden in its glorious enticements as the one that Moses saw.

Gustavus Adolphus Joyner was the proper earth. Gustavus Adolphus Joyner was the chosen rock. And when the lightning struck, Gustavus Adolphus Joyner was ready there and waiting to receive its flash. When he was a child and looked out from Hogwart Heights and saw the distant ranges of the soaring hills, he did not spend much time in thinking of the coves and hollows hidden away among them, or of the quaint and curious world-forgotten people who grubbed and groped there, from whose own blood and flesh and sinew not so long ago he had himself in partial measure been derived. He looked and saw the hills, and in his kindling vision leaped beyond them. His eyes pierced through the mountain wall and swept beyond to daydreams of the golden cities of the plains.

The very sight of these great hills, under the special enchantments of their weather, the blue haze of their tremendous distances, is like some magic vista of time and the imagined kingdoms of the earth. And there is no place among them that is a better vantage point for this *Weltanschauung* than Hogwart Heights. From the summit of that hill the eye commands a prospect in which grandeur and homeliness are uniquely and wonderfully intermingled, in which the far and the near, the sense of strangeness and utter familiarity, are combined in a single panoramic unity of now and forever. Away to the right, miles distant, sweeping up gradually from the edges of the rolling plateau on which Libya Hill stands, the great ramparts of the Smoky Mountains first appear, ranging westward tier on tier until they end in endlessness that carries the vision on into imagined worlds beyond even after the eye can go no further. To the north, east, and south, more intimate, more friendly and familiar, rise the peaks and undulating masses of the Blue Ridge Mountains.

Before one, and below one, lies Libya Hill, the straggling little town strewn widely on its broad plateau, not always lovely at close hand, but very lovely from the crest of Hogwart Heights. The center of the town, the "business section," looks ghostly, unsubstantial, and unreal under its drifting plumes of soft-coal smoke. But out of the heart of this ethereal-looking town, coming as swift and clean as a deliberate act of cold, clear purpose, bends a bright band of what, beneath the summer sun, seems to be an arc of burnished silver. In a graceful curve it sweeps out from the town and bears around the base of Colonel Joyner's hill, then it winds on westward, sinuously but forever westward, till it is lost among the far-flung, blue-hazed mountains. It is a river, just a thread of river, really, when compared to its great brother, the Tennessee, into which it ultimately flows; yet as rivers go in the Catawba hills, where as a rule they are hardly more than creeks, this one is quite impressive. In August, if the weather has been hot and dry, and all the mountain streams are low, the river at this point below the brow of Hogwart Heights will shrink away from banks of cake-dry mud into a mere trickle. But in the freshets of the spring, or later on in June if rains are heavy and a flood time comes, the river will quickly swell and rise up to the very flooring of the wooden bridge. At these times one understands why the first settlers gave it the curiously haunting name of Catawba Broad.

Here on the summit of this hill, bedded in soft grasses, Dolph Joyner lay a thousand times in childhood and traced the shining river's course as it swept out from the town and wound its way beyond his sight and ken; and with soaring certitude he went on following it, through mountain gorges and deep valleys of verdant coolness, until he came out with it into the imagined world upon the other side, and saw it beckoning on before him in a vision of golden lands.

If others had known why the boy spent so many hours in this solitude of hill-top dreaming, they might have guessed that the little world of Libya Hill and the Hogwart Heights Military Academy would soon prove too small for him. His father, of course, wanted him to pursue what he had come to think of as "the family tradition of arms." It was comforting for the Colonel to think that his two sons would join their talents to carry on the school after he was gone. But this was not to be. For, while Drum was as malleable as putty in his parents' hands, Dolph was made of different stuff.

Rather small of figure, erect and graceful as a shaft, Dolph was quick and hard in both mind and body, but this quickness, this lean hardness, was from childhood couched deceptively in a velvet sheath. He inherited all of the Colonel's courtliness of manner without any of the Colonel's bombast and capacity for self-deception. He seemed to be full of grace and gentleness, and his voice, which was never raised in loudness or in violence, was so pleasing in its quiet modulations that it fell on tired ears or on jangled nerves as gratefully as balm. During his college days at Charlottesville he acquired the nickname of "Silk," which was to cling to him throughout his life. Silk was a perfectly accurate tag for him. His whole personality seemed to be summed up in that one word. But it was silk around iron. It was silk carefully overlaid on flint.

The essential quality of Silk Joyner's character was that he not only always knew the right thing when he saw it, but sensed the right thing before anyone else even suspected its existence. And "the right thing" with Silk Joyner was, simply, the advantageous thing. This was his main concern. His vision of life was utterly utilitarian, and the only utility he recognized was that which applied to himself. He was interested in the usefulness of things and of people only insofar as they could be used to further his own purposes. That suave and courtly figure with the silken voice offended no one unless he had to, but he did not waste himself on useless and unprofitable acquaintances. People who could not help him, who could not profit him in some way, were ruthlessly cast out of his life; but the annihilating act was performed with such smooth courtesy and such winning charm that the luckless victim did not even know he had been kicked out of doors into the cold until he felt the icy blast.

At college, Silk knew precisely the right people, joined precisely the right organizations, made precisely the right connections. He squeezed the whole university life dry of the last drop of nourishment it could offer him, and yet did not once betray the fact to those who knew him best that he was anything else but the infinitely pleasant, polished, charming, friendly, and rather indolent fellow whom they took him to be. He got his law degree at Charlottesville within two years after his graduation from the college, and he followed this with a pleasant and profitable term at Heidelberg.

And then, to cap the climax, he did what no one who knew him could possibly have thought he would ever do. But it was the thing he had always had in the back of his head, the thing that his sure instinct told him was inevicably right, so he did it.

He came home—home from his travels, home from Heidelberg, smoother and more silken than he had ever been—and announced that he was going out West, to the Territory of Oklahoma. He said that he was not only going there, but that he intended to settle down there and practice his profession and grow up with the country—there in that raw outpost of civilization which, to his mother's appalled conception, seemed to be as far and wild and grotesquely unfit a place for a gentleman's habitation as an encampment of Sioux Indians.

His mother's tears, his father's entreaties and objurgations, had no more effect upon his purpose than rain against the surface of a cliff. He had made up his mind to go, and go he did. So for the nonce we leave him there, to return to him a little later. In the interim we can be sure of one thing: Silk Joyner is not going to be caught picking daisies out in Oklahoma. While our backs are turned, he will still be cultivating all the right people and doing all the right things, whatever they happen to be in Oklahoma. He will be fitting his silk purse to the sow's ear, and, incidentally, making a very good thing of it.

While Theodore's children were growing up, an event of considerable importance occurred in Libya Hill which, in its sequel, was to reveal as nothing else had ever done the true mettle of the remarkable woman who had given them birth. The impact of this event upon the town was so electrifying that for weeks and months after the first news of it broke upon the awareness of the natives, they could think and talk of nothing else. Everybody was bursting with excitement over it, everybody was adither and agog over the stupendous implications of it, everybody said it was the best thing that could possibly have happened—everybody, that is, except Mrs. Theodore Joyner. From the first, she was totally indifferent to it.

In the late seventies, George Willetts, one of the richest and most benefactory members of that mighty tribe of plunderers which has looted the resources of America for two hundred years, came to Libya Hill and, after looking over all the mountains in the surrounding region, bought up a whole range of them, comprising a major portion of three counties, for his own domain. He imported artists, artisans, and architects by the hundred, brought in from Italy and the great cities of the East the most skilled and cunning craftsmen of their kind—a veritable army of masons, carpenters, stonecutters, and foresters—and put them to work creating on his two hundred thousand princely acres the greatest country house that had yet been built in all America—the greatest private residence, it was said, in the whole wide world.

While everybody in town gasped and buzzed with each new development in this magnificent undertaking, Mrs. Theodore Joyner sat unmoved on Hogwart Heights. From her own verandah, on a summer's day, she sometimes surveyed the proceedings from afar. Across rolling miles of green plateau she could see from her hill the Willetts' mansion rising on its hill, a faery citadel of royal marble gleaming white as alabaster against the smoky backdrop of the distant mountains, upborne richly and sustained by swelling masses of green forest. Poor indeed by comparison was Hogwart Heights and the weathered paint of Mrs. Joyner's old frame house. But Mrs. Joyner sat on her verandah and she never moved. If it ever crossed her mind to draw a comparison, she did so proudly; but what she thought she kept entirely to herself and never said a word to anyone.

George Willetts could have owned six counties for all she cared, and built a marble palace of four hundred rooms instead of the two hundred and sixty-two that were now under construction. He could have spent forty million dollars for all she cared, instead of the twenty million that his plans were costing him, and her feeling toward him would have been the same. That is to say, she would have had no feeling toward him. For she had heard that his grandfather had once run a ferry boat. That settled it. He had no "family." He did not belong. As far as Mrs. Joyner was concerned, he did not exist.

The rest of that small world fairly groveled in the dust before the Willetts' name. People fought for a better glimpse of George Willetts' secluded, legendary person when they saw his chrisomed flesh upon the familiar pavements of the town: they pinched themselves to make sure they were not dreaming, so that they could really tell this marvel as a verity to wide-eyed grandchildren sixty years from then. The name of George Willetts and his enchanted domain came to dominate the life of the little town like a magic spell. But through the whole of this, Mrs. Theodore Joyner sat on Hogwart Heights and gave no sign at all.

It is not likely that the Willetts family cared at first. But the years rolled by, the mansion was completed, the Willetts took possession, and as the whole community save the dame on Hogwart Heights sank before them in the obeisance of abject vassalage, the sheer effrontery of the thing began to fascinate them, then to stun them, until finally it overcame them. As time went on, the word was whispered back into the porches of the Willetts' ears that the lady on the Heights had totally ignored them, had shown no interest in their great proceedings, had said, indeed, that Mr. Willetts had no "family," and that she—God save the mark!—the lady on Hogwart Heights, the mistress of a shabby house and of a one-horse military school—would not receive them!

It was funny. It was unbelievable. It was absurd. It was—it was —it was—great God! it was simply horrible, that's what it was! It was not to be endured! It had never before happened to a member of the Willetts family, and it had to stop!

The upshot of it was that there came a day—a memorable,

never-to-be-forgotten day—when the Willetts family did what it had never done before. It put its pride into its pocket and went to call upon a total stranger—and to make the circumstance still more incredible, if that can be, a total stranger who had snubbed the Willetts family dead and cold.

History does not record that on that memorable day the bells were rung backward, or the flags hung at half mast in Libya Hill, or the streets lined with silent throngs, their heads uncovered, as Mrs. Willetts drove through town on her way to Hogwart Heights. There is a rumor that there was a partial eclipse of the sun, but scientific research does not confirm it. Still, everyone who remembers anything about it agrees that it was a day of days.

The coronation of a king may be witnessed by the populace, but the solemn investiture of the royal robes is reserved for the royal family and members of the most select nobility. Accordingly the full and satisfying record of what happened on that famous day will always be concealed somewhat in mystery. Yet rumor, like a fine and subtle smoke, can insinuate itself through solid walls, and rumor whispers that upon that day Mrs. Willetts got up at the crack of dawn—a thing unknown to her before—and ate the lightest kind of breakfast. Henchmen of the royal preserve, game wardens, foresters, French maids, and such like folk were known to have hinted discreetly afterwards that on this day Mrs. Willetts was not utterly herself. She looked pale and haggard in the mirror, her small, jeweled hand was seen to tremble slightly as she put the cup back on the tray, she is said to have called for her smelling salts and to have taken two sharp sniffs, one more than was her customary average.

Driving down along the eight miles of lovely road that wound from the mansion to the lodge gates of the great estate, behind a pair of spanking bays, two liveried coachmen perched above her, and two more with folded arms behind, in a princely equipage of which the very harness studs were solid silver, the lady was said to have betrayed the tension of her nerves, the agitation of her mind, by the way in which she twirled the handle of her parasol with one small gloved hand and nervously kept clenching and unclenching the fingers of the other. She swept through the arches of the lodge gate with set and rigid features, and for the first time in her life failed to respond with her customary gracious little nod and smile to the bows of the venerable retainer who kept the gate.

These symptoms of internal stress were likewise noted by the populace as Mrs. Willetts passed through town. At a spanking trot the splendid carriage swept smoothly through the streets on velvet wheels. The sun was shining and the silver harness sparkled like a maiden's dream. The flowers were blooming, the month was May, the laughter of young children and of lovers could be heard upon the air. All nature wore a smile that day, but Mrs. Willetts did not smile. Her face was rigid and her eyes were blank. Had she been carved of stone she could not have been more preoccupied, more unaware of all the eyes, the hats, the faces, and the smiles that were raised hopefully to her in greeting.

The carriage swept smartly up South Main Street, turned the corner into College at the Square, rolled out College to Montgomery, trotted swiftly down the long slope of Montgomery to the bottom, then up the hill beyond and out of town. Dust arose now beneath those shining hooves, dust arose around that shining equipage, around the coachmen and the footmen and the flunkeys; dust swirled up around the fashionable figure of George Willetts' wife, obscuring her designs and purposes, clouding all her hopes, smothering whatever thoughts she had been thinking. At last the carriage crossed the old wooden bridge that spanned the river at the base of Hogwart Heights and heaved up as it struck a bump upon the other side. It lurched into the rutted and uneven roadway that wound up around the hill to the academy, and then, still toiling and lurching upward, disappeared from sight around a bend.

Mrs. Willetts finally arrived, got out, mounted the wooden steps to the verandah, and there, straight and cold at journey's end, stood Mrs. Theodore Joyner. They went into the house together—and the rest is silence. Only Rumor knows what happened then, and Rumor was not slow to tell it.

They are supposed to have had tea together, and it is said that for some moments neither spoke a word. Then after a long and painful silence Mrs. Willetts remarked that she had heard so much of Mrs. Joyner and had looked forward to this meeting for quite some time.

Mrs. Joyner, after a perceptible pause, replied: "You are a stranger in this part of the country, I believe?"

Mrs. Willetts strove to assimilate the meaning of this question, and is said to have gasped a little and finally to have managed: "Yes—I—I—I suppose I am. We have been here just six years."

This information was received with another long and attentive silence.

Finally Mrs. Willetts said: "I—I do hope you will come to see us soon."

Mrs. Joyner inclined her head ever so slightly in a gesture that was committal of nothing, and, without answering directly the lady's invitation, is rumored to have said: "I believe you and your husband are both Northern people, are you not?"

"Yes—" Mrs. Willetts blurted out—"but my grandmother was a Southern woman."

"Of what family?" Mrs. Joyner asked with an accent of sharp interest.

"Of the Marsden family—" Mrs. Willetts answered quickly— "the Marsden family of Virginia."

"Which branch?" Mrs. Joyner asked with glacial sternness. "The Southwestern or the Tidewater?"

"The Tidewater," Mrs. Willetts cried out with almost desperate hopefulness.

Mrs. Joyner inclined her head ever so slightly and said, "Ah!"

It is not to be supposed for a moment that this "Ah!" was a warm "Ah!"—an "Ah!" of friendly surrender. It was no such "Ah!" as this at all. But it is reported that there was in it just a perceptible relenting into interest, a suggestion that a very mild thaw had set in, an indication that here at last was something that could be taken into consideration and examined seriously.

"And your mother?" Mrs. Joyner now said, as she put down her cup. "Was she a Southern woman, too?"

"No," Mrs. Willetts answered somewhat wretchedly, "she—she was a Northern woman." Here Mrs. Joyner is said to have stiffened visibly again, and Mrs. Willetts rushed on recklessly: "But she was a Dyckman—a New York Dyckman."

"Was that one of the Dutch families?" Mrs. Joyner asked sharply.

"Yes, one of the very first Dutch families. I do assure you, one of the very oldest Dutch families!"

Mrs. Joyner said nothing for a moment, then, taking up her saucer and teacup again, she remarked with the first faint flush of condescension in her voice: "I have heard that there are some very good Dutch families."

Here Mrs. Joyner sipped her tea, and carefully put cup and saucer down again, and Mrs. Willetts is said to have heaved a long, slow, and quite audible sigh of relief.

Finally Mrs. Joyner spoke again. "I should be glad," she said, smiling graciously as she framed the words, "to come to see you when I am next in town."

Chapter 7

A STRANGER WHOSE SERMON WAS BRICK

FIFTY YEARS AGO, ONE OF THE MOST EXTRAORDINARY PEOPLE IN the town of Libya Hill was a man named Webber. In a great many curious and interesting ways which no one could have foreseen, he was destined to influence the life of the whole town. John Webber came to Libya Hill in 1881, and since the story of his arrival there involved the celebrated Zachariah Joyner, it attained a considerable local notoriety.

It was in the autumn—early October—of 1881. Judge Robert Joyner, Zachariah's brother, had gone to Millerton, twenty-four miles away, to attend the session of the Circuit Court which was being held there at the time. Zachariah had been in Washington, and on the way back had stopped to meet his brother in Millerton.

Millerton was as far as the railroad went in those days. The line had not yet reached Libya Hill, but it was under construction at the time. The building of this particular stretch of the railroad was a tremendous job of engineering for those days. As anyone can see who rides over it today, the line winds back and forth with corkscrew bends and hairpin turns for eight miles between Millerton at the base of the mountains and Ridgepole Gap at the crest, some fourteen hundred feet above. It is a beautiful and thrilling ride—one of the most beautiful in America--and there are places where one can see the track below one seven times.

In 1881, all of this was in the process of construction. The crews were just finishing the grading of the right of way: the tracks were laid, and work cars and shifting engines were already moving over them, but there were no scheduled trains. To get to Libya Hill people had to take the stage. It left Millerton every afternoon at one o'clock and reached Libya Hill at six, which was not bad time considering the tremendous pull and climb of those first eight miles.

The stage wasn't much of a contraption, judged by romantic or Wild Western standards. It was just a wagon with seats for six people, and it was drawn by two horses. When it rained, the dirt road winding up around the mountainside to Ridgepole Gap became a swamp of sticky mire. And usually, when this happened, the passengers got out and walked.

On this day, Zack Joyner had come down from Washington on the train which arrived in Millerton at noon. He and his brother had dinner at a place called Crandall's Tavern, which was a country hotel from which the stage departed. The man Webber had himself arrived on the same train. Zachariah had noticed him, and while they were eating at the tavern Zack commented to his brother on the stranger's peculiar appearance. Afterwards Webber got in the stage with them, and almost immediately Zack, as was his custom with anyone whose appearance interested him, struck up a conversation.

The stage had three rows of seats. In front was the driver's seat, with room for one passenger beside him; behind this and backing up against it was the second seat, and facing the second was a third. There were only five passengers that trip. Judge Robert Joyner sat up front beside the driver, Zack sat behind the driver facing Webber on the left side of the coach, and there were two ladies, a mother and her daughter, who were going as far as Ridgepole Gap.

Zachariah started off at once in his usual way. Webber did

not know who he was, but the other people did. In a few minutes he had them laughing at his jokes, and Webber was looking at him with a kind of puzzled grin. Presently Zack asked Webber where he was bound for and if he was a stranger in those parts, knowing full well that he was. Webber answered that he had never been in Old Catawba before and said that he was bound for Libya Hill. Still curious, Zack asked him if he was not "a Northern man." Webber said he was, and that he came from Pennsylvania.

The stranger had answered these questions readily enough but had volunteered no additional information about himself, so Zack now asked him if he was on a visit. Webber said no, that he was a brick mason and general builder, and that he was coming to Libya Hill to take charge of work on the new hotel which the Corcorans were putting up on Belmont Hill, in the center of the town, and for which ground had already been broken. Zack had already concluded that the man was a laborer of some sort, for his hands were thick and strong and had the look of having known much hard work; and Zack had also noticed on the index finger of the man's right hand a horny callous, which Zack now took to be the mark of persistent wielding of the trowel. Even in later years, when Webber became prosperous and confined himself to superintending the labor of others, this callous remained, and one always felt it in shaking hands with him.

The news of his occupation and purpose was received by everyone with considerable interest and satisfaction. The Corcorans were rich people who had recently come into that section and bought up tracts of property and laid out plans for large enterprises, of which the hotel was the central one. And only a few years before, George Willetts, the great Northern millionaire, had built and moved into his fabulous country estate near by. New people were coming to town all the time, new faces were being seen upon the streets. And now that the railroad would soon be opened, there was a general feeling in the air that great events were just around the corner for them all, and that an important destiny was in store for Libya Hill.

It was the time when they were just hatching from the shell, when the place was changing from a little isolated mountain village, lost to the world, with its few thousand native population, to a briskly-moving modern town, with railway connections to all parts, and with a growing population of wealthy people who had heard about the beauties of the setting and were coming there to live. It was, in fact, the beginning of their "boom"—a boom which at times was to lapse, to lie dormant, but never to die out utterly until the final explosion fifty years later. People had already begun to learn the language and to talk the jargon with a practiced tongue. Even then one was hearing a great deal about the beautiful scenery, the magnificent climate, the purity of the crystal water. The whole vocabulary of the tourist community was just waiting to be translated into the lush phrases of the professional rhapsodist and the Chamber of Commerce guide.

Zachariah Joyner assured the stranger that he was coming to "the greatest country in the world," and enlarged upon the theme in the syllables of the ornate rhetoric of which he was a master. What Webber said is not on record, but it can be assumed from his character that his comment was bluntly noncommittal, quiet, to the point.

The talk then turned to travel and to railway journeys, which in those days were considerably more complicated and difficult than they are now. Webber remarked that he had come all the way from Baltimore, that the trip had been a long and wearing one, with many changes, and that he would be glad when it was over because he was pretty tired. Zachariah then told a story

about "Greasy" Wray, a country lawyer out in Zebulon whom
Joyner had appointed a Circuit Judge during his first term as
Governor. Greasy Wray had never been anywhere, and when
he received his first instructions to hold court in Harrington, a
seacoast town four hundred miles away, he was delighted at the
prospect of seeing so much of the world and proceeded at once
to heed the call of civic duty. He set out on horseback to Libya
Hill; then he went by stage to Millerton; then by the Exeter
and West Catawba Railway to Exeter; then by the Belmont,
Fletcher, and West Central to Sanderson; then by the Sanderson
and Northeastern to Dover; then by the Dover and Mount Arthur
to Redfern; then by the Redfern and Eastern Shore to Bellamy,
where, all exhausted from his three-day journey, he arrived to
find the boat waiting. Greasy Wray got on board at once and went
to sleep, and woke up the next morning to find the boat docked at
its destination. He saw a great crowd of Negroes on the wharf,
went ashore and hired a hack, was driven to a hotel, and demanded of the astounded clerk that the sheriff be sent for right
away. Fifteen minutes later he welcomed the no less astounded
sheriff in his room and said: "I am Judge Wray of Zebulon, and
I have been sent here to open court in Harrington." The sheriff
was speechless for a moment, then he replied: "Hell, man, this
ain't Harrington. It's *Baltimore!*"

This story was one of Zachariah's favorites, and he told it with
gusto. He was off to a good start now, and as the stage toiled up
the mountainside the stories rolled from him in a swelling tide.
Just before the stage reached Ridgepole Gap, on the last bend of
the road as the team pulled toward the crest, the wheels lurched
down into a heavy rut. The two women were almost tossed out
of their seats. They screamed, and then, as the team pulled out
of it again, one of the ladies turned to Zachariah and, giggling
apprehensively, remarked:

"Oh, Senator! I do declare! It seems as if all the holes are on our side!"

"Yes, madam," Zachariah boomed out gallantly and without a moment's hesitation, "and all the roots on ours."

His face did not change expression as he spoke these words, nor his blue eyes lose a vestige of their innocence. But Robert Joyner had to take vigorous recourse to his handkerchief and blow his nose loudly for some time; and when he finally looked back, Zachariah was blandly surveying the landscape, while Webber was staring rigidly out across the side of the stage, and his thick neck and ruddy face were purple.

The ladies got out at Ridgepole Gap, and from that point on Zack Joyner gave free play to his bawdy vein. He asked Webber where he planned to stay when he got to town. Webber said he didn't know, but supposed there was a boarding house or a hotel.

"Well," said Zachariah gravely, "I usually put up at Joyner's place myself."

Mr. Webber very innocently inquired: "Is that a good place?"

"Yes," said Zachariah. "Taking it all in all it suits me about as well as any place I've found. You get a good bed and good accommodation there, and Mrs. Joyner's known as one of the best cooks in these parts. And say—" here Zack looked around slyly, then leaned forward, and, tapping Webber on the knee, said confidentially—"she's not a bad-looking woman either. As a matter of fact—" again he looked round slyly—"when I go there, I usually sleep with her."

It was shameless and outrageous, but it was Zack Joyner, too. One look, however, at John Webber's astounded face was too much for Zack. He burst into a roar of laughter, in which the driver and Judge Robert Joyner joined, and then he introduced himself.

Just after this the thing happened. The stage came to a little rise where the road crossed the right of way of the new railroad tracks. The crews were working here. Just as the team pulled up to the crossing, a shifting engine with a string of dump cars came by. The horses reared and snorted, and the driver lashed them with his whip. Then the train clanked past, the horses pulled skittishly across the tracks, the engine whistled—and the horses ran away.

The team plunged down the mountain road at breakneck speed. The driver clamped his foot upon the brake, the brake rod snapped, and as they neared the bend, Judge Robert Joyner reached over, grabbed the reins, and swerved the team around. The stage skidded to one side and almost overturned, and Zachariah pitched out on his head. Judge Robert Joyner and John Webber bent over him while the driver pulled the team around. His head had struck a rock, and there was a great blue swelling on his forehead. They opened his collar and his shirt, chafed his wrists, and spoke to him. He didn't stir. Robert said he thought Zack was a dead man, because his eyelids were half open and his eyeballs looked like glass.

Then Webber got up, went over to the stage, spoke to the driver, reached in underneath the seat, and pulled out a bottle of Glover's Mange Cure. He came back, uncorked the bottle, bent over Zack, forced the bottle neck between his lips, and poured its contents down his throat.

Robert said later that if Webber had held a blowtorch to Zack's behind, the effect could not have been more instantaneous. He did not *get* up, big, heavy man that he was—he *rose* up, shot up into the air as if he had been fired out of a gun.

"Great God!" he roared. "You've burnt me up!"

That was the way John Webber came to town.

The story lost nothing in the telling that Zachariah gave it. *sc* that in no time at all John Webber became known to everyone as "the man who burnt Zack Joyner up." And the story typified the man: the stark remedy and the blunt, unspoken way in which he administered it were characteristic of everything he ever did. And, most characteristic of all, as Zack himself was the first to admit, was the fact that "it worked." That was the beginning of the sound respect that both Zack Joyner and his brother Robert had for Mr. Webber throughout the remainder of their lives.

Although there was undoubtedly a touch of the grotesque in his appearance, one forgot it quickly on acquaintance, because of the natural dignity—the sheer animal dignity—of the man. For one thing, John Webber never in his life felt a moment's embarrassment because of the way he looked. He was certainly not vain of his appearance: he was the last person in the world to deceive himself. He would even laugh good-naturedly and say: "No one's ever going to give me the prize for beauty at the county fair, and no matter—I've got to work for *my* living, anyway." But he was not ashamed, either. He could resent an insult or an affront to his self-respect as quickly as any man, but he was entirely without morbid sensitivity. He accepted the well-intentioned but sometimes rather crude jokes of his fellows with quiet amusement, and could even turn a joke against a man as well as enjoy one at his own expense.

The wise thing about his attitude was that he accepted his appearance sensibly and without self-consciousness. "I'm not much for looks," he would say, "but I've no complaint to make. I've always had a good constitution, and that was lucky, because I've had to work hard all my life, ever since I was twelve years old. I've had my share of the hard knocks, I can assure you, and done my share of the hard labor; so even if I'm no parlor beauty I guess I can still be pretty thankful that I was strong enough to stand up and take the hard knocks as fast as they came." This innate dignity of the man enabled him to keep at all times what other people sometimes lost—his own self-respect.

Judge Robert Joyner used to say that if Webber had been "an educated man" he could have "gone far in the world"—a statement which he would conclude emphatically by saying: "He would have made a fine lawyer." Judge Joyner's only son, Edward, first heard his father say these words when he could not have been more than twelve years old. He never forgot them, and later on it struck him as curious that he should have remembered them at all. Ordinarily a boy of that age is not very much concerned with the merits of the gentlemen who either adorn or might have adorned the legal profession—even when one's father is a lawyer, and a judge of the Circuit Court to boot. Young Edward Joyner was certainly no different from most other boys in this respect. He was interested in a great number of things at that time, but the law was emphatically not one of them.

Among the things that did interest young Edward Joyner was the circus. He saw his first circus some six months after Mr. Webber arrived in town, and at the same time caught his first glimpse of Mr. Webber. Perhaps that is why he remembered Mr. Webber and his father's opinion of him—why, indeed, Mr. Webber and the circus became interfused in his mind forever after—because he would never forget how Mr. Webber helped the circus come to town. From that time on, young Edward Joyner was pretty well convinced, like his father, that John Webber could do anything he attempted, and do it well.

This great event concerned a very modest version of Barnum's Mammoth Circus and Combined Shows. Since the last stretch of the new railroad was still under construction, the whole thing had been brought in by wagon across the mountains all the way from Millerton. They even had an elephant named Jumbo, and they had marched him up across the Blue Ridge, too—and it was just like Hannibal crossing the Alps. And as Edward Joyner later remembered it, one of the things he wanted to be at that time, and for a long time afterwards, was the man who sat on Jumbo's skull and rode up across the mountains; and if he could not be that man, then he was willing to be that man's man—or his boy or his apprentice—or his valet—or his valet's man—or to take any office, however humble, that the retinue of such a princely officer could furnish—and then, of course, work his way up from there.

It was the spring of the year. The snows were melting in the mountains and the river had flooded the bottoms. The big circus vans, coming into town, had mired up on the river road a mile or two away and were stuck there in the mud up to the axle hubs. The circus people tried to get the vans out of the mud. It was a hard job, they had more than they could do, and they sent out calls for teamsters. Mr. Webber had two teams of iron-gray mules which he used for hauling: he rented them to the circus men that morning and came along himself to see that they got handled right.

It was Sunday morning. The weather had cleared after a week of rain and it was one of the first fine days of April. Judge Joyner and his son had hitched up the buggy and driven out to see the fun, and when they got there it seemed to the boy that everyone in town had come out to meet the circus. They found that part of the circus procession had gotten through all right, but the rest of it was stuck in the mud, with the circus people standing around the vans, cursing, cracking their whips at the big, straining horses, and making no progress whatever. They might as well have tried to pull those heavy vans out of the Everglades. Like Mercutio's wound, the mudhole in the road may not have been as deep as a well or as wide as a barn door, but it served, and the vans and wagons which had already managed to traverse it successfully had churned it up into something resembling the consistency of liquid glue.

So the horses tugged and strained, the circus people cracked their whips and cursed, the whole town looked on and marveled —the sunshine and the hills were the same as they had always been in April—and the big vans never budged. At this moment Mr. Webber arrived from town with two wagonloads of lumber and his four gray mules.

It was the first time the boy had ever seen him. When we are children, our initial impression of a man is likely to color everything we feel about him the rest of our lives, and certainly young Edward Joyner could have had no better introduction to the sharp and strong excitement of Mr. Webber's personality than he had on that bright morning. Everything about the bizarre situation—all so new and strange to the boy—with the brightly painted circus wagons and the big horses lined up along the road, the shining and enchanting day with every leaf still a-sparkle with the rain, and the rocky river, flooded to its muddy rim as he had never seen it before, rushing along with a full and almost soundless violence, and carrying with it the heavy, wet, and rotten, yet curiously fresh and pungent, smell of vegetation—all this gave to the occasion the thrill of a strange and wonderful excitement, as sharp and piercing as a blade.

Mr. Webber as he first appeared on the scene was one of the most extraordinary-looking people that young Edward Joyner had ever seen in his whole life. And this, apparently, was also the verdict of the crowd. As he came up, a kind of involuntary snort or gasp of laughter—more of sheer astonishment than anything else—rose upon the Sunday morning air. The little boys giggled, and Edward heard a man behind him saying softly, in a tone of wonder:

"Hell, I knew they had an elephant—but somebody must have left the monkey cage unlocked!"

At this remark, almost unpremeditated in its humor, there was louder and more open laughter, a growing wave of it throughout the crowd.

John Webber stood there on his wagonload of lumber, and, seen from below as the others had to look up at him, he did seem to fit the man's remark. Although he was somewhat above the average height, being about five feet ten inches tall, he gave the curious impression of being inches shorter. This came from a variety of causes, chief of which was a slightly "bowed" formation of his body. At first sight there was something distinctly simian in his short legs, bowed a little outward, his large, flat-looking feet, the powerful, barrel-like torso, and the tremendous gorilla-like length of his arms, with the huge paws dangling almost even with his knees. He had a thick, short neck that seemed to sink right down into the burly shoulders, and close sandy-reddish hair that grew down almost to the edges of the cheek bones and to just an inch or so above the eyes. His eyebrows were extremely thick and bushy, and he had the trick of peering out from under them with head out-thrust in an attitude of intensely still attentiveness. His nose was short, pointed, and turned up so sharply at the end that the nostrils almost seemed to flare; and consequently, he had an extremely long and simian upper lip. What was most startling of all, perhaps, was the extraordinary smallness—the extraordinary delicacy—of the features when contrasted with the power and weight of the big torso.

His costume on that sparkling Sunday morning was also remarkable. He was wearing his "good Sunday clothes." It was a suit of black broadcloth, heavy and well cut, the coat half cutaway, a stiff white shirt with starched cuffs, a wing collar with a cravat of black silk tied in a thick knot, and a remarkable-looking derby hat, pearl-gray in color and of a squarish cut. As he stood on his wagonload of lumber, he took off the hat and scratched his head thoughtfully, revealing as he did so that his sandy-reddish hair was thin on top, with a wide bald swathe right down the center of his skull.

It was at this instant that the crowd laughed. John Webber paid no attention. One would have thought that he did not hear the laughter, so unself-conscious was the dignity of his attitude, and almost instantly the crowd's disposition to laugh at him died out. He continued to survey the scene a moment, attentively and quietly, then got down off his wagon and said to one of the circus people:

"Take your horses out of the traces."

This was quickly done. The big horses were unhitched and plodded jangling down the road.

"Now," said Mr. Webber to his own teamsters, "unhitch those mules."

This was also done.

"You'd better let us use our horses," one of the circus people said. "We know how to handle horses."

"I know how to handle mules," said Mr. Webber. "Give me six of your men and help unload the lumber from my wagons."

The lumber was unloaded. In just a few minutes Mr. Webber had shored some stout timbers down into that sea of glue and got his two mule teams hitched up to the leading van; the big mules braced their muscles, strained, and the big van heaved up out of the mudhole and lurched forward onto solid earth.

Then Mr. Webber began to use the rest of his lumber. In a wonderfully short time, under his direction, the men had laid down a bridge across that treacherous sink, and one by one the big circus vans rolled forward and over it to safety.

Later, Mr. Webber came over to the buggy where Edward and

his father sat, and stood for a moment talking to Judge Joyner. Edward noticed that the man's good Sunday clothes were now spattered with mud, and that his big hand, as he rested it upon the buggy seat, was also caked with mud; but Mr. Webber seemed not to notice it at all. He just stood there talking quietly, as if such events as this were all in the day's work and must be taken as they came. Of what was said, the boy had no clear recollection later, except that Judge Joyner made some observation about the poor condition of the road, and that Mr. Webber, after looking at the slough again, shook his head with a short, strong movement, and said bluntly:

"We have pikes in Pennsylvania that have been good a hundred years."

Then he turned and walked away. And Judge Robert Joyner, as he gathered up the reins, said quietly to his son:

"There goes a very remarkable man."

It must have been only a month or two after this when young Edward saw the man again. Certainly it was that same year. Since the cornerstone of Judge Robert Joyner's old law office bears the date 1882, it is easy enough to fix the time.

Edward came out of the house one morning about nine o'clock and found Mr. Webber talking with his father in the yard.

"Now, Mr. Webber," he heard his father say, "what I have in mind is this: an office big enough for two good-sized rooms, one for my clerk and for any people who may be kept waiting, and one for my private use. I thought we'd put it about here—" he indicated the upper corner of the yard. "That would be, say, about twenty feet across, and about so deep—" he paced off the distance to which he thought the structure might extend. "Now, it's not going to be anything very fancy. I'm not even going to have an architect draw up the plans. I've sketched them out myself, and I think they will do. But what I had in mind was something plain and substantial, and I'd like to get an estimate from you on the cost."

"What material do you want to use?" asked Mr. Webber.

"Why—" Judge Joyner looked puzzled for a moment, then, glancing back toward the rambling gables of his house, with its clapboard covering, he said—"something like the house there, I suppose. Wouldn't you use pine?"

"No, sir," Mr. Webber answered firmly. "I'd build it with brick."

Young Edward was looking at Mr. Webber when he said this, and now for the first time it occurred to the boy that Mr. Webber was somewhat like a brick himself: the squat figure, the powerful shoulders, the thick neck, the red-weathered face, and the bald head, all had a compact solidity and coloring that suggested that he might be shaped from the materials in which he dealt. To the boy the idea seemed sensational and exciting. Mr. Webber's words surprised his father, too, for it had not occurred to him to use brick; and for a moment, while Mr. Webber waited stolidly, Judge Joyner was silent. Then, rather doubtfully, as if he were not sure he had heard a-right, he said:

"Brick?"

"Yes, sir," said Mr. Webber inflexibly, "brick. It's not going to cost you so much more than lumber by the time you're done, and," he went on quietly, and with conviction, "it's the only way to build. You can't rot it out. You can't rattle it or shake it. You can't kick holes in it. It will keep you warm in winter and cool in summer. And fifty years from now, or a hundred for that matter, it will still be here. I don't like lumber," Mr. Webber continued doggedly. "I don't like wooden houses. I come from Pennsylvania"—ah, there it was again!—"where they know how to build. Why," said Mr. Webber, with one of his rare displays of boastfulness, "we've got stone barns up there that are built better and will last longer than any house you've got in this whole section of the country. In my opinion there are only two materials for a house—stone or brick. And if I had my way," he added a trifle grimly, "that's how I'd build all of them."

The idea, once planted in Judge Joyner's mind, took firm root. So brick it was. Ground was broken for the office within a month, and before the summer was over the place was built and the Judge had moved into it.

And it's there yet, in between the corner filling station and the dilapidation of the old frame house, which now functions dismally as a "tourist home." The old office is still there, squat, blunt, rusty-looking, certainly not an architectural triumph, but living up in every respect to the specifications that John Webber laid down almost sixty years ago. Amid the wreckage of Libya Hill's recent boom it stands as a substantial survivor of an earlier time, a token that someone was here who believed in making things to last.

From that moment on, young Edward's memory of John Webber was tied up with brick. Also from that time on, the appearance of the town began to change, to take on here and there a more substantial look. And John Webber was himself so much the cause and agent of that change that if his whole life story, his epitaph, had to be written in eight words, there could be no better one than:

"Here lies a man who believed in brick."

Chapter 8

THE DEAD WORLD RELIVED

YOUNG EDWARD JOYNER'S OWN VIEW OF THINGS WAS BEGINNING to change about this time. Probably it would have changed anyway in the course of events, but because the impressions of boyhood are so influenced by personality, the whole change which was going on in him was always later to be identified with John Webber. Webber arrived in town just at the time when the old order was "yielding place to new"—when new forces and new faces were coming in, when the townspeople's thoughts and visionings were going *out*, when the town was first establishing its connections with the world. And because Webber was coincident with that process—indeed, did so much himself to fashion it—he always stood, in Edward Joyner's memory, as the incarnation of it.

Later, as he looked back upon his childhood, there was a kind of geographic dividing line which separated his conception of the world into two periods. It was a kind of Before Webber and After Webber time. It seemed to him that After Webber the color of life began to be different. In this time A. W., the world came in. Not only the look of things, but his whole sense of temporal events—his sense of time, the way he felt about the world—began to change. Seen in this perspective, the time B. W. had a curiously lost and lonely look, like the memory of a cloud shadow floating on a hill. Perhaps this is to say that, before, he had been a lost boy in the mountains; now he became a boy thinking of the world.

And because that earlier time—B. W.—is the harder to recapture, we shall begin by trying to describe it.

Sixty years ago, in Edward Joyner's childhood, Libya Hill was little more than a crossroads country village. The population was small, and most of the people had come there fairly recently. The "old settlers" were few in number; there were not many families who had lived in Libya Hill longer than young Edward Joyner's own. There may have been half a dozen other families of similar antiquity—the Blands, the Kennedys, the Duncans, the Owenbys, the McIntyres, and the Sheppertons—they could all be named in a minute.

This is not to say that any of them were really aliens, or, as the saying went, "outsiders." Most of them, even if they were not native to the town, were native to the region. Nine-tenths of them had been born within a radius of forty miles.

During Edward's early boyhood the print of the Civil War was still heavy on the memory of the town. Judge Joyner had been himself a soldier, and while Edward was growing up the boy came to see and know a great many of his father's comrades in the war. They were coming to the house to visit all the time. They liked his father, as most men did, and, in spite of Judge Joyner's instinctive and deep-rooted feeling against war, and his reticence in almost never speaking of his own part in it, he had a deep and quiet affection for these soldiers he had known. His son never heard him say a word that could be construed as criticism of any of them, either as a man or as a soldier. Sometimes other soldiers who had been with him in the war would criticise some General for what they conceived to be a strategic or a critical mistake—Hooker at Chancellorsville, Ewell at Gettysburg, Stuart on his raid through Pennsylvania. Yes! there were even times when the sacred name of Lee himself was mentioned critically, his judgment questioned. In discussions such as these the elder Joyner listened quietly, but took almost no part at all.

His son could remember only one occasion when he did express an active opinion on the conduct of the war. This was once when General Gordon, who was a friend, had been talking about Gettysburg; there was silence for a moment when he finished speaking. Then Judge Robert Joyner turned to him, his square face reddened painfully, and he blurted out: "We could have *had* it! We could have *had* it!" Then he turned away and muttered: "The whole truth is we didn't really *want* it! . . . We didn't really *want* to win!"

Gordon looked at him for a moment with a startled expression, seemed about to speak, and changed his mind. But this was the only time the boy ever heard his father utter an opinion of any sort about the conduct of the war.

Nevertheless, he heard hundreds of discussions such as these during his boyhood; the soldiers were always coming to the house to visit his father. At one time or another, a good many of the Generals stayed there: Pettigrew, McLaws, Iverson and Heth, Jenkins, Hood, and John B. Gordon, that generous and gallant soldier who stood in the boy's adoring vision as the ideal of what a man and soldier ought to be. It was a glorious experience for a boy to sit in breathless silence while these brave men talked, to drink the war in to the very limits of idolatry beneath the magic spell of the war's great men. Their talk was meat to him, their talk was drink to him, the sparkling of bright wine to him! He felt the pulse of it, he breathed the glorious air of it, he felt the singing and the joy of it!

It was all sweet smells and sounds and sights . . . with Jubal Early swinging in his saddle on the skirts of Washington. It was all good tastes and glorious war, like perfumes . . . with Stuart's cavalry pounding up the roads of Pennsylvania. It was the lovely smells of smoking flanks and sweating withers, the glorious smells of sweated leather, the smell of worn saddles, the good reek of the cavalry! And it was apple-blossom smell with troops among it; and campfire smells, and brown-coffee smells, and wheatfield smells in Pennsylvania, and cornfield smells in Maryland, and hayloft smells and troopers up and down Virginia, and all the dogwood and the laurel in the Shenandoah Valley in the spring! And, best of all, it was the acrid battle smells, the smells of gunshot and of powder, the smells of cannon-shot, the sultry thunder of artillery, the smells of cartridges, shrapnel, grapeshot, minnie balls, and canister!

When these men talked, he saw it all, he felt it all, he breathed and tasted it all—all of the glory, joy, and fragrance of the war— none of its stench and filth and misery. It was not in the boy's heart to understand the sadness and the sorrow in the talking of the Generals. He never saw the failure and defeat of it, the passionate regret of it, the constant repetition of its bitter and incessant litany of *"Why?"*

Why, they would earnestly demand, had someone left his right flank unprotected, when he should have had sufficient warning of the pressure of Hancock's infantry behind the wood? *Why* had someone mistaken a picket fence for a line of soldiers? *Why* had there been a mile's interval between someone's line and his support? *Why* had someone waited from eleven-thirty in the morning until two-thirty in the afternoon to follow up his own advance and effect the total rout of an exhausted enemy? *Why* had someone not instantly taken possession of the hill, when he must have known it was undefended?

Why had Jubal Early, Gordon passionately demanded, not followed up the rout of Cedar Creek with one single, crushing, and conclusive blow? *Why,* when Hancock's army was in a state of almost total rout, its divisions scattered and its force demoialized, when only a single corps of the whole army was intact— *Why* in God's name had Early failed to give the order for capture and annihilation of that corps, and pounded it to pieces, which a few batteries of artillery could have done? *Why,* when a glorious victory was ours, had he refrained from making it complete, and allowed a vanquished enemy to gather up its shattered forces, and so had let a glorious victory be turned to terrible defeat?

Embattled *"Why?"* and wildly-longing *"If"*—the two great dirges of defeated men! *If* someone had not acted as he had; *If* someone had not gone where he had gone, or stayed where he had stayed; *If* someone had only seen what others saw, believed what others told him, known what others knew; *If* only someone hadn't waited, or had done at once what others would have done without delay—"Yes, *If,*" as Zachariah Joyner said with bitter irony, *"If* only men were gods instead of children; *If* they were seers and prophets gifted with prevision and foresight; *If* battlefields were checkerboards of logic instead of fields of chance; *If* someone had not been just what he was at the place and moment where he was—in short, *If* flesh were not flesh, and brain not brain, and man's nature, feeling, thought, and error not the things they are—then there would never be defeats and victory, there would be faultless logic, but no war!"

As for the boy, he saw the thrill of it, he saw the glory of it; he never saw the defeated hopes and passionate regrets of it, in these earnest conversations of the Generals. For, no matter what their sorrow, how deep and unassuaged their resignation, the Generals were grand men. Inhuman war had fostered in them all a wise and deep humanity; fatherless death upon the battlefield, a kind of deep and powerful paternity; awful responsibility, a calm and unperturbed serenity, a total fearlessness of death or life, a tenderness toward man and child, and to all living. He heard them talk of another's error, and confess their own. He heard them question another's judgment, not his courage. He heard them engage in hot debate and open criticism, but there was no recrimination. They were good men, the Generals. They were not jealous, vengeful, petty, mean, and bitter people; theirs was the grief of grief, the sorrow of irrevocable loss; theirs was the sadness for the shattered past, all of the lost joy and the singing—but there was no hate.

And to the boy it seemed a good life that they lived then— sixty years ago. He saw and heard them talk, he listened breath- lessly to everything they had to say, he devoured every scrap that they had written—memoirs, reminiscences, autobiographies, personal experiences in the war, as well as complex and highly technical discussions about battles and campaigns, errors in strategy, technical maneuvers. As a result of it, his studies in school suffered disastrously. His grammar was a thing of shreds and patches, his algebra was worse than negligible. To his father's blunt and frequently outspoken disgust, he was deep in "flanking operations" of all sorts, and a "covering movement" held no terrors for him. He had small Latin, and less Greek, but his knowledge of his rear, his wings, his right, his left, his center, and the position of his supporting columns was encyclopædic and profound.

He was, as he admitted in his later years, obsessed. He would go for days at a time completely lost to all around him, sunk in a whole dream-world of war, a war in which *he* played the con- spicuous part, a war exclusively concerned with *his* tactics, *his* strategies, *his* battles, *his* campaigns, *his* final and decisive vic- tories—for, since he was a warrior of twelve years, *his* victories were always final and decisive. In all his gory struggles, *he* never lost a battle, or made a technical mistake.

In his mind's eye, and in his war-drunk heart and spirit, he composed entire histories, extraordinary documents woven of a dozen different styles, and cunningly combining the most exciting features in the works of all his literary masters—the cold and dry precisions, the technical analysis of the Northern General Doubleday, the flaming and impulsive rhetoric of John B. Gordon. Like Molière and Shakespeare, the boy took what he wanted where he found it, and, like both his illustrious predecessors, he may sometimes have improved upon his theft:

"The scene upon our left was one of indescribable confusion. Early, unaware of Hancock's movements in the morning, and, through an error of his faulty vision mistakenly assuming that a picket fence somewhat to his right and rear was a supporting column of his own troops, had rashly thrown out his left to the very edges of the wood—when the attack occurred. At this moment, when the Southern line was still resting on its arms, a solid wall of flame and fire burst from the wood. At the same instant, Hancock's right, under the command of Hays, swept out behind the cover of the wood around the flank of Early's unsuspecting line. Under the murderous cross fire of this enfilading movement and the solid frontal wall of Hazard's guns, the whole left crumpled like a piece of paper, and was driven in upon the weakened center. The Union cavalry under Pleasanton now dashed from the woods and drove through the thinned and shattered lines, and the rout was complete.

"It was at just this moment that Lee turned to that young and brilliant officer who, alone of all his Generals, had from the outset of the battle rightly judged the movements through the wood of Hancock's men.

" 'General Joyner,' he said gravely—for he was speaking to

none other than the famous Edward Zebulon Joyner, the youngest general officer in the Confederate Army, the commander of
the famous Iron-Wall Brigade, a stripling in years and in appearance, but a scarred veteran of battle despite his youth, and in
tactical judgment and strategic skill perhaps the superior of any
other officer in the whole Army of Virginia—'General Joyner,'
said Lee gravely, as he pointed toward the fatal wood, 'do you
think that position there is tenable and may be taken by our men?'

"For a moment the young officer was silent. A look of deep
sadness and resignation overspread his handsome countenance,
for he, better than all others, knew at what fearful cost of men—
the men of his own gallant and beloved command—the operation
might succeed. He of all men realized the tragic blunder that
had been committed—the tragic consequence of Early's obstinate
refusal to heed the warnings he had given him that morning—
but no matter what he felt or thought, he masked his feelings
bravely, his hesitation was only momentary. Looking Lee directly
in the eyes, he answered firmly:

" 'Yes, General Lee, I think that the position in the wood *is*
tenable and may be held.'

" 'Then, General,' said Lee quietly, 'I have just one other
question. Do you think that course the only one that is left us?'

"The young hero's answer came this time without an instant's
hesitation, as clear and ringing as a shot:

" 'Sir, I do!'

"Lee was silent for a moment; when he spoke, his voice was
very sad.

" 'Then, Sir,' he said, 'you may advance.'

"Without an instant of delay, the young leader gave the order;
his veteran troops swept forward, the great attack had begun."

This was the kind of thing, as Edward Joyner later on confessed, to which his fantasy was susceptible in the eighties. He not only thought and dreamed volumes of it in his mind and heart—he actually *wrote* whole reams and packets of it out on paper; and one of the most painful experiences of his life occurred when he came home one afternoon and found his father sitting at his roll-top desk reading a great batch of it. The boy had thought his secret safe, but had very imprudently stuffed the manuscript away in an unused drawer, and the Judge had come upon it unexpectedly while going through his desk to find some letters.

He looked up at his son briefly, very grimly, when he entered; then, without a word of greeting, he went back to his interrupted reading of that damning scrawl, that devastating revelation of his miserable soul.

And Edward sat there wretchedly and watched him, as he read page after page. His father sat at the desk, with his broad back turned on the boy, the late light gleaming on the polished surface of his bald head, with only his thick red neck, the angle of his square red jaw, a small portion of his square red face, exposed. Although the boy could not see the expression of that square red face, he did not have to use much of his imagination to vision its grim intensity. And as Edward sat there, staring wretchedly, he could see that red neck turn a redder hue, the red jaw thickening to an angry purple. Near the end of his perusal, which, like everything he did, was most deliberate and thorough —*horribly* complete, it seemed to the boy, as he watched him read each page slowly and carefully from top to bottom, turning each page face down carefully with a thick and hairy hand when he had finished it—his father began to give utterance to certain harsh, explosive sounds indicative of partial strangulation, and to certain fragmentary expletives which were translatable to his offspring's tortured ears as follows:

"'. . . flanking operations!' . . . Pah!"

And bang! The offending sheet would be thumped down on its miserable face.

"'. . . murderous enfilading fire which drove his whole left back upon his center—which crumpled like a sheet of tissue paper!' . . . What damned rubbish is this anyway?"

Bang! And down went this one on its miserable face.

"'. . . that brilliant and gallant young Commander, the flower of the Confederate cavalry, as he was the pride of their success, whose superb tactical manipulations might alone have served to save the day if only——'"

This, finally, was too much for him! He banged the offending sheet of paper down upon his desk with a tremendous thump, he raised his square red face, and roared out like a bewildered man imploring heaven:

"Great God! Whoever read such Goddamned stuff as this since time began?"

Then he composed himself again, and went back to his reading. Slowly, deliberately, with agonizing thoroughness, he read the whole thing through to the bitter, miserable end. When he had finished, he sat silent for a moment, his thick hands clenched upon the desk, his burly shoulders leaning forward, breathing somewhat slowly and stertorously, like a man trying to think his way through some problem to a laborious conclusion. At last he gathered up the manuscript in his thick fingers, carefully arranged it, put it into the little drawer from which it had come— where the boy had thought it was so safe—and, fumbling in his vest pocket for a small key, locked the drawer. Then he swung around in his old swivel chair, and faced his son grimly and in silence for a moment. And now he took a sheet of paper from his pocket—a sheet which obviously had been crumpled violently in his hand, and at whose telltale and abhorred appearance the boy's heart stopped beating—and, smoothing it out carefully with his big fingers, he presented it to his son:

"Here's your report card. It just came today. Among your other academic victories I notice you got forty-two in history."

Then he got up, still breathing loudly, and limped heavily and slowly from the room.

Edward's father never spoke to him of this humiliating episode again. One of the greatest elements of that blunt, inarticulate, and desperately shy man was his generosity, the warmth and understanding of his essential humanity. His words could be as direct and brutal as a blow of the fist, but once he had spoken, he was done with it; what was past was past, he didn't bear grudges, or try to persuade people to his own judgments or beliefs by the ignoble practices of incessant argument, recessive bickerings.

Nevertheless, he was seriously perturbed by the strength and virulence of the boy's obsession. By the time Edward was fourteen, he was openly and passionately announcing that he was going to West Point if he could get an appointment. Although the father's usual comment on this was a scornful grunt, or a blunt comment that "You'd better be thinking of some means of earning an honest living and being a useful citizen," he was deeply and seriously alarmed. The truth was that Judge Joyner would rather have had his son choose any other profession in the world than that of the soldier; every instinct of his nature, every element of his character, abhorred the whole idea and the life of war.

"It's not a life, anyway," he said. "It's death. It's true the finest men I ever knew, I knew because I went to war. But I went to war because I *had* to go—and that was the reason that the others went. But the reason that you meet fine men in war is because it is fine men who have to go to war; it is not war that makes them fine. War is the filthiest, rottenest, corruptest, and most damnable disease that man and the devil have invented; and because it is the filthiest, rottenest, corruptest, and most damnable disease, it brings out the most heroic and ennobling qualities that men have. But don't deceive yourself; the reason that war brings out these qualities is not because war is good, but because war is bad. These qualities come out in men who go to war because without these qualities men could not suffer and endure it. Sherman said that war is hell; well, he was wrong. War is not hell, war is worse than hell, war is death!"

He was silent for a moment, his square face reddening as he strove to speak:

"To hell with death!" he grunted.

His son pointed out to him, with all the earnestness and persuasiveness of youth, the advantages of getting "a good education" at West Point free of charge, and added that, even though he went to West Point and got an officer's commission, "I might not even have to go to war; there might not ever be another war."

"That would be a fine life, wouldn't it?" Judge Joyner said. "If that's all the value you put upon your life, why don't you just chuck it off the top of Mount Mitchell and be done with it?"

The boy was troubled and bewildered. "Why? How do you mean?"

"I mean you'd be doing something just as useful, for yourself and for your country—and at just a fraction of the expense. No!" he shook his head doggedly. "A peacetime soldier is no good at all. He is a parasite, a fool, and his head is about as useful to him, or to society, as a doorknob. . . . No! You find good men in an army in time of war; in time of peace you find tin soldiers."

He was very scornful of "tin soldiers." No man was ever more generous or fair when he spoke of his own comrades in the war, but, like Zachariah, his contempt for the military pretensions of people such as Theodore was frank and pitiless.

Robert Joyner was especially exasperated to see that the terrible experience of the war had taught so many people nothing. His homely character abhorred romantic flummery. He was an intelligent and experienced observer of men and customs, and perfectly aware of a fatal weakness in the Southern temperament —its capacity for romantic self-deception and mythology. The very root and source of his practical and hopeful character was a spirit that would not yield an atom to defeat. He was the type of man who, had his own house burned down, would have begun to build a new one before the smoking embers had grown cold; and, had he needed them, he would have pulled the very nails out of the smoking embers.

At the moment of Lee's surrender, he undoubtedly had his plans made and knew what work he had to do, and do at once. When he got home, he began immediately to rebuild his life, and from that time on he never faltered at his task—which was, which *always* was, the task before him, the work at hand.

"If there's a job to do," he told his son—"and you will find as you grow older that there always *is* a job to do—for God's sake, lay a-hold of it, and *shove!* Don't shilly-shally, and don't mess around! That's the trouble with so many of us now! It's always been a trouble in the South. I hoped the war would have knocked some of that foolishness out of us, but you can see yourself what has happened, can't you? God knows, before the war the thing was bad enough—Sir Walter Scott, fake chivalry, fake lords and ladies, fake ideals of honor, fake wooden columns on the houses—everything fake except the plumbing, which wasn't fake because it didn't exist at all. And now, look at the thing that's happened to us. I hoped the war would have knocked all that rubbish into a cocked hat, that the beating which we had to take would wake us up, and that when we got home, we'd start off with a clean slate, make a fresh start. That's the thing,

Ed!" Robert Joyner cried, and smote his big hand down upon the desk. "*Get really started!* Don't you realize that that's the thing that ails us in the South? It's not the war. It's not the war that ruined us. Most of us," he went on grimly, "were ruined long before the war! It's all rubbish for most of us to talk of what we lost, because we had nothing to begin with. And the real truth of the matter is that we got off on the wrong foot at the beginning—we made a bad *start*! Why," cried Robert Joyner earnestly, and brought his big fist down upon the desk again, "looked at it in one way, that war might have been the best thing that ever happened to us—if we had only seen it in the proper light. It gave us the chance to *start off with a clean slate*—to wipe out that whole fake and shoddy way of life—and to begin anew! —to get started *right*! And now just see the thing that's happened!" In his earnestness, he leaned forward and tapped his son on the knee with one big finger. "For every fake we had before the war we have ten new ones nowadays, and each of them is ten times as bad! Some of the people back before the war *did* have some basis for their pretensions. If they lived in houses with fake columns, at least some of them did own such houses; and although their niggers ate them out of house and home, at least some of them did own niggers. But look at the kind of people you meet everywhere today. You have people talking of the great estates and houses that they lost who were born in shacks and raised on hog and hominy. You find people—like Old Looky Thar!" cried Robert Joyner scornfully, mentioning a local character to whom Zachariah had given this strange name for reasons that shall presently appear. "You find people like Old Looky Thar—who calls himself a 'Major' now, and never even rose up to a corporal's chevrons. Yes! and tells you of all the land and property he owned, and all the niggers that he lost! You've heard him, haven't you?"

" 'No, Suh!' " Zachariah broke in at this point, imitating perfectly the exact tone and quality of Old Looky Thar's high-
pitched, cracked, and drawling voice. " 'We wa'nt no common
trash. We owned *niggers*, we did!—We had big estates an' great
plantations, *we* did!—We were *big* folks in the community, I
tell you!—Why, up to the time I was twenty-two, I nevah had to
lace up my own shoes. We had *niggers* fo' *that* kind of work!' . . .
Shoes!" roared Zachariah, and banged his big hand down. "Why,
damn his soul, that old mountain grill was lucky if he ever *saw*
a pair of shoes before he was twenty-two years old, much less
own a pair! And as for niggers, I *know* he never saw a nigger until
he came to Libya Hill, just before the war, for he was born
and raised on Thumb Toe Creek out in Zebulon, where niggers
were unknown. As we all know, the mountain people hated
them. And as for great estates and houses—why, Goddamn his
lying hide!" yelled Zack. "He was brought up in a lean-to shanty
—he was lucky if he had a corncob—and if he went out in the
woods, he had to take a stick along to kill the snakes with! There's
your fine old Southern gentry—Looky Thar!"

"And it's not the Looky Thars alone, my boy," Judge Robert
Joyner went on earnestly. "It's all the people who *might* do something and who never do—the people who sit around on their
behinds mourning the loss of something that they never *had*.
Did you ever hear the scientist's description of a certain phi-
losopher as a blind man searching in a dark room for a black
cat that wasn't *there?*—Well, the South is full of just such
people—people who sit around and sit around, mourning the
loss of something that they never had, or are better off without—
and there's *work* to be done! A whole new world to build, a
whole new life, better than anything we ever had before! . . .
And . . . we ought to be up and *doing* it. We ought to lay

a-hold and shove—there's nothing to delay us. As old Salmon P. Chase said: 'The only way to resumption is to *resume*!' "

"Well," young Edward said, "why are you always poking fun at Uncle Theodore and his school? He *resumed*, didn't he? He started up the school again just as soon as he got back from the war."

"Yes, he did," his father answered, "but you ought not to resume making a fool of yourself. You ought not to resume tin-soldierdom. You ought not to resume turning out little tin soldiers for a world that has need of *men*. You ought not to resume training little tin soldiers for a war that has already been fought! That's like locking the barn door after the horse is stolen."

"An occupation, by the way," Zachariah put in at this point, "in which your Uncle Theodore excels!"

"You ought not to resume the kind of foolishness and fakery and lying that ruined you in the first place," his father went on. "You ought to resume being what God made you for—what you were intended to be."

"What is that?" asked the boy.

His father looked at him a moment with his round blue eyes, his own strangely boyish earnestness.

"A *man*!" he said. "A fellow who doesn't whine about the past or groan about what can't be helped! A fellow who is willing to *work* like a man—and *act* like a man—and—*be* a man!"

"Like who?" asked young Edward pointedly.

"Why—why—" his father breathed heavily, craned his thick red neck, looked around from side to side, and suddenly found his answer—"like John Webber! That's who! There's a *man* for you!" And he thumped his big fist on the desk.

"Well," young Edward said and laughed, "he may be. But some people think he *looks* like a monkey."

"I don't care what they say," the Judge said doggedly. "There's a *man*! He goes ahead and does things. That's the kind of fellow that we need!"

At this moment, as if to remind him that he himself had things to do, the courthouse bell began to ring, and he got up to go.

Chapter 9

THE BELL STRIKES THREE

LATER, IT SEEMED TO EDWARD JOYNER THAT HIS WHOLE CHILDHOOD had been haunted by the ringing of the courthouse bell. It got into almost every memory he had of early youth. It beat wildly, with advancing and receding waves of sound through stormy autumn days. In the sharp, sweet loveliness of spring, the bloom of April and the green of May, the courthouse bell was also there: it gave a brazen pulse to haunting solitudes of June, getting into the rustling of a leaf, speaking to morning with its wake-o'-day of "Come to court," and jarring the drowsy torpor of the afternoon with "Court again."

It was a rapid and full-throated cry, a fast stroke beating on the heels of sound. Its brazen tongue, its hard and quickening beat, were always just the same, yet never seemed the same. The constant rhythm of its strokes beat through his heart and brain and soul with all the passionate and mad excitements of man's fate and error, and he read into the sound his own imagined meanings.

He never heard it as a boy without a faster beating of the pulse, a sharp, dry tightening of the throat, a numb aerial bouyancy of deep excitement. At morning, shining morning in the spring, it would seem to speak to him of work-a-day, to tell him that the world was up and doing, advancing to the rattling traffics of full noon. In afternoon it spoke with still another tongue, breaking the dull-eyed hush of somnolent repose with its demand for action. It spoke to bodies drowsing in the midday warmth, and told them they must rudely break their languorous siesta. It spoke to stomachs drugged with heavy food, crammed full of turnip greens and corn, string beans and pork, hot biscuits and hot apple pie, and it told them it was time to gird their swollen loins for labor, that man's will and character must rise above his belly, that work was doing, and that night was not yet come.

Again, in morning, it would speak of civil actions, of men at law and the contentions of a suit. Its tone was full of writs and summonses, of appearances and pleadings. Sometimes its hard, fast tongue would now cry out: "Appear!"

"Appear, appear, appear, appear, appear, appear, appear!"
Again:
"Your property is mine—is mine—is mine—is mine—is mine!"
Or, yet again, harsh, peremptory, unyielding, unexplained:
"You come to court—to court—to court—to court—to court— to court!"
Or, more brusque and more commanding still, just:
"Court—court—court—court—court—court—court!"

In afternoon, the courthouse bell would speak of much more fatal punishment—of murder on trial, of death through the heated air, of a dull, slow-witted mountain wretch who sat there in the box, with a hundred pairs of greedy eyes upon him, and, still half unaware of what he did, let out the killer's sudden sob, itself like blood and choking in the throat, and instantly the sun went blood-smeared in the eyes, with the feel and taste of blood throughout, upon the sultry air, upon the tongue and in the mouth, and across the very visage of the sun itself, with all the brightness of the day gone out. Then, as the clanging stroke continued, a cloud-shape passed upon the massed green of a mountain flank, and the gold-bright sun of day returned, and suddenly there were bird-thrumming wood notes everywhere, swift and secret, bullet-wise within the wilderness, and the drowsy stitch and drone of three o'clock through coarse, sweet grasses of the daisied fields, and there beneath his feet the boy beheld the life-blood of a murdered man soaking quietly down before him into an unsuspected hand's breadth of familiar earth—all as sudden, swift, and casual as this, all softly done as the soft thrummings in the wood. And as the brazen strokes went on, he saw again the prisoner in the box, all unknowing still of the reason why he did it, a stunned animal caught in the steel traps of law, and now, with those hundred pairs of greedy eyes upon him, the courthouse bell was pounding on the torpor of hot afternoon the stark imperative of its inflexible command:

"To kill—to kill—to kill—to kill—to kill—to kill!"

And then, dying out upon the heated air, just:

"Kill—kill—kill kill kill kill killkillkill . . . !"

It is doubtful if people of a younger and more urban generation can realize the way the county courthouse shaped human life and destiny through all America some sixty years ago. In Libya Hill the courthouse was the center of the community, for Libya Hill had been the county courthouse before it was a town. The town grew up around the courthouse, made a Square, and straggled out along the roads that led away to the four quarters of the earth.

And for the country people round about, the courthouse was even more the center of life and interest than it was for the townsfolk. The countrymen came into town to trade and barter, to buy and sell; but when their work was over, it was always to the courthouse that they turned. When court was being held, one could always find them here. Here, in the Square outside, were their mules, their horses, their ox-teams, and their covered wagons. Here, inside the building, were their social converse and their criminal life. Here were their trials, suits, and punishments, their relatives accused, their friends and enemies acquitted or convicted, their drawling talk of rape and lust and murder— the whole shape and pattern of their life, their look, their feel, their taste, their smell.

Here was, in sum, the whole framework of America—the abysmal gap between its preachment and performance, its grain of righteousness and its hill of wrong. Not only in the voices and the persons of these country people, these mountaineers who sat and spat and drawled and loitered on the courthouse steps, but in the very design and structure of the courthouse building itself did the shape and substance of their life appear. Here in the pseudo-Greek façade with the false front of its swelling columns, as well as in the high, square dimensions of the trial courtroom, the judge's bench, the prisoner's box, the witness stand, the lawyers' table, the railed-off area for participants, the benches for spectators behind, the crossed flags of the state and of the nation, the steel engraving of George Washington—in all these furnishings of office there was some effort to maintain the pomp of high authority, the outward symbols of a dignified, impartial execution of the law. But, alas, the execution of the law was, like the design and structure of the courthouse itself, not free from error, and not always sound. The imposing Doric and Corinthian columns were often found, upon inspection, to be just lath and brick and plaster trying to be stone. No matter what pretensions to a classic austerity the courtroom itself might try to make, the tall and gloomy-looking windows were generally unwashed. No matter what effect of Attic graces the fake façade might have upon the slow mind of the countryman, the wide, dark corridors were full of drafts and unexpected ventilations, darkness, creaking boards, squeaking stairways, and the ominous dripping of an unseen tap.

And the courthouse smell was like the smell of terror, crime, and justice in America—a certain essence of our life, a certain sweat out of ourselves, a certain substance that is ours alone, and unmistakable. What was this smell of courthouse justice in America? What were the smells of terror, law, and crime in this great land? It was a single and yet most high, subtle, and composite stink: made up of many things, yet, like the great union that produced it, one smell and one alone—one and indivisible!

It was—to get down to its basic chemistries—a smell of sweat, tobacco juice, and urine; a smell of sour flesh, feet, clogged urinals, and broken-down latrines. It was, mixed in and subtly interposed with these, a smell of tarry disinfectant, a kind of lime and alum, a strong ammoniac smell. It was a smell of old dark halls and old used floorways, a cool, dark, dank, and musty cellar-smell. It was a smell of old used chairs with creaking bottoms, a smell of sweated woods and grimy surfaces; a smell of rubbed-off arm rests, bench rests, chair rests, of counters, desks, and tables; a smell as if every inch of woodwork in the building had been oiled, stewed, sweated, grimed, and polished by man's flesh.

In addition to all these, it was a smell of rump-worn leathers, a smell of thumb-worn calfskin, yellowed papers, and black ink. It was a smell of brogans, shirt-sleeves, overalls, and sweat and hay and butter. It was a kind of dry, exciting smell of chalk, of starched cuffs that rattled—a smell that went with the incessant rattling of dry papers, the crackling of dry knuckles and parched fingers, the rubbing of dry, chalky hands—a country lawyer smell of starch and broadcloth.

And oh, much more than these—and *all* of these—it was a smell of fascination and of terror, a smell of throbbing pulse and beating heart and the tight and dry constriction of the throat. It was a smell made up of all the hate, the horror, the fear, the chicanery, and the loathing that the world could know; a smell made up of the intolerable anguish of man's nerve and heart and sinew, the sweat and madness of man's perjured soul enmeshed in trickery—a whole huge smell of violence and crime and murder, of shyster villainies and broken faith. And to this high and mountainous stench of error, passion, guilt, graft, and wrong, there was added one small smell of justice, fairness, truth, and hope.

The county courthouse was, in short, America—the wilderness America, the sprawling, huge, chaotic, criminal America. It was murderous America soaked with murdered blood, tortured and purposeless America, savage, blind, and mad America, exploding through its puny laws, its pitiful pretense. It was America with all its almost hopeless hopes, its almost faithless faiths—America with the huge blight on her of her own error, the broken promise of her lost dream and her unachieved desire; and it was America as well with her unspoken prophecies, her unfound language, her unuttered song. And just for all these reasons it was for us all our own America—with all her horror, beauty, tenderness, and terror —with all we know of her that never has been proved, that has never yet been uttered—the only one we know, the only one there is.

Young Edward Joyner's interest in the courthouse and the courthouse bell was a double one: the sound of that great and brazen bell not only punctuated almost every experience of his youth, but it also punctuated almost every memory that he had of his father. Since his father was a judge of the Circuit Court of Appeals, the whole record of the boy's life during this period might have been chronicled in the ringing of the bell. When the bell rang, court was in session and his father was in town; when the bell did not ring, court was not in session, and his father was holding court in some other town.

Moreover, when the bell began to ring, his father was at home; and before the bell had finished ringing he was on his way to court. The ceremony of his going was always the same; his son watched him perform it a thousand times, and it never changed or varied by a fraction. He would get home at one o'clock for lunch—or "dinner" as they called it in those days. He would eat in a preoccupied silence, speaking rarely, and probably thinking of the case that he was trying at the moment. After dinner, he would go into his office or "study," stretch himself out on his old leather sofa, and nap or doze for three-quarters of an hour. His son often watched him while he took this brief siesta; he slept with a handkerchief spread out across his face, and with only the top of his bald head visible. Often, these naps or dozes produced snores of very formidable proportions, and the big hand-kerchief would blow up beneath the blast like a sail that catches a full wind.

But no matter how profound or deep these slumbers seemed to be, he would always rouse himself at the first stroke of the courthouse bell, snatch the handkerchief from his face, and sit bolt upright with an expression of intense and almost startled surprise on his red face and in his round blue eyes:

"There's the *bell*!" he would cry, as if this was the last thing on earth he had expected. Then he would get up, limp over to his desk, stuff papers, briefs, and documents into his old worn briefcase, jam a battered old slouch hat upon his head, and limp heavily down the hall to the sitting room, where young Edward's mother would be busy at her sewing.

"I'm going now!" he would announce in a tone that seemed to convey a kind of abrupt and startled warning. To this his wife would make no answer whatever, but would continue placidly at her sewing, as if she had been expecting this surprising information all the time.

Then Edward's father, after staring at her for a minute in a somewhat puzzled, undecided manner, would limp off down the hall, pause halfway, limp back to the open door, and fairly shout:

"I say, *I'm going!*"

"Yes, Robert," his wife would answer placidly, still busy with her needle. "I heard you."

Whereupon, he would glare at her again, in a surprised and baffled manner, and finally blurt out:

"Is there anything you want from town?"

To which she would say nothing for a moment, but would lift the needle to the light, and, squinting, thread it.

"I say," he shouted, as if he were yelling to someone on top of a mountain, *"is—there—anything—you—want—from—town?"*

"No, Robert," she would presently reply, with the same maddening placidity, "I think not. We have everything we need."

At these words, Edward's father would stare at her fixedly, breathing heavily, with a look of baffled indecision and surprise. Then he would turn abruptly, grunting, "Well, good-bye then," and limp down the hall and down the steps, and heavily and rapidly away across the yard. And the last thing Edward would see of his father until evening would be the sight of his stocky figure, with the battered old brief case underneath his arm, limping away up the straggling street of the little town, while the courthouse bell still beat out its hard and rapid stroke.

Judge Joyner often said that, outside of a battlefield, a courtroom could be the most exciting place on earth, because it provided the greatest opportunity there was for observing life and character. And it seemed to his son that he was right.

When an interesting case was being tried, he sometimes took his son with him. Young Edward saw and heard a great many wonderful and fascinating things, a great many brutal and revolting things, as well. By the time he was fifteen he was not only pretty familiar with courtroom procedure, but he had seen men on trial for their lives. He had watched the thrilling and terrible adventure of pursuit and capture, the cunning effort of the hounds of law to break down evidence, to compel confession, to entrap and snare—the hounds full running, and the fox at bay. And he heard trials for every other thing on earth as well—for theft, assault, and robbery; for blackmail, arson, rape, and petty larceny; for deep-dyed guilt and perjured innocence—all of the passion, guilt, and cunning, all of the humor, love, and faithfulness, all of the filth and ignorance, the triumph and defeat, the pain and the fulfillment, that the earth can know, or of which man's life is capable.

Yes, the courthouse in those days was a wonderful place to observe the drama of man's life and character: not only in the proceedings of the trials themselves, but in the people who attended them—the crowd of "courthouse loafers" that were always hanging round. A good deal of the life of the whole town was here—and if not a good deal of its "character," at least most of its "characters."

Although his father's house on School Street was just a few blocks from the courthouse on the Square—so near, in fact, that he could be in court before the bell had finished with its brazen ringing—in those days they would pass a large part of the town's population in the course of that short journey. Every step of their way was punctuated by greetings, such as "Hello, Judge," or "Good morning, Judge," or "Good afternoon"—and his father's brief, grunted-out replies as he limped along:

" 'Lo, Sam."

"Morning, Jim."

"Day, Tom."

He was a good walker in spite of his limp, and, when in a hurry, he could cover ground fast—so fast, indeed, that the boy had to "stir his stumps" to keep abreast of him.

Arrived at the courthouse, they were greeted by the usual nondescript conglomeration of drawling countryfolk, tobacco-chewing mountaineers, and just plain loafers who made the porches, steps, and walls of the old courthouse their club, their prop, their stay, their fixed abode—and almost, it seemed to the boy, their final resting place. Certainly some of them were, in his father's phrase, "as old as God," and had been sitting on the courthouse steps, or leaning against the courthouse walls, longer than most people could remember.

Chief among these ancient sons of leisure—he was, by tacit consent, generally considered chief of them—was the venerable old reprobate who was always referred to, when his back was turned, as "Looky Thar." Zachariah Joyner had given him that title, and it stuck forever after, chiefly because of its exceeding fitness. Looky Thar's real name was Old Man Purtle. Although he called himself Major Purtle, and was generally addressed as "Major" by his familiars, friends, and acquaintances, the title was self-bestowed, and had no other basis in fact or actuality.

Old Looky Thar had been a soldier in the war, and, in addition to the loss of a leg, he had suffered a remarkable injury which had earned for him his irreverent and flippant name. This injury was a *hole* in the roof of his mouth, "big enough to stick your hull fist through," in Looky Thar's own description of its dimensions, the result of an extraordinary shrapnel wound which had miraculously spared his life, but had unfortunately not impaired his powers of speech. He was one of the lewdest, profanest, dirtiest-minded old men that ever lived, and his obscenities were published in a high, cracked falsetto and accompanied by a high, cracked cackle, easily heard by people one hundred yards away.

He was, if anything, prouder of that great hole in his mouth than he was of his wooden leg; he was, in fact, more pleased about it than he would have been over election to the Legion of Honor. That hole in the roof of his mouth not only became the be-all and the sufficient reason for his right to live, it became the be-all for his right to loaf. The hole in the roof of his mouth justified him in everything he said or thought or felt or did, for he apparently believed that it gave to all his acts and utterances a kind of holy and inspired authority, a divine and undebatable correctness. If anyone had the effrontery—was upstart enough— to question any of Looky Thar's opinions (and his opinions were incessant and embraced the universe), whether on history, politics, religion, mathematics, hog raising, peanut growing, or astrology, he might look forward to being promptly, ruthlessly, and utterly subdued—discomfited—annihilated—put in his place at once by the instant and infallible authority of Old Looky Thar's chief "frame of reference"—the huge hole in the roof of his mouth.

It did not matter what the subject was, what the occasion, what the debate; Old Looky Thar might argue black was white, or top was bottom, that the earth was flat instead of round; whatever his position, everything he said or thought—*was right,* because he said it, because a man who had a big hole in the roof of his mouth could never possibly be wrong in anything.

On these occasions, whenever he was questioned or opposed in anything, his whole demeanor would change in the wink of an eye. In spite of his wooden leg he would leap up out of his old split-bottomed chair as quick as a monkey, and so angry that he punctuated almost every word by digging the end of his wooden peg into the earth with vicious emphasis. Then. opening his horrible old mouth so wide that one wondered how he would ever get it closed again, exposing a few old yellow fangs of teeth, he would point a palsied finger at the big hole in his mouth, and, in a high, cracked voice that shook with passion, scream:

"Looky thar!"

"I know, Major, but——"

"*You* know!" Old Looky Thar would sneer. "Whut do *you* know, sir?—a miserable little upstart that don't know *nothin'* tryin' to talk back to a man that went all through the Wah an' come out of it with *this*! Looky thar!"

And, stretching his mouth open until one could hear his jaws crack, he would point a trembling finger at the all-embracing hole again.

"I know, Major—I can see that hole all right. But the argument was whether the earth was round or flat, and *I* say it's round!"

"*You* say it's round!" sneered Looky Thar. "Whut do *you* know about it, sir? How do *you* know whether it's round or flat— a little two-by-fo' snotnose like y*ou* that ain't *been* nowhere, an' ain't *seen* nothin' yet! *You*—talkin' back to a man that's fit all up an' down Virginy an' that's got a hole in the roof of his mouth big enough to stick your hull fist through! Looky thar!"

And once more he would dig viciously into the earth with his wooden peg, crack his jaws wide open, and point to the all-justifying hole with a palsied but triumphant hand.

If not opposed in any way, Old Looky Thar was amiable enough, and would talk endlessly and incessantly to anyone within hearing distance who might have leisure or the inclination to listen to unending anecdotes about his experiences in war, in peace, with horses, liquor, niggers, men, and women—especially with women. His alleged relations with the female sex were lecherously recounted in a high, cracked voice, punctuated by bursts of bawdry, all audible a hundred yards away.

Judge Robert Joyner loathed him. Looky Thar represented everything he hated most—shiftlessness, ignorance, filth, lechery, and professional veteranism. But hate, loathing, anger, or contempt were not sufficient to prevail over Old Looky Thar; he was a curse, a burden, and a cause of untold agony, but he was there in his split-bottomed seat against the courthouse porch, and there to stay—a burden to be suffered and endured.

Every time Judge Joyner went to court, he always glanced up quickly as he came up the courthouse steps to see if Looky Thar was there—as if he hoped some merciful act of Providence had taken him away. But Looky Thar was always there. Fire, famine, floods, and pestilence could devastate the earth—but Looky Thar remained. He could always be heard endlessly relating his war experiences to the courthouse loafers. And as the Judge limped up the steps, and the loafers would obsequiously and with scrambling haste remove their sprawling, drawling carcasses out of his way, Old Looky Thar was always there to greet young Edward's father. It was a form of greeting which his father especially loathed.

Although Old Looky Thar could pop up from his chair as quick and nimble as a monkey when he was mad, and someone had opposed him, when he greeted the Judge he became the aged and enfeebled veteran, crippled from his wounds, but resolved at the cost of no matter how much suffering to make a proper and respectful salutation to his honored chief. If it had not been for the intense embarrassment and angry suffering which this spectacle cost the Judge each time he was compelled to witness and endure it, the absurd show which this old reprobate put on would have been a most amusing one. As it was, it was a remarkable exhibition, even to one who was not familiar with the hypocrisy behind it.

At Judge Joyner's approach, Old Looky Thar—who would have been regaling his tobacco-chewing audience with tall tales of "how we fit 'em up and down Virginy"—would cease talking suddenly, tilt his chair forward to the ground, place his palsied hands upon the arms of the chair, and claw frantically and futilely at the floor with his wooden stump, all the time grunting, groaning, and almost sobbing for breath, like a man at the last gasp of his strength, but resolved to do or die at any cost. Then he would pause, and, still panting heavily for breath, would gasp out in a voice mealy with hypocrisy and assumed humility:

"Boys, I'm shamed to have to ask fer help, but I'm afraid I got to! Here comes the Judge an' I *got* to get up on my feet. Will one of you fellers lend a hand?"

Of course a dozen sympathetic hands were instantly available to pull and hoist Old Looky Thar erect. He would stagger about drunkenly and claw frantically at the floor with his wooden leg in an effort to get his balance, catch hold of numerous shoulders to steady himself, and then, with a magnificent show of concentrated purpose, he would bring his arm up slowly to the salute. It was the most florid salute imaginable, the salute of a veteran of the Old Guard acknowledging the presence of the Emperor at Waterloo.

There were times when young Edward was afraid his father was going to strangle the brave veteran. The elder Joyner's face would redden to the hue of a large and very ripe tomato, the veins of his neck and forehead would swell up like whipcording, his big fingers would work convulsively for a moment into his palms while he glared at Looky Thar; then, without a word, he would turn and limp away into the courthouse.

To his son, however, he would unburden himself of his feelings, which, though briefly expressed, were violent and explosive.

"There's one of your famous veterans," he growled. "Four

years in war, and he'll spend the next forty years on his hind end! There's a fine old veteran for you!"

"Yes, father," the boy protested, "but the man *has* got a wooden leg."

His father stopped abruptly and faced him, his square face reddened painfully as he fixed his son with the earnest, boyish look of his blue eyes.

"Listen to me, my boy," he said very quietly, and tapped him on the shoulder with a peculiar and extraordinarily intense gesture of conviction. "Listen to me. His wooden leg has nothing to do with it. He is simply a product of war, an example of what war does to eight men out of ten. Don't drag his wooden leg into it. If you do, it will blind you with false pity and you'll never be able to see the thing straight. Then you'll be as big a sentimental fool as he is."

Young Edward stared at him, too astonished to say anything, and not knowing what reply to make to what seemed to him at the moment one of the most meaningless remarks he had ever heard.

"Just remember what I tell you," his father went on, slowly and impressively. *"A wooden leg is no excuse for anything."*

Then, his face very red, he turned and limped heavily and rapidly away into his courtroom, leaving his son staring in gape-mouthed astonishment at his broad back, wondering what on earth such an extraordinary statement of opinion could mean.

He was soon to find out.

Chapter 10

THE LOST DAY

YOUNG EDWARD GREW UP IN WHAT THE HISTORIAN HAS SO OFTEN called "the dark period of Reconstruction," yet he remembered his boyhood as a happy time.

He had a good life in the eighties. As he looked back upon it later, it seemed to him that their little world, their little town, was full of life and hope and growth. They escaped, almost totally, the kind of apathy and desolation of which a great part of the South was victim.

People did not feel the sadness of the war so much in Libya Hill. As Judge Joyner said, they had not had much to lose before the war, so there was not so much later to regret. The mountain people had never been wealthy. They had not been slave owners. They were a backwoods folk—a small-farm, hunting, hewing, clearing, trapping, and log-cabin sort of people. In many of the mountain counties, Negroes were unknown before the war; many mountaineers had never seen a Negro before the war broke out.

Even in Libya Hill it is doubtful if there were more than half a dozen people who had owned slaves. Old Captain Duncan had had by far the most—some forty or fifty Negroes: he owned a great deal of land and had a sawmill, and he had used them there. The Blands had had a few slaves. Zack Joyner may have had half a dozen, and Robert three. Perhaps there were a few more families scattered here and there who had owned a slave or two apiece, but such families were rare.

Thus, since western Catawba did not belong to the rich cotton- and tobacco-growing, plantation-owning, and slave-holding South, its losses from the war were less than they otherwise would have been. Libya Hill, in fact, was still an undeveloped, almost pioneer community. The wilderness of the Blue Ridge Mountains surrounded it and had cut it off from the main lines of development that had been going on in the other regions of the South. Its growth was still to come.

So, as far as young Edward's own life and that of his immediate family were concerned, the business of living in the eighties was an interesting and hopeful experience. Although they were very far from being rich, their circumstances were a good deal more comfortable and secure than those of most of their neighbors. Edward's father had his judge's salary—a modest one—and a little money coming in from rents. Besides, he owned the old house on School Street, the land on which it stood having been inherited from his father, as well as a place six miles out of town, also a part of old Bear Joyner's holdings. This last was farmed and lived on by a tenant, but the family went there in the summer. All told, they had some three thousand dollars a year to live on, in addition to owning these two places. It was not affluence, but it was a good deal of money in the South in the 1880's.

More important than all this, Judge Joyner, like John Webber, was what was known as "a forward-looking man" (this was probably the real basis for their friendship), and the atmosphere around the house, as around everything with which young Edward's father had to do, was busy, cheerful, and hospitable. Someone was always paying them a visit; someone was always staying with them; someone was always coming or going. This gave to their life a perpetual atmosphere of eager preparation and expectancy, with all the accompanying bustle of arrivals and departures, the joy of greetings and the fond regretfulness of farewells.

And, as we have seen, the town itself was stirring at that time with its first delicious pangs of growth, of bursting from its shell. Edward Joyner, like all the rest, shared the feeling of agreeable excitement and elation, the sense of sparkling things that lay ahead. It was in the air.

As a sign and symbol of their golden future, the railroad was coming up the mountain. People waited for its coming with eagerness and a buoyant impatience. And at last the great day came. The last rail was laid, the last spike driven, and Edward Joyner would never forget the carnival exhilaration of that day in April, 1884, when old Captain Billy Joslin brought his engine, "Puffing Billy," around the bend and down the rails into the station, its brass bell clanging, its whistle tooting, the whole thing festooned with bright bunting, to be welcomed by every man, woman, and child in town with loud cheers and yelling jubilation.

And young Edward, as he stood beside his father and his mother on the platform, did not know it at the time, but he realized later that with that puffing little engine the world came in.

Not long after this event, and only a few months after his father had spoken so mysteriously about Old Looky Thar, the boy was in the study late one afternoon and his nose was buried in a book. He was reading an account of the Battle of Spotsylvania by one of the Generals in Hancock's command who had been present at the fight. He had finished reading a description of the first two movements of that bloody battle—Hancock's charge upon the Confederate position, and the thrilling counter-charge of the Confederate troops—and was now reading about the final movement—the hand-to-hand fighting over the earth embankment, a struggle so savage and prolonged that, in the words of this officer, "almost every foot of earth over which they fought was red with blood." Suddenly he came upon this passage:

There have been other battles of the war in which more troops were engaged, the losses greater, the operations carried on in a more extensive scale, but in my own estimation there has been no fighting in modern times that was as savage and destructive as was the hand-to-hand fighting that was waged back and forth over the earth embankment there at Spotsylvania in the final hours of the battle. The men of both armies fought toe to toe; the troops of both sides stood on top of the embankment firing point-blank in the faces of the enemy, getting fresh muskets constantly from their comrades down below. When one man fell, another from below sprang up to take his place. No one was spared, from private soldier up to Captain, from Captain to Brigade Commander. I saw general officers fighting in the thick of it, shoulder to shoulder with the men of their own ranks; among others, I saw Joyner among his gallant mountaineers firing and loading until he was himself shot down and borne away by his own men, his right leg so shattered by a minie ball that amputation was imperative. . . .

Something blurred and passed across the eyes of the boy, and suddenly all of the gold and singing had gone out of the day. He got up and walked out of the study, and down the hallway, holding the book open in his hand. When he got to the sitting room he saw his mother there. She glanced up placidly, then looked at him quickly, startled, and got up, putting her sewing things down upon the table as she rose.

"What is it? What's the matter with you?"

He walked over to her, very steadily, but on legs which felt as light and hollow as a cork.

"This book," he mumbled and held the page up to her, pointing at the place—"this book—read what it says here."

She took it quickly, and read. In a moment she handed it back to him, and her fingers shook a little, but she spoke calmly:

"Well?"

"What the book says—is that father?"

"Yes," she said.

"Then," he said, staring slowly at her and swallowing hard, "does that mean that father——"

And suddenly, he saw that she was crying; she put her arms around his shoulders, as she answered:

"My dear child, your father is so proud, and in some ways a child himself. He wouldn't tell you. He could not bear to have his son think that his father was a cripple."

And all at once the boy remembered what his father had once said to him; and knew what he had meant.

A cripple!

Fifty years and more have passed since then, but every time the memory returned to Robert Joyner's son, the vision blurred, and something tightened in the throat, and the gold and singing passed out of the sun as it did on that lost day in spring, long, long ago.

A cripple—he, a cripple!

He could see the bald head and red face, the stocky figure limping heavily away to court . . . and hear the fast, hard ringing of the bell . . . and remember Looky Thar, the courthouse loafers, and the people passing . . . the trials, the lawyers, and the men accused . . . the soldiers coming to the house . . . the things they talked of and the magic that they brought . . . and his war-young heart boy-drunk with dreams of war and glory . . . the splendid Generals, and his father so unwarlike, as he

thought . . . and the unworthiness of his romantic unbelief . . .
to see that burly and prosaic figure as it limped away toward
court . . . and tried to vision him with Gordon in the Wilderness . . . or charging through the shot-torn fields and woods at
Gettysburg . . . or wounded, sinking to his knees at Spotsylvania . . . and failing miserably to see him so; and, boylike,
failing to envision how much of madness or of magic even brick-
red faces and bald heads may be familiar with . . . down the
Valley of Virginia more than seventy years ago.

But a cripple?—No! no cripple. One of the strongest, straight-
est, plainest, most uncrippled men his son would ever know.

Half a century has gone since then, but when Robert Joyner's
son would think of that lost day, it would all come back . . .
the memory of each blade, each leaf, each flower . . . the rustling
of each leaf and every light and shade that came and went
against the sun . . . the dusty Square, the hitching posts, the
mules, the ox-teams, and the horses, the hay-sweet bedding of
the country wagons . . . the courthouse loafers . . . and Old
Looky Thar . . . and Webber's mule teams trotting across the
Square . . . each door that opened . . . and each gate that
slammed . . . and everything that passed throughout the town
that day . . . the women sitting on the latticed porches of their
brothels at the edge of "Niggertown" . . . the whores respiring
in warm afternoon, and certain only of one thing—that night
would come! . . . and all things known, as well as things unseen, a part of his whole consciousness . . . a little mountain
town down South one afternoon in May some fifty years ago
. . . and time passing like the humming of a bee . . . time passing like the thrumming in a wood . . . time passing as cloud
shadows pass above the hill-flanks of the mountain meadows, or
like the hard, fast pounding of the courthouse bell. . . .

And now, his father dead, and long since buried, who limped

his way to court and who had been at Gettysburg . . . another
man since dead and buried with the gorilla arm-length of an
ape. . . .

And time still passing . . . passing like a leaf . . . time passing, fading like a flower . . . time passing like a river flowing
. . . time passing . . . and remembered suddenly, like the forgotten hoof and wheel. . . .

Time passing as men pass who never will come back again
. . . and leaving us, Great God, with only this . . . knowing
that this earth, this time, this life, are stranger than a dream.